HYDDENWORLD

William Horwood is the author of the bestselling classic Duncton Wood and Wolves of Time series. He has returned to his hallmark fantasy in this epic series following the flow of the seasons. *Hyddenworld* is the first of four books.

William lives and works in Oxford. He is currently working on the second book in the series.

Find out more about the author at: www.williamhorwood.co.uk

Praise for Hyddenworld

'The writing is beautiful, and should appeal to readers who enjoy the fictions of Philip Pullman, J. R. R. Tolkien or Trudi Canavan'
Waterstone's Books Quarterly

'A wonderful book'
FantasyBookReview.co.uk

'The writing is rich and emotive'
SFX

'This new series could prove to be one of the classics. If anyone is going to stand a chance of rivalling Tolkien it is William Horwood. I can't wait to read more'
Scott Pack, MeAndMyBigMouth.typepad.com

'An intimate, delicate and delightfully written novel that instils a sense of the "Old English" like no other'
TotalSciFiOnline.com

'A real gem of a novel . . . It's colourful, it's incredibly creative and this new series is one that will soon become a firm favourite'
Falcatatimes.blogspot.com

T0353338

ALSO BY WILLIAM HORWOOD

The Duncton Chronicles

Duncton Wood
Duncton Quest
Duncton Found

The Book of Silence

Duncton Tales
Duncton Rising
Duncton Stone

The Wolves of Time

Journeys to the Heartland
Seekers at the Wulf Rock

Tales of the Willows

The Willows in Winter
Toad Triumphant
The Willows and Beyond
The Willows at Christmas

Other works

The Stonor Eagles
Callanish
Skallagrigg
The Boy with No Shoes (Memoir)

HYDDENWORLD

WILLIAM
HORWOOD

PAN BOOKS

To Deborah, with love

First published in Great Britain 2010 by Macmillan
This edition published 2013 by Pan Books
an imprint of Pan Macmillan, a division of Macmillan Publishers Limited
Pan Macmillan, 20 New Wharf Road, London N1 9RR
Basingstoke and Oxford
Associated companies throughout the world
www.panmacmillan.com

ISBN 978-1-4472-6147-6

A CIP catalogue record for this book is available from
the British Library.

Typeset by SetSystems Ltd, Saffron Walden, Essex

Visit **www.panmacmillan.com** to read more about all our books
and to buy them. You will also find features, author interviews and
news of any author events, and you can sign up for e-newsletters
so that you're always first to hear about our new releases.

CONTENTS

I   THE RIDER AND HER QUEST   1

II   FIRES OF THE UNIVERSE   25

III   TWELVE YEARS LATER   105

IV   INTO THE HYDDENWORLD   219

V   BRUM   331

VI   SPRING   455

VII   SHIELD MAIDEN   489

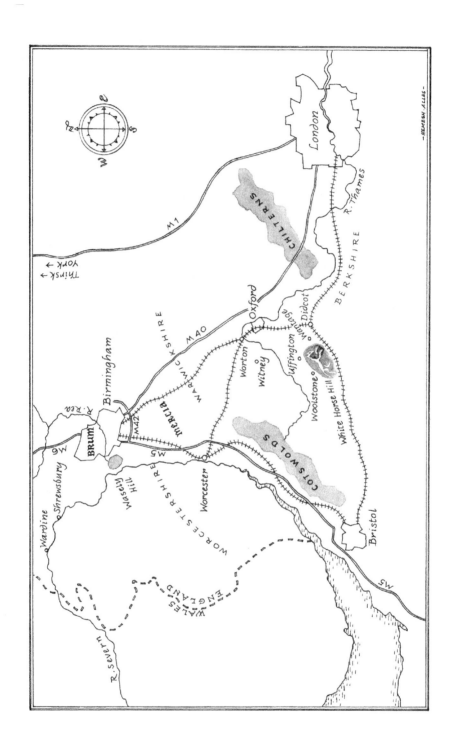

I

THE RIDER AND HER QUEST

I

THE RIDER AND
HER QUEST

A few moments before dawn on the first day of Spring the White Horse and its rider came out of the darkness of winter and paused awhile on a hill near Brum in Englalond.

Wraiths of cold mist lingered in the hollows and ditches nearby, stirring with the horse's hoofs. Its rider was female and nothing much to look at, being barely more than a wraith herself.

Her papery face was wrinkled, her hands and fingers crooked, her eyes rheumy, her white hair thin and her body bent with long centuries of journeying. As she was too old to dismount in comfort the White Horse dropped to its knees to let her down. Afterwards she clung to its reins for support.

Around her neck she wore a disc of gold. It was worn and battered and its four main settings were all now empty of stones. They had represented the seasons – one for Spring, a second for Summer, the third for Autumn and the last for Winter – but time had loosened them and they had been lost.

The rider's name was Imbolc, which in the old language means Spring. She stood bowed now, the White Horse protective over her as, with mixed emotions, she remembered her last days in the place where she now stood.

This was Waseley Hill, where the metal-smith Beornamund, a Mercian CraftLord and maker of objects of power and majesty, had kept his forge fifteen hundred years before. In those days Imbolc was a mortal, beautiful of form and spirit and loved by Beornamund. But their love was cut tragically short. On the day of their betrothal Imbolc was killed by a devastating flood caused by an argument among the selfish gods of the sky. He decided to wreak revenge upon them by making a flawless sphere of metal and glass of supernatural power, which he hurled into the heavens among them.

The gods laughed at his mortal pride. Only when the sphere began to draw to itself the fires of the Universe and the colours of Earth's seasons did they stop their squabbling and see the danger to mortal- and immortal-kind. They united to destroy it, doing their work so well that only four small fragments of the sphere, seemingly of no conse- quence, fell back to Earth. Returning to their own concerns they did not see something Beornamund saw, that each piece that fell was an exquisite gem which held fast to itself the light and power of one of the seasons. He recovered three of the gems easily enough but the most important of them, the gem of Spring, he could not find.

Angry still, he warned the gods that if ever the four gems were reunited then his original sphere would re-form itself more powerfully than before and the gods and their universe be threatened once again. He made a pendant disc of gold to hold the three he had found, leaving an empty place for the gem of Spring in case it came to light one day.

But the impulse of youth often gives way to wisdom and it was so with Beornamund. He grew ashamed of having challenged the gods and put the Universe at risk. From that time on he dedicated his life to making objects in celebration of Imbolc's beauty and their great love. So extraordinary were his skills, so deep his understanding of the nature of universal life, that when he died the gods offered to make him an immortal.

But because he loved Imbolc still, he told them he would only agree if they did the same for her, whose spirit had been an unhappy wanderer across the Earth since the day of her untimely death.

The gods talked secretly among themselves about his request and set a condition that must be satisfied if it was to be granted.

'Before you are reunited with Imbolc she must complete a task for us. The Earth is in need of a Peace-Weaver to heal the strife between the mortals and repair the ills they cause the Earth. Let her ride the White Horse until the day comes . . .'

Wise Beornamund saw through their trickery and understood that they still wished to punish him for what he had done when he was young. He knew well that mortal strife is born of such greed and desire for plunder that it reigns eternal. He therefore feared that she could never complete her task and be free to return to him.

The gods shrugged and said, 'Well then, give her the pendant you made in defiance of us so many years ago, proud Beornamund. When its last gem, that of Winter, finally loosens and falls to Earth we will accept that she has truly lived through all the seasons of her life, one as a human, the last three in immortal time. Then, like you, she will have gained the wisdom to be immortal. But . . .'

Beornamund frowned, suspecting another trick.

'. . . but before she returns to you she must find her true successor, her sister, the Shield Maiden. For by then the greedy mortals will have need of someone more fearsome than a Peace-Weaver. And . . .'

Beornamund's frown deepened.

'. . . and while she's at it,' they added lightly, 'let her use mortal help to find what mortal made: the gem of Spring. We are curious to know where it has hidden itself all these years! Do that successfully and *then* can she finally return!'

He thought for a few moments and finally smiled, for he saw that they had overlooked something. The gods had asked merely that the gem be found, not brought to them. He knew very well that no mortal would be satisfied with a single gem, even if it was that of Spring. Once started on such a quest they would not stop until they found the others, which had been scattered across the Earth during Imbolc's journey down the centuries. Who could say with whom the power would lie if the day ever came when all the gems were united once more? Neither the gods nor himself, Beornamund decided. Which seemed just.

'Let it be so!' he said. 'There is the wyrd of destiny in all things and there will be in this.'

With that conclusion the gods also seemed satisfied.

✷

So now Imbolc stood on the hill near Brum where Beornamund once had his forge, with the gem of Winter finally gone and her last quest now before her – to find the Shield Maiden and the gem of Spring. She had no doubt that in finding one the other would be found as well.

She leaned against the White Horse pondering these things and fearing that she was too old now for much journeying and that her energies were all but gone. Then she remembered advice she had had from the wise woman mortals call Modor. She had helped Imbolc in her early years as Peace-Weaver and been a close friend ever since. She often said, 'We can do nothing without the help of others for we are all one with the Earth and the Universe.'

Imbolc looked about and guessed that the White Horse had brought her to Waseley Hill for a reason. She reached a hand into the swirling mists which formed and re-formed about her and she sensed that mortal help was very close at hand and that the Modor was thinking of her too, far distant though she was. She relaxed and let go the reins, stronger now. What would be, would be.

The mist began to clear and the White Horse moved across the breaking light of dawn to protect Imbolc's old eyes from the rising sun, as her final quest began.

2

BEDWYN STORT

Three hydden and a half – the half being a thin, gawky, fair-haired boy of eleven – lay huddled and asleep in one of the ditches not far below where Imbolc stood.

One was Brief, Master Scrivener of Brum and the most eminent archivist of his age. He was tall for a hydden, nearly three feet high, and was wrapped in a thick, grubby red cloak with the black woollen cap of a scholar on his head to keep him warm.

Next to him lay the stocky well-made figure of Mister Pike who, at thirty years, was a good many years younger than Brief. He was a staverman: a hydden trained in the military arts, and his role just then was to protect Brief against those who might wish to harm him and his own occasional folly in venturing where he should not go. Pike's heavy ironclad, a stave hooped at either end with cast-iron, lay beside him.

Further on still in this muddy abode was Barklice, one of the city's most renowned verderers, whose ancient role involved travelling about Brum and its environs dealing with matters of dispute and litigation and soothing the troubled waters and sometimes intemperate spirits of different hydden communities thereabout.

As such, and as a by-product of his demanding work, he was not only one of the most experienced route-finders alive in Englalond but also spare of build, thin of face and free of spirit.

All were dressed in trews and jerkins, their shoes home-made, the uppers of leather and the black soles of the best material available to them: pieces of tread taken from the discarded car tyres of humans.

None of these three had wyfkin or living family, which was why they had chosen each other's company to trek out of the city the evening before to welcome the coming of Spring with story and chatter, shared jokes at themselves and the world at large, a few simple rituals that went to the deep core of their faith in Mother Earth. More deeply still they were worshippers of the Mirror-of-All in whose vast reflection they believed all mortals, hydden and human alike, had their reality and being.

To hydden such as these, the first day of Spring was a very different thing than that which humans usually celebrate. For humans live mainly in cities and homes which isolate them from the elements. Which means that by the time humans recognize that Spring is in the air Spring is in fact already well begun.

Hydden are closer to the Earth and know that the loveliest of seasons starts much earlier than March or April. It arrives with the first stirrings in the cold ground, and certain yawnings and scratchings in deep burrows, occasional glimmerings of softer light through clouds still bleak with winter chill and in the new-found life and joy of the rilling of the streams that comes with the thawing of winter snow and late January rain.

No one can say with certainty at what hour or day Spring actually begins, but in the northern part of the Hyddenworld the first day of Spring is arbitrarily set at February 1st, using the human calendar, and that was why despite the cold, dank weather Master Brief and his friends had made the trek south-west out of Brum to Waseley Hill to welcome the season in with a warm brew and open fire. The mead had been strong and they snored still.

The fourth among their number, the 'half' as Brief sometimes called him, though he was tall for his age, was his assistant Bedwyn Stort. He lay separately from the others wrapped tight in a discarded black plastic refuse sack – a logical if eccentric protection from the damp. He looked as he was, a restless sleeper, and he never imbibed. One foot, shoeless, had forced itself out of the bag on one side, the other had twisted and stuck uncomfortably into one of its corners.

An arm, ending in a freckled hand, had thrown itself up the side of the ditch as if attempting to escape his body. The other hand was clasped tight over the face and eyes to protect them from the dawning light.

But to no avail.

Fingers parted, an eye opened and then closed again before the hand moved away altogether and Stort slowly opened his eyes and peered with such curious intensity that it was as if he was not sure where he was or even who he was.

His nose, which was long, sniffled at the air and as he looked at the mist swirling just above it, and over his sleeping companions, his expression changed to one of surprise, even astonishment.

He sat up and disentangled himself from the bag to reveal his normal garb, which was a suit of Harris tweed, made by himself to his own design, which had so many bulging pockets of different shapes and sizes that it was impossible to work out where one began and another ended.

It was the mist that puzzled him.

'Strange,' he murmured, 'it's moving as if stirred, which means that something has stirred it, something big.'

He heard the snorting of a horse.

'A horse,' he told himself aloud, which was how he often worked things out, 'but no ordinary horse. *No ordinary horse!*'

He glanced at his companions, saw they were fast asleep and heaved himself out of the ditch onto the grass above, where he stood quite still, his tousled head with its protruding ears to one side, listening.

'Very weird,' he told himself, adding with playful but serious irony, '*wyrd* indeed!'

For 'wyrd' is what humans sometimes call fate or destiny. But for the hydden, wyrd is a matter of choice rather than inevitability and they know that to make the choice may change a life for ever. So wyrd was to be taken seriously.

Stort hesitated only briefly before, without a thought for his personal safety, he began striding up the hill into the mist. For even at eleven Bedwyn Stort's scientific curiosity and quest for answers ran far ahead of any danger his actions might attract.

3
PACT

Whatever else Imbolc expected to appear in the form of help on her final quest, it was not a strangely dressed and gangly young hydden, barely more than a boy, climbing up the wet grass towards her.

The White Horse had made itself scarce, so she stood alone pondering whether or not to change her guise, for there are few mortals able to look into the eyes of an immortal. On this occasion instinct told her to stay as she was.

Peace-Weavers do not see like mortals only the latest, newest reflection from the Mirror of reality of what comes before them. They see as well what the Mirror has held in the past and will one day hold in the future. They see these things as not-quite-shadows, light grey with an occasional dash of real colour, vague precedents and prefigurings, fragments of time that add up to a life.

As she now set eyes on Bedwyn Stort, Imbolc was astounded at what she saw. Image after image affirmed him as a most extraordinary hydden.

An infant who from the first moments of his birth saw the world with the curiosity of a child; a child who bore himself with the courage of youth; a youth who wandered the world and bore with fortitude the loss of his family with the wisdom of an adult; an adult who cried out early with the pains of age and loss; and finally one of the old ones, his first innocence still intact and his eyes filled with that same light of life as when they first opened, despite the ravages of suffering and old age.

Such seemed to be the past and present and future of Bedwyn Stort.

Most of all she saw in his eyes as he came up to her, undimmed by the times he must live through, the light of great love. She knew it as she knew her own. In that she guessed she had found at last one of those who, if they were true to their wyrd, and had the courage and strength to journey to the furthest end of the pilgrim road, would be the ones to help the Shield Maiden fulfil her difficult task.

Stort stared at her and then at the pendant that she wore, old and battered as it was, its gems all gone, its gold dinted with many knocks, the white quartz in its centre worn and dull, with no hope, it seemed, of ever shining with the light of love again. He guessed who she was.

'Is that the pendant Beornamund made for you?' he asked, undaunted by her stare.

'It is, Master Stort, the very same. Its gems are gone now, scattered across the Earth.'

He stared at it more closely and said, 'Master Brief believes . . .'

'Sssh . . .' she whispered, reaching towards him and placing a finger on his lips, 'do not say what Brief said, it is better that I am not told.'

She knew at once that she had done wrong, not through her words but by her touch, for it is said that a mortal touched by an immortal may be given thereby a burden too great to bear.

Stort fell silent and felt flow through him a storm that began as an icy wind but ended with an elemental blizzard. It left him hollowed and aged, wore him to his knees and began to steal his life away right there on Waseley Hill.

But it is said as well that what the mortal loses the immortal gains, and Imbolc the Peace-Weaver felt his youth pass briefly into her so that what once she had been to Beornamund the CraftLord she became again: young, beautiful, filled with the life and love of the season that bore her name.

At once she knelt down by Bedwyn Stort, held him close and whispered, 'You shall not leave us yet, for you have work to do . . .'

Then she told him that someone was coming to Englalond alone soon who was in danger and might need help.

'. . . he's the giant-born on his way already . . . find him and do what you can. Do this and I will ask the Mirror-of-All to return your life to you by the light of this rising sun. Can you do it for me?'

Stort nodded and reached up his hand and touched her lips as she had his. At once his youth returned and she began to age again.

'There!' she said, 'It is good! It is as it had to be. See him now through the coming years so that he is ready to help find the Shield Maiden and change all your lives through the dark decades ahead when I shall be here no longer to help . . .'

Stort fell into a deep sleep, and it was then that the White Horse returned, bent its head, and Imbolc, youthful a few moments more, climbed on its back and sped away. The sun rose and the mists cleared before its warmth, and she and her horse were no more than clouds across the sky.

The sun woke Brief and the others. They saw that Stort was gone and, thinking all was not well, rose up, looked up the hill and saw him laid upon the grass.

Pike reached him first, Barklice found the signs of a horse's hoofs, but it was Brief who guessed that Master Stort had been chasing more than wraiths of mist.

They made him a brew, they brought him round and they gave thanks for youth and the first light of Spring.

When he told them what had happened and that he had been given a task to perform, but he might need their help, they were ready to believe him.

'What's the task?' asked Brief.

'I don't exactly know,' said Stort.

'Who's the enemy?' asked Pike, his right hand already firm upon his stave.

'I'm not sure,' said Stort.

'Tell me the place and I'll take you there,' declared Barklice.

'Um . . .' began Bedwyn Stort uncertainly, 'I can't remember, but she said I'd find it if I looked hard enough.'

'Who did?'

'Imbolc. She touched me and . . .'

They looked at each other in dismay, for every hydden knows that immortals never touch mortals but to harm them. They looked at

Stort more closely and saw what he said must be true. For on his right brow and in a small patch at the back of his head they saw something that had not been there the night before – white hair, which in a youth is a sign of innocence and ancient wisdom.

'All I know is that someone's coming and he's younger than me, that he's in danger and that we can help . . .'

'Gentlemen,' said Master Brief, rising at once, 'I believe we have work to do. You say "he is coming" but the rest you can't remember?'

Stort nodded.

'Well,' said Master Brief, 'that at least is a start and we know he's a boy! Your hands on mine if you please!'

Pike and then Barklice reached their hands to his.

'You too Master Stort!'

They made a pact then to pursue the task that Stort had been set, as if it was their own, right to its end.

'Now gentlemen, I suggest we climb this hill to see if Stort can get a better sense of where exactly it is we must go.'

But it was not to be.

'*Humans*,' growled Pike in a low and urgent voice, 'and near. I can hear 'em tramping over the hill.'

They retreated then as only hydden can, into the hollows and ditches of the hill as the mist had done before them, and disappeared as it also had, before the rising sun.

4
STRANGE SITE

P ike was nearly right, but it was one human, not several.
Arthur Foale, former Professor of Astral Archaeology at
Cambridge University, now dismissed and out of work, would
have arrived earlier but for the mist.

He had allowed two hours for the car journey from his home in
Berkshire but it had taken three and he had missed the rising of the
sun, though only by minutes.

He had walked up by the public footpath that started at the car
park at the bottom of the hill. He was big, bearded, and wore the
kind of lived-in boots and muddied trousers, as well as a thick fleece
against the morning cold, that suggested he was well used to such
conditions.

He wore a backpack and there hung from his neck a pair of
binoculars and a small digital camera. His trousers were belted and to
this was attached a small round leather pouch, robustly stitched and
with a well-made strap and buckle. It was an army-issue prismatic
compass.

He held a blue, plastic clipboard which he opened and peered at
before veering off the path to cross the fields at roughly the same
contour where Stort had found Imbolc a little earlier.

The clipboard held the relevant part of the local large-scale Ordnance Survey map, a geophysical survey of the area which looked
mainly blank, and some A4 sheets on which he intended to take
notes.

He took the compass from its pouch and pushing his thumb

through its ring attempted to take a bearing on the corner of the field some way above where he stood. He shook his head in apparent wonderment at the result and turned his attention to a location below him where part of the car park showed. Again he attempted to take a bearing and again he shook his head.

He moved forward, stared at these two locations again, and from them straight ahead, and waited for the mist to clear some more. He spotted a distant feature of the landscape, located it on the map and then drew a few lines on the survey.

In this way, dispensing with the compass and doing everything by eye, he proceeded by fits and starts across the field until half an hour later, checking his position with bearings all around him, he seemed satisfied. He took off his backpack and placed it on the ground where the slanting sun caught it and made it nicely visible. The spot was within two feet of where Imbolc and Stort had met.

Arthur Foale then squatted on the ground and peered along it this way and that, like a golfer looking at the lie of a green before making an important putt. What he was doing was not dissimilar. He was looking at slight variations in the ground brought out as shadows by the sun.

Finally satisfied, he moved the backpack a few yards downhill and to one side, where the stream that came from the hill above flowed near where Imbolc had first arrived. He then climbed up the hill with vigour and some excitement, not looking back until he was two hundred yards away and perhaps fifty feet higher.

He looked back downslope to his pack, searching out again the variations in height he had made out earlier. He took some time doing this, so long in fact that the sun rose further and the shadows disappeared.

But he had seen enough and seemed well satisfied.

He pulled out his mobile and made a call home.

His wife Margaret answered.

'It fits,' he said. 'If I'm right, this is where Beornamund did his work. I . . .'

He said no more.

A fickle wind had twisted and turned across the face of the hill and strands of mist risen from the bed of the stream and briefly obscured the site he was looking at. With the coming of the mist his signal was gone.

But that did not really surprise him. The geophysical survey and the difficulty he had found in taking bearings had prepared him for anything.

The site was the strangest he had ever known in a career of busy and often controversial archaeology.

Compasses went wild. Mobiles cut out. And the geophysical survey he had privately commissioned and which he now held in his hand showed absolutely no results of any kind at all in a wide circle around the spot where he had first placed the backpack. It was a bizarre white-out. Which was a first in his career and theoretically impossible, because there is always variation in the Earth and the only thing that could wipe the slate clean was a source of power so great that nothing quite like it had ever been found before.

The mist's brief return was over and the sun shone again but it was higher now, the shadows gone.

His mobile rang.

'Are you *sure*?' asked his wife, who was Professor Foale too, but unlike him still in gainful employment. Her subject was Anglo-Saxon literature and her speciality the most extraordinary legend to emerge out of the Dark Ages. It concerned Beornamund, greatest of the Mercian CraftLords, who had given his name to the great manufacturing city of Birmingham or Beornamund's Ham, which some dialects, now lost, were known to have corrupted to Brummagem or Brum.

'Arthur, can you hear me?'

Arthur Foale stood transfixed by the singular beauty that morning of the light across the hill and it made him think of the two objects for which Beornamund was most famous, both now lost.

'*Arthur?*'

'Yes,' he said, 'I'm here but . . . give me a moment. I'm thinking.'

'Thinking of what?' demanded Margaret finally.

'I am thinking that this is a site that should not be desecrated by excavation,' he replied, as astonished by this strange impulse as she was. Excavation was what he did. Otherwise how was he going to unearth the story the site might tell?

'I'll have to find some other way of exploring its secrets,' he said rather lamely.

'Such as?' Margaret wondered.

Arthur's methods could be unusual. Very unusual. They tended to get him into trouble.

'I'm looking at my shadow on the hill, the sun being bright here this morning,' he replied for no obvious reason.

'Meaning . . . ?'

Margaret was feeling ever more uneasy.

'My shadow's compressed by angle and slope. It's perfectly formed but it's something less than three foot high and makes me feel rather large as a matter of fact. Like a giant.'

She knew the reference was to Beornamund and guessed that Arthur had just made a quantum leap of some kind in his thinking.

For Anglo-Saxon legend said that the CraftLord was a child of the little people but, as the old language puts it, 'giant-born' – an aberrant, a mutant, a potential outcast. Most such were killed when their abnormal size began to show, but the CraftLord escaped and passed himself off as human. Then at the end of his life it was claimed he returned to the world into which he had been born, transmuted back to the size he should have been. It was mystery for which no one had an answer.

But Arthur Foale had long had a theory, and the shadow at his feet had suggested a way of putting it to the test.

'I'm coming home,' he told Margaret, 'I've found what I needed to here.'

'*Arthur . . .*' said Margaret warningly.

It was too late and the phone was dead again.

An idea had been sown and Arthur Foale was not the kind of man to give up on an idea until it had been proved false or true.

I'll have to find some other way of exploring its secrets he had said.

Margaret did not like the sound of that at all.

5

GIANT-BORN

That same morning, across the North Sea from Englalond in the uplands of Germany, an extraordinary conversation was taking place in German.

'So *this* is the boy? The one?'

'*Das ist der Junge*?'

The three hydden nodded at the woman addressing them, fear and fatigue in their eyes in equal measure. They stared at a sturdy boy of about six.

'How can you be sure?'

'*Look* at him! He's the one they're looking for, the one they've been trying to kill.'

It was the oldest and most respected of them who spoke – he was the Ealdor, the leader of their village. He was frailest but the most passionate and his face was grey and drawn with the effort of their journey up into the mountains, and with the constant fear that they would be betrayed.

They need not have feared.

The hydden of the Harz Mountains in middle Germany were renowned for keeping their secrets close and their mouths shut. The natural adversaries of authority, they were the sworn enemies of the Sinistral, who dominated the Hyddenworld with their dark armies, the Fyrd.

Right across the globe, old kingdoms, ancient republics and entire tribal structures that had stood the test of time collapsed before the advance of a single, unified, system, that of the Fyrd, a word which in the old language means 'occupying army'.

Not since the rise of Imperial Rome in the human world, two thousand years before, had mortalkind seen how a combination of military might and technological innovation, fuelled by the spoils of victory, could so rapidly and completely take over the old and replace it with the new.

So the Harz Mountains, like Englalond, were a bastion of liberty.

Their female leader is called Modor, from which the word 'Mother' derives. Her consort is known as the Wita or Wise Man.

They looked ordinary enough, perhaps even poorly dressed. But they carried themselves with the calm authority and simplicity which experience and wisdom bring.

The Modor looked carefully at the boy who, in hydden terms, was already adult size. Apart from his height he looked normal – most unusual in one who suffered his rare condition, which healers called giantism and could not be cured.

His head, his feet, his hands, his limbs were perfectly proportioned. Better still, he had bright eyes, an intelligent look, a cheerful face, and he was still a happy child.

His size made him seem more human than hydden.

The Modor frowned and looked at the Ealdor. 'You're his grand-father, aren't you?'

The Ealdor nodded and sat down. The boy moved closer to him, as much out of love as for reassurance. The old hydden patted the lad's shoulder affectionately.

'His mother gave him to me for safekeeping after the Sinistral sent their people to kill him, and I fled here with the help of my two friends, to bring him straight to you. I fear now that our village will have been destroyed and that you see before you its only survivors.'

The Modor shook her head sadly. 'Does he speak German yet?'

'His first language is our own Thüringian dialect, but German proper . . . well, that's coming. English not at all.'

'He's definitely still growing?'

'Fast,' sighed the Ealdor.

'Then he'll need to learn quickly. He cannot stay with us long because it will not be safe for him. We must train him at once to the stage that he is ready to leave the Hyddenworld. It is the only way he can survive, and he's still young enough to learn to pass himself off as human.'

The Ealdor nodded sadly.

'Where will you send him?'

'To the one place in the world where the Fyrd have not yet destroyed all freedom. He will be taken across the sea to Englalond. Once he has finished growing, the Sinistral will not be able to find him there, and nor will they think they even need to, for they will believe he can never come back into our world.

'We shall teach him English, which fortunately shares roots with his own language. We shall also teach him to use his strength. We shall teach him to trust his intelligence.'

The Ealdor sighed. 'And the Hyddenworld? Will he learn to forget that too?'

The Modor and the Wita looked at each other, but it was he who answered.

'We cannot do that now, even if we wished to, for we can see that you have put into him something that means he can never forget where he came from, not in his inner being at least. These mountains he may forget, or your village, and all of us gathered here, but in his heart the Hyddenworld and its wonders and its wisdoms will always remain his home. Look at the boy! Look into his eyes! You and your kin put love into him, Ealdor, and he will never forget that.'

'But he will never be able to come back. He will be . . . a giant. Like a human. He cannot *ever* . . .'

But the Wita shook his head.

'. . . Oh, but he can,' he said. 'The journey back and forth between human and hydden is not an art that has been entirely forgotten, Ealdor, even in these most forsaken of times. There have always been those, on both sides, who have discovered how to travel between each other's worlds. It is done through the henges, whether of wood or stone, living tree and living water – there are many kinds and they exist the world over. The only difference between a human and a hydden is one of size, and that is a relative thing, a matter of perception. Your grandson will come back.'

The Ealdor looked puzzled.

'But the henges are fallen, the White Horse not heard of in centuries, the rituals forgotten . . .'

They smiled.

'Yet we still preserve that ancient skill, and have ourselves some-times journeyed back and forth. Recently, too, for we have been expecting you to bring the boy to us, so we have already found a place in Englalond where he can go, and people there who will watch over him.'

'Other free hydden, you mean? Not the Sinistral – or the Fyrd who are under their control?'

The Fyrd of whom he spoke were the strong arm of the ruling Sinistral: an army of fierce warriors with no pity or compunction in their creation. They controlled the hydden cities and routes through-out Englalond, as they now controlled them all the Hyddenworld over. Over recent years the Fyrd had become liberty's shadow, freedom's bane.

The Wita said, 'We've known for centuries that once the giant came, then the hydden and the humans he needed to help him would come too. They *know* he's coming. They're readying themselves.'

The Ealdor looked fearful again. '*Humans*?'

The Modor laughed, her consort joining with her: the joyful laughter of free spirits.

'Humans aren't all bad,' she said. 'Two of them even came to these parts ten years ago trying to find us. We nearly let them, but . . . we felt it better to wait for the boy. They came before their time but were not to know that.'

'But he wasn't even born then.'

'Nor were you a century ago, but we knew you must come before he did, and you did. The timing of things is not what it seems, and the wyrd of things is not entirely beyond our control. Remember, the coming of the giant was predicted by Beornamund himself fifteen hundred years ago, at the time when he made the Sphere and captured the Fires of the Universe.

'This boy's task is greater than we can even conceive, as was the nature of the Sphere itself. The whole Universe held in only two hands – just imagine it!'

'He's just a boy.'

'He's a giant in the making and his time is coming. You have done your part. We shall now do ours, and then . . . then . . .'

The Modor suddenly dug deep inside her pockets and pulled out a single scrap of paper with human writing scribbled on it. 'Humans are the most trusting and foolish creatures in the world, as well as the most destructive.

'The woman merely left behind a cross of twigs and a wreath of wild flowers on a stone. Touching really, because I think she assumed we must be pagans. The man was more practical and left this.' She held up the piece of paper.

'What is it? What must you do with it?'

The Modor began laughing again, the boy joining in.

'After a millennium and a half, he expected us to break the silence between hydden and humans just like that!' explained the Wita more seriously. 'It takes your breath away, such simple trust! Yet it makes a certain amount of sense. For how else will they know the boy is coming?'

The Ealdor took the torn paper and stared at it. 'What is it?' he asked in puzzlement.

The Modor retrieved it and put it back in the folds of her dress. 'They call it a telephone number. He hoped we'd make a telephone call just like humans do.'

She laughed again for a moment at that.

'And will you?' The Ealdor looked appalled, as did his companions.

'Me? I'm too scared of such things,' admitted the Modor. She looked at the Wita. 'But *him*? Do you know I think he's crazy enough to do it!'

The Ealdor stared at them both in wonder: actually thinking of talking to humans? That was the greatest taboo of all.

'But—'

The Modor raised a hand to silence him, her expression serious again. 'We have said enough now. It is generally best to leave the future unspoken,' she said, 'for fear that by talking of it we make it turn out differently.' She turned to the boy and signalled him to come near her. 'Now, what is his name?'

He went over to her, obediently.

'His name is Yakob, as is my own,' the Ealdor replied. 'That is the tradition in our village.'

She looked at the younger Yakob, deep in thought for a moment, then reached an old hand out to touch him. He was a well-made boy, as strong as they come. He grinned at her, and then he too looked serious.

'From this moment on, boy, your name is Jack. Do you understand me?'

'He doesn't speak English.'

'Well, he'll not learn it if I continue to speak German!' she replied sharply. 'Do you understand, your name now is Jack. So . . . My name is . . .'

The boy stared at her, his eyes alight with this new challenge. He concentrated as she repeated what she had just said.

He nodded carefully, thinking how to form his first words in this new language.

'My . . .' he began.

'*My name is . . .*'

'My name is Jack,' he said.

II

FIRES OF THE UNIVERSE

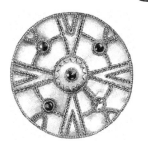

6

THE CALL

A telephone rang in Berkshire, England, a month later.
It was old-fashioned and made of black Bakelite and it was mislaid somewhere in a room full of papers, books, ashtrays, files, a baseball cap, several walking sticks, African carvings, a model Inuit canoe, three empty glasses, which had contained shots of whisky now evaporated, and a cat ... so that when it rang, it proved impossible to find.

Arthur Foale knew it was there because he could hear it ringing, but whether it was actually on his desk or under it, or in the heaps of things to one side, he had no idea.

His wife Margaret looked up from her own desk in the tidy half of the room and said, 'Good heavens, is that *your* phone ringing?'

She sounded surprised because hardly anyone called Arthur these days.

'It's a mistake obviously,' he replied as he scrabbled about. 'I'm just trying to find it so I can stop it ringing.'

'It may not be a wrong number,' she suggested.

'Well it *is*,' he said, when he finally found the phone, just after the ringing stopped. 'Or it was.'

His wife glanced at him sympathetically and returned to her work. She knew there was only so much she could say or do in the unfortunate circumstances in which Arthur now found himself – out of work and without any prospect of paid employment. Someone had to earn the money for them to live on and it could no longer be him.

Until just three years before they had been considered one of the most interesting couples in the British archaeological firmament, each holding a full professorship in one of its oldest universities.

Then Arthur had been stripped of his position as Professor of Astral Archaeology at Cambridge University for causing a public ruckus with the Director of the National Physical Laboratory, and several others, during a live televised debate about Creationism.

It would have been funny in other circumstances but not in those. Arthur was a big man with a big heart, but he didn't suffer fools gladly and sometimes lost his temper. He had now lost it one time too many and, though it made good television, he'd been blackballed professionally.

Since then he had been unable to obtain a paid position in any college within reach of their home in Berkshire, or even to get his controversial work published in journals.

A television series he had made on Anglo-Saxon Cosmology was shelved and his American publisher dropped the series of lucrative textbooks of which he was author. No one was interested any more in a middle-aged ex-professor with a reputation for being too outspoken. And too controversial: for instance his theory that prehistoric wood and stone henges were not 'cosmic calendars', as people liked to think, but portals into other worlds.

'Mad Professor Says Stonehenge Is a Time Machine' was not the kind of subsequent headline that did Arthur any good. In a matter of months he had gone from being an expert with too many demands on his time to someone nobody in the media wanted to talk to.

Sighing at the missed call, he heaved his large, shambolic body from the chair, grunted and grumbled for a bit, and then headed off towards the conservatory and through its wide open doors out into the garden.

Five minutes later his phone rang again.

Margaret Foale picked it up. 'Yes?' she said, hoping there was enough distance in her voice to discourage unwanted callers.

A strange voice spoke. She listened.

'Can you repeat that?' she said finally. 'I am finding you rather hard to hear.'

She listened again and then said, 'I'll fetch him. I think he's in the garden. Please do not hang up.'

She went to the conservatory and from there through its open doors.

Arthur was standing looking up at his trees.

She stared at him for a few moments before speaking.

If she had known how to tell him how much she loved him just then, she would have done so, but there were not words enough and if there were she did not even know the right ones.

'It's for you,' she called finally, trying to sound as if such an occurrence was entirely normal. Even so there was a touch of excitement to her voice. For the call she had taken was either a prank by some former student or else something that might change the world. She did not know which of the two she would prefer.

'For you!' she called out again.

'What is?' he said, turning to face her.

Two great trees rose up behind him, on the far side of the rough lawn. They were magnificent as they caught the evening light.

'The phone call,' she said.

'Who is it?' he asked.

But she had already gone back inside.

Arthur Foale followed her and took the phone from her tense grasp.

'Yes?' he said cautiously.

'Professor Foale?'

'Er, yes?'

The caller began talking very softly.

'Can you speak up, please?'

The caller continued, but the voice sounded little louder, just clearer. It was really no more than a whisper and it might have been male, it might have been female. It was old and it was heavily accented and it was other-worldly.

Arthur Foale listened closely, at first unable to make much sense of it, then beginning to understand. And then his head began to spin as if what he heard was beyond belief. He signalled Margaret to come and listen in.

'*You understand? The boy is coming. He is ready now and he must come. It is too dangerous here. He comes. All is ready.*'

'Is he . . . ?' Arthur began hesitantly.

'*He is the giant-born.*'

'But where? Where will he be?'

There was no answer to that.

'When?'

'*Tomorrow.*'

'Tomorrow?' repeated Arthur faintly.

'*You do nothing. Wyrd will decide. Wyrd . . .*'

'But . . . ?'

'*There is no more to say. The boy is coming to Englalond. The time has come.*'

The phone went dead.

7

INTO THE WORLD
OF HUMANS

The boy appeared early the next morning at the front door of a
foster home on the North Yorkshire Moors, in the north-east
of England, as if from nowhere. There had been the hammer-
ing sound of a horse's hoofs just before the unexpected ring at the
door, but when it was opened the only sign of a horse was a magnificent white mare in a field some way off across the moor, its white
mane and tail brilliantly catching the morning sun.

The boy smiled at them, evoking a similar response, but when they
looked up from his face the horse was gone, and there was only a
streak of white cloud across the bright blue sky to suggest that it had
ever been there.

His arrival on the first day of March coincided with the first warm
days of Spring, so mild and warm that in the weeks that followed the
sloe blossom came out early, shoots pushed through soil still moist
from the snows of February, and the buds on trees grew fat and sticky
as birds paired up and busied themselves with their nests.

The boy was of average height but stocky, and he looked exceptionally strong and healthy. Whoever had abandoned him had thought to
dress him sensibly against the chill winds that blow across the North
Yorkshire Moors. But there was an odd thing about his clothes, in
that they carried no clothing company labels. They were old-fashioned
and hand-made, as if someone from a bygone era had dressed him.
He was carrying a suitably child-sized backpack made of old, worn

leather, most beautifully stitched and preserved, unlike anything that could be bought nowadays in a shop. It looked as if it came from another time and culture and it was certainly a lot older than its owner. It showed signs of having done a lot of travelling.

The oddest thing of all was that there was nothing inside it except for a ragged but obviously much-loved soft toy, a horse that was once white but now grubby. The boy let the staff examine the pack but kept a tight hold of the horse.

Some numbers and a name were inscribed inside the flap of the backpack in Gothic script of the kind that used to be common only in Germany. The name was 'Yakob', but when they repeated it the boy shook his head firmly. Despite their best efforts to question him he remained silent, so they named him Jacob or usually Jack for short.

There was no record of a missing child of his description to be found on any of the national or international registers, nothing at all. But, for the time being, the newspapers were kept out of it because, in such cases, something usually turned up.

Just then, anyway, the newspapers had something better to shout about than a missing child, namely the strange behaviour of the weather. All over the world it was out of kilter with both latitude and season, and was acting as if it was feeling deliberately malevolent towards mankind. It was as if a band of mean old gods, long since banished even from folk memory, had returned to say just how much they disliked mortals.

Their violent breath, in the form of freakish winds, scattered the sands of deserts and felled the bushes and trees of the temperate zones; their rough old hands tore clouds apart and caused such deluges of rain that people the world over were not just drowned, they were swept away; and what the roaring thunder in their voices did not scare to death, their cold stare froze wherever it stood, even in places that had not experienced a frost in decades.

Not yet, however, on the North Yorkshire Moors, or any other part of the British Isles either, which continued to enjoy that strange and beautiful early Spring, even if uncertainty about the coming days was growing as such extreme weather began to encroach on neighbouring parts of Europe.

The authorities decided to keep the boy there in the foster home where he had arrived so mysteriously, until inquiries about him bore fruit and a decision about his future could be made.

But, six weeks after his arrival, he made it for them.

The boy, for all his obvious physical well-being, was a natural target among the other children, some of whom had problems with controlling anger and aggression. He didn't speak or answer to 'Jack', the name they generally used, and he had a habit, annoying to others, of being nearly incapable of being by a window or door without wanting it wide open. He seemed not to feel the cold.

In the common room one evening after supper, an older boy of ten, who along with two others mildly terrorized the younger ones, grabbed the new boy's pack and pulled out his toy horse.

Until then the boy had said nothing in all the time he had been there, and certainly nothing provocative or in any way aggressive, but now he spoke out.

'Give it back,' he said firmly.

But the older one said he wouldn't until the boy told them his name.

'You do have one, yeh?' he taunted.

The boy fell silent, seeming more surprised than scared.

'But it's mine,' he said finally, stepping forward and stretching his arm up as the older boy raised the horse just out of reach. That was when someone else tripped the newcomer up.

As the boy tried to rise to his feet, someone pushed him back down.

Then they all moved in, kicking and punching and shouting at him.

What happened next was as extraordinary as it was unexpected.

The boy rolled away from his tormentors, stood up, and looked around the room for a weapon. The only thing he could find was a tatty TV magazine, which he rolled up tight.

His attackers stood back and then laughed as they saw what he hoped to defend himself with. They began to close in, and the atmosphere turned ugly with excitement and bloodlust.

There was another derisive laugh as the boy raised the baton of newsprint in front of him. Maybe they should have been warned by the expression on his face, but he was smaller than the bullies, despite his muscular build.

If they had known how to assess it, they would have recognized unusual determination and self-control.

He rolled the magazine even tighter, his calm and measured movements sufficiently intimidating for them to pause. Too late: like a firework exploding the boy lunged hard and fast against the first and tallest bully. He thrust one end of the rolled magazine up hard into his throat.

As his victim gasped with pain and began gagging, the boy pulled back to consider for a moment, then lunged forward again, this time thrusting the magazine hard into the other's groin. The bully collapsed straight to the floor, his mouth gaping in pain, his skin turning pallid in shock as he tried desperately to catch his breath.

The boy turned instantly on another of his attackers, thrusting the makeshift weapon straight into his armpit. His second victim clutched there instinctively, leaving his solar plexus open to a further jab, then he doubled up and toppled slowly backwards, hitting his head against the arm of a chair.

By now the others sensibly backed off, and the sound of screaming and moaning had brought a member of staff into the room. The boy calmly retrieved the toy horse and returned it to his backpack.

'My name is Jack,' he said quietly.

Of the pair he had attacked, one was taken for treatment by a doctor, while the other was obliged to go and lie down for several hours.

The foster home isolated Jack instantly, and phoned the authorities. The incident was so strange that reports of it very quickly went from local to regional level.

'Are you sure there's no clue at all about who he is? He hasn't mentioned anything at all about someone who might know him?'

They confirmed there were no clues at all. Even though Jack was talking now, he would not or could not shed any light on where he'd come from.

'Check again carefully. Things easily get missed.'

They did, and found that something had indeed been missed.

It was the jumble of numbers written, alongside the name Yakob, in his backpack. They were oddly spaced but, looked at the right way, might resemble a telephone number.

It was Arthur Foale's number.

They rang it the following morning.

8

ON BORROWED TIME

At about the same time that day, the White Horse arrived with Imbolc as if from nowhere out of a cloudy sky. It landed in a fallow field in Warwickshire, in the realm of Englalond, its great hoofs sending mud and grass flying to right and left as it skidded to a stop in the lee of a blackthorn hedge, whose white blossoms trembled briefly and then stilled.

The Peace-Weaver's work was hard, so many were the conflicts between the hydden and human worlds, so hard and complex their resolution. But that day Imbolc's eyes shone bright, excited by the coming of the giant-born and her meeting ten weeks before with Bedwyn Stort. A new generation was taking over and things were as they needed to be.

Without thinking, she touched the pendant around her neck to remind her of Beornamund, as she had so often over the centuries. The gem of Spring had never been there, lost as it was before the pendant was made to hold the others. But the three Beornamund had retrieved had all been in place at the start of the journey, falling out one by one through the years. The last had been the gem of Winter, a dark and brooding thing, lost only a few weeks previously. Its absence still shocked her. She really was living on borrowed time.

'Oh, Beornamund, my journey is almost over and now . . . now . . .'

Across the field she saw some people approaching, tiny figures in a landscape.

'This,' said Imbolc the Peace-Weaver, 'is the beginning of my final task, and the greatest. Like it or not, my years now being numbered to but a few, I *have* to find the Shield Maiden.'

One of the figures across the field called out, 'Is it this way or that, eh? We're getting cold. Make up your mind!'

Imbolc smiled, for a Peace-Weaver's work is never done even when she is living on borrowed time.

'To work!' she murmured.

9

ASSIGNMENT

Arthur Foale had been hoping for weeks that his old-fashioned telephone would ring a second time, with further news of the boy. But when it finally did ring, the call was not quite what he expected.

It came from Roger Lynas, a senior child-welfare officer with the North Yorkshire Health Authority. He was circumspect, very. There was an unidentified boy, who was in trouble. Arthur's number was found written on his backpack and—

Arthur broke in to ask some questions.

The replies were evasive. It was their primary job to protect the child, so they wanted information, though were not prepared to give any. Arthur, never good in such situations, felt his hackles rising.

His voice began to rise, he began to bluster, but just as he was beginning to shout, Margaret came into the room.

She arched a questioning eyebrow and he calmed down at once.

'Just a moment,' he said. His hand covered the receiver.

'Who is it, Arthur?'

'It's a Mister Lynas of the North Yorkshire Health Authority, and he . . .'

Arthur then explained as best he could. As he did, the feeling began to grow in him that he was in the process of making a mess of what might be the most important telephone call he would ever receive.

He took up the phone again.

'I think,' he said as mildly as he could, 'that you should be talking to my wife. Could you hold on, please?'

Margaret took the receiver and started the conversation over.

'Hello, I'm Margaret Foale. Could you . . . ?'

By the time Margaret was finished she had established a friendly rapport with Roger Lynas, found out that the boy's name was Jack and extracted a promise that they were now to be kept in the loop. She had succeeded in conveying the impression, without telling any actual lies, that they knew a good deal more about this boy than they did, and managed to establish the idea that she and her husband should now be involved further. However, a meeting would be necessary before they could help.

She was given a number to call, received effusive thanks, and, most important of all, got information that Jack was being sent that same day to London for further assessment.

'Tomorrow, then, you'll call us,' she finally agreed.

But as she put down the phone she looked pale. She began breathing rapidly so she had to sit down.

'What is it?' asked Arthur.

They had not been able to have children, though both had much wanted them. They had always known that this huge and ramshackle country house, which was Margaret's inheritance, needed children. It was that kind of home, full of space for children to play and a garden with trees to climb, and places to build dens and to hide in, which needed young life.

The phone-call had stirred something in Margaret's emotions deeply, and pushed her to a place she had never thought she would have the opportunity to go to.

Arthur went over to her. 'What is it?' he asked gently.

'That conversation,' she said. 'It is the first I have ever had about any child as if . . . as if . . .'

She bowed her head and reached blindly for him.

'. . . as if it were my own.'

'But, darling—'

'I know, I know but . . . this boy has no one. Absolutely no one. Can you imagine that?'

'Yes, but—'

'Something's happening, Arthur, and it's something important. It's a beginning of something, and that boy *is* its beginning. I've never been a mother so I supposed I'd never have a mother's instinct, but there's something about the boy – they're calling him Jack – which has changed something in me.'

She fell silent.

'Tomorrow; we'll know more tomorrow,' was all he could say.

Sudden rain lashed against the window. They heard the conservatory door crash shut.

'It's started already,' she said suddenly. 'It's happening *now* . . .'

Arthur looked baffled.

'. . . and do you know something?'

He shook his head.

'There's another thing I feel, which I have never felt before. I think it's what every parent feels about their child – or fears, anyway. I feel something awful's going to happen to Jack, and it's a kind of torture because there's nothing I can do, nothing . . .'

Arthur held her tight as the storm hit the house hard, and Margaret wept the pent-up grief of years. Inside the house and outside, it felt to Arthur as if the world was coming to an end and they were suddenly caught up in it.

10

MASTER BRIEF
AND FRIENDS

I mbolc watched the slow advance of Brief, Pike and some others across the field towards her. They were being led by Master Stort, whose hesitant progress seemed to irritate them, used as they were to more decisive leadership than an eleven-year-old could offer.

She gave the White Horse its instructions, which were to linger thereabouts in the form of a wraith of mist across the vale, and to be ready when her present task was completed during the coming hours. Then, with her steed safely out of both hydden and human sight, she pondered which of her many disguises to adopt.

Imbolc very rarely manifested before other folk as her true self. She decided to adopt her favourite guise. She muttered a simple spell, waved her arthritic hands about, and was suddenly transformed into a middle-aged hydden pedlar from Ireland, for whom her Celtic name seemed well suited.

She wore a large portersac on her back and in front of her carried a tray of combs, laces and charms for travellers, which was supported by a strap that went around her neck. Her stoop instantly disappeared, her step grew more sprightly. Even though it now began raining quite heavily she was humming a catchy tune.

She knew no better than Stort where he was meant to be going, for a Peace-Weaver cannot see all that is to be, just its general direction. About even that she was often wrong, since wyrd might be wonderful but it was subject to mortal whim.

Stort looked even more odd than she remembered him. He was clad in an old-fashioned jacket and kept stopping and starting and then stopping again, staring here and there, peering at the ground and then up at the sky, before appearing to sniff at the air for inspiration before finally waving a hand to signal the group forward once more. No wonder the rest of the group looked so dispirited.

But even as she watched, their young leader suddenly regained his sense of direction and purpose. She heard a cry, as of one who has just had a revelation, and Stort made a sudden turn left and dived almost headlong through the thorny hedge without apparent discomfort before climbing the railway embankment that rose on the far side of it, soon to be followed by the rest of his grumbling party.

Most of them were dressed in the garb of stavermen, out doing their civic duty: leather trews, a tunic made of good-cloth and sturdy boots, and each with a stave ironclad at top and bottom in his hand.

She studied their faces hoping to find one that was familiar, and was glad to see Master Brief was among them. In all of Englalond there was not a hydden she respected more than this one, even if now getting close enough to talk to him involved negotiating the thorny hedge.

As it was thick and damp, she wished the White Horse, being thoughtful in so much else, had had the foresight to arrange her arrival to take place on the other side of this obstacle. But once on the ground she had to suffer as mortals do. So she pushed and heaved her way through the hedge, holding her tray of goods close against her chest, hampered by the weight of her pedlar's pack, until she too was able to climb the embankment.

By the time she reached the top, the group she was pursuing had moved on along the path of the railway line and disappeared. The line itself had long since been abandoned and the rails and sleepers salvaged for scrap. There were however the remnants of a platform where a country station must have once stood, though its buildings, too, were all gone.

Imbolc pressed on along the empty track and not long after saw that a quiet country road ran under the line, and realized that the hydden had done the sensible thing and clambered back down the embankment to shelter from the rain under the bridge that had once carried the line above it. She found them variously huddled on the ground. They merely nodded their heads on hearing her greeting, and continued to scowl at the rain.

Except, of course, for Brief, who knew her true identity and was delighted to see her.

'Well, well, well,' he began, with obvious pleasure, 'and what brings you here this miserable day, Imbolc?'

His grey beard had droplets of rain in it, his cloak was wet, but he carried himself as he usually did, with authority and good humour.

She smiled and reached out a hand to his by way of greeting.

'The same thing that has brought you here, Master Brief, I dare say. That you should stray so far from your beloved library in Brum is rare indeed, but to find you in such a desolate spot, with such a ragbag of companions, confirms my suspicion that something very strange is afoot. Am I right?'

She knew already that it was Stort who had brought them here, but she wanted Brief's version of this most unusual young hydden.

He did not reply to her question, growling instead at the weather, which was getting worse by the moment. This storm was set to develop into something very bad indeed, as the wind grew wilder and the air about them was filled with flying rain. Soon the sky filled with lightning and their ears with the deafening thunder that followed.

'It is worse than you know,' she confided, for his ears only. 'I have travelled a great distance across the entire continent of Europe to get here, and I can safely say that this is the worst weather in living memory – and *my* memory goes back to the Dark Ages. I can tell you that *this* particular storm is about to get a lot worse.'

'Is that a guess or a prophecy?' he asked, finally.

'It's a prediction based on long experience.'

'Like your prediction about our world coming to an end when the Earth starts to fight back?' he jibed lightly. Brief had never for one moment believed that her frequent warnings would come to pass.

'That's already started and will get a lot worse unless you do something about it,' she replied tartly. 'But I have come to the conclusion that until you all realize that the Earth is not merely a larder to raid, or a well to drain dry before finding another one, but your equal partner in life, then you will continue to proceed on the road to disaster. Meanwhile, Master Brief, your beard needs a comb.'

She gave him one from the stock she was carrying, more out of gratitude that he had made it easy for her to join his group than from any real desire to improve his appearance.

Had he not welcomed her personally, the others of his group would probably have told her to find some other place to shelter, because seven is a number of good fortune, eight much less so.

Hydden were superstitious about numbers and, when venturing out, much preferred odds to evens, and if they *must* travel in an even-number group, then it had better be one of the luckier numbers.

Eight happened to be one of the unluckiest.

So Brief had to appeal to the others' good nature to persuade them to let this grubby-looking female pedlar share their arch. Now the others squatted a little way off, scowling at her suspiciously.

But Brief knew that Imbolc never made an appearance without reason and, when she did, some good generally came of it.

'So, why are you here?'

'I'm looking for my successor,' she replied briefly.

'I didn't know you were retiring,' he rejoined.

She smiled thinly. 'I'm not retiring, I'm fading. Have you genuinely forgotten how old I am?'

'No, I have not.' Then he added hastily, 'And I don't want any visual reminders of your great age.'

She had once made the mistake of appearing before him as she really looked, and the sight had quite upset him. Her present transformation into a down-at-heel female pedlar of middle age was much easier to live with.

'Well, anyway,' she continued, 'my final years have come, and someone else must take on this job because fifteen hundred years is more than enough for anyone.'

'When do you expect to, er . . . fade away?' he asked.

'In about ten years' time I should think,' she said calmly, 'so right now I'm already living on borrowed time. We Peace-Weavers don't exactly disappear, you know – we pass on to other, hopefully better, things. It depends what the Mirror-of-All has in store for us. Even so, that only gives me a decade to find my successor, and train her in readiness.'

'How long have you already been searching?'

'She's been on my mind for about three hundred years,' said Imbolc matter-of-factly.

'Doesn't the Mirror-of-All sort those kind of things out?' Brief lowered his voice respectfully as he said that, with a glance directed out from under the bridge towards the dark, wild sky beyond, as if expecting the power that ruled all their lives to suddenly show itself. He knew of course it never did, or maybe could not, appear in any obvious way.

'No,' responded Imbolc, 'the Mirror does *not* sort it out. With respect to my successor, that's *my* task – maybe my last and most important one. Especially as my successor may have to cope with the end of the Earth as we know it . . .'

'There you go again!' said Brief, resignedly.

She turned from him and stared at the others, noticing for the first time that Stort had produced a black plastic bin-bag, scavenged from humans, and put it over his head, puncturing a hole in it through which he had thrust his long thin nose so he could breathe. It was one of the oddest things she had ever seen.

'Is that the youngster who was leading you?' Imbolc asked, not revealing she already knew his name and his importance to her quest. But of the details of his life she as yet knew nothing.

'Please don't ask about *him*,' groaned Brief. 'It's . . . *complicated*. He's not a staverman like the others. He's . . . no, I don't want to go there right now. I'll explain about him later. It's enough to say he's the reason we're hanging about in this horrible place in the middle of a storm.'

Imbolc stared at Bedwyn Stort with renewed interest.

'In that case maybe he's why *I'm* here,' she said softly. 'So tell me something about him.'

'*Later*,' repeated Brief frowning.

'Hmm,' she murmured softly, suddenly lost in thought, her attention again on Stort in the black plastic bag.

'You were saying,' Brief murmured, bringing her back to the present, 'that you were currently looking for the next Peace-Weaver.'

'I said I was looking for my successor. That doesn't mean she will be a Peace-Weaver. Has it never occurred to you that it's not a Peace-Weaver we need most in the troubled years ahead?'

'But I assumed your successor would fulfil the same role?' said Brief, now rather puzzled.

He stared at her, his heart thumping, overcome by a horrible pre-monition of what she would say next. If she did, and if she was right, it meant that the years ahead would be hard for all of them, and demand much sacrifice and courage. He knew the myths and legends as well as anyone alive, and therefore understood there was only one alternative to a Peace-Weaver – and it was not a pleasant thought.

'I hope you don't mean . . . ?' he whispered, his voice shaking, not daring speak his thought aloud.

'I mean,' said Imbolc very firmly, 'that my successor will be a *Shield Maiden!*'

Even she herself uttered the two words with a certain awe.

Master Brief gulped and glanced nervously around at the others to see if they had overheard. Fortunately it seemed not.

Shield Maidens were reputedly not benign and reasonable entities like Peace-Weavers. They were fierce and warlike and took no nonsense from anyone, either hydden or human, female or male, old or young. When a Shield Maiden was on the prowl, the Earth supposedly became a very dark and unpredictable kind of place indeed. Not that Brief, or anyone else living, had personal experience of such an occurrence, but he knew of it through his lifelong study of myth and legend. The last Shield Maiden to fly across the Earth had done so over two millennia before.

'And you think she will make an appearance here today?' he enquired in a trembling voice.

'She might do. And if she does, my days will be shorter on this Earth than I thought.'

'But surely no sensible hydden, especially a Shield Maiden, would be out on a day like this.'

There was a rumble of thunder, a flash of lightning.

'Who said she had to be hydden? The Mirror-of-All does not make those kind of distinctions.'

Brief looked dumbstruck. 'You mean she might be a *human*?'

Imbolc eased her back to rest more comfortably against the wet brick wall of the arch, as the gloom of the strange day deepened and their huddled forms were caught again in the flash of lightning and shaken by a crash of thunder.

'I think she might be,' she admitted, feeling the kind of relief that comes with knowing a problem of long standing might be on its way to being solved. 'Yes, indeed, I think she very well might be human. And I have a feeling she's going to show up on or near this very spot before the night is done.'

He looked utterly appalled.

'While we're waiting for my successor to make her appearance, Master Brief,' she continued good-humouredly, and nodded towards the plastic bin-bag, 'why not tell me about *him*? Who is it exactly that has had the strength of personality to drag experienced hydden like yourselves so many miles away from home, and shows the common sense and inventiveness not to care what others think of him, and takes shelter under that plastic bag to keep himself dry?'

Brief glowered at the black bag and the long, thin nose that protruded from it.

'I was given to understand,' said Brief, 'that it was you yourself who instructed him to lead us here.'

Imbolc looked innocent and avoided answering by asking, 'Have you known him long?'

'Not very,' replied Brief shortly.

'But he's a hydden with some experience?'

'Just the opposite.' Brief shook his head. 'He's eleven years old and has no experience whatsoever of the real world.'

Imbolc looked even more interested. 'Yet he still contrived to get you all here?'

'He's very ... persuasive,' replied Brief grudgingly, and yet not without a tinge of admiration in his voice.

'Go on, Master Brief, go on.'

A conflict of emotions showed in his expression, before one alone triumphed. It was simple excitement.

'He says – and he's not the kind who says anything without meaning it, and feeling confident of proving himself correct – that a, well, *the* ... I mean to say he is quite certain that ...'

'What, Master Brief? *"The"* what?'

'He claims,' murmured the scrivener, 'that somebody important to us all will appear hereabout this very day. He says you told him so!'

'Does he now!' said Imbolc ambiguously. 'And just how important will this person be?'

'You're more likely to know that than a humble scrivener like me,' said Brief. 'But since you ask the question I'll answer it in good faith. The timing, the bad weather, and the fact you're involved in some way tells me that we are about to meet one who is giant-born. Am I right?'

'If you are,' said Imbolc, 'then this would be the one who by prophecy and tradition is going to save the Earth and through that the Universe.'

They fell silent, both of them pondering this mystery.

To Imbolc the mystery was how the hydden had ever got into their heads that Beornamund had made such a 'prophecy' about the end of all things, tied up in a confusing way with the emergence of hydden and human heroes. Unless the idea had come in some way from her which, come to think of it, maybe it had. She was inclined to talk too much. For now her old head went into a spin thinking about it all and she was content to know that she would not be around when really bad things started happening. She had sometimes seen what it was like when the Earth got angry and never wanted to see it again. If that ever came to pass then she trusted that by then the White Horse would have taken her back to Beornamund and a long and peaceful immortality . . .

Meanwhile she needed to concentrate on her quest for the Shield Maiden and the gem. She nodded again towards the animated refuse bag.

'Tell me about him. What's he like?'

Brief sighed, shook his head as if in disbelief at the strange times in which he was living, and finally announced with that same tremor of excitement in his voice, 'The honest truth is that, in all my years, I've never met anyone quite like him and, well, I do believe he's the most extraordinary hydden I have ever met!'

11

STORM WARNING

J ack was sitting alone in the waiting room of a health centre in Thirsk, a small market town in the Vale of York and a few miles east of the motorway to London.

It was the health centre the foster home regularly used and was now a convenient transfer point for Jack from the custody of one health authority to another, after the incident with the other boys. The only problem was that the woman due to pick him up and take him to London hadn't arrived yet. Bad weather had slowed progress on the motorway, but she had checked in with them on her mobile to confirm she was on her way.

The health centre had agreed to keep an eye on the lad while he waited to be picked up for his further journey south.

Jack sat there expressionless, seemingly confident that somebody would eventually come for him. In the small square outside the trees fretted under gusting winds, while patterns of raindrops slanted down the exterior plate-glass wall. Inside everything felt just fine.

Nothing much happened for quite a while, until a frown unexpectedly settled on the boy's forehead. He suddenly loosened the strap of his leather backpack and dug inside it. Finding what he wanted, he paused in thought for a moment more before pulling it out, a decision finally made.

He got up and went over to the pile of toys in the corner, and carefully laid the item he had taken from his bag on top of it.

It was his soft toy horse, but a white horse shaped unlike any other – long extended legs, a single eye, pointy ears and head, a long lithe body. A horse so old and worn with travel and time that only the essentials of its life and form remained, with a tail that swirled back into the past just as far as its flowing motion and eager eyes led it forward into the future.

Jack stared at it, muttered something, nodded briefly as if some secret agreement had just been made, and then went back to his seat and to his silent waiting.

He didn't look at the horse again, rather it stared at him and the world all about it, or seemed to.

Across the room the television flickered as a wild wind outside beat garbage against the clear glass looking onto the square beyond. A sequence of words flashed onto the screen and the grim images that followed made the message's meaning plain enough. It was a warning of particularly severe weather.

A nationwide alert.

Jack closed his bag and gazed at the television. He looked as if he was carrying the burden of the whole world on his shoulders, but was resigned to that fact uncomplaining.

People arrived and people left, but Jack remained seated in his chair, his backpack clutched tight, waiting patiently.

The alert on the television was repeated a few times more, while the receptionist continued to keep an eye on things in general, and the lone boy in particular.

Outside the first really heavy drops of rain began falling out of an ugly sky. It was no day for a journey.

12

PRODIGY

The chill wind gusting around the railway-bridge arch under which the hydden were sheltering was stronger now and as the rain grew heavier the day darkened.

The five stavermen huddled over to one side, while Imbolc and Master Brief continued talking quietly on the other. The subject of their conversation was now Bedwyn Stort, who had detached himself from them all and gone to squat down at the far end of the arch, resting his back against the dank brickwork.

From time to time the Peace-Weaver glanced discreetly in his direction, hoping to catch a clearer glimpse of him now that she knew something of his history. But he remained almost totally covered by a black plastic bin-bag, from which only his nose and feet protruded.

His story was a strange one, as she had now discovered.

It began when Brief received an unusual request from a retired scrivener living in an obscure hydden village on Englalond's bleak borderland with Wales. The place itself was called Wardine-on-Severn, and it seemed one of the scrivener's pupils had expressed a strong desire to learn Welsh.

'I confess I thought that a little strange,' commented Brief, 'but, even in these troubled times, learning is not quite dead.'

As Master Scrivener, it was one of his duties to assist in all matters of education and learning within the former capital city of Brum, which, as all hydden with any love of lore and tradition will know, lay within the heart of the human city of Birmingham, but far down out of sight among its sewers, conduits and waterways, in the tunnels and subterranean arches of its railways, and in the interstices of roads and buildings which humans cannot reach. Brum's rich and fabled culture was in sorry decline, yet not quite lost.

'Our archives remain the best in Englalond, and there I found a text that might serve this special purpose. As it was rare and valuable, I entrusted it to a staverman whose integrity was well known to me, namely Mister Pike yonder – the same who is the leader of the five accompanying me today.'

Brief discreetly pointed out the fiercest-looking of the small group. He had the familiar bearing of one who has done military service, his garb clean and well pressed, his cloak heavy but short, his bare arms muscular and his hair cut close.

Brief added confidentially, 'Pike is very intelligent, utterly dependable, and a fearsome fighter when need be. He also has experience of the Welsh Marches, which is no terrain for the faint-hearted. The grammar I sent him to convey covered the basics of the Welsh language, as well as the topography, history and the strange folklore of that wild and dangerous country. I did not expect to hear much more regarding Wardine, and on his return Pike revealed little about his mission.

'But, not long after, I had a further missive from my former colleague. He explained that his pupil, who you'll guess was Bedwyn Stort, now required something rather more advanced so far as his Welsh studies were concerned. He also wanted any similar texts dealing with the other Celtic languages, such as Breton and Irish, but also the lost languages of Pictish, Ivernic and Lube – the last being the mystic language of the ancient bards, of which even I had barely heard.'

Imbolc looked both surprised and impressed.

'You may very well imagine that my interest was now aroused,' continued Brief. 'Again I sent Pike off to deliver the texts. On his return he this time expressed the view that young Stort might benefit from a little of my attention, but . . . I was busy and I put the matter to one side.

'A year passed and then I had a further request, this time for texts on a much wider variety of subjects.'

'Such as?' asked the Peace-Weaver.

'Well . . . certain other lost languages, also mathematics, the history and lore of the Mirror-of-All, something on Beornamund, founder of Brum, as well as a tome or two on cosmology and mystic knotting, which, as you know, are somewhat complex subjects for someone barely more than a child.'

Imbolc nodded. Mystic knotting was not a subject most youngsters even knew about let alone desired to study, even assuming a topic so abstruse could be studied at all.

'So what did you do, Master Brief?' She noticed that Pike was watching them carefully.

'I immediately summoned Pike again, and asked him to tell me more about this talented student. What he told me . . . but let him tell you for himself. I think he realizes we're now talking about him and Stort – of whom he can be somewhat protective.'

He signalled to the staverman, who came over, still looking at Imbolc suspiciously. Close to, he exuded a definite aura of physical strength and strong purpose.

Not a hydden ever to cross lightly, thought the Peace-Weaver.

'Is she making inquiries after Master Stort?' Pike growled, eyeing her coldly.

Brief admitted that was so but added, 'She may be trusted, Mister Pike.'

'Which means she ain't really a pedlar,' he replied at once, 'seeing as pedlars and their kind are not to be trusted, eh?'

He stood looming over Imbolc, who smiled and said, 'You're right, Mister Pike, I'm not a pedlar . . .'

It is given to Peace-Weavers to pass on to mortals the sense of the wider Universe of which they are part. In Imbolc's eyes Pike saw briefly the beauty of the stars, the orbits of the planets and the colour and vast shifting of the galaxies beyond.

Or was it but the light of love that shone from her to him? Whatever it was, the impression was enough to fill Pike's eyes with awe, while Brief, who knew the Peace-Weaver's way of doing things, smiled to see that even one as wary as Pike could be won over so quickly.

'Oh, yes, she may be trusted, Mister Pike,' repeated Brief softly.

'Aye, well,' said Pike, raising a hand to his eyes as if not sure what had just happened, 'of that I am glad, for I'd lay down my life for the lad, seeing as he once saved mine. Master Stort yonder has a powerful wyrd about him, which seems to carry mine along with it.'

Imbolc let the matter of wyrd pass without comment, it being too large and profound a subject to discuss in the fading light of a cold wet day under a railway bridge. Anyway, as the weather worsened and the day darkened, there was the sense that things thereabouts would soon come to a head and they should all be ready when they did so, however that might be.

But one thing was clear. For a hydden of Pike's strength and accomplishments to concede so freely that his own wyrd was subject to a mere child's was unusual, to say the least.

'Tell me how it came about that one so young saved your life?' she asked quietly.

Pike looked both rueful and embarrassed. 'He did warn me but I did not listen. He has the power of prediction, has Master Stort.'

'Warn you about what?'

'Quagmire, down by the River Severn. He would insist on going out and about without protection, refusing even to carry a stave. So I felt it my duty to accompany him, thinking that Master Brief would not like it if all that bookwork came to naught because young Stort had been waylaid and harmed, or worse, by the thieves and robbers who infest those parts.

'As it was, it was me who nearly died. I ignored his warnings about the dangers of the place, and the next thing I knew I was stuck in it and sinking fast, and would have drowned there and then if he had not acted.'

'He had the strength to pull you out?'

Pike shook his head. 'A hundred folk working together couldn't have got me out. The ground, you see, was treacherous, so they couldn't have got near without sinking in it themselves. I thought I was properly done for.'

'So how . . . ?'

'I'm coming to that. You know what the lad did next, calm as you please? He makes himself comfortable on the nearest solid ground, pulls out a slate and chalk from his pocket, for the purpose of working a few things out, produces a chronometer from another pocket and proceeds to time my rate of sinkage.

'Naturally, I cursed a bit, but he calmly says, "Mister Pike, I advise you to stop fidgeting, and spread your arms out horizontally. That'll slow you down a bit." I did as he said, but even so I continued to sink.

'"Do something!" says I, beginning to get desperate, for the mud was up to my chest by then. He ignored me, his brow furrowing, and it was then that the humming began.'

'Humming?'

Pike nodded, his gesture a mixture of weariness and affection.

'He hums whenever he's working out a problem. Only trouble is there's no hydden alive less able to hold a tune or even produce a harmonious note, come to that. Stort's humming is an agony to all about him, and I almost began longing for that mud to rise right up over my ears. Hum, hum, hum . . .

'I may have cursed a bit and he may have said, "More haste less speed," or words to that effect. I know we both got angry with each other for a while. By then the mud was up over my chest, and with the pressure of it even breathing was becoming hard.

'Then his infernal humming suddenly stopped – always a good sign as I have since discovered – and he stood up and said, "I know what I need. We have seventeen minutes, twenty-three at the most, depending, I suspect, on how deeply you breathe. Try to keep your chest well expanded while I'm gone."

'With that he set off in that lop-sided gallop that passes for Stort running, and he headed across the fields to Wardine. I continued to sink and, as the mud reached my chin, I cursed the Mirror and all that reside within it, including Master Stort, Wardine, Master Brief, book-learning and much else beside.'

The Peace-Weaver nodded sympathetically. 'You must have been terrified.'

'I was,' said Pike, 'but be that as it may . . . as the mud reached my mouth, Master Stort reappeared with some villagers carrying poles and ropes, and various other things they had assembled at his instruction. In no time at all they had rigged up a sort of . . . well, I would say it was . . . a *contraption*.'

'Actually, Mister Pike, it was a block and tackle,' interrupted a voice off to their right. It came from the black bin-bag, and it seemed Master Stort was about to emerge.

Pike grinned. 'Whatever it was, he and those others rigged it up, and they somehow got a rope under my arm, pulled steady at the tackle he had made, and about thirty seconds later I popped out from all that mud like a cork from a flagon of fermented mead. And ever since that day, he has my loyalty and trust in all things. Eh, Stort?'

The bin-bag shuffled about a bit, and the nose disappeared inside.

'Yes, thank you Mister Pike,' came a muffled voice. 'Our wyrds are as one, yet together make more than two! That's a riddle as well as being a mystery!'

'Yeh, well . . .'

Pike went back to sit with the other stavermen; the bin-bag continued to rustle and shift.

'It must be said,' Brief continued quietly 'that Stort has an independence of spirit bordering on the eccentric. It's a quality not helped by the fact that he sincerely believes that everything he does is entirely logical.'

'Is that such a problem, Master Brief?' asked Imbolc.

'Yes, it is, because it means he does not know how odd his behaviour can seem to others, like wearing a bin-bag for a cloak. He'll merely argue that it's easier to carry.'

'He's right, of course.'

'And he won't carry a fighting stave, because he insists that fighting is not the best way to settle disputes, and that history shows it just provokes more of them.'

'He's right about that too.'

'Maybe he is,' sighed Brief, 'but that kind of thing is hard for others to take, especially those of his own age, amongst whom, you'll not be surprised to learn, he has very few friends. But Pike's right about his gift for predicting things.'

'For example?'

'Things big, things small, from weather change to who's about to come round the corner next. You'll find out for yourself soon enough I daresay.'

'So let me guess. You went off to see him in Wardine for yourself, and then brought him back to Brum to study further under your direct instruction?'

'In a nutshell, yes,' confessed Brief.

'And now he's led you here?'

'Thanks to you, Imbolc, it would seem. But quite what we can expect to *happen* I have no idea.'

He waited for Imbolc to enlighten him. Peace-Weavers don't suddenly turn up in the back of beyond unless they have a very good reason. Brief was feeling increasingly uneasy.

All Imbolc said was, 'I am here merely as an observer. I cannot influence a thing, merely watch and take note, even though . . .'

'What?'

'I know only that what will happen here will influence all our lives, and therefore Mister Pike is right to be wary, as you are right to feel nervous. When Shield Maidens begin to show themselves we'd better all watch out . . .'

They looked around expectantly as if they thought that the critical moment would come just by talking about it.

What happened instead was that Master Bedwyn Stort finally cast off his bin-bag and emerged.

He was indeed an extraordinary sight, with his wild hair and beanpole legs and arms. He said nothing but looked about for a moment and then went straight to the far end of the railway arch, looked out at the violent sky and began to hum loudly.

A tuneless, disturbing, thinking kind of hum.

A hum to get right to the heart of things.

He raised one foot to scratch the calf of his other leg and all the while his humming intensified.

Then suddenly it stopped and he put his foot back on the ground, whereupon he turned round to face them.

Imbolc stared at him curiously, recollecting their previous close encounter in the mist of Waseley Hill.

Most eleven-year-olds would wear ordinary clothes: a pair of short trews, perhaps, a light tunic of some kind, and an ordinary style of boots. Their most distinctive feature, usually, was the stave they all carried, on which they stuck various emblems and marks denoting which town or village they came from, what gang they belonged to, and even their size of fortune.

Stort looked nothing like this.

He wore a suit of such ancient design that Imbolc had to cast her memory back to the late nineteenth century to remember when she had last seen anyone wearing such, and that was a human, on a walking vacation in the Alps. The suit comprised a jacket, trousers and waistcoat – the buttons mostly missing – whose green tweedy material looked so rough that it seemed more fitting to scour pots with than wear close to the skin. It was obviously home-made, the stitches sewn so crooked and loose, while the arms of the jacket were of slightly different lengths.

I do believe he's made it himself! Imbolc thought in surprise.

The innumerable pockets were all bulging with contents: a thin strip of coiled car tyre was trying to escape from one, and some plasticized wire from another. A computer part kept company with a piece of vaguely medical-looking red rubber hose, and the black bin-bag was now thrust in alongside them.

The slate Pike had recently mentioned protruded from the breast pocket of Stort's waistcoat along with some pieces of chalk and several sharpened pencils of human manufacture; while, secured through a buttonhole on his lapel, a chunky silver chain disappeared into a waistcoat pocket, where it was doubtless attached to a chronometer.

But that was as far as Imbolc's observations proceeded, because suddenly the boy spoke up and his voice was urgent.

'Got to get out of here,' he urged. 'Er, very soon.'

Mister Pike went over to him and they conversed in low voices, Stort gesticulating in an oddly disjointed way, while Pike nodded and looked even grimmer.

Then the staverman turned to them. 'When Master Stort says "soon" he means "now!" That means we have to move straight away.'

'Where to?' said one of the stavermen.

'Up above,' said Pike tersely. 'On top of the bridge.'

'But we'll get cold and wet,' protested another of them.

'And down here you'll get even colder, because you'll be dead,' said Pike.

With that, they all moved.

Fast.

Except, strangely enough, for Bedwyn Stort, who stayed right where he was, staring at Imbolc.

'Have we met before?' he asked, frowning.

'Yes,' said Imbolc, 'but I looked a little different.'

He came closer, peered into her eyes and then at the pendant that hung from her neck. Normally she kept it covered, but it had somehow worked loose and was now plain to see on her jerkin.

'The old woman on Waseley Hill,' he said eventually. It had been given to very few mortals to make the connection.

'The same,' she admitted.

'You're the Peace-Weaver!' he said, with all the excitement of discovery.

'Am I?'

'Looks like it,' said Stort. 'Same eyes and same pendant. This arch is no longer a good place to be.'

'Thank you for the advice, Master Stort,' she said.

They followed the others out into the rain, up the embankment to the rail track above.

13

DECISION

Two hundred miles to the north, Clare Shore pulled into the car park of the health centre in Thirsk where her husband Richard worked as a doctor.

It was a Friday and the plan was for Richard to get off early to avoid the weekend traffic, so they could head south and stay overnight in London for a wedding they were attending the following day. With luck their journey should take just three hours, so they would get to the house of the friends they were staying with by early evening.

But as Clare climbed out of the car, the sky, which had been dark and threatening all day, grew darker still and the expected downpour began in earnest.

'We'll make a run for it,' she decided, grabbing the hand of Katherine, her five-year-old daughter. They got inside, breathless and laughing, the rain now torrential.

Clare was medium-height, dark-haired, cheerful-looking. Katherine was fair, unlike her mother, but tall for her age, and thin, which she got from Richard. She wore corrective glasses which made her look too studious for such a young age.

'He'll be a few more minutes,' one of the receptionists told Clare. 'You'd better wait for him here in the dry. You're only going to get wetter if you go back to the car.'

The reception was now nearly empty of patients, except the stalwarts undaunted by the weather. Once they had sat down, Katherine stared through the plate-glass window at the rain outside and then up at the strange black-purple sky.

Sitting opposite there was a boy about her age doing the same thing.

The two children looked at each other appraisingly. Katherine gave the boy a half-smile, and he smiled back at once as if recognizing her. She looked away, not yet ready to make friends. He was dark, stolidly built, with a confident but wary air about him. There was a small neat backpack made of dark leather on the floor by his chair.

Their brief exchange of glances became more frequent, as if he was somehow watching over her.

Clare watched this interaction with interest. Katherine did not make friends easily and for her to smile at another child, and especially a complete stranger, was unusual.

But there was something else.

Clare happened to know that the same boy had been there for at least two and a half hours already, because he had been sitting in the same chair earlier that morning when she popped in to have a word with Richard about their journey.

Feeling the natural concern any mother feels for a child left alone for so long, she got up to ask a woman at reception about him.

'He's waiting to be picked up and taken down south,' she explained. 'We're keeping an eye on him until his new case worker gets here. She's coming all the way from London, but there's thunderstorms on the M1, and the traffic is chaos, and maybe that's the cause of the mix-up.'

'What mix-up?'

'The lady who brought him had to go, but said she would come back to see the pick-up had been made, but she's not checked back in yet, and some mobiles are down, so . . . Anyway the boy, he seems fine. Been good as gold.'

'Which part of London is he meant to be going to?'

'His case worker's from Wembley, I think . . . but she's still not responding.'

'Wembley's near . . . where *we're* going,' Clare blurted before she could stop herself.

She looked back at the boy and studied him more carefully. She had already noted a certain wariness of the world about him, but there was also a strength of character that bordered on defiance.

From her own experience in voluntary work, she had seen that combination before in children like this, who had been let down so many times by the system that they found it hard to trust anyone or any circumstance. But there was something more about him, something quite arresting. She smiled at him and he gave a shy smile in return.

By the time Richard finally emerged from his clinic, Clare had made up her mind what she wanted to do. She suggested that they should take the boy south themselves.

'I'm not the practice manager,' he replied reasonably. 'This is for her to work out.'

Clare explained what had happened so far.

Richard discreetly studied the boy, and soon came to the same conclusion about him as Clare had – that what he didn't need now was yet another let-down by the system, but people who cared. Richard needed no further persuading. If the person coming to pick him up was showing no sign of arriving, he couldn't just leave the child sitting here all day with no alternative plan.

'Okay, let's see what we can do, but it's going to delay us a bit. Do we even know his name?'

'Jack,' said the same receptionist, who had been listening to this exchange.

'Come on,' said Clare to Katherine. 'Let's try and make friends with him while Daddy sorts something out.'

Richard Shore started making phone-calls, first inside the building and then outside it, having been given a number written on the card that the woman who had originally dropped the boy off had left at reception. He didn't manage to reach her in person, but instead got Roger Lynas of the North Yorkshire child-welfare agency. Yes, he knew of the case. No, he was unable to pass on the details. Yes, severe weather was causing chaos everywhere, so that the case worker coming from London to pick him up had finally been obliged to abandon her journey; and yes, it might well be very convenient if the boy could travel with them, so long as they would deliver him to where he was going in West London.

But, no, not until someone more senior had confirmed this new arrangement.

'Strange,' Richard told Clare. 'We shouldn't have to pick up someone else's mess and take on the troubles of the world, but—'

'But we can't just leave him sitting here, can we?'

'Well, we could, as a matter of fact,' said Richard, still hesitating.

They moved away a little, so they could talk further without being overheard. The boy stayed right where he was, his eyes occasionally flicking back to Katherine. They had exchanged a couple of words, and several more glances, but now she had begun playing separately. She got up and wandered over to the pile of toys, which another child was sifting through. There was something she wanted and she knew the score: you gave one or you took one, it didn't matter which. But being the daughter of one of the partners in the practice, Katherine had always given rather than taken.

It was the white horse which had attracted her. It looked as if it was galloping proudly across all the other toys, as if they formed the world below and it was now heading for the stars.

'I want this one,' she said to herself, a shade timid now. Not touching it yet and wondering if anyone was watching.

The boy was.

So were Clare and Richard.

The boy got up off his chair, went to the pile of toys, picked up the horse and offered it to Katherine.

'You can have it,' he said, and returned to his seat.

Katherine took it and then held it up for her mother to see. Clare smiled and nodded.

'It's a white horse,' the girl said, clasping it to her face despite its raggedy age and grinning.

Richard smiled, looking resigned as, for some reason, he let this simple statement clinch things in his mind.

'Decision made,' he said.

When Clare broke the news to Jack that he was to go with them, he gave a brief smile of relief, but there was still a wariness about him.

Natural enough in the circumstances thought Clare, adding aloud, and she hoped reassuringly, 'You can sit in the back with . . . well, this is Katherine.'

The boy looked serious again. 'I'm Jack,' he said, finally breaking the ice.

'Hello, Jack,' said Katherine with an easy smile.

That's a first, Clare told herself. 'This is my husband Richard, who's a doctor here,' she explained. 'He'll be driving us.'

Richard squatted down and reached out a hand to touch Jack's shoulder. 'Okay with you?'

Jack nodded.

'Shall I take your bag?'

Jack shook his head firmly. He leant down off the chair and picked it up.

'*I* will,' he said, holding it close, as if it was all he had in the world – which maybe it was. That was when Clare saw that it wasn't the usual cheap nylon style branded with sports logos.

It was dark leather, beautifully stitched, like an Edwardian valise, except it was so worn and shiny with use that it looked infinitely older than that.

Clare noticed something else. Jack's accent was rich, warm, rolling. She couldn't place it exactly but he sounded like a country boy.

'Come on, everybody,' urged Richard.

They rushed out through the rain, the two children laughing as they got wet. Richard slipped behind the wheel, Clare into the passenger seat beside him, Katherine sitting behind her in the back, Jack behind Richard.

They turned out of the Health Centre car park into heavy Friday traffic, any advantage of an early start now completely lost.

'This rain's forecast to get even worse,' said Richard. 'I think I'll get on the motorway by the longer, country route, which might avoid the worst of the home-bound traffic.'

Their long journey began.

14

HAIL

Ten minutes later the Shore family and Jack had left the last of Thirsk's street lights behind and were driving on a country road. The sky was now a lurid grey, but occasionally filled with sheet lightning.

'Don't be frightened!' Richard called out to his passengers.

Clare turned to look behind her. 'They're not frightened, they're fascinated,' she told him in a low voice, turning forward again.

A short while later there was a bright flash and a crackling roll of thunder so loud that it shook the car.

Katherine stared open-mouthed, Jack wide-eyed.

A few minutes later they ran straight into a hailstorm. It sounded as if a truckload of pebbles was suddenly being poured on to the roof of the car. Richard just had time to pull over into a lay-by before the wipers failed, seizing up under the onslaught of the golfball-sized hailstones.

They were coming down so hard the noise was deafening, and Clare was worried whether the windscreen would come out the other side of the storm in one piece. Already nuggets of grey-white frozen water were piled on top of each other, obscuring the lower half of the screen. The tops of the posts of the wooden fence alongside which they had stopped were piled with hail.

For a few moments they felt transported to another world, one hemmed in by ice. Then a light slanted across the windscreen, signalling the approach of another car, and lit up the posts as well.

Richard turned on the wipers again and, as the windscreen cleared, began to pull out into the road. He braked too hard, the approaching car being on the wrong side of the road, and they all crashed forward into their seat belts. The headlights of the other vehicle came straight at them through the rain. The car missed them by inches before disappearing into the night.

'That was close,' murmured Richard uneasily.

'Go carefully,' said Clare, who was not normally a back-seat driver but was now feeling apprehensive – just as Jack had been. *'Please.'*

As Richard eased the car slowly back on to the road, they snatched a final glance at the fence posts where the hail had collected. All that was left now was dripping water which, catching the tail-lights of the receding car, turned the colour of blood.

'Weird,' said Richard as they finally continued their journey.

15
STANDING GUARD

Master Brief, Imbolc and the others had all moved to the top of the bridge, on Stort's warning. He felt nervous staying under it, even if standing on top meant getting very wet.

'Why stay at all?' muttered one of the stavermen. 'Nothing's happening here.'

'Because Master Stort wishes it,' said Pike who, alone of them, was not hunkering down against the rain. Ever alert and restless, he was watchful of everything in the dark. He sensed a general danger and a specific threat, and he remained standing up so he could look one way more easily, then another, and then a third.

His fear?

That they had been seen and followed by a patrol of Fyrd and even now were being watched, though even the Fyrd might remain under shelter in weather like this.

Englalond had long since suffered under the rule of this army of occupation sent to run the country by the Sinistral, ruling dynasty of the Hyddenworld, whose headquarters were across the Channel in the Rhineland.

Fyrd! Many were the hydden's dark songs that rhymed Fyrd with wyrd, all of them bad; and, as the songsters put it, many were the good and decent folk the Fyrd had cast into grave-grip.

Pike knew very well that an expedition such as their present one was, strictly speaking, illegal. They had crept out of Brum under cover of night, so that the hydden city's guardians, as, ironically, they called themselves, would not notice them leave. No easy feat for a hydden of Brief's importance, and he must already have been missed.

So Pike stood guard in the rain, alert and menacing.

He glanced over at Bedwyn Stort, back now in his bin-bag, then at the other stavermen, dripping with rain; at Brief, who also stood as solid as a rock against the storm; and finally 'the pedlar' who he had long since guessed was a lot more than she seemed to be.

He leant on the parapet of the bridge, eyes screwed up against wind and rain, his face shiny wet when caught by lightning.

Finally he looked down along the nearly invisible road below.

Something wasn't right.

He went coolly to the other stavermen and spoke to them quietly. 'There's a something in the air, a Fyrd kind of something. So you all keep alert, every one of you. You keep your stave to hand and your knives ready on your belts, understood?'

They nodded grimly. Pike had a nose for danger and they knew it.

'Whatever it is, what it's going to be, I don't know. But it's not good, not good at all. Most of all I want no harm falling on Master Stort.'

They nodded again.

Pike knew that Master Brief could look after himself, and anyway no Fyrd would dare harm him, for things hadn't got that bad in Englalond yet and his official position should be enough to deter them. As for the pedlar, she looked like she would know how to keep herself safe. He returned to where he had been standing before, and peered again into the darkness below.

For a human standing at the edge, the brick-built parapet on the bridge would have been much too low to conceal him. But for a hydden wishing to remain more or less unobserved, at two and a half feet it was just right.

Pike was the only one among the stavermen feeling absolute confidence that young Stort was not leading them on a wild-goose chase. He didn't know why he felt like that or why, from the first moment he met the youngster nearly three years before, he had felt so strongly that his destiny had changed direction.

As he now leaned on the parapet, alert, uneasy, the rain seemed to trickle down inside his cloak as well as through it – cold and hungry again, but not wishing to be anywhere else.

For he sensed ... something. It was Fyrd certainly ... but something more.

Pike eyed the now nearly impenetrable darkness, his stubbly chin hard and purposeful. He was just able to make out a sharp bend turning off to the left further along when lightning glimmered in the sky and then again, striking closer to hand. The bend up ahead then became a brief crescent of streaming light.

'Master Stort ...'

He never called the youngster by his first name. He liked such formality of address and the fact that Stort called him Mister Pike in return.

The bag moved.

Water, which had collected over those parts of it where Stort's hands and arms stuck out a bit, now spilled to the ground. His nose retreated and, unfolding himself vertically, he stood up, almost as tall as Pike himself, then removed his bag and came closer.

'Mister Pike?'

'I don't like the feel of things,' said Pike. 'I swear, by the Mirror itself, there's Fyrd about down there in the dark, but there's something more than that.'

Stort sniffed at the rain and darkness, hair flattening almost immediately in the downpour, a shiny drop hanging on the end of his nose.

'Hmm ...' he said noncommittally and then, 'Odd. I smell something.'

'Fyrd!' snorted Pike, who together with his stavermen here, felt a match for anyone that night.

'No, it's more than just something in my imagination,' said Stort. 'Even in this wind I smell ... oil.'

'Oil?'

Even as he said it another flash of lightning lit the road below, which glistening with water as it was, looked like a stream except that two figures were there, both holding something in their hands.

'Fyrd!' snarled Pike.

'Oil,' said Stort. 'They're spilling it on the road ... but why would they be doing that?'

16

VERY WYRD

The rest of the Shores' journey was on the motorway. Car lights flashed by continually as Richard drove on steadily through the spray-filled murk, and Jack and Katherine soon fell asleep in the back of the car.

Sometime later, Clare turned on the traffic news. Freak storms were raging right across England, causing chaos and hold-ups and diversions everywhere, including further south on the motorway they were driving on.

'We'll just have to hope for the best,' said Richard.

Meanwhile, total darkness had fallen, so the drive had now become a slog and an endurance test. A brief stop at a service station made them feel no better, but the children had woken up and they needed something to eat.

'Do you want me to drive?' said Clare, as they set off again.

Richard shook his head.

Behind them the children stayed awake for a time. But they were not talking, just staring out of the windows at passing cars and lights, darkness and lightning and rain, their eyes beginning to close again.

The lightning was intermittent right across the night sky ahead of them, and the traffic reports got steadily worse. They ran into squalls of heavier rain, sudden crosswinds, and lengthy periods when the traffic slowed right down to a standstill. But somehow they continued to make progress.

'Tired?' said Clare, reaching out a hand to him.

'I was for a time, but I'm through it now. If we stop again, we could lose a lot of time. It's all right, don't worry, I'm safe to drive.'

A short time later he slowed the car again.

'We could turn off at the next junction and go right back to Yorkshire now, if you're really worried about the weather getting worse,' said Richard, 'or we could stop off in a roadside lodge and stay overnight.'

Clare considered this and finally murmured sleepily, 'Let's continue.'

Jack suddenly woke for a moment and mumbled something. Then he said, quite distinctly, '. . . All right.'

Clare turned in surprise and stared at him, but he was already drifting off to asleep again, his bag still clutched tightly in his lap.

The car was buffeted again by winds. The rain teemed down.

It had turned into a slog of a drive out of alien darkness and back into it, mile after mile.

A short while later, as they neared Birmingham, the traffic slowed and soon traffic police were illuminated in their headlights, signalling them over onto the hard shoulder.

Clare opened a window to ask what was going on.

'Heading on south?' said an officer. 'OK, follow the diversion signs and they'll take you back onto the motorway at the next junction.'

'Has there been an accident?'

'Something like that,' he replied noncommittally. 'Just follow the signs.'

Richard smiled as they drove on again and turned off the road. 'A Brummie accent's a lot different from a Yorkshire one,' he said.

'Yes,' said Clare, absently, now concentrating on the road.

The diversion signs were easy to follow at first, until the rain came down heavily again, driving straight at them so as to reduce visibility. As the roads grew dark and narrow, they even lost sight of the car in front.

Ten minutes later, after seeing no further signs or any other traffic heading in either direction, Richard knew they were lost.

'We must have missed one of the signs,' he confessed.

'Now what do we do?' said Clare.

72 WILLIAM HORWOOD

'Go and buy a Satnav,' said Richard ironically, 'but meanwhile we do it the old-fashioned way and watch out for a road sign. We can't have gone that far wrong.'

Clare looked back at the children. Both must have picked up on her own worry, for they were wide awake again, Katherine looking anxious, Jack wary.

The boy turned to Katherine. 'It's all right,' he said again.

Clare smiled at this and turned to study the road ahead, watching out carefully for signs. But now there was just darkness and high hedges, and then lightning. Next there came a crash of thunder and they ran into truly torrential rain.

'It *will* be all right,' said Clare softly, as much for her own benefit as anyone else's. The rain was thunderous and the wipers struggling so much to keep going that suddenly the road ahead was no more than a blur of rain.

She sat up straight and leaned forward to peer through the windscreen.

'Richard, we'd better stop, we can't see anything . . .'

The car lights made little impact on the raging darkness, but it was obvious the road ahead was too narrow to stop in.

'I'll pull over when I can and we'll wait until this downpour passes,' said Richard, his voice tight with concentration.

They topped a rise and the road ahead dropped steeply down so suddenly that it felt like a roller-coaster ride, but one in darkness, in rain caught by the headlights rushing wildly at them as the car speeded up.

'Richard . . . ? *Richard!*'

'*Daddy!*'

Katherine's eyes were wide with fear as she saw the hedge to her right veer towards her and nearly hit the car.

Lightning struck somewhere so close that the thunder that followed was as good as simultaneous, a huge loud crack that sent a vibration right through the vehicle.

Clare had time to see by its sudden light that Richard's face was tense and desperate as he struggled with the steering wheel to slow the car down

'I can't seem to control . . .' he shouted.

Clare felt a sliding sensation under them, the hedge to her left swinging slowly away, as if the car was beginning to turn around.

'Richard!!!'

For a moment the car straightened up, but then she saw the road ahead shift laterally again, twisting like a snake before them, first one way and then another, and then back too far again as the car slipped out of Richard's control.

'Clare, I . . . I . . .'

He struggled with the wheel, Clare half reached towards him and began to scream.

Jack shouted, 'No!' and twisted against his seat belt towards Katherine, his right hand trying to get to her, to hold her and protect her as the car's wheels began to leave the ground.

17

CRASH

The moment Pike saw the Fyrd, he had sent two of the stavermen to investigate but not engage.

Their report confirmed what Pike and Stort had seen, that oil had been spilt on the road.

'There's only one reason for doing that,' Pike told Brief. 'They mean to cause an accident.'

Brief shook his head in despair. There were rumours that the Fyrd's patrols sometimes meddled in the human world, but this was the first time he had witnessed it. Time was when any such an intervention in human affairs was unthinkable, but a new generation of Sinistral were taking control of the empire and they were using the might of the Fyrd in ever more extreme ways.

Some hydden believed that what the Fyrd did was a matter of timely revenge on humans for the damage they had done to the world through their thoughtless exploitation of the environment, but others wondered if there was a more sinister agenda behind it. There had in recent months been a spate of deliberate accidents with no regard for life, so that certain elements of the Fyrd could raid the crashed cars for their contents.

'We may be about to witness for ourselves what the Fyrd always deny their people do,' said Brief, 'in which case some good might come of this night's work.'

Stort had begun humming loudly in an effort to work out a way to deal with the danger presenting itself on the road below.

'We could try and wipe away the oil,' he rattled off impulsively, 'or leave warning signs of some kind, or we could . . . no, no, that won't work in this kind of weather'.

'What won't?' enquired one of the stavermen.

They knew that Master Stort was endlessly inventive, often to no great effect, but sometimes impressively so – occasionally with comical results which were all the funnier because he himself did not think them amusing. Whatever else, he was never less than interesting in all he attempted.

That evening he was being very serious indeed.

'In dryer conditions we could burn it off,' he said, 'which would serve the twin purpose of clearing away the problem and warning anyone approaching, but tonight that is not possible because oil is not combustible without great heat, and there is no way of achieving that here and now.'

They discussed a little more until Brief decided, 'All we can do is wait and watch. What we have already seen has confirmed Stort's suspicions about this night. If the oil is on the road, we cannot remove it. Nor, if something else happens, should we intervene.

'Mister Pike, let us continue to keep a watchful eye open!'

A short time later the Fyrd reappeared below, unaware that they were being watched. They examined the road, and seemed satisfied with their work.

Pike signalled silently to the others, moving closer to Stort and gripping his stave tighter. 'You stay close to me, Mister Stort, and you'll be all right.'

Stort half-smiled. 'Usually, Mister Pike, it's you who stays close by me!'

'Well, whatever . . . just be . . . careful!'

The other stavermen crept nearer. 'There's another on the other side,' whispered one of them, 'but I don't think any of them know we're here.'

'Mister Pike!' a voice hissed urgently. It was Stort.

Pike went back and stood by his side, peeping over the parapet.

'Did you hear that?' The youngster had the ears of a roe deer.

Then Pike did hear it: the squeal of car tyres on a road.

'See that?' Stort had the eyes of an eagle.

Pike saw it just moments later – a glimmer of light low down near the bend in the road, and this time most definitely not lightning.

'It's a vehicle,' he said, 'and it's coming at speed.'

'It's skidding,' said one of the stavermen, staring in alarm at the swinging headlights, the red back lights occasionally visible as well.

'By the good Earth herself,' swore another, 'it's heading straight for the bridge we're standing on.'

They watched in horror as the shafting glare of the headlights of the skidding vehicle arced horribly up the hedge, and above that into the leafless branches of an oak tree, as its wheels left the ground before thumping hard back onto the road in a shower of sparks, amid grinding and squealing, its engine racing as it shot out of the darkness straight into one of the piers of the bridge, colliding so hard that it shook everything about them.

They leaned right over and helplessly watched what happened next.

The back of the car swung right round into the arch beneath them as the front end of the car, too, now facing the wrong way, disappeared from their sight into the same arch in which they had been sheltering and in which, were they still there, they would all most certainly now have been killed.

All thought of the Fyrd momentarily fled their minds as they rushed across to the other side of the bridge to see what happened. The car emerged, sliding and rolling into view again, before crashing back down onto the road, glass splintering, the boot and a rear door shooting open. Then the door peeled away and cartwheeled ahead into the darkness, and they saw a human figure thrown clear through the sparks and wildly gyrating lights, briefly rising like a rag doll through the air before falling onto the grassy verge as the vehicle finally ground to a halt on the road below him.

The figure lay still.

Brief and the others stayed as they were because hydden tried not to intervene in human affairs.

The car below them was beginning to burn with a fire too strong even for the rain to put out. The flickering flames lit up the verge on either side, and the body of the person thrown clear. It moved and sat up. It was a boy who looked human.

'The giant-born?' said Brief, glancing at Imbolc.

'But still a boy?' said Stort, bewildered. They had always assumed that Beornamund's legend meant it would be an adult giant who came with the maid.

Stort turned to Brief for an explanation.

But Brief was looking as thoughtful as he was and just as confused.

'I thought it was the arrival of the Shield Maiden we were here to bear witness to,' he muttered.

Seconds later, after a few light flames flickered out of the crushed front of the car, it exploded in a ball of flame shooting into the air. By its dying light they saw that the windscreen and the front end of the car's roof had completely gone, exposing the seats, in which three figures still sat immobile, two in the front and one behind.

Brief turned to the Peace-Weaver. 'Who's inside that burning car?' he asked her urgently. 'Who *exactly*?'

She hesitated. This was not how it was meant to be. But then . . . she suddenly relaxed. She almost smiled.

Wyrd had its own way of working things for good and for ill; for worse as well as for better; for the least important person, and also for the entire Universe. And in the Mirror were reflected all things.

'I think the Shield Maiden is in there,' said Imbolc, sure now that her search was near its end – or at least at its proper beginning. She knew Beornamund's prophecy too.

It was Stort who acted. Before Pike and the others could stop him Stort slipped behind them and along the bridge to where he could climb over the parapet and jump down onto the embankment on the same side where the boy had been thrown.

He was away into darkness before the others had even realized he'd gone, crashing his way down through the vegetation of the embankment – aiming to break the most ancient of the Hyddenworld's taboos.

While from out of the wreckage and flames came the strangest of sounds, pitched just so its insistent sound could be heard above everything, even the wind.

It was the sound of a mobile phone ringing.

Then it stopped.

18

WORRIED

Roger Lynas, the officer in charge of Jack's case, stared at the phone he had just put down. Outside the weather was bad. The road reports were appalling. Now, worse still, the Shores weren't picking up his calls.

This had always been a strange case and he felt, for reasons he could not work out, that he was not only out of his depth but the case itself was hurtling out of his control.

One good thing was that Dr Richard Shore and his family were known to him.

The other positive was that the police checks done on the mysterious Foales, whose number had been in Jack's backpack, were as good as they get. No criminal record, no offences of any kind, good references all around. In fact it turned out that Arthur Foale was, or had been, a semi-public figure. Lynas thought he recalled seeing him on telly talking about the Dark Ages.

How he and his wife were connected to the boy Jack, Lynas had no idea, but intended to find out. Meanwhile they were the best option he had where Jack was concerned, and his primary concern was the lad's welfare.

He had promised to keep Mrs Foale informed, and he decided to do so now. He picked up the phone again and tried the Foales' number. He got an answer straight away.

'Just to say Jack's on his way to London now, and as soon as he's arrived I'll let you know. If you're free tomorrow . . .'

'I'm free any time,' said Margaret Foale, 'but . . .' she hesitated.

'What?' Lynas was trained to notice anything and everything.

'It's the weather. It's bad now and the forecast says it's getting even worse. It's not the best evening to be travelling, so couldn't Jack have been brought down tomorrow?'

Lynas smiled slightly. She sounded like a worried parent. That was a good sign. 'I'm sure he'll be fine,' he said.

Wind thumped against the side of the building he sat in, which suddenly shook with the strength of it.

Lynas went to his office window and stared into wild darkness at an indifferent world: trees, people, buildings, cars, clouds and beyond it, far beyond it, the Universe itself.

'It's certainly a wild night, Mrs Foale, but Jack is with a doctor and his family known to me and will be safe I'm sure.'

'Well . . . that's good then,' said Margaret Foale doubtfully.

'Yes,' said Lynas, hoping his reassuring words worked more successfully for her than they did for him.

As he ended the call the building was hit by violent wind again.

19

FLAMES

R ichard Shore slowly emerged back into consciousness. He
found himself still sitting in the driver's seat but with the roof
of his car gone and a dark patch of sky above him. The car
was surrounded by the light of flames shooting up all around, and the
hiss of steaming rain.

Puzzled and bewildered but not yet feeling the pain of any injuries
or burns, instinct made him rise, his seat belt melted away and the
air-bag, which had briefly blown up, now deflated.

He turned very slowly, flames licking at his lower body, to see his
wife Clare scrabbling uselessly at her seat-belt fastener. He reached
down through flames to try and free her, but failed, and his hair
started sizzling in the intense heat.

He turned further still to look behind him, and saw that Jack had
inexplicably disappeared, but Katherine was still there, sitting calmly,
probably in shock but seemingly unhurt.

Richard turned back to Clare, moving so slowly that time itself might
have been on holiday, and saw that she had now half-turned to try to
reach out towards Katherine, except that the seat belt prevented her.

She began screaming desperately at him, but her words remained
silent, his eardrums, like the rest of him, still in shock and trauma.

Then, inexplicably, his wife's beautiful dark hair darted one way
and then another, tugged by the hot and violent gusts of wind all
about them, and her eyes closed as her hands wandered aimlessly
here and there through the flames, becoming increasingly useless.

It was then that Richard's world speeded up again, and his hearing returned, and he heard another explosion and saw the sudden roaring of flames.

Then, astonishingly, he heard something else, and if anything restored him to his senses it was that sound: the cool, calm, voice of the man inside the radio he could no longer see, still reporting the news. Then that too was gone.

Richard reached down and slid his own arms under Clare's flailing arms. With a strength born of panic and love and the primeval need to keep his wife alive, he heaved her bodily from her seat and shoved her through the now non-existent door at her side.

As he did so both the arms of his jacket burst into flame.

'I feel no pain,' he told himself aloud and wonderingly, 'not a thing.'

One of his eyes blistered with heat and turned blind.

He then turned back to where Katherine sat and tried to free her too, but failed. Instead he half-dived, half-fell out of the car after Clare, picked her up again and threw her onto the far verge well clear of danger, before returning to the car and instinctively turning towards Katherine's door, so as to open it and set her free.

But the door handle had already turned black with heat.

On the verge onto which he had been thrown, Jack finally came to, and at once sat bolt upright.

His eyes took in the wreckage of the car and then what looked like a rag doll on the opposite verge, its hands moving ever so slowly. With a shock, he realized it was the woman, the girl's mother.

Nearer to him, but on the far side of the car, he saw a figure in flames trying to wrestle open the girl's door.

Then Jack saw Katherine still stuck in her seat, though his own door was gone, all that part of the interior now no more than a tangled skein of springs and metal struts that had once been his seat.

But Jack did not hesitate further.

He leapt up and began to run back towards the burning vehicle, each step seeming to take a lifetime as the flames from the front of the car started to encroach on the seat in which she was still trapped.

Then, hearing her scream as the flames now almost reached her, Jack found himself running faster still.

✳

Richard's world, briefly so fast and urgent, had begun to slow down once more, as the scalding pain heralding his own descent into a darkness from which he would never return began to overwhelm him.

Even then the instinct to save his child's life was more powerful than the desire to save his own.

He reached for the handle of Katherine's door, but as he gripped the hot metal he smelt his own flesh burning and felt his fingers curl into uselessness. He saw Katherine's face staring out at him through the glass, and realized she was so afraid, so frightened now, in a way no child should ever be . . .

Then a moment of terrible, heavy sadness as the darkness closed in around him – creeping up his body, into his head and then blinding his other eye – a feeling of despair that might have been the last thing he knew, except that he saw her turn her head away from him to look the other way and reach a hand out towards the boy, who was suddenly there now, there to help her, there to see her to safety.

Which was the last thing Richard knew before darkness came, pain fled and he was no more.

At that same moment Jack reached the ragged gap in the car where the passenger doorframe on his side had been, and saw the man through glass, a dark form surrounded by orange, slowly sinking away and out of sight on the far side of the car.

Katherine, hearing him shout, turned in Jack's direction and reached out her hand. Jack took it but for a moment he didn't think he'd be able to move her. He leaned further in, grabbed her arm and pulled harder still. The buckle of her seat belt burst open, and he was finally able to heave her out of the car and right over himself as the flames erupted brightly again from the footwell in the front.

She fell on to the road, beyond the blazing car, and he landed on top of her with a thump.

She rolled out from under him and, as he tried to heave himself to his feet, he felt her hand clutching at his jacket, hauling him upright.

Then, together, back on their feet, the flames rushing after them, they ran from the road and the exploding car towards the same verge where Jack had lain before, heaving, pulling, shoving each other up the slippery grass into the darkness above.

At the end, as Jack felt something like hot water coursing down his back, he kept her moving ahead of him and sheltered from the worst of it until, with one last desperate exertion, they reached the top of the manmade embankment and tumbled down its far side into blissful darkness.

Jack felt himself slip again into unconsciousness and, as he did so, Katherine took hold of him with one hand while in the other she clutched his little leather bag as if, in the midst of all this tragedy, pain and death, it was the most important thing of all.

It was then that she looked up and saw them coming across the field, three strangers in black, looming and purposeful. They were not much bigger than herself but they were broader, stronger – and seemingly adult.

She let go of Jack and the bag, and stood up in the dark, the flames of the wrecked car still lighting up the sky on the other side of the embankment they had slithered down. She took up position in front of Jack as if to protect him from them.

'No!' she said quietly.

But the Fyrd, three of them, faces shining in the firelight, eyes dark-set and glittering with night, came on until they were almost within reach. The leader, taller than the others, was sleek of hair and had an unpleasant smile even more distorted by the flickering light of the flames. His eyes were cold.

'It's not you we want but the boy!' he announced, his voice an icy whisper in the dark. One of them had a knife in his hand.

'*No!*' she said again.

The other two moved closer.

One was an ordinary Fyrd, stern, fit, in his thirties, with a flat, emotionless gaze.

The last one, the one with the weapon, was different. He was younger and looked as if he came from tough Polish stock. He was broader of body and face, his expression a natural smile, his hair curly and dark, his eyes hazel and his manner warm. But his eyes were gimlet-sharp, his hands large and strong, his stance firmly grounded.

He was dressed in the light grey uniform of an untried Fyrd, one seconded to a senior officer to watch and learn. The only weapons such trainees were permitted to use were knives, of which he wore two, to front and back respectively.

He stood silent and respectful, shadowing his leader.

It was the other who now spoke.

'We want to look at the boy,' he said.

'*No!*' cried Katherine again, her eyes defiant, her little form protective over Jack. '*Noooo!*' she screamed.

It was then that Bedwyn Stort arrived.

He had as good as fallen down the embankment from the bridge in his haste to reach Katherine and Jack before the Fyrd did.

Now, breathless from running, scratched by brambles, his trews half falling down, his tunic torn open by barbed wire, looking completely shambolic, he pushed Katherine behind him before raising his fists to the Fyrd in an apparent attempt to engage all three of them at once.

Astonishingly the Fyrd pulled back, suspecting a bigger ambush. They stood half-smiling while they considered what to do with someone who was nowhere near their size or weight, who did not carry a stave, and who quite plainly had never fought anyone before in his life.

The younger Fyrd, thinking perhaps that charm would do better than threats, squatted down in front of Stort, smiling falsely, glanced at Katherine in a speculative way, and then looked past them both to Jack and said, 'We only want to help the boy.'

But his knife glittered in the dark.

20

FROM THE EDGE
OF THE UNIVERSE

Pike had reacted swiftly to Stort's impulsive decision to intervene down below. The moment he realized what his protégé
was up to, he alerted the others. Then, ordering Brief and the
pedlar to stay where they were, he and the other stavermen followed
Stort down the embankment as silently as they could.

The evident surprise among the Fyrd at Stort's arrival told Pike
that the newcomers had no idea any other hydden were present, and
he wanted to retain this element of surprise as long as he could.

In the brief moments while the Fyrd considered how to deal with
Master Stort, Pike was able to study them unseen.

Even though there were only three of them, they looked formidable; that much was certain. And, as was the custom of the Fyrd
when on military duty, they were dressed in well-made black garb
shot through with the clear synthetic thread that diffused their
outlines and made their form indistinct.

It was instantly obvious to Pike which of them was the leader –
he'd had to deal with his like many times back in Brum. Tall,
aristocratic, self-confident, indifferent to those beneath him, contemp-
tuous of ordinary civilians but far too young for such a role.

Unless . . . Pike told himself, *this is a well-connected junior member
of the Sinistral establishment on his way to Brum to take up an
appointment which would give him the experience he needs to be
pushed through the ranks very fast.*

Pike guessed that the present assignment was ordered by a more senior member of the Sinistral clan still, someone who had come to know of the boy's movements.

Which said much for the Fyrd's network of intelligence and their ability to get things organized on the ground. It also told Pike that this was a situation fraught with danger and implications that he and the others were not fully aware of.

The Fyrd officer's number two was the usual sort, military through and through: well-set and orderly, with close-cut hair. The kind trained to take orders as well as give them, up to his level of competence. Such as had made the Fyrd the formidably successful occupying force it was.

The third had the broad good looks of someone from Eastern Europe, whence a large number of the reinforcements for the Fyrd and its administration came from, their home territory of the Rhine-lands not supplying enough as their empire expanded. Many such had come to Brum, often to take up menial roles, to give support to the Sinistral's army of occupation.

All in all the three Fyrd did not look too much of a challenge for Pike and his stavermen, but then they could not have expected opposition.

'Follow me straight in,' Pike whispered to the others, glad that Brief and the pedlar had had the sense to stay out of sight. 'Their leader is armed only with stave and crossbow, and that not primed, probably because he was not expecting any trouble. I'll take the one to his left, you deal with the young one on the right who is kneeling before Stort with knife drawn. Then we'll see what they have to say for themselves.'

Pike emerged with the others slowly from the shadows of the embankment, not wishing to seem too much of a threat and thus precipitate an attack.

He called out, 'That boy's under our protection.'

The young Fyrd stood up and backed off immediately.

His leader, as cool as Pike himself, half-smiled and said, 'If that's the case, you're not doing such a good job. He appears to be as good as dead.'

It was not the best of moments for Bedwyn Stort to renew his intervention, but that's what he did. Except for the appearance of Pike and the stavermen, things might have gone very badly for him, but the smiling young Fyrd acted coolly.

He restrained him with one hand but held out the knife with the other to show he meant business.

The tall Fyrd laughed aloud and drawled, 'This little drama seems suddenly to have moved from laughable comedy to potential tragedy, so would you care to bring your dog to heel before my assistant Brunte kills him? He likes the taste of blood, so I would not advise provoking him unnecessarily.'

Pike looked at Brunte and had no doubt that, young though he was, he meant business.

'Mister Stort . . .' he growled warningly.

Bedwyn Stort had the sense to scramble away but, to his credit, only as far as the two children. For her part, Katherine stood stock-still, now in an apparent state of shock, while Jack lay unmoving on the ground, the burns to his back and right shoulder all too visible.

'So,' said the Fyrd, with a sardonic smile, 'are there any more in your motley group we should be aware of?'

Pike hesitated, unsure whether to reveal the presence of Brief and the pedlar.

But the decision was made for him.

Brief himself appeared from the shadows of his own accord, tall and bold, his stave of office held proudly in his right hand.

'Well, this gets more astonishing by the moment!' said the Fyrd. 'Our orders were simply to detain the boy, but now it seems that half of Brum is here in an attempt to do the same thing. You are none other than Brief, Master Scrivener of Brum, am I right?'

'Yes,' said Brief, taking his place next to Pike, who now realized that the pedlar, or whatever she was, was nowhere to be seen. Much good she was going to be to anyone in a crisis!

'You realize, Master Brief, that your presence here is illegal?' continued the Fyrd. 'If you, of all people, had applied for permission to depart the environs of Brum, I would have known about it, so I guess you did not?'

'You being who, sir?' replied Brief with no sign of nervousness.

The Fyrd smiled grimly. 'I am the newly appointed Quentor of

Brum on my way to take up office. Apprehending this boy is but a small diversion.' His eyes hardened. His voice too. 'But you know what, Brief? I have been travelling for some days now and I am cold and tired and bored. This boy is of interest to us, but he cannot possibly be of interest to you. Therefore I am ordering you and your friends to return to Brum at once. Get there before me and your transgressions will go unnoticed. Get there afterwards and I regret that you will not go unpunished, and even your position will not protect you, Master Brief.'

The Fyrd readied their weapons, as did Pike and the stavermen.

'The boy is a human and there should be no contact between hydden and human,' said Brief. 'That is the law! As for your purpose – quite plainly it is not to apprehend but to murder.'

The Fyrd's eyes grew cold.

'You do not know what Fyrd I am. My name is Lavin Sinistral . . . and I will have my way over this boy and you will retreat!'

At the mention of the name Sinistral a chill hush fell across them all. They knew at once that they were dealing with a situation as difficult as it was dangerous. This new Quentor was young, but if he was a Sinistral it meant his post was merely a training ground. Arguing with such a one had consequences, defying him was as good as death, young though he was. The Sinistral watched over their own.

But Brief stood firm, while Pike looked yet more threatening. Neither was intimidated. If a member of the Sinistral family had been sent in person to deal with the boy then Stort's premonitions of his importance were correct.

A shadow crossed over the Quentor's face, and Pike realized too late that he had misjudged the situation entirely. It seemed a new breed of Fyrd was on its way to Brum, one that was more resolute than ever before.

'Goodbye, Master Brief,' said Lavin Sinistral calmly, without a hint of what was coming. 'It was interesting but hardly a pleasure to meet you. The times are changing, and you and your kind are now the past.'

With that, and before Pike or the other stavermen could respond, he primed his crossbow, raised it and pulled the trigger in a swift double action which released two bolts straight at Brief's heart from point-blank range.

Master Brief was as good as dead.

Yet it didn't happen.

There came a sudden icy mist to the air and everything slowed down – the metal bolts from the Quentor's crossbow, which started so fast, lost speed until the rotation of their lethal heads was plainly visible.

Then, as suddenly as it had appeared, the mist was gone and what had taken its place was the flank of a white horse sliding between the Fyrd and Brief, the bolts from the crossbow shattering into a thousand shards of light as they hit the great steed, twisting and turning and spiralling away in all directions, their sound like the tinkling of glass shaken in a void of time.

The White Horse reared. Its rider was a woman, ancient in one aspect, youthful in another, and hanging from her neck was a disc of gold. *The Peace-Weaver* they told themselves in awe and wonder, for well known as she was in legend and song, in woven tapestry and painted image, it was given to few ever to see her. Even Brief, who knew Imbolc of old, felt the same wonder and surprise.

The White Horse turned away, its rider with it, her hair streaming, her robes shimmering with light and a spectrum of colour flowing behind her. This fell to earth as a sudden chilling torrent of hail, the like of which they had never seen before – huge lumps and shards of ice filled with a strange light which faded where it fell.

In that endless-seeming moment each side retreated from further conflict, the Fyrd fleeing into the darkness of the distant fields, unwilling to risk their lives against adversaries with such an ally as the Peace-Weaver herself. Then she was gone over their heads as an arc of light that got ever thinner, reaching away through the storm of wind and rain, through the clouds beyond and right over the moon.

In the stillness that followed, with the danger of the Fyrd now gone, Pike, Brief and the others moved nearer to Katherine and Jack.

'Why has he retreated?' Pike murmured to Brief.

'Because he found something far more important here tonight than a mere boy,' said Brief soberly. 'He has had confirmation that both these children are protected by the Peace-Weaver herself, and therefore more valuable alive. But be certain of this, Pike, that Quentor will be back one day to claim them if he can. He is a pure-blood Sinistral and they never give up.'

21

TREACHERY

B ut a force was present that night of which even the wise Brief and the other hydden were not aware, or the Fyrd leader either. For what stalked among them, as vast and magnificent in its own dark way as any White Horse or Peace-Weaver or mortal purity of soul, was mortal ambition, driver of destiny and turner of souls to right and to wrong, to good and to bad.

It was there among them and it wore a smiling face.

Like a seed waiting for the nurturing of clear water and warm sun, ambition needs only opportunity to step forward and grasp the moment. It sniffs out opportunity as crows do carrion, and such was the impulse that now flowed through the blood and sinews of the Fyrd leader's young assistant, Igor Brunte.

He was not actually a Fyrd by birth, but by creation. He was – as he looked – Polish or, as the Fyrd liked to call his kind, a Polack. When the Fyrd took dominance over the hydden of Warsaw, he himself was only five, just old enough never to forget or forgive what happened to the city of his birth.

His father had been killed outright, his mother and elder sister ravished, his older brothers burnt alive along with other children. It was a fate that Brunte himself would have suffered had not one of these siblings pushed him forcibly through a metal grille nobody else was small enough to fit through before the fire reached them.

His elder brother had said just three words to him, which he never forgot and which he ever after would act upon: *Survive, remember, avenge.*

Brunte learned the arts of survival through his years of a brutal itinerant childhood that took him all across Europe and eventually to the very heartland of the Fyrd along the Rhine.

There he could study his enemy at close hand, by joining their army, fighting their wars, and studying their ways.

Remember his instructions? He could never forget nor forgive.

Avenge? He did so whenever he could, in small ways and large, but from simply wanting to cause trouble and hurt to a few, he now felt a need to kill them all, especially the Sinistral – every last one, wherever they lived, whatever their rank.

Even those in Brum, connected with the German branch so loosely that there was doubt of there being any real blood connection at all, he had plans to eliminate

That night these youthful but long-held intentions found new fuel. Brunte had also spied the vast, shining light of the White Horse and its rider, and in that brief moment he saw an opportunity so great that his life was changed for ever. He had spotted what the Quentor-elect had seen, and Brief and Pike as well: the pendant disc that hung from the Peace-Weaver's neck. Its gems had all gone. He knew the legends as others did, and the prophecies too.

She is near her end he told himself at once, *which means that her death will happen in my lifetime, perhaps while I am still young. Therefore I must ready myself to take hold of that pendant, which one day will fall from her neck . . . It will give me power over all.*

That was only the first of Brunte's immediate thoughts. Having now caught the sweet scent of opportunity, he decided to take it. But he knew that it was no good seeing what might be if he was not there to take advantage of it. The path to power is littered with the bodies of those who did not know how best to tread it.

So it was that as he and his more senior colleagues retreated from the bridge, Brunte glanced sideways at the Quentor and like the survivor that he was knew at once what he was thinking: something similar to himself.

'*Brunte must die, and my colleague too,*' *is what's in his mind* Brunte told himself. *He knows that we saw what he did, and fears it will thwart his own ambition.*

Igor Brunte did not hesitate once he had worked out what action to take. He never had, and he never would.

'My lord,' he said, the moment their retreat had taken them back into shadows, 'a word in your ear if you please . . .'

He glanced meaningfully at the other Fyrd, as if mutely accusing him of those same dark thoughts of which he himself was guilty. The Quentor understood at once and fell into the trap.

'Yes?' he said softly, inviting him close.

Brunte had his back to the other Fyrd, blocking his view. In his left hand he now held the longer of his knives.

'I have something here for you, my lord,' he said softly, plunging the knife into his leader's side so that its point went straight to his heart.

The Fyrd leader did no more than let out a little gasp of surprise, before falling sideways to the ground.

Brunte turned at once to the other one.

Shocked, speechless, and surprised – all emotions Brunte noted with cold interest – the second Fyrd's training deserted him, the more so because of Brunte's strangely hypnotic smile. He succeeded in uttering only a single word: 'No!'

'Oh yes, my friend, you too. For the secret of this night I share with no one.'

This time he used both his knives together, each cruelly: one upward into the eye, the other downward to the gut. Then, letting go of them, he shoved his calloused fist hard into the stricken Fyrd's open mouth, reducing his dying scream to a mere grunting sob.

The job done, Brunte retrieved his knives and turned away into the night. Without further delay, he set forth to Brum, fabricating a tale of murderous attack and thinking of ways he might himself in time assume senior office of some kind and ready himself for greater power still.

22

HEALING

Imbolc's intervention had saved Brief's life and left them free to do what they could for Jack. He lay awkwardly and still, the blackened flesh of his burnt back bare to the night, while his face, caught by the flickering light of the still-burning car, bore the pallor of death.

Brief examined him.

'Well, he's still alive, that much we can say. But unless I can treat these burns . . .'

He bent closer, hardly daring to touch Jack's clothes, which had melted into his skin.

'I don't think I have ever seen anything so brave as what this boy did,' murmured Brief, 'which rather confirms that he is what we think he is – a giant-born. In fact *the* giant-born. But . . .' He sat back on his haunches and dug inside his robe to remove a flat pouch secured on a woven cord around his waist. 'It's a long time since I treated wounds of this severity. I fear that unless I can first cool these burns I will only do worse damage if I try to apply a salve, even one as sovereign as I have here.'

He looked up at Pike, despair written on his face. 'I'm not sure what to do, but if he's to have any hope then we need to use something cold, very cold – and quickly.'

Stort loomed up suddenly from the shadow of the embankment, covered in mud and grime. He carried a black bin-bag, heavy and dripping, in his hands.

'Some of the hail which fell just now,' he announced. 'Master

Brief, I have a feeling this might help the boy's burns if you can apply it.'

Brief took the load thankfully and knelt down beside Jack.

'So he's putting to one side his doubts about tradition and taboos concerning hydden and human!' Stort whispered to Pike.

'If he hadn't I most certainly would have done what I could myself,' replied the staverman.

'Yes, I am,' muttered Brief irritably. 'Now could you kindly stop chattering and Master Stort, please find me some more ice.'

'I will try,' said Stort. 'Meanwhile, Mister Pike, I think the human lady lying on the far verge may need some of this hail as well, so perhaps you could set your stavermen to collecting some.'

He dug into one of his pockets and produced a roll of bin-bags. 'Please tell them that I will wish to have any they do not use returned to me. It was no easy matter getting hold of this lot.' Despite his otherworldliness, Bedwyn Stort had a streak of practicality about him, odd though his methods sometimes were.

Pike stared across the road, past the wreckage of the car, to the opposite verge where the dark form of Clare Shore lay exactly where she had been thrown.

He sent two of the stavermen across to examine her, while Stort and some others busily gathered more hail. Katherine, wide-eyed, stared after them, but made no attempt to move from Jack's side, as if, for the moment at least, he needed her presence most.

Brief applied the bin-bags of ice and water as Stort brought them to him, successfully easing Jack onto his side, and grunting with satisfaction when he heard the boy's breathing grow deeper and more regular.

Then Jack began to shiver, his body and legs shaking more and more violently.

Brief took off his own robe and laid it over him, covering the makeshift ice packs as well, then he dug into his pouch and produced a small vial of liquid from which he shook some drops into Jack's half-open mouth.

He coughed faintly, and for a moment he even tried to move.

But it was Katherine who did the moving. She got up, went closer to him and knelt down, her head so close to Brief's that they were touching.

'It's all right, Jack,' she whispered, and impulsively reached out a hand to his cheek. His own right hand moved in the dark, reaching for hers.

'It's all right,' she murmured, as much to reassure herself as him.

Stort said to Brief, 'The boy might need this.' It was the leather backpack he had been carrying with him earlier.

'Plainly it's hydden-made,' observed Stort. 'Confirmation if we needed it of what the boy's origins really are.'

Moments later there came a quiet whistle from the far side of road, and one of the stavermen attending to Clare Shore raised his hand.

'It's Mum,' said Katherine to Jack, as if instinctively understanding that he must know why she was now leaving him.

Only one of the stavermen stayed with Jack, while the others crossed the road to approach Clare.

'Not a sign of life,' Brief informed them heavily, 'not even a tremor. But she's an adult human, so I don't know if . . .'

They all stared at her, in awe.

To them she was a giant, their feet smaller than her hands, her twisted limbs massive compared to their own.

'I can find no burns to speak of, nor any real injury,' Brief told Pike, 'but there is no sign of a pulse, assuming humans have them too. Since they bleed, as we do, I assume they must. I can only think she's sustained some terrible internal injury we cannot see.'

Pike stared at her, never having seen a female human at such close range. She looked monstrous.

'Did you apply that same balm that brought the boy round?' asked Pike.

Brief nodded bleakly. 'But no result.'

'And the girl?' said Pike quietly, nodding towards Katherine, who knelt beside her mother, staring into her face.

'Hasn't even touched her or tried to say anything. I think perhaps she realizes her mother is—'

'Master Brief!'

It was Stort and he was pointing towards the area of the night sky towards which the Peace-Weaver had ridden. It was not dark but like a vast open wound, a violent cut of a knife across the Universe which burned with cosmic fire.

As they stared in astonishment the fire burned bright and shone its light briefly where Katherine knelt by her mother.

Clare Shore stirred and moaned. Then, opening her eyes, she reached out to her daughter, seeming not to see the rest of them at all.

She couldn't sit up, or speak, in fact could hardly even move.

Clare was quite evidently very badly hurt.

But she was most definitely alive.

The strange light in the sky, which after all might have been no more than swirling low clouds catching in some way the burning wreck of the car, for a moment shone brighter still.

'We see the Fires of the Universe,' whispered Brief in awe, speaking for them all, 'as the Mirror turns . . . and with its light shining on that girl and her mother we glimpse something of the Shield Maiden!'

Brief fell silent as if in prayer, before adding in a different voice, 'They'll be all right now. Our work, gentlemen, is done.'

Then, one by one, the hydden backed away and left the human mother and daughter by themselves.

Instead they crossed the road and went back to Jack.

'He seems more comfortable,' announced the staverman who had stayed with him.

'Well, then,' said Brief, 'there's no more that we can do here. But we'll watch over them all until help arrives.'

Less than ten minutes later, the storm having considerably abated, they heard the sound of a vehicle. It came slowly towards them in the same direction Richard Shore had originally approached from.

Brief removed his cloak from Jack, and they all retreated behind the parapet of the railway bridge above.

Below them the lone car slowed to a halt just before reaching the smouldering wreck. A man got out, looked about him in shock, retreated inside his vehicle and emerged again to make a call on his mobile. He then climbed up the verge to where Jack lay, took off his jacket and spread it over him.

Only then did he notice Katherine and her mother.

Very slowly, cautiously, he went over to them, and knelt down by them.

He made a second call on his mobile.

Twenty minutes later the first ambulance arrived, its headlights and blue flashing lights finally revealing the scene in all its true horror of injury and death and destruction.

The police turned up next, and then a second ambulance.

The three of them were placed in separate ambulances, the girl remaining with her mother.

The body of Richard Shore was removed last of all.

Meanwhile, unseen up on the railway bridge, the hydden watched these developments to the very last.

Pike looked grim and resolute, and Stort looked saddened, while Master Brief, feeling all those emotions, raised his stave to the sky and whispered prayers for the living and a prayer for the dead; and finally a prayer for the hydden themselves, summoning them all to him before he spoke further.

'Gentlemen,' he said, 'we who have been witnesses to the events of this night will be its guardians. We shall not speak of what we have seen, and we swear to watch over these three surviving humans whose paths have crossed ours during the turning of the Mirror-of-All which has shown itself this night. The boy, the girl, the woman and ourselves remain as witnesses; the man who died here goes on ahead.'

'And the Fyrd,' interrupted Stort, 'they are part of it, too.'

'Indeed they are,' acknowledged Brief. 'They are witnesses caught like us in the wyrd of things.'

With that they shook each other's hands in solemn acknowledgement of their sense of shared responsibility, before turning away to begin the journey back to Brum.

Except it seemed that they had forgotten something.

'Master Brief . . . ?'

For the second time that night Bedwyn Stort slipped away and down the embankment. Pike followed him, the others watched.

'It's here somewhere,' said Stort, searching through the shadowed undergrowth furtively lest humans near the crash scene saw him.

'What is?' asked Pike, hand firmly on his stave in case the Fyrd reappeared.

'This!' said Stort.

He reached into the grass and moments later was holding some-thing in the air.

'It's the giant-born's portersac. One day he'll need it again.'

He climbed back up the embankment and joined the others.

Pike took the old bag and opened it.

'Nothing inside,' he pronounced.

'Just so,' said Brief, taking the bag and carefully folding it and putting it in his own. 'It's waiting to be filled with the things he'll need for his life's journey. Now, gentlemen . . . let us leave!'

They headed back along the track the way they had originally come until, the hedges on either side rising higher and the sky above dark before dawn, they were gone into shadows to ponder all they had witnessed and trek through the many seasons yet to come before their wyrd, and Jack's and Katherine's, might bring them together again.

23
AFTERMATH

'Please say that again,' said Margaret Foale.

She was talking on the phone to Roger Lynas, the same case officer from North Yorkshire who had been looking after Jack.

She had assumed this call was about Jack, and it had been until now. It seemed, however, that Jack was going to need years of operations and a long-term rehabilitation programme. The burns to his back, incurred while endeavouring to protect Katherine, were deep and particularly severe. That the boy had survived them at all was astonishing.

So any idea Margaret had harboured that she and Arthur might adopt him was out of the question. His situation was just too complex, the care he would need too specialist.

'We have had incidents like this before,' Lynas continued, 'and there are very good homes for such cases.'

'Institutions?' Margaret had said.

'Homes is the preferred word,' said Lynas.

Then the sudden change.

'But, Mrs Foale . . . I wanted to talk with you about the future of Katherine.'

Margaret blinked and her heart felt as though it was stopping.

She had been thinking about Katherine just before the call. The truth was that in the days and weeks since the crash she had begun to think a lot about Jack and Katherine.

Roger Lynas had promised to keep the Foales informed of what became of him, never expecting for a moment the drama and tragedy of what actually happened. Naturally when Margaret Foale learnt of the events, she and Arthur had visited Jack in the Birmingham hospital where he was taken after the crash.

They went again and that time met Clare and Katherine. A bond was formed, and it soon became clear how much support Clare would need. She took to the Foales – attracted by Margaret's natural warmth and Arthur's irascible good humour. Katherine took to them too, and they took her for walks in the hospital grounds when Clare was receiving treatment. No one was surprised, given the circumstances, that she attached herself to them more and more, as if in the Foales she found the kind of support that grandparents might have given had there been any, which there were not.

'I want to talk to you about Katherine's future. You and Professor Foale both. But this is not a conversation to have by telephone. Would you both be prepared to come over and talk about things?'

'What things exactly . . . ?'

Her mind was beginning to race. So many emotions experienced in the past weeks, since their original conversation about Jack; so many changes in her inner world.

Now Lynas wanted to talk about Katherine.

'Arthur?' she called, after promising to call Roger Lynas back that same day.

'Whatever is it?' he said when he she called more urgently a second time. She was in tears. She knew it was rarely given to a couple such as them, who were unable to have children, to have such an opportunity later in life. Of course she had harboured hopes – from the first moment Katherine held her hand in the hospital grounds and Clare began to confide her fears for the future to her. Now . . .

'I'm not sure what he wants to talk about but . . .'

'We'll go, of course,' said Arthur.

Later that day she and Arthur found themselves seated in a makeshift conference room at Northfield General Hospital, the one nearest the scene of the accident which possessed the specialist staff able to help Clare Shore.

Katherine had been well looked after within the same hospital, while Jack had been taken off to a specialist burns unit in London.

'But surely there are relatives she can go to?'

'None on either side,' said Lynas, 'and Clare Shore has asked if you would be willing to be involved. Katherine wants it too, though of course she's only a child. Even so, her attitude is important.'

'What do they want exactly?' said Arthur.

'For you, to act as guardian. They trust you.'

Margaret had cried then. Their wish implied the greatest possible trust.

If she knew they were observing her closely, as professionals must, assessing, thinking ahead, working out what was best for the child, taking on board the mother's wishes, weighing up the Foales' suitability . . . Margaret didn't show it.

What she said was, 'I think perhaps that we ought to talk with them both, and then spend a little time with Katherine. That's what we should do,'

Lynas smiled. He could not have wished for a better response.

They found Katherine sitting by her mother's bed. She was clutching a soft toy, an old white horse.

'Hello,' she said, looking at Margaret. At Arthur she grinned.

Clare eased herself up in bed, her face lined with loss and pain, her eyes filled with worry for the future.

'Hello, Katherine,' Margaret said as she reached a hand out to Clare and smiled.

Clare's return smile was bleak and tired.

Sedated, Margaret guessed.

'Katherine wants you to take her out again.'

'Do you?' Margaret asked the child.

'And McDonald's again.'

Margaret glanced at Clare. The child's mother nodded.

'Of course,' said Margaret.

She never subsequently called herself a 'parent', nor did she much like the idea of 'guardian', but whatever she and Arthur became as a result, it started right there and then when Katherine got up and reached out a small hand for Arthur to take.

'Where are we going today?' she asked.

Margaret was lost for words, but Arthur improvised.

'Waseley Hill,' he said promptly. 'It's only minutes away. Plenty of wet grass there! Is Mister Lynas going to come, too?'

Katherine looked appraisingly at Roger Lynas. 'No,' she replied.

So Arthur and Katherine went off alone, leaving the others behind with Clare Shore.

'I think this could work out,' said Roger Lynas, smiling at them both and starting to leave the room for them to talk.

Clare nodded, daring to think that she might have found a way forward for her child out of this tragedy and their deep loss.

'And Jack?' she whispered.

'Just extraordinary,' said Lynas at the doorway. 'He's the toughest child I've ever known in all my years in this job. By rights he shouldn't be alive, but he is recovering much faster than the doctors could hope.'

Clare was already closing her eyes when he left, daring to finally sleep properly and begin to heal, knowing she had done all a mother could, but she still wanted to say something more.

'What is it, Clare?'

'Jack looked after Katherine so closely during the . . . accident,' she whispered, before adding, 'and I think he always will. And then . . .'

'What?' asked Margaret.

There were people who came and helped before the ambulance came. I thought they were in my imagination but Katherine told me she saw them. Little people . . .

But Clare did not voice this aloud. It was too strange, too quirky and too irrational.

'That night of the crash the sky seemed to crack open and I saw such a fire, as if the Universe itself had opened. Its light shone on Katherine. Margaret . . .'

'My dear?'

'I think this was meant to be and that you and Arthur were meant to come into our lives now. I really believe that. That's why it feels right for you and Arthur to look after her.'

Her eyes closed and she looked more comfortable and at peace than for days.

'Will you . . . ?' she whispered.

'We'll look after you both,' said Margaret Foale, taking her hand. 'Now sleep, just sleep.'

So Clare finally let herself do so – comforted by a woman who was barely more than a stranger to her but felt like the mother she had never known.

III

TWELVE YEARS LATER

24
THE CALL

'Jack?'

Katherine spoke his name hesitantly, beginning to doubt it was really him. His voice sounded different.

'Er . . . yes?' he said uncertainly. She didn't sound like a little girl any more.

'*Jack?*'

'Yes.'

'It's *Katherine*. Katherine Shore.'

'Yes?' he repeated, as if keeping his distance.

Clare Shore had been chronically incapacitated since the car accident that had killed her husband, and nearly killed Jack as well. Katherine had come sometimes to see Jack in the hospital afterwards, but even those visits had trailed off when he was about eleven. Since then there had only been the regular cards at Christmas and on his birthday.

'It's Mum . . .'

He assumed at once that her mother must have died. But that wasn't quite the reason Katherine had phoned.

'She's near the end now, Jack, and she wants to see you.'

But Jack found he didn't want to revisit those memories. They had left too many painful scars both in his mind and on his body.

'Jack?'

'It might not be easy,' he said evasively.

'She *needs* to see you and . . . and I . . .'

I need to see you because I don't know where else to turn.

Something switched back on in Jack's mind. She needed him.

He breathed in deep and asked her, 'What's wrong? Apart from your mother that is?'

'Something happened.'

'What happened?'

His voice was suddenly protective. He didn't understand why he felt like this for someone he hardly knew, and who reminded him only of hard times. But he did.

The burns to his back and neck he had suffered while saving her life had been so bad that he had since had to endure years of skin grafts and general rehabilitation. Each operation, each bout of post-operative care, had been arduous.

Three people especially had helped see him through those early years: Margaret Foale and Katherine and Roger Lynas, his original social worker. Arthur had always stayed in the background.

Clare Shore was never well enough to travel comfortably, so she had remained in the periphery of Jack's life. But what he did know was that she and Katherine were now sharing the Foales' huge house in Berkshire. It had started as an arrangement of mutual convenience, with Clare providing an injection of capital into their home, while needing a new home for herself and her young daughter. But what had started out as a temporary arrangement had almost inevitably become permanent. And so the childless Margaret suddenly found she had two children to think about.

Yet the early friendship between Jack and Katherine was only tenuous at best, based on a chance meeting that had ended in tragedy for all concerned.

As time went on, both children found her visits increasingly difficult, and their interests developed in different directions – Jack towards the conventional urban activities of the other children with whom he shared a home, Katherine towards country pursuits like a pre-teen passion for horses.

Then the disastrous day when Katherine came to visit him in the children's hospital, and he complained angrily that the doctors were insisting on yet another operation.

'They're doctors,' she argued conclusively, as if that made them gods. At the time she was only ten, he eleven.

Jack was in pain, angry and frightened, and was stung by this seeming lack of sympathy, otherwise he'd never have said what he did. What he said next he regretted too late.

'You're on their side,' he yelled, 'like everyone else around here. You know nothing about what I'm going through, *nothing* . . . If it hadn't been for . . .'

He stopped, the words half out.

If it hadn't been for your parents picking me up this might never have happened to me.

Katherine didn't need to hear the words to know what he had been going to say.

'And if it hadn't been for you . . .' she shouted back.

. . . then my father might still be alive and my mother not permanently ill.

Maybe it was worse that the words were never properly said on either side, because the hurt and anger remained and grew.

Katherine hadn't seen him since, and although he'd bitterly regretted what he'd said, he'd never had the courage to apologize. While Katherine, feeling that in some way it was her fault that Jack had suffered the way he had, couldn't bear to face him and see that recrimination in his face again. Eventually Mrs Foale started visiting alone, having come to accept that the two of them probably needed some time apart, and to find better circumstances for meeting than a hospital bedside.

So, apart from cards at Christmas and on birthdays, the silence between them had lasted five long years.

But now Katherine was on the phone, claiming that something had happened. Something she needed to talk about.

'*What* happened?' he said again.

'It's about Arthur.'

'Arthur?'

'What about him?'

'He's disappeared.' There was a wobble in her voice. 'And with Mum so weak, I didn't know . . . I needed . . .'

'What?' said Jack.

There was a long silence.

Eventually Katherine spoke more calmly. 'Jack, I need someone to talk to.'

The clock turned back twelve years in a flash, and all pain, all doubt, all anger over their long time apart, fled away and was no more.

It wasn't just for her mother she had rung; it was for herself, and that was different.

'I'll have to make some arrangements this end,' said Jack impulsively, 'but it's all right, I'll come.'

25
TALK

Jack called Katherine back the next day.

They began talking and then didn't stop, sharing the details of their lives during the recent years. That same evening they talked again.

'When you think about it, we don't seem to have much in common,' Katherine said, amazed how easy it was just talking to him, but . . .

'You're right, maybe I'd better not come,' said Jack, misinterpreting what she meant.

'Don't be ridiculous,' she said, though suddenly uncertain.

There was a long silence.

'Of course I want to come,' he said finally.

He found himself astonished by what he had so nearly added, which was: *I've missed talking to you all these years, Katherine, and lately I've been thinking of, well, a lot of things. I've kept thinking of you and I don't know why. Now this has happened, and it feels right.*

It was true. For months before her phone call she had been on his mind.

That Spring he began noticing what he never had before – the new warmth in the air, the colours of life, buds on the urban trees, and sometimes, overhead in the evening, flocks of birds migrating from southern Europe. It had made him feel imprisoned and restless – made him think of the Foales, their country house and Katherine, and wish he was in touch with her again. Now here she was on the end of the line, a wish come true.

But Jack wasn't going to admit any of that.

Instead, embarrassed by his own thoughts, and not guessing she was thinking much the same, he protested again, 'Of course I want to see you.'

Me too she thought. *Me too, Jack . . .* But all she managed was, 'That's cool!'

'Tell me about where you live,' said Jack impulsively, to change the subject.

'The house is right across the valley from White Horse Hill,' she said. 'The White Horse is a carving in the chalk. I sent you a picture of it once.'

That same little card was, for no reason he ever understood, one of the very few things he truly treasured. It had pride of place in his postcard collection, and had come to represent all kind of things to him, the greatest of these being freedom. He had often imagined visiting all those places in Katherine's postcards, riding on a great White Horse, but he never imagined visiting the White Horse itself.

'I've still got it,' he said. Then added: 'Do you remember what you wrote on the back of the card?'

'Yes,' she said, softly.

It had come to mean everything to him because she gave it to him in hospital soon after some especially painful and difficult surgery, and just before their argument.

Look at this horse when you need to, like I do, she wrote. *Imagine you're on its back and it can take you anywhere you want at any time . . . to a place where there's no pain, just good things. Love, Katherine.*

He had read those words a thousand times, and travelled the whole world with her on that horse.

Love, Katherine.

He doubted he would ever tell her, or anyone, how he treasured those last two words inscribed on her postcards.

Next day he called her again.

'I'm coming this afternoon,' he said.

'Great. I'll arrange for a taxi to meet you.'

'It's already done. They're paying for a cab.'

'The whole way?'

Jack laughed. 'That's social services for you. It's to do with spare funding of transport for people like me. Very weird – just shows sometimes they get things right. I'll be turning up about four.'

'In time for tea.'

'Sounds quaint.'

'You remember how Mrs Foale likes that kind of thing and . . .'

'What?'

'. . . so do I.'

26

ROOM WITH A VIEW

atherine Shore sat in her first-floor bedroom in Woolstone
House, looking out across the fields to the steep wooded
escarpment that was White Horse Hill. The horse itself
looked as it always did, as it had done for nearly five millennia: either
galloping in from the left-hand side, or leaping off to the right,
depending on her mood.

Many was the journey she and that horse had made together, many
the tears she had shed on its back, many the times it took her through
the wild winds of her mind to distant shores – first, on simple
adventures, when she was younger; later on journeys of impossible
platonic love.

Now, more recently, into unspoken yearnings that left her restless
and irritable. The truth was she wanted something from Jack she
couldn't name and maybe he couldn't either, however long they had
talked.

That morning, lying in front of her on the desk were her text
workbooks for English and history, which she was now revising for
exams in June. She had been studying by distance learning ever since
her mother had become permanently housebound, thus making
Katherine and Mrs Foale her primary carers. Katherine still went
into the school in Wantage occasionally, to check she was still on
course, but she had inevitably become isolated from her contemp-
oraries. Having a dying mother is not conducive to making friends
because, however sympathetic, other kids just don't know what to
say.

But even if they did, Katherine would never have been one of the most popular pupils. She was already tall and skinny for her age and shunned cliques; she also knew too much and preferred books to company. Besides, there was a constant look of strain in her eyes that made people wary.

During her first year at school, this sense of exclusion hadn't mattered too much, because Katherine had bonded instantly with a chubby, red-haired, freckly girl called Samantha Fullerton. Sam also liked stories, had impossible dreams, and, best of all, had the strength and courage to stand up against the group, remaining impervious to peer pressure and youthful female spite. It said a great deal for Sam's parents that their daughter felt so secure in herself and had her feet so firmly planted on the ground.

Sam was Katherine's first and only school friend invited to stay at Woolstone House over the weekends, allowing the pair of them long walks over White Horse Hill and secret conversations long into the night.

Then halfway through their fourth year together at school, Sam's father moved the family to Hong Kong. Within weeks she was gone, leaving Katherine alone once again.

It seemed too late now to find a wider circle of friendship at school, so she retreated further into her books.

Then, nearly a year later, after only a couple of garishly coloured postcards from Hong Kong, the first real letter from Sam: friendly, chatty, full of news. Full of longing for England, concerned about Clare, a little lonesome too.

Katherine wrote back at once and the friendship, never truly dead, sprang to life again.

The year before, at Easter, with GCSEs almost upon them, Samantha's father brought her back to England and left her for a few days at Woolstone House. It was as if the two girls had never been separated, not for an instant, though each looked quite different from what they remembered.

They were the happiest few days of Katherine's adolescent life.

It was from this time on that Katherine opened up about her strange feelings of close affinity with Jack, confused and unresolved as they were. Was it that she owed him a debt for saving her life or was there something deeper? It sometimes felt to her that destiny meant them to be together. The trouble was she knew that could be just a romantic dream she liked the idea of!

'Maybe destiny and dreams are the same thing!' Sam wrote.

'. . . and maybe he feels the same!' replied Katherine.

Sam texted back: 'You'll never know if he does if you don't ask him. Mum says men need prompting!'

Katherine dithered for days.

'We haven't spoken to each other for years,' she eventually emailed Sam, 'and I bet he won't want to hear from me or he would have written himself. I bet he has loads of other friends, by now. Meaning girlfriends.'

Jack, she calculated, would have by now turned seventeen.

'Write to him,' Sam counselled her. By then her family was living in Sydney.

She didn't, but Katherine's thoughts about Jack shifted and changed. He was beginning to become tangible again. Meanwhile her strange dreams about him had to be theoretical, as were most of her thoughts involving the opposite sex.

Most, but, it turned out, not quite all.

The previous year she attended a Christmas social in the church hall where Mrs Foale was parish helper. It was, it turned out, a village event involving a whole mix of different people. At one point in the evening, a nice-looking boy came dancing close and, what with one thing, then another, and the lure of old-time mistletoe, they kissed in the cold darkness outside from which, breaking away as she imagined a violated heroine might do, she began laughing, as did he.

'Only did that for a dare,' he confessed, grinning.

Hearing which, she realized, to her surprise, that she would have done the same.

It was all right with him after that, and it lasted a few weeks into February, and it wasn't bad, in fact it was exciting. Except he wasn't as tall as her, and he didn't spark any strong emotion in her, which she thought should probably be present if he was 'the one'. Which is maybe where her recurrent fantasies about Jack came in.

So the boy from the village was ultimately a bit of a disappointment, though she let his hands wander until there came a point where he became too insistent. He had no more idea of what he was doing than she did.

But at least he had a sense of humour, and they shared rueful laughter, and agreed that it wasn't all it was cracked up to be. Their secret, however; no one else need know.

Then he found someone else more compliant and drifted away, and she felt relieved that whatever it had been it was over. It was a journey into the unknown which went only far enough for her to come back safely. But she knew she wanted more of wherever her dreams and fantasies were leading her.

Sam got told all the details, and sent details of her own encounters back. They didn't add up to that much for two girls aged sixteen in the twenty-first century.

Then everything changed. Arthur Foale, back only a short time from one of his mysterious trips, disappeared again. This time without warning or contact from him – to the stage where Margaret Foale, well used to her husband's wandering ways, was also concerned.

Then, too, Katherine's mother began deteriorating rapidly. When Clare said she wanted Jack to come and stay, it gave Katherine the excuse she needed to make that call.

Only when they started talking did she realize how much she needed to see him again.

Now the day had come and Katherine was sitting in her room, staring at the view and weighing up one final thing she was uncertain about concerning his bedroom, which Mrs Foale said it was her job to get ready.

People very rarely stayed at Woolstone House, and when they did they were not usually male or, well . . . *Jack*.

So Katherine, in a panic, had finally decided on the plain cream sheets and not the pink ones, and had changed the picture on the wall twice, in favour of a painting of boats.

When she couldn't think of anything else she headed downstairs and into the garden.

'Katherine, is that you?'

'Yes, Mum.'

'Where are you off to? It's cold.'

'I'm just going out into the garden.'

Mrs Foale, hearing Clare call out, came to see if she needed anything, and found her weeping.

'What is it my dear?' she asked, hugging her gently. She knew Clare was in almost constant pain, though she rarely complained, but certain small things upset her. Like her daughter not stopping to say hello before going out.

'It's Katherine,' Clare whispered. 'What's she *doing* out there?'

Mrs Foale went to the conservatory doors, and watched Katherine wandering across the great garden, stopping sometimes to bend down to look at flowers, and then choose with care.

'I think she's finding something for Jack's bedside table.'

'What sort of things?'

'She's looking for the flowers of the Spring.'

27

WHITE HORSE

Thirty minutes after leaving the outskirts of London, Jack's cab driver suddenly announced, 'Now *that's* a view!'

They were on a dual carriageway heading downhill through a steep-sided cutting excavated in chalk, whose sides framed the vast expanse of the Vale of Oxfordshire stretching ahead below them.

For Jack it seemed an unexpected portal to another world, because countryside like this was not something he had any previous experience of.

His first reaction was to wonder why the driver even bothered to comment on a landscape that looked so featureless and flat.

But then it drew him in, as at the beginning of a film, when the blank screen fills out and the action begins and all else is forgotten. Maybe it was the misty blue horizon, maybe some of the details he now began to see: an old farm building here, a church spire there, and then the shining silver ribbon of a stream reflecting the sky, and snaking away out of sight almost before he noticed it.

As they journeyed further, Jack began to realize he had been living in a city too long. He felt he had never seen such lush countryside before, not *this* type of countryside. Quiet villages, neat hedges, undulating fields, and stands of trees, their leaves already showing, while beyond them extended inner, shadowy, depths of woodland inviting exploration and discovery.

'England can be a beautiful country,' murmured the driver, as if picking up on his reverie.

Jack had to agree, as the earlier apprehension he had felt about this trip began to ease a little, replaced by a new excitement. He might not have seen this part of England before, but a memory of his brief childhood stay on the North Yorkshire Moors had come back, and before, vague though it was, another deeper memory of somewhere else: of mountains, biting cold air, and views across deep valleys. It put a yearning and restlessness into him that he could not explain but which made him feel alive in a way he hadn't felt for a long time.

'Mind you,' added the driver, '*that* thing spoils it a bit.' He pointed towards six great cooling towers, off to the left, from whose summits thick white steam billowed upwards into the sky.

'What is it?' he asked.

'Didcot Power Station, biggest of its kind in Europe. Spewing God knows what into the sky. We have to drive past it to get to where you're heading, so you'll get a closer look later. It's not that far now before we turn off . . . Oops, spoke too soon, as usual!'

At that moment, the traffic news broke in automatically on the car radio, and the driver turned it up so they could listen. The traffic began to slow to a crawl, as the announcement warned of delays occurring just after Junction 6, caused by an obstruction on the highway somewhere further on.

'No problem,' said the driver cheerily. 'We turn off at that junction anyway, so with luck we'll miss the worst of it.'

With a sideways wink at Jack, he pressed the button on a hands-free earpiece.

'Let's see if I can find out what's causing the obstruction.'

For a moment he listened in to some waveband chat he had linked to, and then switched his headpiece back on mute.

'That's a new one on me. It seems there's a horse loose on the motorway, and the traffic's backing up while they restrain it. Shouldn't be too . . . no, it's all right, here we go.'

The traffic ahead was starting to move, and a short time later they were able to turn left onto the slip road and head south, rapidly leaving the motorway behind.

'Could have been worse. They must have got their horse.'

But they hadn't, because Jack could see it through a gap in the hedge on his right and then a few more times after that, galloping parallel with them, keeping pace with the car, its coat an undulating white-grey sheen like the sky itself.

He lost sight of it then for a minute or two as the car turned a corner, before the hedge transmuted into a plain wire fence and then he could see it again, clear as anything, further off now but still magnificent. It veered nearer, was briefly lost to view again, and then was right in the field next to them, head pressed forward, muscles straining. But this time on their left side? That was strange.

'It's quite a horse,' said the driver, who had caught sight of it again as well.

For just a few moments more the white horse was so close that Jack could clearly see its eyes and questing nostrils, and the long hair of its mane and tail flying behind it in the wind. He even imagined he could hear the thunder of its hoofs.

Then it disappeared again and, though he strained to glimpse it, and turned his head round and tried to see through the rear window, the view was obscured, and he saw it no more. Moments later the car slowed right down as they entered a large village.

Fifteen minutes later they reached their next turn-off, and took a series of minor roads across the Berkshire countryside.

'We're nearly there,' said the driver, consulting his Satnav. The car turned smoothly between two big blue gateposts, paint peeling and standing crooked, the gate itself long gone. The wheels crunched over weed-filled gravel till they pulled to a halt in front of a great dilapidated house.

Jack climbed out of the cab and looked up five shallow stone steps to the double front door. One half of it suddenly opened and there stood Katherine, but looking nothing like he remembered her.

She was taller, her hair longer, and she was dressed differently from many of the London girls he knew: dowdy, sombre, serious.

'Hello, Jack,' she called out, her smile a bit crooked, her wave a little self-conscious.

He grabbed his backpack and climbed up the steps and shook her hand, his grip maybe too strong. Back in London girls hugged him and did the pretence of a peck on the cheek. This formal gesture felt strange, yet more sincere.

They gazed at each other, both nervous and both maybe a little disappointed. Jack was a shade shorter than she had imagined; she plainer than he expected.

Yet even in that first clumsy moment, it felt like a great old door, under-used and stiff with age, was slowly opening.

I saw a white horse he wanted to say, or even shout.

Instead he just stared at her in silence, his head thrust a little forward in that intense, disconcerting way of his, and she at him. Their initial disappointments were almost at once replaced by something else.

'*What?*' she said finally, curiosity in her voice.

'You look different – taller than I expected.'

What he really wanted to say took him by surprise: *The clothes don't matter, Katherine, because your eyes are beautiful and the way you hold yourself as well and . . . and . . . there's something that makes me want to be sure that no one ever hurts you.*

Katherine had her own thoughts too: *You look different, Jack. You look stronger and self-confident, like you know your place in life and aren't afraid of it – that makes me a bit scared of you.*

But neither one of them said any of this.

'Come this way,' she said, feeling she was inviting something powerful and unpredictable into the house. 'Um . . . through here,' she gestured.

The dark interior of the house loomed around him.

'I saw a white horse,' he muttered, following through the darkness this girl whose back and hips were now more like a woman's.

'Mum wants to say hello,' said Katherine over her shoulder, not having heard what he said. He didn't repeat it.

So they journeyed on together into the shadowy recesses of a house that had known illness too long and was ready for new life again.

'Jack?'

She had stopped in the shadows by a door ajar. He could see it led to a conservatory.

'Jack, Mum's not her normal self . . . I mean . . . there's something I didn't tell you.'

He stared at her, saying nothing.

Close-to he could see her nervousness. Of him? Of the situation? He felt nervous too.

'What?'

'Mum talks strangely sometimes and . . . I mean she's in a lot of pain. And there's the drugs which affect her mind so she seems to see things. I mean . . .'

'What do you mean?'

Jack felt he was more used to straight talking than she was. Where he came from if you weren't clear what you wanted you didn't get it. You had to say what you meant.

'I thought you might not come if I told you she . . . has delusions. Sees things that aren't there.'

'What things?'

She took a deep breath.

'Little people.'

'Like dwarfs?'

'No, not like dwarfs. Like . . . people. She might talk to you about them – maybe. She talks to Mrs Foale. Not to me though, not directly.'

'It's all right Katherine, I won't be embarrassed. I've been ill too, the mind plays tricks. Did she really want me to come or did you make that up?'

'Of course she did. I don't make things up.'

He grinned, more relaxed than she was.

'Let's go and see her,' he said, 'and then I'll make my own mind up.'

She looked relieved.

'Right,' she said, 'here goes . . .'

28

CLARE

J ack had never been in the same room as a dying person before, and it shocked him. It felt as if something else was hovering there in the shadows whose name was Death.

Jack knew of the Grim Reaper from his computer games. In real life he seemed much more scary. He also found that, strictly speaking, Clare was not in a room at all, which added to the odd, disturbing quality of the situation.

Weeks before, when she had become too weak to make it upstairs to her bedroom anymore, they had, at her suggestion, brought her bed downstairs and put it into the conservatory.

It was overheated, the more so when the sun shone, but its humid air helped her breathing and she could keep the doors open without getting cold.

The conservatory was huge, crumbling and Victorian, its slanting glazed ceiling supported by rusting Gothic cast-iron pillars up which vines grew from the earthen floor itself, their roots cracking the tiles around them. It was stuffed with potted plants amongst which, near the two sagging doors that opened wide onto a ruined terrace, stood Clare's bed.

Outside, growing up and across the glass panes of the conservatory, were the thick and still leafless stems of vines and wisteria, and an out-of-control rambling rose. In one corner the wisteria had broken through like the advance party of on invasion force. It felt almost as if the garden was trying to reclaim the house.

The garden itself stretched away outside in all directions, and from where Jack stood it appeared to have no boundaries or any end to it. There was a rough lawn, bumpy and badly mown, with a few formal and once elegant flowerbeds now gone to seed and weed. At a distance of a hundred yards, the 'lawn' gave way to shrubs and trees dominated nearest the house by two enormous conifers whose thick straight trunks rose nearly black against the cloudy sky.

They looked like two dark sentinels standing guard at the entrance to a world beyond; or maybe standing guard over Clare Shore against the world outside.

Or both.

Between them Jack could see that the ground beyond was a patch of rough grass around which other trees seemed to be closing in.

Jack hardly recognized Clare lying there among the untidy sheets and blankets and the many pillows scattered on her bed. The last time he had seen her was when he was only eight, and she could still travel. She had then visited him in hospital in London, pushed in a wheelchair by Mrs Foale, who had not yet made an appearance.

Clare's hair had been dark-brown then and, despite the wheelchair, he vaguely remembered her as cheerful and full of life and energy.

Now her hair was grey and lifeless, her skin pale and shrunken, and she looked so tiny and frail that the pillow propping up her head looked huge.

But then, noticing him at last, she slowly smiled and her dark, still-bright eyes took over from everything else, and he knew her again. His heart leapt because she had always looked at him like that on her visits, as if filled with joy to see him.

'Hello, Jack,' she said, raising her right hand weakly from the blankets towards him. He instinctively reached out and grasped it, as if that was the most natural thing in the world.

'Hello, Clare . . .' he said gently, not sure what to say to her.

She held his hand tight and just looked up at him.

Then: 'Closer,' she whispered.

He leant closer and closer still, and very slowly she did something to him that no one else ever had.

She reached her other hand up to his face and cupped one cheek with it, before letting go his hand and using her other one to do the same. Thus holding his face, she started feeling it as if to possess it with her touch.

Her smiling eyes were dark pools of welcome and acceptance.

'Thank you for coming,' she murmured very softly. 'Thank you, Jack.'

What he noticed next was not the bony chill of her touch, or the intensity of her gaze, but an endless tinkling of glass on glass. It was like a far-off waterfall of sound that had drifted in from the garden.

He turned slightly towards the open doors to see if he could catch the source of this sound, but he could not detect one.

'Aren't they beautiful?' she whispered.

He nodded. 'What are they?'

'Chimes for our protection,' she said, 'to make us safe. They are like the reflections of our lives forever mingling to confuse those who do not love us.'

She turned her head a fraction towards the outside world, then closed her eyes to simply listen and to sigh.

Then she said something strange.

'You'll understand about the chimes soon enough, Jack, and though I could explain it's better you find out for yourself.'

Jack hesitated over what to say next. He didn't want to patronize or humour her, but Katherine had warned him about her 'delusions' and that intrigued him: he wanted to know more. There was something he had not said out in the corridor, something he had never told anyone, not ever. The crash scene often came back to him in dreams and nightmares. Often he was trying to reach Katherine but couldn't. Other times she was just standing there and he was burning on the ground, people helping him. It had been years before he worked out what was strange about them. Two of them were obviously adults, because they had beards, but neither was any taller than Katherine. *Little people.*

'What do they protect us from?' he asked Clare evenly.

Katherine, who was sitting at the foot of the bed, tensed up.

'Mum didn't mean . . .'

Jack raised a hand and she fell silent.

Clare whispered, 'I don't know, Jack, but I know I feel safer when I hear them.'

The chimes tinkled in the background.

'Aren't they beautiful?' she said.

He nodded.

'You were iller than me. Things are heightened when you're ill, seeming worse or better than they really are. Ill people are said to get closer sometimes to the other side. Did you know that?'

'No,' he said, shaking his head.

Katherine relaxed. She liked the way Jack was listening and the gentle way he talked to her mother.

She took the opportunity to really look at him for the first time. He looked quite fierce and his head jutted forward very slightly to one side. She could see the scar tissue on his neck above his collar, rough and ugly.

You got that saving my life she told herself.

One of Clare's hands dropped away from him, back to the bed. The other moved on to touch the nape of his neck, and run its fingers over the places where he was burnt, lingering and feeling, caressing the rough, scarred skin.

No one had ever done that either, and whenever they had tried he had flinched. Not now, however, because her touch felt like a healing balm.

Katherine's hand touched his shoulder. 'She'll sleep now,' she whispered. 'She stayed awake just for you to come. Now she'll sleep.'

He looked round at Katherine, and then back at her mother, and then beyond them both into the garden.

The clouds had turned orange with the late-afternoon sun, which now caught the tops of the two conifers and made them seem aflame. He saw the dark rise of a steep chalk ridge beyond the trees. Then a blazing patch of light sped across it, a travelling, racing, run of brightness spilling through a gap in the cloud. It gradually turned the ridge of the Downs bright and pale, until suddenly it turned something that, until now, had been lost in the gloom, bright white and seemingly alive. It was the chalk outline of the White Horse of Uffington: its legs were just simple curves, its single eye bright, its ears pricked, its tail flowing behind it, seeming to be racing through sunlight towards the sky.

Framed between the two tallest trees it shone with startling brightness, but then the sunlight moved on, and the horse faded, until it was no more than a grey shadow.

'That's it,' said Katherine. 'That's our horse.' Her hand touched his arm very lightly as she nodded towards the hill. Then she whispered, 'She'll talk to you tomorrow afternoon, that's her best time. Let her sleep now.'

Jack looked back at Clare and saw she was fast asleep. He let go of her hand after placing it back on the bed and, without any embarrassment, he leaned forward and kissed her cheek.

'I'll look after Katherine *always*,' he found himself whispering. 'From now until the end of time.'

She stirred, half raised one hand towards him, gave a murmur of understanding and turned her head back into sleep.

Neither she, nor Jack, saw Katherine mouthing the words: 'And I'll look after him.'

29

HOUSE

'Mrs Foale's out late tonight, and she sleeps over the Stables, so you may not meet her till tomorrow morning,' explained Katherine later. 'Maybe you want to put your bag in your room upstairs? Come on – I'll show you.'

The stairs were wide and they creaked. They turned a corner halfway up, which created a little gallery of balustrades from which the hall below was visible. Except there were no lights on, and Katherine was in the habit of not using them unless absolutely necessary.

They went on up the stairs into shadows, the only source of illumination a skylight in the ceiling high above their heads.

Katherine led Jack next down a long corridor which had just a strip of carpet running along the middle, with bare boards on either side. It made the passage look even narrower.

'My room's back there, Mum used to sleep here until she couldn't manage the stairs, and you're in what's called the guest room, except we never have any guests.'

'You have now,' said Jack.

'But you're family,' said Katherine, without thinking. 'Well, anyway, something like that. It's in here.'

She opened the door but didn't go in because that felt a step too far, now Jack had arrived. She had made up his room with infinite care, cleaning, dusting, polishing, folding and refolding the sheets on his old Edwardian single bed at least three times to get them right.

But now he was here, a disturbing, unfamiliar presence, it was suddenly his space and not hers.

'Um, well ... I'll leave you then. Supper at six-thirty? We can entertain ourselves tonight. Mrs Foale's made one of her murky stews, so beware.'

He gazed at her, not wanting her to go but unsure how to ask her to stay. The whole day had been weird and he was tired and a bit confused, and there was something about the house – an unsettling feeling of sadness and waiting. 'Thanks, then. Six-thirty.'

'There's a gong, and I'll bang it. Mum likes to hear the routines, as they help pass her day.'

'Okay, then.'

Then she hurried away and Jack found himself alone. The room took him by surprise: it was huge compared with what he was used to. The tall casement windows, covered in cracked and peeling cream paint, looked out on to the darkening garden and beyond it to White Horse Hill, now just a dark and lowering mass against a mauve sky. They had shutters folded into the frame on either side.

There was a wooden bed, a bedside table with an old crooked lamp made out of an ornate wine bottle, and a big threadbare rug which covered less than half the black-painted floorboards. A picture of boats on the wall helped it look like a seaside boarding-house room from the Fifties, and made Jack feel he had walked on to the set of a movie produced in an English film studio, story unknown.

There was also a desk by one of the windows, a wardrobe with a door hanging crooked and ajar, a cream light shade with burn marks round the top because at some time in the past it had been fitted with a bulb too powerful and hot for its size.

Jack dropped his bag on the floor and sat down on the bed, and let the gloom descend on him. Except it wasn't quite like that because, though it got darker inside the room, the sky over the hill got lighter, brighter and redder for a time.

He watched it and heard his own breathing subside.

Today was an ending and a beginning like no other he could remember.

He reached his hand behind him to the bed, which had soft pillows and sheets which were smooth, clean and ironed with carefully turned-over blankets on it. He lay back on the bed and stared at the ceiling, following its cracks to the furthest corner of the room until, his eyes closing, he began to drift off. He fell asleep into familiar nightmare: him on his back in the dark burning, the little girl that once was Katherine standing nearby staring at him, the bearded person coming and coolness on his back and the bang bang bang of . . .

The gong awoke him and he sat up at once, his bag at his feet and still unpacked. He looked around groggily, and saw something he had not noticed before. It was a bunch of flowers, not much more than a spring posy of daffodils and sweet-smelling hyacinths, which Katherine had put in a jam jar placed neatly on a round crocheted mat to protect the wooden surface beneath.

Next to it was a box of matches and next to that in turn a smaller jar with a tea light in it. Jack lit it and placed it a little way further from the posy but still within the frame of the three-part mirror, so it not only lit up the flowers but was reflected in the mirror.

The posy was bound by threads of dried grass cleverly tied in a bow.

Earlier, Katherine had let slip she saw him as family.

That was one thing, this quite another. He had never in his life been made to feel at home in such a way.

Movement reflected in the glass but he didn't look around. He saw Katherine silhouetted at the door behind him, watching.

'I didn't hear any movement,' she said, 'so I thought you might be sleeping. Did I wake you with the gong?'

He nodded, but it didn't matter whether she had or not; it was the flowers that he was thinking about.

'Thanks,' he said. 'No one's ever done something like this for me before.'

'There's food on the table, Jack,' she said nervously, 'if you're hungry.'

'I'm always hungry,' he said.

'Come on then,' she said awkwardly.

He strode along behind her, his steps louder than she was used to in the usually quiet house. She wouldn't have been surprised if the plant stand at the top of the stairs went flying or Arthur's umbrella stand in the hall below skittered across the oak floor when they reached it, its contents flying and bashing into the walls and the great front door.

'You don't put lights on much, do you?' he observed.

'Generally not,' she agreed, adding, 'and anyway the bulbs always blow and there's no one to change them.'

Supper was not murky stew. It was Welsh rarebit and salad with a dressing, and the moment Jack sat at the table Katherine realized it wasn't nearly enough. He looked like a shaggy lion being offered peanuts.

The truth was she had put Mrs Foale's murky stew back in the fridge, thinking it too crude and unpalatable-looking for the occasion. She saw now that it would have been perfect.

'That was starters,' she lied when the rarebit disappeared and he looked around hungrily, 'because . . . well . . .'

'What?' he asked.

She began laughing.

'What?'

'Nothing.'

'*What?*'

She told him about the stew. They both started laughing, like children in a playground, but laughing too from the strong under-currents that came with being children no more; and with the pleasure of realizing that things were all right.

'So, do you want some murky stew?' she asked.

'*Yes!*'

She heated him some and left him to begin to devour it, while she tended to Clare.

'She's sleeping again,' said Katherine heavily when she came back.

She sat down without expression.

'It must be hard for you,' he said.

She nodded without looking at him and answered, 'It gets harder. But there are good moments and she's mostly positive. Doesn't want to upset me I suppose. Just now she said she could hear us laughing earlier, which she liked. She's glad there's new life in the house. Do you want some more?'

Jack nodded and she fetched him some. They began to catch up all down the years. Their voices, now loud, now soft, and their laughter spread throughout the old house, threads of light in darkness reaching into the furthermost corners.

'I'm sorry about what happened, Jack, you know – not talking for years.'

'It was my fault too.'

'I liked the way you talked to Mum.'

'It wasn't hard,' he said.

The angry silence of the years was broken and new trust building. By the time they said good night they were friends again.

Much later, all lights out, Mrs Foale returned by cab.

She went to check on Clare, who was awake, eyes open.

Mrs Foale turned her over, made sure she was set for the rest of the night.

'You look better,' she said.

'Can you tell the difference? In the house?'

Mrs Foale sat back and considered. 'Maybe I can. I'll check the kitchen and come back.'

It was neat as two pins except that the drying-up cloth was hung in a different place. She checked the fridge, then made herself a mug of tea and went back to Clare.

'Well, well,' she said, 'someone round here finally appreciates my murky stews. It's all gone, every last scrap.'

'Can you feel the change?' Clare asked again.

'Yes, I can. Maybe the house will start coming alive again . . . ?' said Mrs Foale with a sad smile. 'I wish Arthur was here.'

Clare nodded, sad too.

Her friend rarely mentioned Arthur these days, but his absence was palpable around the house, he being such a big, alive person. There was a lot about his disappearance that Clare did not understand, not least Mrs Foale's unwillingness to involve outside authorities in it. Plainly she knew more than she was saying, so Clare had felt it best to say nothing much herself unless the opportunity arose. Now it had.

'It's three months now, isn't it?'

Mrs Foale nodded.

'And you've heard nothing?'

'Nothing. But . . .'

'What?'

'There have never been lies between us or anything left unspoken. So it's better you ask nothing more. There's things I can't say. Please?'

Clare nodded, but not willingly. Katherine missed Arthur too. *She* did as well. He was father to one, older brother to the other. Now he was gone without any satisfactory explanation.

'It's hard not to talk about him,' said Clare. 'It feels we're denying his existence.'

'Please,' said Mrs Foale again, unhappily.

'His going had to do with his work didn't it?'

'I . . . really . . . he made me promise not to talk about it.'

Clare fell silent. She was thinking she had done right to ask that Jack come and stay.

'He's a very remarkable young man,' said Clare. 'He talked to me like a man, not a boy. He's suffered greatly, Margaret. I think you'll see the changes in him. And it'll be good for Katherine to have him here . . .'

Margaret Foale caught a look in her friend's eye and she laughed.

'I do believe you're match-making already, Clare! He's only been in the house a few hours.'

'Don't be ridiculous!'

But she laughed too.

'. . . .now would you like me to read to you? Or turn on the radio maybe?'

Clare shook her head slowly from side to side. 'No, you go to bed and I'll make up a story in my head. By the time I get to the end, I'll be asleep. And, Margaret . . . ?'

'My dear?'

'Are you going to talk to Jack about Arthur? He's not a fool and will start asking questions if you don't.'

'When the time's right.'

'The time will never be right,' said Clare firmly, 'so it's best you do it as soon as possible.'

'What do I say?'

Clare thought for a moment.

'Tell him what you haven't exactly told me,' she said. 'The truth.'

'That's not as easy as it sounds because I don't "exactly" know it myself.'

30

FIRST STEPS OF THE DANCE

J ack woke the following morning into a world so different from what he was used to that he might as well have been on another planet.

No traffic noise; no shouting or swearing or the clatter of feet outside his door; no institutional cooking; no set time to get up.

Everything was different.

He sat up in bed and stared out over the garden towards White Horse Hill, hoping to see the chalk figure again. Eventually he did, as the morning mist drifting across the hill from right to left began to break up, revealing the horse behind it and giving the illusion that it was the horse that was moving, not the mist.

He heard the sound of Spring outside, and the tinkling of glass chimes.

Someone was playing the piano and he could smell fresh coffee and bacon, while sunshine played across the windows of his huge room and all down the pale curtains. He lay back on the pillows, listened to the music, and promptly fell asleep again.

When he awoke the second time, the piano playing had stopped, and this time he got up, very slowly, enjoying the moment.

The bathroom was old and primitive, with a high cobwebbed ceiling, and a shower head hanging loosely over a stained roll-top bath with griffin's feet, from which water dribbled out so slowly it took a while to get hot. But there were fresh old worn towels laid out, some rose-scented soap and a faded photograph of a younger Mr and Mrs Foale posed by a standing stone, on which 'Avebury, 1957' had been written in black ink.

He drifted downstairs and made his way into what Katherine had grandly called the dining room during their brief tour of the house the day before. There was a hotplate with bacon, mushrooms and scrambled eggs keeping warm, and a blue plastic radio playing softly, with an electric cable running from its rear to a small socket on the wall.

The coffee he had smelt was in an old-fashioned Bakelite flask, and the only cereal on offer was a box of Kellogg's Cornflakes, with a little sugar bowl next to it covered by a square of lace, weighted at the edges with amber beads.

His first impression from the day before was right: this house was stuck in a time warp, and he was beginning to think its inhabitants, including Katherine, might be as well.

A clock on the mantelpiece ticked steadily, a sound he had not heard in a long time. To his astonishment he saw it was nearly ten o'clock. Maybe he was drifting into a time warp too.

Jack had his breakfast alone but not feeling at all lonely, because the house all around him seemed to have a life of its own – drifting voices, the piano again, a bell ringing, a door opening, soft footsteps on a stone floor and, somewhere over his head, the floorboards creaking before someone stopped and opened a window.

Only when the lace curtain at one of the windows stirred slightly did he realize that the windows in the room were actually open as well, so quiet and still was the world outside. But soon after there was a distant rumble of thunder, and a darkening that brought a sense of ominous change to the air.

Katherine suddenly appeared. She was in belted jeans, an apricot-coloured T-shirt and wore leather flip-flops. She had a good figure which she must have noticed him assessing because she flushed very slightly and stared boldly back at him, making a considerable effort not to be fazed.

'Morning, Jack,' she said.

To her he remained inscrutable. By the light of day, after a good night's sleep, he looked attractive in a tousled sort of way – which were the exact same words she had used that morning in an excited email sent to Sam. She had also used the word 'sweet', as if he was some charming boy who had popped in for tea.

But in fact 'sweet' was something she didn't feel he was at all.

'Morning, Katherine,' he replied, finally smiling.

'Mrs Foale made the breakfast, so it's my job to clear away and do the washing up,' she explained.

'*Our* job,' said Jack, getting up. It seemed the right thing to do, and anyway he always did his own washing up.

'Oh!' she said, obviously not used to someone else helping. 'Er . . . right.'

She didn't seem quite to know how to let him help, which was how she had been the previous evening. Now, as then, he did so anyway.

But, as he dried the crockery and cutlery, he poked restlessly about like a cat getting to know its territory.

'Do you want to see the house properly in daylight?'

He grunted abstractedly.

'So you do?'

He did.

She took him on a full tour of the house.

They went up the main stairs at the front, and came down some narrow ones at the back, and in-between there were many different worlds of rooms, boxes, pictures of people gone, things half put away, things waiting to be found.

There were two floors plus an attic, so substantial in itself that it had little rooms with doors in the eaves and another door out on to the roof. These attic rooms, like a few on the floor below, were unused and dusty from fallen plaster. They were filled with a clutter of old furniture, tea chests and cardboard boxes. Many of these had been opened and rummaged through, as if someone had been searching for something specific over many years but never quite found it.

'That's Mrs Foale and me,' explained Katherine, 'looking for various things. She keeps remembering items she once had, but hasn't seen for years, and we do usually find them in the end. But there's no gold and silver that I've ever seen! No secrets and no surprises!'

It didn't feel like that to Jack, however.

The steep back stairs led down to a green-painted door that opened into a huge old kitchen, also dusty and unused, along with an adjacent scullery, a boot room, an old laundry, and a huge walk-in larder with a thick stone slab to keep things cool on. In places, Katherine told him, the building went back to the thirteenth century, there being, to prove it, the vestiges of two stone arches in the corridor leading to the rickety back door.

'This bit used to be the granary,' continued Katherine, as if all normal homes had a medieval arch or two.

There were great stone slabs on the kitchen floor, while the back corridors were covered with grubby, mouldering rugs. Hooks in beams projected above their heads, on which, Katherine claimed, pork sides had once been hung.

'Mrs Foale has no money now and she keeps threatening to let out this part of the house, but I don't expect she will.'

'Nobody would want it,' suggested Jack.

'They would,' said Katherine rather tartly, 'but they'd want to clear out the rubbish, knock down the walls and change everything. We don't want that to ever happen.'

'Why not?'

'Because we love it – it's home,' she replied quietly.

'I wouldn't know what that means,' Jack said without thinking. He didn't notice Katherine's discomfort at this remark. Instead he reached a hand to one wall and felt it carefully, and then stretched his fingers up to one of the old hooks above them, caressing its rusty point, trying it.

'Let the tour continue,' she said, awkwardly changing the subject.

The front of the house was more modern, meaning early nineteenth-century: high ceilings, rectangular paned windows with shutters, and an Adam-style fireplace in the drawing room. The wide, worn oak floorboards creaked and were weak with woodworm in places, and some of the doors had thick felt hangings over them to keep out the draughts in winter.

The radiators were great cast-iron monstrosities connected to each other by ugly pipes as thick as Jack's arm, which ran along the top of skirting boards and up walls and through the ceiling above, where plaster had fallen away leaving ugly holes.

The smaller kitchen, which Clare and Katherine regularly used, and where they started this tour, was a poky little modern one located in a former cloakroom near the front door. But they hadn't finished yet . . .

They turned in a new direction. There was a music room with a huge grand piano, with music sheets on it, and to Jack's surprise there was a fire guttering in a grate and the room felt warm.

'I heard someone playing this morning,' said Jack.

'Mrs Foale plays most mornings. She tends to use only this room and the library . . .'

They went on through a big oak door and stood on the threshold of an oak-panelled library. In its centre were two desks facing each other back to back. One was very tidy, the other a mess.

'Guess which one's Arthur's!' said Katherine, looking at the untidy one.

When she had first called Jack, Arthur's disappearance was one of the first things she had mentioned.

'You said he disappeared . . .'

'Well, there's no other word for it. One day he was here and the next not. Mum was as puzzled as I was and Margaret's explanations didn't add up.'

'Why not?'

'She said he had gone to do some important work, but if that were true he would have mentioned it to one of us as well. Then she said she wasn't sure when he was coming back, which might have been reasonable if she looked happy about it, but she didn't. But he's been gone for three months now.'

'You mean he might have gone off with someone?'

Katherine shook her head and laughed.

'Not Arthur, he's too obsessed with his work and relies too much on Margaret's expertise to even think about someone else!'

'Only a suggestion,' said Jack. 'What's your theory?'

'That Margaret knows a lot more than she's saying.'

'This house gets more interesting by the moment.'

'I miss him,' said Katherine impulsively, adding, 'It's like losing my dad all over again. Jack, Mum wanted you to come but I did too.' She said this in a rush and very quietly. She was embarrassed to admit she needed him.

'Well I won't disappear, unless you want to get rid of me,' he said lightly.

She grinned.

'I'll tell you when I do! Want to see the garden now?'

Jack nodded but didn't move.

They had reached the library but he had not yet taken it in. It contained more books than he had ever seen in one room. The shelves, which went from floor to ceiling, and had even been extended over the two doors and between the windows, were jam-packed with every kind. Most of the books looked old, some very old.

'Mrs Foale doesn't like people coming in here much. Since Arthur went I've not liked being here at all. Let's go.'

Yet still Jack stood there.

There was something about the room, or was it the things in the room, things by Arthur's desk? He would have liked to take a closer look.

'Yes, let's go,' he said.

'We'll go out through the old kitchen,' she said, setting off again. 'It'll take us round the side of the house, which is a nice way to approach the garden. It's quite big, I must warn you, and your trainers . . .' – she darted a glance at his trainers, which were a lot less substantial than the leather shoes she herself was wearing – 'might get wet. Did you bring some boots?'

He hadn't, because living in the city he didn't have footwear suitable for the country.

He shook his head.

'You could use those, maybe.' She nodded at a pair of old black army boots deposited by the back door. They were mouldy with age and one of them had a cobweb inside. 'They're a pair of Arthur's old ones, but I'm sure Mrs Foale won't mind.'

He eyed the boots dubiously, but then relaxed and grinned. 'Why not?' He kicked off his trainers, shook out the boot with the spider web, and stepped into them tentatively.

'They look like they fit you,' said Katherine.

'They're okay,' said Jack, walking up and down a bit before tying up the laces. He was surprised to find how comfortable they were.

'I'll wait for you outside then,' she said, before slipping through the back door.

If he could have followed straight away, he would have, but one of the laces in the boots was so rotten it snapped, and when he tried to re-tie it, it snapped again.

By the time he had sorted himself out and stepped outside, Katherine had disappeared from sight. Which wouldn't have mattered much except that he found the cobbled back yard he was now in had three different exits, and he had no idea which way she had gone.

He made a left and then a right through a door in the wall.

He found himself in a walled vegetable garden which, like the house itself, was a relic from another age. Its regular, rectangular beds had been abandoned to weeds, and the espaliered fruit trees tied back to the great brick walls still carried the dried and desiccated remnants of fruit unpicked from the previous season.

An old barrel served as a rain butt, but it was so full of unused water that it spilled over whenever a slight breeze caught its dark, algae-covered surface.

He heard movement.

'Katherine?' he called.

'She went through to the old rose garden,' a female voice said nearby.

He turned and found himself facing Mrs Foale.

'Hello, Jack,' she said. 'It's been far too long!'

He smiled warmly and gave her a hug. She was as he remembered her – with a wrinkled, healthy, outdoors face, hair kept in place at the back with a tortoiseshell comb, the green cardigan a man's. Arthur's probably.

'It's so good to see you,' she beamed. 'I hope you slept well last night. It's quite a long journey from London, isn't it?'

'It was fine,' he said. 'I like the house.'

'We like it too! It's home. Katherine's shown you round?'

He nodded.

'. . . and Katherine said about Arthur. Disappearing was the word she used.'

It wasn't very subtle, but Jack's curiosity had been piqued by what Katherine had said earlier.

'Er, yes. His work takes him all over the world.'

She waved a hand about vaguely as if to convey an image of Arthur going walkabout. He could see what Katherine meant about her avoiding the subject.

'I'll put out some lunch later. Katherine will show you where. Now you'd better hurry and find her. The garden is rather large and overgrown, I'm afraid. Try going through that door over there, the one that's half off its hinges. I'm afraid that Arthur was never very practical about such things.'

She trailed off unhappily and looked away. Then, turning back to him, she pointed the trowel at his feet and brightened up.

'Arthur's boots! They've been all over the world, you know, and visited some strange, forgotten places. It's so good to see them on you.'

'Katherine said I could wear them.'

She nodded and smiled.

'Please do,' she said. 'As for Arthur . . . I do need to talk to you about him but . . . not yet. There's things you need to know. Clare and Katherine are angry with me for being so vague about it all, but it isn't easy . . .'

She seemed to be taking him into her confidence, but what about he had no idea.

'I'll do anything I can to help,' he said. 'I'm just not sure what.'

'We'll have to discuss it one day soon.'

'Okay,' he said.

31

INTO THE GARDEN

F inding Katherine in the garden was not as simple as it seemed. It was large and its boundaries elusive, hidden beyond thick bushes, stretching away beyond trees.

Right in front of the house was a wide expanse of ruined lawn, potholed by rabbits, mounded by moles and badly mown. To the right were dilapidated rose gardens, box hedges no one had cut for years, and overgrown shrubberies beneath whose overextended and broken branches leaves had collected over the years and fallen branches rotted.

To the left were outbuildings containing abandoned cast-iron rollers, wooden rakes with woodworm, sacks infested by vermin, and roof spaces obscured by spiders' webs heavy with dust, and brambles and other climbers which, having found a way through the walls, sought a way out towards the light from broken tiles above.

But straight ahead from the conservatory were the great evergreen trees Jack had noticed the day before, and between them a large circle of green, damp grass, surrounded by more trees.

Jack searched for Katherine long enough to begin to think she must be avoiding him, or at least moving from one area of the garden to another, unconsciously keeping her distance.

She needs space he told himself when he finally understood what was happening. *She's not used to having someone like me about.*

Jack knew about needing space from the group and individual counselling sessions he had been subjected to through the years. Often he had said nothing, resolutely refusing to get involved in other people's problems and pain, bored by their slow journeys to self-discovery. Until, in the last year or two, he had begun to make those journeys himself.

So it didn't take long to work out where Katherine might be coming from. And going to.

And Arthur, she's lost Arthur but got me instead he thought ruefully. *Not much of an exchange!*

So he found somewhere to sit and took time out for some space of his own until, in her own way, she came back to him, pretending she hadn't known he was there.

'That's okay,' he said. 'I needed time by myself.'

Which was just what she needed to hear.

'Can I join you?'

He made space for her on the damp grass.

It was a moment of silence, except for the chimes.

'You'll get used to them,' she said, seeming by saying so to convey that she wanted him around the place a while longer.

The first morning became the pattern for the weeks that followed. Katherine took to using the garden as her sanctuary when things inside the house, including Jack, got too much for her. She was elusive, complex and uncertain of herself; and the vast garden turned out to be a shifting, changing labyrinth which echoed the shifts and deepening patterns of their friendship.

'What's your favourite book?' she asked one day.

Jack didn't have one, he had never read much.

'Mine's *The Secret Garden*,' she said softly, as if it was a secret she was sharing with him.

When he said he had seen the film she turned up her nose. But he ordered the DVD online anyway, when he discovered that Arthur had a DVD player and flat screen televison which Margaret never used. They all watched it one evening with Clare in the conservatory, the dying light through the glass behind the picture the perfect background.

'Not as good as the book,' muttered an obviously moved Katherine afterwards.

She left the book by the door of his bedroom and he read it, the first book in a long time.

When it was finished he scribbled one word on a Post-it note and left it with the book by her bedroom door.

Agreed it said.

After that she felt more confident around him, more able to say what she felt, more able to go off by herself.

She was right about the garden, but it was more than an echo of their growing friendship, it was the interface between them. She had see-sawing needs sometimes to be close to Jack, sometimes nowhere near him.

Jack found it hard at first even if, in the self-awareness stakes, his troubled background and the support he had had in the past had taken him further down the road.

He couldn't understand why one moment Katherine would be happy, laughing and easy with his company, seeming to want to do things with him, then at other times would make bitter comments about his life in the city, make fun of him and argue with him over the smallest thing. It seemed as if one moment she liked him, and at others almost hated him. It left him angry and frustrated – until the sunny Katherine emerged again and all was forgiven.

This left him with a wild, almost savage wish at times to be able to reach out and touch her, and tell her what she made him feel.

Not that anyone seeing them in those first weeks would have known, or even guessed, that such torrents of feeling and uncertainty ran beneath the calm surface of their everyday lives. They said nothing to each other about them, barely admitting anything to themselves, directing their energies instead towards activities that kept them physically busy and their minds well occupied.

Both had work to do before the end of May and had different ways of dealing with the workloads. Katherine locked herself away in her bedroom, emerging sometimes for a cup of something or a walk in the garden, or just to sit with her mother.

Jack's final exams took place in June, but he was on top of the basic work and now in revision mode. He had it all sorted on cards, and when the weather was good, which mostly it was, he would find a nook in the garden and then do his revision lying on his back out in the sun.

It was while he was lying there with his eyes closed one day that

Jack had the sudden disconcerting feeling that he was being watched. He knew it wasn't by Katherine because she was working up in her room in the house. He could see her head bent over books.

It wasn't Margaret Foale because she was out shopping.

It couldn't be Clare.

He sat up and looked about.

The sense of it went deeper than just thinking someone could see him and he couldn't see them. It was the sense of being watched that was the most powerful thing he felt.

He stood up slowly. He was by one of the two great conifers and he was conscious of it towering away above him as if, as if . . .

What had disturbed him was the feeling of having been in this place before, except it wasn't this place, meaning the garden, it was here, right here, but different, and the tree soaring away above him, its thick trunk far too wide for him to put his arms even halfway round, gave him the uncomfortable sense that he was smaller than he was; or had been.

He was a child, but not a child.

He was the size of Katherine in his recurring dreams, but he was not like Katherine.

He was the bearded man in the nightmare, but he was not him. He was in their world, of their world, and in that world someone was watching him.

He was being watched from another place.

He stood still and acknowledged something he had been avoiding for months before coming to Woolstone.

He had often thought, or dreamed, or imagined, that there was another world just beyond his reach which, if only he could find a way into it . . .

'Back into it!' he muttered to himself now. 'I'm sure I've been there before . . .'

If he could he would feel less restless, more at home.

Home.

The word was almost painful to think of because it represented loss.

Home.

Home was still where he wanted to get.

He felt an overwhelming need to turn these powerful, unarticulated feelings into some kind of reality. He went to one of the conifers and touched it, caressed it, looked up into its soaring heights wishing its stiff branches could take him to it. Then he peered beyond it, as if to catch sight of someone there.

'Jack! Jack what are you *doing*!?'

It was Katherine calling from her window.

She had looked out, seen Jack touching the tree before very slowly peering around the tree to the encircled area of grass beyond.

'*Jack!*'

'I'm looking for someone,' he called back, knowing the reply would infuriate her, 'so get on with your work!'

The sense of being watched from a world other than his own increased in the following days, and to make it worse Katherine wouldn't leave the subject alone, annoyed with him for not explaining what he had originally meant. Why it should matter to her he had no idea, but he gave nothing away.

The garden extended over at least eight acres, and evidence of its rich history since medieval times explained the confusion and false trails inherent in its walls and hedges, its abandoned terraces and obscure ponds all overgrown with brambles and bamboo.

As the days advanced through April, and encouraged by some days of rain followed by humid warmth, the vegetation grew ever more verdant and lush.

The flowers of Spring, from which Katherine made his welcome posy, gave way to those of early Summer.

The rough lawn close by the house grew green with moss and a light blue dusting of creeping speedwell; while in the spaces among the trees, dog's mercury – vigorous and poisonous and always the first greenery to spread across the forest floor – yielded place to a carpet of bluebells, their ranks softly interrupted by the cream-white flowers of wood anemone.

Elsewhere all manner of vegetation grew, seeming almost to burst forth from itself in a series of green explosions one after the other so that, day after day, wherever he looked, Jack found something new to see and a different routeway of life to explore.

The mauve curling flowers of comfrey, in whose thick entangling hairs the bumble-bees struggled and fought in their quest for nectar; the first flush of willow herb, its form like tribal spears; or red campion, whose pert flowers were as much pink as red; among all these appeared sunbursts of cowslip and dandelion and then, of course, the first buttercups. While in among the trees on lower wetter ground sloping to one side of the property, where the sun rarely reached, were garlic-scented ramsons and . . .

It was a plant Jack had never seen before, but which like all the others Katherine taught him the name of.

'Euphorbia,' she said lightly, coming across Jack kneeling in this semi-dark of woodland shade on a bright May day, only a few days before her first exam. 'Fancy a walk?'

Their walks were casual and spontaneous, and never prearranged. Tiring of revision, one or the other would suggest that they go off. Katherine led the way at first, because she knew the highways and byways of the area well from the many country walks Arthur had taken her on when she was just a little girl.

'He taught me the names of all the flowers of the fields, or if I found one he didn't know, he encouraged me to look it up.'

She often mentioned Arthur, as did Mrs Foale, but his disappearance was rarely referred to and after that brief discussion with Mrs Foale on his first day at Woolstone, when she hinted there were things she wanted to talk about, she had never mentioned the conversation again. His occasional attempts to do so were rebuffed and he decided to leave it to her to choose a time.

One clear day he and Katherine decided to walk all the way to the River Thames, lying eight miles to the north across the Vale of the White Horse.

'Arthur often claimed it's one of the great natural boundaries of England,' volunteered Katherine, 'and that there is a magic in its crossing. He said its spirit – like the spirit of the other great rivers of England such as the Severn, the Great Ouse, the Trent – is on your side if you respect and honour it. If you don't, it might turn against you.'

Jack stayed silent at that, not sure what to say. Katherine knew a lot about a lot of other things, and spoke about them with an eloquence of which he was a little in awe.

'How do you honour a river?' he asked eventually, several minutes later.

Katherine shrugged, uncertain about that herself. 'I think you throw an offering to it,' she said. 'That's why a lot of old and valuable things have been discovered in rivers – like money and swords.'

They found a wooden humped-back bridge over the river, and Jack impulsively rushed to climb to its highest point. Katherine followed him more slowly.

'So,' he said, 'let's honour it.'

He had a sense that he had done something like that before, and recognized at once it was all part of those feelings he had about having once known a world beyond the one he was now in. Yet another glimpse of a past memory.

'What is it?' she asked, seeing him staring down into the river with a blank expression.

'I feel like I've done this before, but I can't remember when.'

'*Déjà vu*,' she suggested.

'Meaning?'

'French for "seen before". People often get feelings like that when they happen to be in a situation that repeats something that occurred in their past.'

Jack went silent again.

'Jack, what's on your mind?'

'I don't have a past,' he said, 'or not one I can remember. Nobody even knows where I come from!'

'It must be horrible to feel like that.'

'It feels ... empty. Except lately I've begun to feel I have one, after all, only it's just out of reach.'

She came closer. 'Tell me.'

He thought a bit. 'All right, like those mirrors and chimes hanging in the garden, which your mother likes so much. I think I've seen or heard them before. I think I know what they're for ... except I couldn't know.'

'Know *what*?'

He turned and looked at her.

There had been moments lately, whenever they talked, that they felt they really reached right into each other's minds.

'What they're meant for. Even how they work.'

'And . . . ?'

'They're for protection,' he said. 'They work by breaking up the world into fragments of reflections, so you can't see past them.'

'But . . . how could you know that?'

'I know, I know, it's ridiculous. But you did ask.'

She waited.

'. . . because,' he said slowly, daring finally to admit it, 'I've seen them before. They were used once to protect me.'

'From what?'

'People. Dark shadowy people. I could feel their cold getting to me, freezing my mind, but they couldn't find a way through the mirrors because they reflected themselves back and broke them up.'

'Jack, that's strange. It's similar to something Arthur once said about the chimes, that they alter our perception of the world and maybe that of harmful people who want to get to us. Then he said . . .'

'What?'

'Something weird which I've thought more about since I caught you peering around that tree.'

He grinned.

'Did you think I was crazy?'

She shook her head.

'Arthur's a scientist so he deduces things and tests them. He said about the chimes that they offered a clue about how to get into another world.'

'Why would he think that?'

'Have you ever wondered how the chimes got there?'

'I presumed you and Clare and everybody put them there.'

'We did, most of them. But Mum admitted once that the first ones were not put there by her or Mrs Foale. They just appeared one morning. Mum said they made her safer. Before that she had felt watched.'

Jack breathed deeply, trying to control the sense of relief that came with affirmation that a feeling he had thought unique to himself was shared by someone else.

'So we began to add to them as the years went by, but sometimes I noticed that others appeared by themselves. I told Mum once what I thought. She said to ask Arthur about it. He listened, nodded, thought a bit and finally said, "It's the little people." I thought he was joking, but what with what Mum has been saying recently and now you . . . maybe he wasn't.'

Jack just stared at her.

'Jack? There's more, isn't there?'

He nodded. The sense of relief he'd felt earlier shifted now to a need for release. He felt emotional and couldn't hold her gaze.

He turned away and said, 'Sometimes when we're out walking I feel we're going the wrong way. As if there's a better way. As if there are other paths we could take but don't.'

'Like unmarked public footpaths?'

He shook his head. 'Like paths that have been there a very long time.'

It was her turn to give him a strange look, and then turn away to the river.

He waited.

Eventually she said, 'This gets weirder by the moment. That's what Arthur said once – or something like it. Just before he disappeared.'

Jack waited in silence a bit more.

'He told me never to try those paths because they lead to dangerous places. He said not to go to the world they lay in, but he wouldn't explain more. I think Mrs Foale knows more about his disappearance than she's ever said. I think maybe Mum does too, but they don't want me to know.'

'Makes sense,' Jack nodded. 'Probably trying to protect you.'

'I don't need protecting.'

Jack shook his head and said, 'I think you do.'

'From what?'

'I don't know exactly but I feel it. The sense of being watched isn't always pleasant. Sometimes it feels benign, sometimes malign. The watchers are the people who use those paths that I sense, and Arthur maybe sensed. Time to talk properly with Mrs Foale about all this. Meanwhile . . . let's honour the river.'

He dug into his pocket and produced two fifty-pence pieces, took her wrist and put one into her palm.

Then he held her hand together with his over the river.

'Now,' he said.

They watched the coins fall, standing with their heads and bodies close, the coins seeming to turn only slowly as they tumbled towards the moving surface of the water beneath them, where, with two nearly silent splashes, they disappeared into the mysterious underworld beneath.

Their hands touched a few moments longer, Jack's body close to Katherine's, and the bridge seeming to vibrate a little. Both were breathless, each acutely aware of the other, a light breeze blowing strands of her hair across his cheek. He glanced at her, and saw her face was flushed.

She caught his eyes and pulled away embarrassed, both staring into the reflections in the river below, their eyes staying focused on those rather than on each other.

'I made a wish,' said Jack, suddenly turning to face her.

'You mustn't reveal it,' she whispered, all awkwardness gone as she impulsively put a finger to his lips.

'Does this bridge have a name, Katherine?' said Jack as they turned and headed back down the bridge to the riverbank.

'It's called Old Man's Bridge,' she replied, setting off back along the path towards Woolstone. It felt like they still had a long walk home.

But briefly Jack lingered and looked back at the bridge where they had stood.

I'll come back here again, I expect, he told himself, and . . .

Then the world grew silent about him, all of it gone but the bridge and the river and himself. It was surely an epiphany, a moment of sensing what must be.

When I'm an old man I'll come back here, and I'll stand where we just stood, and I'll be alone then but Katherine will be safe, and we'll have done what we need to do. She'll be safe for ever then.

'Jack?' Her voice brought him back to the present, and he liked the sound of it as she spoke his name.

He turned to look at her.

She was tall and fair and, though she wore old jeans and boots and a raggedy grey fleece, right then she looked like the most beautiful girl he had ever seen.

She took half a step towards him. 'What is it?' she said.

'Nothing, just thinking,' he answered, joining her.

She turned as he did, the pair of them at one together, and he put a hand briefly on her shoulder.

As they walked back into the garden Mrs Foale called to them from the doorway, 'Jack, there's something I want to talk to you about – along with Clare.'

Jack whispered, 'She's beaten me to it!'

'Well, obviously they don't want *me* there!' Katherine whispered on return, but without rancour. 'Tell me about it later. Okay?'

'Okay,' agreed Jack.

32

REVELATION

Later, with the light fading and Katherine upstairs revising, Jack and Margaret Foale went and sat by Clare's bed in the conservatory.

Jack had no idea what to expect but he felt subdued and nervous.

'It's about Arthur isn't it?'

'Yes,' said Margaret, 'and also yourself. And Katherine too. But let's start with Arthur. Do you remember him?'

Jack shook his head. Except for a shadowy male figure on one of their visits, he had little recollection of him at all.

Margaret produced a photograph. 'This was taken when he was a guest lecturer at Imperial College in London, just before he disappeared. I want you to have a good idea what he now looks like.'

The photograph was in digital colour and quite clear.

It was of a big man, black-bearded, wild-haired, with a ruddy, weather-beaten English country face and sharp twinkling eyes. He was wearing a check shirt and grey trousers that were somewhat too short for him and standing by a pull-down blackboard, with an old-fashioned piece of chalk in his hand. A dark misshapen jacket hung over a chair to one side, a laptop sat on the table in front of him, and there was part of a projected image on the screen just behind his head. The lecture room looked archaic, with a great window to his right, the cords to open and shut it dangling down the wall.

'So, that's Arthur,' continued Margaret. 'He once told me most emphatically that if ever he went off on one of his field trips and didn't reappear within two weeks, we were to ask you to come here at once. That's why Katherine called you, because I asked her to, but she doesn't know the full reason why.'

Jack nodded.

'She was scared after he disappeared. But . . .'

He got up and paced about.

'I'm not comfortable talking about this without Katherine here. You shouldn't keep all this from her.'

'But she's just a . . .' began Clare.

Jack raised his eyebrows and looked quizzically at Margaret Foale.

'Just a girl?' he said ironically.

'Well . . .'

'I don't think so,' said Jack.

They both looked sheepish, even defensive.

Margaret Foale got up and said, 'He's quite right, Clare. I'll go and get her.'

It seemed that everything at Woolstone was shifting and changing before their eyes. The perceptions of all of them, both of themselves and of the world outside, were altering, fracturing, regrouping into something new, separate and together, like the world seen in the reflective chimes whose continual music was the only thing that kept things together, lightly, beautifully, made by the lightest of breezes, powerful as the greatest hurricane.

When Katherine finally joined them they all talked that evening in a way they had not before, sharing the doubts and discoveries of their separate journeys to the same time and place. Journeys of loss and grief, of love and realization, of the past into the present and on, moment by moment, into the future. Fragments of memory turned into a thousand different stories of which they were made but which, as they talked, they unmade and remade.

Mrs Foale had been going to tell Jack alone that evening all that she knew about Arthur's disappearance. She finally did so with them all present a few days later.

The way it was done was unexpected. She handed Jack a computer disk.

'Arthur said to give this to you, Jack, only after you'd got used to things here, and to us too, and when we felt the time was right. Well the time's right and I'm going to do what he probably wouldn't have done seeing as he was over-protective of you, Katherine. I'm going to give it to both of you to watch. All right?'

'Very all right,' said Katherine.

Arthur had written the words *For Jack* on the disk in black felt-tip. She had added 'and Katherine' in blue.

'The time's right to share this now,' said Clare matter-of-factly. 'I'm dying and we all know it. You've got the right to have some questions answered before I go, Jack.'

'About the accident?'

Clare nodded. 'Yes, that . . . and what happened before that, which Margaret knows about. About your past, in other words.'

Katherine looked at Jack and said, 'Yes, he needs to know about that.'

'Well, we don't know much,' said Margaret, 'but certainly more than has been said. Arthur put what he knows and believes on that disk, in case he didn't come back. Where from will become clear when you watch it. He said it's both an explanation and a warning, and that it would be better if you watched it with us present, so we could answer any questions. That now includes you, Katherine.'

Jack took the disk and inserted it in the DVD player.

'Okay, shall we watch it?'

Margaret reached over and touched Jack's arm.

'Arthur could be a bit insensitive sometimes, thinking other people had his intelligence and his thick skin. What you're going to see and hear, if it's what I think it is, might be a bit of a shock. That's why we're here.'

'To pick up the pieces?'

'Maybe.'

'I think I'll sit next to Katherine then,' he said softly.

They exchanged another glance. There was friendship there, and trust. There was nervousness too.

She reached a hand to his arm, unconsciously copying the way Clare made contact at important moments.

'It'll be all right,' she said.

'Let's go for it,' said Jack, turning off the light in the conservatory so they could see the screen better.

The film was amateurishly made by Arthur himself. It started with a shaky webcam recording of him talking straight to camera.

'Jack, we know only that you came from Germany, probably from the Harz Mountains, and that was when you were about six. Margaret will explain the background to that. Anyway, you came to England only a few weeks before the accident in which you got so badly injured. Now this is going to be hard to take but, astonishing as it may seem to most people, to you it might not come as a total surprise. Most people who never knew their earliest years actually retain what are called vestigial memories of them buried deep in their unconscious, which then begin to surface in their teens. I wouldn't mind betting that something like that has been happening with you, too.

'So let's get to the point. I believe you're very special because you're a genetic crossover between two worlds, one of which is our own, the human world, with which we are comfortable and which we see as the solid and material reality of our lives, and the other . . . well, that's the one I need to explain. The other, which I call the Hyddenworld, we humans do not see at all. This is for many reasons, but most of all because we do not believe it to be there. We have been taught, for two thousand years at least, that it is *not* there, and people, indeed whole communities, have been slaughtered for suggesting that it is. We have lost the ability to see it just as someone who loses their sight for many years may not see in the same way as sighted people can until they have learned how to. So far as the Hyddenworld is concerned, humans have become unsighted to its presence among us and, as important, what that means to our understanding of the world.

'The good news is that in many of us the belief survives that this Hyddenworld – the world of little people – does actually exist. It has its own reality. It is just as real as our own. Indeed you will find hardly a society or a culture throughout the world that does not have so much traditional and cultural reference to the little people that, were it anything else but them, this evidence would be regarded as sufficient proof of their existence by most rational thinkers.

'But there is also evidence of a more specific kind, which very few know about and which has been kept well away from the public domain. Such evidence is in the form of some film and early security-camera footage taken before the inhabitants of this otherworld came to realize the threat cameras posed to them, and took evasive action. I began collecting such material many years ago . . .'

The film switched suddenly from webcam to the grainy black-and-white footage familiar from old film stock. Arthur's voice then continued as a background commentary.

'This exterior footage comes from a film made in 1948 at Elstree Studios in Surrey. Keep a close watch on the top left-hand corner.'

It showed a woodland scene near a river, as two actors in Forties dress appeared in the foreground. Then someone else, seemingly dressed in a period costume of some kind, appeared suddenly on the far side of the river.

'Watch out for the scale of things when he passes that bicycle leaning against the tree . . .'

Jack leaned forward, watching now with growing fascination. The figure in the film could suddenly be seen to be standing little higher than the cycle wheel, no bigger than a child.

The footage changed again, and Arthur's voice-over continued.

'Berlin, 1945 and some footage on a news camera accidentally switched on at dusk. Watch carefully! We've got the familiar war-damaged city-scape, but this time including two figures, strangely dressed as if they were peasants from a medieval village . . .'

These figures appeared and disappeared several times, as if they were searching for something among the rubble. An adjacent doorway indicated the scale, and again, they were no bigger than young children.

'One last clip, from 1991, taken by an early security camera at night in a shopping mall in Manchester.'

Again, an ordinary urban scene, and again diminutive little people, caught on camera. After that the film reverted to Foale talking directly to camera.

'I could show more examples, but let's leave it at that for now. Here's the interesting thing. In the three years from 1993, all such images disappear from the record, first in Germany and then gradually across the world. They suddenly stop. We think that's because these people learned ways to avoid ever being caught on camera. You might think that these clips could have been faked, but I've had them very carefully examined and there's absolutely no evidence of that.

'Now, it's true that we don't generally believe in beings such as the little people, and will prefer any explanation but the true one, but that's good, in a way, because it makes my investigative work a lot simpler.

'Meanwhile, the Hyddenworld and its people certainly know *we* exist. They have to, because they live among us constantly in real time, in real space, being born, living, dying, subtly interacting with us. They see us as clumsy giants, doltish and highly destructive of ourselves and the environment, yet they also piggy-back on our technology, though to what extent I'm not yet sure. What I do know for sure is that one of them telephoned me twelve years ago from a public telephone in Germany just before your own mysterious arrival.

'Why contact me? you may ask. That's probably because I am the only human being who actually believes in them, not excepting my wife, who remains sceptical still. And why now particularly? Because a crisis looms. This brings me back to you, Jack.

'I said earlier that you're a genetic crossover. By that I mean that though we humans and hydden come from a common ancestry, separating off in the primeval past, what hydden call a "giant-born" retains certain qualities of both races, and yet crucially something unique to himself. More of that in a moment, but let me stress that such crossovers are not unique among the hydden, but they do seem to occur extremely rarely.

'Because their recessive genes mean that they can grow to human size, giants are seen as objects of dread and superstition amongst their own kind. And though they usually turn out exceptionally able and physically strong, the hydden fear them so much that they almost invariably kill them in childhood. Because of the timing of that mysterious phone call and your sudden arrival, it is my firm belief that you are one of these prodigies, and that you were sent into the human world to save you from destruction by your own kind.'

The film came to an abrupt stop.

Jack looked totally stunned.

After a while, he finally broke the silence.

'These trips of Arthur's, are they to do with the Hyddenworld?'

'Yes,' said Margaret after a pause, 'that's exactly what they are to do with, but can you see why it would be impossible to tell anyone? If it's true it's something beyond extraordinary. If it's not it means that Arthur is mad. Either way it's fraught with danger.'

'And he thinks that I come from that world?'

'He does and so do I. Let me tell you a bit more about what we think it means to be what the hydden call "giant-born" . . .'

She began telling him what she knew, what Arthur and she had worked out, and about the legendary giants-born, most particularly Beornamund of Brum.

Old stories, new times.

Jack listened but asked hardly any more questions. At some point during that long evening, which went into the night, Katherine found courage to reach over and put her hand on his. Just a touch for reassurance and empathy. She couldn't begin to imagine what it all meant to him but she guessed it ran deep.

In the absence of questions from him and his silence as he tried to come to terms with an entirely new perception of himself and his world, she asked questions for him.

'But . . . but . . . but . . .'

So many ifs and buts, and more questions remaining than answers given.

Finally they had all had enough for the time being and went off to their rooms.

'Thanks, Katherine,' he said outside her door. 'I'm glad you were there.'

She hugged him.

'Always,' she whispered.

'Yes,' he said.

Katherine said, 'I think that Arthur was primarily trying to *tell* you something, without actually spelling it out. He must have guessed that Mrs Foale would see the film, too, and he didn't want to worry her unduly.'

He went to his room.

Arthur had been right in what he said: none of this was exactly a surprise. Jack had sensed something like this was coming. It shook him, even shocked him, but it also brought a sense of relief. For the first time in his life, he felt he was beginning to get a sense of who he really was.

Later that night he suddenly woke up feeling certain that Katherine was right. Arthur had been trying to warn him about something – but what?

Jack got up and opened the window, staring through the darkness towards the trees.

He stood there a long time, but somehow couldn't work it out.

Eventually he went back to bed, and slept fitfully, until he reawakened feeling much more worried than before.

Dawn was breaking and the sky was red.

'Red sky in the morning, shepherd's warning,' he murmured aloud.

But that was merely a caution about the weather. What was nagging at him was something that hinted at dangers far greater than the weather.

Then he got it.

The warning's not just about me, it's about Katherine too. They might try and get at me through her. He didn't want her or the others to know that because it would 'alarm them unduly' as Katherine herself puts it.

Then he got something else.

He's telling me the Hyddenworld is my world and I've got to protect Katherine from it.

The sky over White Horse Hill changed to the colour of warning red as rain clouds loomed and then, the wind shifting, retreated.

'For the time being,' murmured Jack, his eyes purposeful, his movements assured. 'All I can do is watch and wait.'

He got up, washed and dressed and went out into the garden before breakfast, prowling about as if in search of the enemy. He didn't see one but he didn't doubt any more that one was there and it was dark and shadowed and some day, probably sooner than later, it was going to emerge out of his dreams and nightmares and show its face.

33

RIDGEWAY

Their daily walks became longer, faster and more vigorous, as if providing an antidote to the shocks of Arthur's DVD. They tried not to think what it might mean for the future and put all their thoughts and actions into the present.

They began at last to explore the chalk escarpment immediately to the north of Woolstone, and then the chalk Downs beyond. Their mysterious dry valleys and rolling slopes, littered with ancient monuments, including the White Horse itself, were as changeable in appearance as the weather which swept continually across it.

The ridge enticed both Jack and Katherine and they explored every aspect of it from the huge hill fort nearby, and even down to the solitary hawthorn that added drama to the smooth sward of grass below it.

But they did not walk those few extra yards up to the Horse itself. It didn't feel as if it was time.

'Not yet,' said Katherine, her fair hair wild in the strong wind that was always blowing up the scarp face.

'No,' murmured Jack in agreement, hands stuck into his fleece pockets, feet solid on the grass, mouth firm over jutting jaw, eyes narrowed against the wind.

Instead they would turn back from that final exploration, and head over the crest of the scarp to the ancient Ridgeway that ran west-to-east in its lee, echoing the run of the Thames flowing to the north.

This Neolithic highway was said to be the oldest road still in use in Europe and there was the feeling, as they started along its chalky, rutted path, so hard on the ankles in dry weather, so slippery in wet, that they were joining a stream of travellers who had gone the same way since time began.

It started twenty miles to their west, at the stone circle of Avebury, rising up the scarp slope before beginning its high-level journey east and then north, a great arc of a route that ended nearly ninety miles away on Ivinghoe Beacon.

'Except it doesn't,' Katherine informed Jack one stormy day. 'Arthur said it once joined other routes and went much further, all the way up into Norfolk where it joins the Peddar's Way, and on to the Wash . . .'

They stood, as they often did, in silent contemplation of the landscape and their place in it. Katherine had the whole route fixed as an image in her mind; Jack felt it in his very guts, and wanted to walk it then and there, right to where the North Sea's waves hit the East Anglian shore.

'You and I learn things in different ways,' observed Jack, looking along the Ridgeway as if to discern its distant end. 'You read it in books, or learn it from people like Arthur, and then you discover it on the ground itself. I do it the other way round, and learn what I'm feeling from you and Mrs Foale and your Mum.'

Their arms and shoulders brushed each other as they stood leaning against the wind.

'Shall we walk the whole way one day?' suggested Katherine. 'Right to the sea? We could go for a swim in celebration.'

'If we do, when we get there I'll strip off and dive straight into the water.'

He turned away because he knew it was something he would not want to do with her watching.

Katherine glanced at him, puzzled and slightly distressed – not for the first time with Jack. She looked at the scars that disfigured his neck, rightly guessing what had made him fall silent. He had let his guard down.

'Jack . . . ?'

That was the first time she wanted to reach out to him as a woman might, to take him in her arms and run her fingers over his wounds.

'Let's head on,' he said, shutting down, stepping forward once more. But he was not silent for long. He wasn't good at silences or sulking.

The moment over, he suddenly laughed and said with a rueful grin, 'Except I'm not sure where we're going right now, are *you?*'

His face had caught the wind and sun and he looked bronzed and healthy, his eyes brighter and more alight than when he had first arrived, weeks before.

She too looked different, more relaxed, her hair more blonde, made curly by the wind.

'I always feel safe on the Ridgeway,' she said slowly. 'The spirits of the past protect the likes of us up here. You know what I think? I think we should go to Avebury tomorrow.'

Avebury had been one of Arthur's favourite stone circles, even more so than Stonehenge, and Jack had never been there.

'Isn't it too far to walk?'

'We could get a bus there, or Mrs Foale could drop us off early in the morning, and we could start walking back. It's only twenty miles.'

'Only!'

Jack was as fit as Katherine but had never been used to walking the distances she had. He still thought of them as much longer than they were.

'We could see it as the beginning of our walk to the North Sea. We'll do it in stages, bit by bit, year by year, and when we get there we'll become different people and . . .'

She stood staring at him, heart thumping, about to step out into a void.

'Then what?'

Until that moment she had no idea what she was going to say, but instinct took over and she blurted it out. 'Then you'll know it doesn't matter if you take your shirt off and I see your burns. That just won't matter any more.'

She felt at once it was the wrong thing to say, because his face darkened, his grin faded.

'It'll always matter,' said Jack, retreating, unable yet to go so far. 'It'll always matter.'

She stood staring at him in alarm. She had said too much and made too many presumptions. But it felt unfair. Sometimes that instinct and bluntness was all right for Jack to display but not for her.

'I'm sorry,' she said.

They walked home in uncomfortable silence, each lost in their thoughts and in regret that finding a common language was so hard.

They didn't do the trip to Avebury the next day, or the day after that.

Clare Shore was dying and everything was on hold.

34
EYE OF THE HORSE

The doctor was just leaving when they arrived back at Woolstone House, late from seeing a film in Newbury. He reported that Clare was now as weak as she had ever been.

She was heavily sedated when they looked in on her.

'Tomorrow . . . maybe the next day,' said Mrs Foale quietly. 'I'm afraid she hasn't got long.'

The tears started pouring down Katherine's face. Even though she had accepted the inevitable a long time ago, it was still a shock. Jack put his arms around her and pulled her close – she buried her head in his shoulder and sobbed.

When she'd calmed down a little she found a warm change of clothes and prepared to sit with her mother through the night. She was there when Clare woke up just after eight next morning and asked, 'Where's Jack? I want to talk to him.'

He came at once and sat on the edge of her bed, taking her hand as he had done when he first arrived.

'Alone,' whispered Clare.

Katherine and Mrs Foale left the room.

Jack looked into her dark eyes, no longer so bright, which had now given up the struggle against pain. He knew it was goodbye. The stranger ever hovering in this room was at her shoulder now.

Jack had to lean close to hear her.

'You must do for me what I can no longer do for myself. You must climb White Horse Hill.'

'I—' he began.

'Today, this afternoon, go to the White Horse and say I'm ready now. For so very long I've wanted to climb up there myself, but of course I never had the strength. Now you must do it for me.'

They sat for a while.

Then: 'Jack?'

He looked at her.

'Look after her,' she said, 'and listen, *listen* . . . learn to let her look after you. That'll be your greatest gift to her. *Let her look after you, Jack.*'

He nodded as if he understood, but he was unsure if he properly heard what she had said.

Then, with great effort, she reached up and touched his face. 'Thank you,' she whispered, 'for coming to us. Now . . . go and climb that hill for me!'

Jack got up.

Katherine was waiting outside and they took each other in their arms.

'She's near the end isn't she?'

Jack nodded.

He held her tight until she was ready to go to Clare.

Then, when she was gone, he knew what he had to do.

Jack set off after lunch, leaving Katherine and Mrs Foale now to take turns in watching over Clare. He didn't say where he was going but explained it was something Clare had specially asked him to do.

He walked the length of the garden, circling the clump of trees, till he reached the far boundary fence. Then he crossed the field beyond to where the ground dropped away into further trees, where he then lost sight of White Horse Hill. He found the right path and followed it into the oppressive air which was heavy with humidity again, and charged with a dark energy. Rain was imminent once more, which added a sense of urgency to his steps in case, if he did not hurry, he might not reach White Horse Hill in time.

The trees of the copse through which he must pass were so thick and twisted above his head that they formed a canopy blocking out light.

Only when the path turned away from the stream and began to climb again did he feel he was properly on his way. He came to a stile beyond which he was able to see the chalk ridge once more, and what might even be the foreleg of the Horse. But, looking back, he saw no sign of Woolstone House.

The path turned almost parallel to the line of the hill, climbing only slowly, but giving him occasional views of the chalk ridge and finally of the Horse again. Each time he spotted it, it seemed to have shifted and moved in both its shape and direction, as if it really was alive.

He got to a place where he could see its eye, and realized that the eye was gazing at him directly.

'I'll make for there,' he told himself, impulsively leaving the trodden path for a more direct route. The terrain steepened at once and grew rougher, the trees huddling closer to each other, their branches forming claws that tried to hold him back.

The ground grew steeper still, and he had to lower his head and batter his way through undergrowth which tore at his clothes and scratched his face and neck.

A roll of thunder, and a kind of madness overtook him. He began running straight up into the thickets ahead, finding each time that he had only strength enough to make a few strides before he had to stop, his chest heaving, his mouth full of the woody, earthy dust of trees and lichen.

But Jack didn't care. He wanted to fight these trees as if they were his enemy, and continued struggling, pushing, thumping into them.

Then another pause to catch his breath, and another dash upwards, until quite suddenly he was through them and out the other side, tumbling headlong onto open grass, gasping for breath, the thin wire of a livestock fence now all that lay between him and the final climb to the White Horse above, just over the last steep curve of the hill.

As he began to plod up the steep grass slope, he felt a flurry of wind in his hair, colder than before, then the thunder renewed. Moments later the wind's force had doubled, and then redoubled, and a squall of rain came gusting straight at him, throwing him off balance, battering against his face, sending a cold stream of water down his neck.

Head down, he plodded resolutely upwards, watching the grass beneath him grow sodden and shining under the wild sky above. The sky itself was like the surging fears he felt for himself and Katherine. It was not just that she was in danger because of himself, as Arthur seemed to have warned, but that there was some danger she posed in her own right which might make her a target. The very possibility darkened his mind with doubt and fear. For how could he protect her properly, or she herself, if they did not know the nature of the threat she presented?

He turned briefly and looked back across the Vale, half expecting to see something, even in such a downpour. He saw nothing but sheets of grey rain and felt nothing but the chill cold on his face and soaking through his wet clothes and into his body; and he knew only that he must climb this hill for Clare, until he reached the Horse.

The eye of the Horse, he told himself, knowing it to be an objective far beyond a strip of chalk exposed on a hill, for which each step upward required an effort of will.

On and on, a battle against the elements now, Jack's face screwed up against wind and rain and cold as he began to fear he was losing his sense of direction, yet certain he had now to follow no path but the one he chose for himself.

He pushed on, his feet slopping and slushing through rivulets of rain, Arthur's hobnailed boots allowing him a grip that ordinary boots would never give.

He took the steepest course he could, figuring that if he carried straight on up he *must* eventually reach the top, though each next step now felt a near-impossibility.

The wind grew even more violent, wild and fierce. Jack hunched himself forward again, and climbed on, getting ever more tired, but knowing he would not now be beaten into stopping or turning back. Even so, he began to sense around him something new and unsettling.

It was a strange unease, a shift in things, the sense that something vaster even than the landscape itself and the sky above, and all the elements, was changing inside and outside him, re-forming, ending and beginning again.

The hill grew so steep he finally had to scrabble on all fours up the tussocky, chalky, slippery grass, grabbing at whatever gave a handhold, shoving a foot into any rabbit hole that gave him something to push against.

When he felt himself veering right, he corrected himself and carried on up the steep incline. When the rain drove into his eyes, he wiped them clear with the sodden cuff of his jacket. As he felt water trickle into his boots, he ignored it.

Until, panting in short gasps and grunts, he looked up to see, almost shockingly, a sudden line of sodden grey-white chalk exposed to his left.

One limb of the Horse. A leg stretching off into the distance.

Then another to his right, racing far away, as all around him, white against green, chalk amid grass, the ancient White Horse of Uffington began to take a strange shape. Not a horse so much as a tangle of lines conveying a movement that went on for ever.

On he climbed, in amongst its extraordinary elongated limbs and the outline of its body, the rain and wind becoming its energy, and his too, his grunts and gasps becoming incoherent outbursts: screams of fatigue and a lifetime of pain, shouts of anger and rage, bellows and roars that no one but himself could have understood, as he finally reached his journey's end and fell headlong, hands and arms stretched out wide, into the perfect white circle of the eye of the Horse, which seemed to mirror the sky above but whose round shape was that of the earth beneath.

Jack swore and yelled, his mouth now tasting of chalk.

Then he stood up and turned to face the world beneath and the sky above, and to confront the vast unease that had overtaken him on the last part of his climb and which, he now understood, had been with him all his life ever since the accident.

He knew now he was giant-born to the Hyddenworld and Margaret had explained a little of what that might mean. Such folk it seemed had always been targeted and destroyed. The sense of being watched fed the natural anxiety he felt that he was the object of others' hatred and fear.

'Yes,' he whispered, 'that fear was put into me at birth and it won't go until I confront and defeat the people who want to destroy me.'

The wind died, and the rain was reduced to no more than a steady drip from his soaking hair on to his collar, and the squall, now having passed on as swiftly as it had come, left behind it a landscape that was drenched but unbeaten.

Then sun came out and turned the White Horse of Uffington into a maze of lines all around him that suddenly made perfect sense.

Only when the air finally stilled and the sky was clear, and his whole body began to tremble with fatigue and cold, did he notice the woman standing on the ridge above him.

She was tall, solid, almost a silhouette against the bright sky, and her hands were buried in the pockets of her cloak.

She nodded to him slightly, which he took as a signal for him to climb up the last few yards from the eye of the Horse to the crest on which she stood.

A last brief squall flew across the hill between them, and he had to fight through even those few final steps.

'Jack,' she began, 'I have been waiting for you to find me again for so many years.'

Her cloak was rain-sodden, her damp hair slicked back over an ageless face, her eyes filled with a hundred thousand things as they shifted from him to focus on somewhere in the Vale below.

He turned and looked that way too, and far off, as far as he had come, he saw the two tall conifers with Woolstone House framed between them.

He then knew instinctively, not who she was but what she was.

She was the rider of the White Horse.

She had picked him up once when he was young and scared, soothing his fears of exile, whispered courage into him because he had to leave behind everything he knew if he was to survive, and she had told him he could become the giant he was born to be.

If he did that, maybe one day he could go home again.

Then she had sent him off on her horse, across the sky, in among the stars – from where, tumbling like a leaf on the wind, he had come back to Earth and to the life he now knew.

'Do you remember my name?' she asked.

Jack shook his head.

He had chalk and mud on his face; grey chalk slime all over his clothes; water-filled boots, and he was suddenly very cold and very tired.

He had been fearful all the way to the top of the hill, and all through the years before this, but in her presence all fear was gone.

She reached out a hand to him to help him take the final step, so he could stand by her side.

'My name is Imbolc,' the Peace-Weaver said, 'and my journey is almost done. Twelve years ago I reached the end of the winter of my life, and since then I have lived on borrowed time, watching both you and Katherine grow until you became ready to take on the challenge of your lives. That time has now come. So listen to me, learn and remember . . .'

35
GOING HOME

Jack's instinct was right, the dark stranger called Death – whose presence he had felt in the conservatory the day he first came – had finally, that same afternoon, whispered in Clare's ear that her journey through life was over.

While, outside in the garden, the ever-present sound of chimes, briefly so loud when Jack had set off to find the Horse, grew fainter and fainter despite the sudden squalls of wind and rain.

'Katherine? *Katherine!*' It was Mrs Foale.

Clare Shore had weakened further and she was now asking for Jack again.

'But he's gone up the hill, Mum,' said Katherine, taking her hand. 'He'll be gone a while yet. But I could go and try to . . .'

Clare shook her head, her grip on Katherine's hand tightening for a moment.

'Stay,' she whispered, looking over at Mrs Foale, who merely nodded and said nothing. Katherine knew she must obey, for the end was near.

'I wanted to . . .'

'What, Mum?'

'. . . to thank him again. For saving your life. And to tell him . . .'

Only her eyes seemed alive now. The rest of her was no more than a shadow, and one that was almost gone.

'What? Tell him what?'

'Tell him he's ready now, and that you are too. Tell him that.'

Clare struggled with her breathing and began coughing.

Mrs Foale patted her hand soothingly

'And I wanted to tell you about the . . .' continued Clare eventually, her eyes lightening briefly with the joy of remembrance, 'about the chimes and what they bring to us. But they'll come soon now and *they'll* show you. That's better than any telling done by me.'

'*Who'll* come? And show me *what*, Mum?'

Clare Shore looked over at Mrs Foale. There was sadness in her eyes now because she didn't want to go. She didn't want Katherine's hand to slip away from her for ever, but she felt so tired, and they were ready – the children were ready – and it was all right now, she could let go.

'Mrs Foale knows . . . and she'll tell you. She'll . . .'

Margaret Foale nodded, tears welling in her wise eyes. 'I know and I will, my dear,' she whispered.

'Thank you,' said Clare, turning her head now towards the open doors of the conservatory, trying to hear the chimes.

'I can't hear the chimes any more,' she said eventually.

In fact the gusting sound of trees in the wind was so violent that none of them could hear them. She turned her eyes back into the room, beginning finally to give up her long, brave battle with illness and pain.

'Mum . . .' whispered Katherine, but there was nothing else she could say. She could not stop the door opening through which only her mother could go.

'Mum . . .' she repeated.

Her mother smiled and her free hand fretted with the sheets.

Clare had no need to open her eyes to see; it was enough that her other hand had found Katherine's again.

'Never doubt he loves you, my dear,' she said softly, 'or that he needs you and that you need him. Like Richard and I did, like . . .' Clare's hand squeezed Mrs Foale's. 'Like you and Arthur.'

She turned back at Katherine. 'You'll know – you know already. You're both ready now.' She began coughing again.

Earlier she had refused to take any more of the drugs prescribed by the doctor to ease the pain.

Mrs Foale decided to leave Katherine alone with Clare for a time. There was no one else Clare needed to see, except maybe Jack, but he was up on White Horse Hill, where Clare wanted him to be. He was doing for her what she couldn't for herself.

That was his way of being with her at the end.

The right place at the right time, that was Jack from the first and it will be so to the very last. Always where he needs to be.

'What are you thinking, Mum?'

'Good things, my darling – just good things.'

Always trust him to watch over you, my love. I feel it's what he was sent to do and that somehow he's loved you from the beginning of time, as you have him. 'I can't hear the chimes any more,' Clare repeated, as if it was the last thing she had to cling on to.

She opened her eyes a final time to look into Katherine's.

The air fell still, as did the trees and the grass and the plants, and for a moment they heard the chimes again, until they too faded to nothing and silence fell, but for the dripping of the rain as the squalls passed on, taking with them the spirit of Clare Shore.

Katherine raised her mother's hand and, with tears running down her face, put her arm gently around her mother's shoulders and held her close, until the body that had carried her brave soul through so many courageous years lay still at last.

36

WARNING

'Imbolc's a strange name,' Jack said.

The worst of the rainstorm was now over and he was sitting talking with the Peace-Weaver up on White Horse Hill. The sun had broken through racing clouds and shone for the moment across the Vale below where Katherine lived.

'Maybe, but it's my given name and I like it. Do you know what it means?'

He shook his head.

'Spring,' she said, 'in the old language. That was from when I was mortal.'

'You seem real enough to me.'

She laughed. 'Now, there you're very much mistaken. What you see is an illusion and not real at all, and maybe you'll just remember it as vague shadows and wraiths. But that's all you need to remember in order to do the right thing.'

He looked at her appraisingly. She was tall, elegant, about forty-five, with chestnut hair that the rain had darkened. Her cloak looked unlike any garment he had seen before, and fell to her shoes.

'This is my favourite guise here in the human world, but in the Hyddenworld—'

'It's a real place, isn't it?'

'So real you're as good as in it already. You'll soon be learning how to go back and forth. It's one of the great gifts that giants like you possess.'

'Giants?'

'As Arthur Foale told you, yes.'

'You know him?'

'Of course.'

'Is he still alive?'

'Yes,' she said, turning serious. 'And it's one of several things we have to talk about.'

They fell silent for a moment.

'You knew what would happen this afternoon, didn't you, Jack?' she said eventually.

'That Clare would . . .'

He didn't like to say the word.

Imbolc didn't use the word either, because in actuality nobody dies; they simply move on to other planes.

'Yes, that her journey through life would be over. But I was thinking of something more specific than that.'

'That it would happen while I was climbing White Horse Hill? Yes, I think I did.'

'It's Katherine I had in mind. You need to be prepared for the fact she'll suffer extreme grief, which will make her vulnerable to the forces that she needs your protection against, whatever she herself may claim.'

Jack considered her words.

'Don't underestimate the power of such a loss,' she warned him. 'Grief takes you over, clawing at your heart and mind, forcing you to think of nothing else but the person you've lost, and what an endless black void their absence seems to create . . . And with that comes anger, too, because you've been left behind to continue on the stony road alone. Anger at everything and everyone.'

Imbolc had produced a black plastic bin-liner to keep their bottoms dry on the wet grass, off which Jack had since begun to slip. He pulled himself back next to her.

'Clever idea that,' Jack had said with a grin, indicating the bin-bag.

'I wish I could claim it was my invention, but someone called Bedwyn Stort gave me the idea a long time ago. I've carried one ever since, and very useful it's often been.'

'Bedwyn Stort sounds a funny sort of name as well.'

'He's a strange sort of person, or at least seems to be when you first meet him. But you find you get used to him and, as you do, that you can't do without him. That applies to you especially, because he saved your life the same day you saved Katherine's. You're all bound together in a common wyrd, on which a very great deal now depends.'

'He sounds like someone to meet. Where does he live?'

'In a place called Brum, but I don't think he's there right now. In fact, I think he's on his way here.'

'You seem to know a lot of things.'

'Hmm, I know next to nothing really. He's coming here simply because he's worked out that the time's right and that you're ready and, most important, that you're now needed,' she smiled. 'That's what giants are for.'

Jack ignored that remark.

Below them the Vale shone crystal-clear in the afternoon sun, the air thoroughly cleansed by the rain. Jack was beginning to feel warmer and now he felt good.

'What are you looking at?' she asked him.

'I was just looking at the view.'

'Can you see Katherine's house?'

He searched the landscape briefly and pointed.

'How did you locate it so fast?' she asked.

'From the two tall conifers – they're darker and taller than the others.'

'And what else do you notice?'

'I . . . well, *lots* of things.'

'About the garden, I mean.'

He stared but saw nothing out of the ordinary, just trees and a patch of lawn.

'It doesn't matter,' she said finally. 'Maybe you'll see it in time. But you'll need to see it soon or you'll not know where to go.'

'I'll keep looking for it until I see it then.'

Imbolc returned to the subject of Katherine. 'Grief makes people do strange things, including stupid things. It thus makes people vulnerable. Just when you think they've conquered it, it comes back. Two years, three years later . . . that's what it can take to regain stability after a parent dies. But you and Katherine don't have the luxury of that sort of time. A few weeks at the most now, and then you'll be needed.'

'For what?'

'I'm coming to that. First it's important you realize how Clare's passing means that Katherine will be in very great danger. Death of a loved one always leave the bereaved vulnerable and weak to dark influence. Clare's determination to live has been Katherine's protection, and her faith in the chimes as well.'

This made sense to Jack, but he still did not understand the nature of the danger.

'Arthur Foale seemed to warn me that whatever this dark force is it might try to get at me through Katherine. But there's something it fears about Katherine in her own right, isn't there? What's the danger exactly?'

'You should be asking me *who*. The Sinistral, that's who. Stort and the others will explain, so I don't need to.'

He looked puzzled and she immediately reassured him.

'Don't worry, it will become clear soon enough. But mention of the Sinistral reminds me of how you came to get badly hurt when you were six.'

'You mean the car accident?'

'It wasn't an accident,' she said coolly.

'I don't understand.'

'It was deliberate.'

'That's ridiculous. I was there, and I saw it was an accident.'

'So was I, Jack, and I can tell you it was not. The Fyrd were sent by the Sinistral to deliberately cause it.'

Jack shook his head in disbelief.

'But who would want to kill Katherine?'

'It wasn't her they were trying to kill.'

'But . . .' He couldn't continue for a moment.

'Jack, they were trying to kill *you*.'

Grief is far worse, she had told him minutes before. *It takes you over, clawing at your heart and mind.*

Grief had taken him over, after that accident – grief for what he himself had lost.

'I think they partly succeeded,' he said suddenly, at last acknowledging his own suffering.

The Peace-Weaver reached both her hands to his face and then to his damaged neck, as Clare had done when he first met her, in a gesture of understanding and acceptance.

He tried to pull away then, but she was stronger than him, and suddenly bigger by far, as big as the Earth herself and the sky above. When he stood up and struggled and fought and tried to fight and hurt her, she was stronger even then.

Until time passed and his anger subsided.

'They succeeded,' he said again.

'That's the miracle, Jack, because they didn't and, in failing, they made you stronger. That's the way wyrd works: it achieves the opposite of the ill that others try to inflict. But, make no mistake, now Clare's protection has gone from you both, they'll soon be back.'

None of what she was saying made sense, but then quite suddenly something quite different did.

Looking across the Vale again, he finally saw what it was about the far-off garden of Woolstone House that was odd and which Imbolc had been hoping he might eventually see. The sun had dropped lower in the sky, its soft red rays catching the tops of the trees. In particular it caught the tops of the two conifers, and others too, about ten of them, which were shorter but distinctive by their dark foliage, and suddenly became noticeable in a way they were not in the garden itself, there getting lost among all the other trees.

He leaned forward, staring hard, following the top of one tree to the next, and then round to the next, until he had worked out their simple pattern. He had of course noticed these other conifers before, but down on the ground it was next to impossible to make out the pattern they formed.

'What is it?' he asked, puzzled.

'It's a living wood henge, created by Arthur Foale very many years ago. There were conifers already there so he just thinned them out to make the pattern plainer.'

The sunlight faded from the trees for a moment, and then became brighter and stronger on them until he saw they formed an almost perfect hidden circle, its symmetry flawed only by the fact that the two biggest conifers, standing directly opposite the house, had a wider gap between them than the others.

'That's the entrance,' explained Imbolc, 'and if you work it out from the sun, you'll realize that it's on the north-east side of the henge – where such entrances always are. It took Arthur a long time to work that out, and after that he needed to do a lot of research in order to learn how to use it for its most important purpose.'

'Aren't henges astronomical calendars or something?'

She shook her head. 'The trouble with humans is they find it hard to think outside what they already know or believe in, so, because they no longer believe in the hydden, it has proved rather difficult for them to see what's so obvious, namely that the most important function of henges – many of which were built by the hydden, by the way – is to serve as portals between the hydden and human worlds. Of course you need to know how to use them, but that's not so hard. Just remember it's all about illusion, which explains why, being a shape-changer, I'm such an expert.'

'You were going to tell me where Arthur Foale now is.'

'No, I wasn't, and anyway I don't know exactly. But I can tell you what he's doing, which may still be of some help.'

'Which is?'

'He's looking for Spring.'

'That's weird,' said Jack. 'Spring's not a place, it's a season. All he has to do is wait until Spring comes round again.'

Imbolc laughed once more. 'Spring can be many things and is. It's a person, it's a state of being, it's also a gem, or represents one. That is what Arthur's in search of. The trouble is that getting into the Hyddenworld is one thing, getting back out quite another. For that he may need help. Then again, there's legends and prophecies that seem to suggest a giant-born will be needed to find the gem, so Arthur needs help from him.'

'Not me I hope?' said Jack doubtfully.

Imbolc smiled at his bewilderment. The sun faded and the air turned cold again, as mist drifted across the hill. The view below was gone too and, when the mist cleared eventually, the sun had disappeared and he could make out Woolstone no more.

'I can't see the house,' he began, turning towards her.

But she had gone as well.

The storm had finally moved on, and all that was left was the distant thud-thud-thud sound of distant thunder, like a great horse's hoofs galloping across the sky.

37
OUT OF THE DARK

Imbolc was right.

In the wake of Clare's death, grief hit Katherine and it hit Margaret Foale too. It was a grief raw and harsh and impossible to escape.

Katherine's moods changed violently and frequently.

One moment she would sort obsessively through Clare's possessions; the next moment all she wanted was to change yet again the details of her mother's up-coming cremation in Oxford. The undertakers, who had seen it all before, stayed calm and professional.

Only two things were constant throughout: first the date for the actual funeral in eight days' time, second that Katherine was angry with Jack, *very* angry. As if Clare's death was his fault. As if she somehow blamed it on his arrival here.

As if she wanted him now to leave.

It was as if she had forgotten all her mother had ever told her about Jack.

'Go back *now*,' Katherine screamed at him, 'back to wherever you came from. I don't ever want you—'

'Katherine . . .'

'I'm going into the garden, *my* garden, and when I come back I don't want you here, or ever to know where you've gone, because—'

'Katherine . . .'

'Just go, Jack. Can't you see you're not wanted and never were!?'

The truth was that grief put a kind of madness into her, till she became nearly impossible to live with.

But Imbolc had warned Jack and he knew what to do. So whenever Katherine grew mad at him in those first days of grieving and told him she wanted him out of the house, and her life, and out of everything, he stayed calm and watchful, and refused to leave or get angry or even let her out of his sight.

'I wish you'd go,' she would say again and again.

'Well, I'm not going to go,' replied Jack firmly.

The following day Katherine would be all sweetness and light again, as if she had totally forgotten ever asking Jack to leave.

It was at such a moment that she asked him one day, 'Could you do me a favour? It's for Mum really as much as for me.'

'I could,' said Jack, mock-grudgingly.

She came and hugged him and pecked his cheek. 'Sorry about . . . you know, everything.'

'What's the favour?'

'I want us to build a bonfire after all this is over, one bigger than any we've had here before. One so big it can be seen easily from White Horse Hill. It'll be a celebration of Mum's life. She always did like bonfires, and I like them because they're sort of pagan and earthy. Okay?'

'Okay.'

Then, her brief moment of calm over, she rushed off to her room where, once more, Jack would hear her crying inconsolably.

Only slowly, through things she herself said and other comments that Mrs Foale ventured, did Jack begin to understand the full nature of what Katherine felt. For it was a grief felt not only for the passing of Clare Shore's courageous life, but for what the lives of Richard and Clare might have been had they both lived.

Mrs Foale herself, though as helpful as she could be, was rather less patient with Katherine's moods than Jack was. Clare's death had triggered the feelings of desolation she herself had felt since Arthur had left them, and which it had seemed inappropriate to indulge, with Clare having been so ill. So she had been holding these feelings at bay since his disappearance.

Sometimes in those days, though careful never to let Katherine see her, she stood by herself in the vegetable garden, lacking the energy to do anything but weep for the husband – and now the dear friend – she had lost.

Then, pulling herself together, and remembering what a great gift Clare and Katherine had been to her when they came to Woolstone House, she would go to her room for the night, determined to find a way the next day to show Katherine that she still loved her.

While Katherine, bereft as well, cast adrift upon a stormy sea, would sometimes fall silent and sit, inconsolable, in the conservatory or out in the garden listening to the chimes, whatever the weather or the time of day – or night.

Once she put on some loud rock music, another time she started a bath which she forgot about, so everything flooded . . .

So it was left to Jack to hold them together, one way and another.

In doing so, as the day of the funeral approached, he began to understand that grief and loss make people vulnerable to the unseen worlds that swirl about them, but from which, normally, their psyches are geared to protect them.

It was bad enough that by day this onset of grief had set flowing the currents of ill-temper and unreason flowing throughout the house and garden; what was worse, and far more worrying to him, after Imbolc's warning, was that by night there was something darker sneaking about the place – something closing in.

For it was then, when the women were inside, locked down in grief and inclined to eat their meals in frowning strained-face silence or choosing to eat nothing at all up in the privacy of their rooms, that Jack tried to find respite from them out in the garden.

In his special places – a bed of grass that caught radiant sunlight between the three trees that encompassed it, a spring-fed pool around which grew thickets of bamboo, a spot behind one of the ruined rockeries – while lying on his back or sitting cross-legged, trying to meditate like in one of the books he had found in the library, Jack began, bit by bit, to hear the sounds of the very Earth itself.

The events of the past days seemed to heighten his awareness and make him hear all manner of things he had barely noticed before: trees creaking softly, leaves tumbling along branches, the hop-hop scurry of a blackbird's feet in the undergrowth, the breeze across the garden, the occasional patter of rain, the buzz of bees from one flower to the next and, more than once, the rough scurrying of hedgehogs in the undergrowth.

These sounds, and many more, mingled with the tinkling of the glass that Clare and others had hung on the shrubs surrounding the secret henge. As they sounded, Jack began to understand how perhaps it was the way this gentle resonance fragmented things, and how the chimes' dappling reflections of the sun and sky broke up the trees and grass and the very shadows that made it more difficult to see things clearly, and thus offered protection against the mounting sense of dark invasion he was finding harder and harder to keep at bay as the day of the funeral approached. How this might be he did not know, but he felt sure it was so.

Which was why, in daytime, when the breeze blew, and the tinkling of glass was continuous, it felt as if there was nothing much to fear. Jack could lie back, take in the sun, forget the time and place and, most of all, the circumstances. He could feel that Katherine was safe and that Mrs Foale was calm.

But at night, when the reflections of shards of glass and mirrors died with the light, and the loss of the breeze deprived the garden of the safety of their sound, he became ever more certain that dark life both hostile and dangerous was venturing forth from the other worlds to spy and snoop, surreptitiously, on the house and its inhabitants, slipping past where Jack watched and waited.

Then later, returning from a different direction, as if their reconnaissance was now complete, their plans laid and unpleasant possibilities established, those same spirits retreated back past him, biding their time.

38

IN THE LIBRARY

It was midnight and Jack couldn't sleep.

He went downstairs, fixed himself a hot drink, wandered around the ground floor of the house, went to the conservatory doors and peered out into the dark. He then opened them and stepped out onto the cracked paving stones of the terrace outside, felt nothing untoward and went back inside.

'Jack?' It was Mrs Foale.

'I couldn't sleep,' she said. Her grey hair was tousled and she wore a thick granny nightie underneath one of Arthur's dressing gowns.

'Nor me,' said Jack. 'I made myself tea. Would you like some?'

She nodded her head. 'I'll be in the library.'

As he loaded the tray, he heard Katherine moving about upstairs. She liked hot chocolate so he made her a cup, knowing the sweet scent of it would attract her down.

It did.

'Margaret's up.'

They joined her in the library, pulling chairs around to face where she sat at her desk.

'I was thinking, as I lay awake, that when this is over we should all go up to Arthur's cottage in Northumberland. It would do us good. It's a long time since I've been there.'

The last two years of Clare's illness had put a stop to that.

'And I was thinking that we must make a bonfire for Mum's ashes,' said Katherine. 'She would have liked that. I mentioned it to Jack. We could head off after that.'

It felt positive and the right thing to do.

'What's the walking like up there?' asked Jack.

'Fabulous.'

He got up, feeling restless, studied the books on the shelves, peered out of the window, and found himself standing at last by Arthur's chair. It was placed sideways-on to the desk, giving the unnerving impression that he had left in a hurry, intending to come back shortly. The chair itself was made of well-worn light oak and leather, with an old-fashioned, and now rusty, swivel mechanism just above the five-footed base. It looked like something from a museum of the history of furniture.

Jack impulsively sat down in it and then sprang up, thinking it might offend Margaret.

'It's all right,' she said instinctively. 'Arthur wouldn't mind.'

From this new perspective, Jack saw how the library was a room of two halves. Margaret's desk was neat and tidy, as were the shelves on each side of it. Arthur's section was the exact opposite – cluttered, dusty, disordered, drawers half open, an ashtray full of stubbed-out butts and the ash of a single cigarette that had burnt right through. It looked very much as if Arthur had just lit it, when he was suddenly called from his desk and never came back.

There was, among the pile of papers which Jack eyed closely but did not touch, an opened academic journal whose yellowing pages suggested it had been lying there from long before Arthur had left. There was still the musty smell of cigarettes hovering over the desk, as well as . . . he sniffed a bit more and then spied a whisky bottle, and next to it a dusty cut-glass tumbler. He picked the glass up and sniffed it, detecting the tell-tale signs of evaporated liquid in the bottom of it.

'Cigarettes and whisky,' Jack remarked, without thinking.

'He liked his drugs,' said Mrs Foale drolly.

Jack looked more closely at the introduction to the article in the journal left open on the desk. It was one written by Arthur himself, and had an image of him looking exactly as he did in the DVD he had left behind for them.

He found himself peering into the couple of desk drawers that were already half open.

One drawer contained several packs of cigarettes of a brand that Jack had never heard of, their packets as yellowing as the journal's pages. The other contained an ancient calculator, a scattering of pencils, some rubber bands, and a prismatic compass like Jack had once used when being taught to navigate his way across the Welsh mountains with an Ordnance Survey map.

When he picked it up and studied it closely, he saw it was perfectly made, the prism in just the right place, the graduations expertly cut into the brass, the needle swinging easily. But the ring in which a user normally put his thumb, to hold the device to his eye while taking a bearing, was far too small even for his little finger.

'Strange,' murmured Jack.

He put it back and turned his attention to the row of books on the floor-to-ceiling shelves right behind the chair he sat on. They seemed mainly about folklore and looked very well-thumbed. There were more books on the same subject on the shelves further along, and a whole lot besides on everything from astronomy to Anglo-Saxon history.

There were box-files as well, all neatly lettered and numbered in contrast to the general mess and clutter itself, which, the more he examined it, gave a sense of Arthur's wide range of interests. There was a pile of maps on the floor and boxes of seemingly unsorted photographs, a lot of them depicting megaliths and stone circles, and what Jack guessed to be Iron Age hill forts.

There was an Edwardian hat stand, its enclosed base full of walking sticks of all shapes and sizes, while the hooks above held a variety of bashed-up hats. Random shoe boxes contained stones, black seaweed, a dried and curled-up adder skin. Soon the pattern became clearer: everywhere he looked there were things from outdoors, or things to wear for going outdoors; or books which might inform anyone heading outdoors.

It seemed that archaeology involved a bit more than sitting at a desk and reading textbooks.

'What exactly do *you* do, Margaret?' asked Jack impulsively. 'I mean, you never talk about it.'

'People aren't usually too interested. I'm currently working on a text which scholars call the *Codex Exoniensis*. When Leofric was appointed first Bishop of Exeter in the year AD 1050, he gave the codex to the cathedral library. It contains one hundred and thirty-one leaves or pages of manuscript, rescued from other books now lost, and individual manuscripts bound together with the rest for their better preservation. The text itself consists of various riddles, material about Christ himself, two biographies of saints, religious allegories, homilies, and some extraordinary elegies and lyrics.'

'What's Old English sound like?'

'German, Frisian, even like Modern English in places, though you wouldn't recognize that fact if you saw it printed.'

'Read us some,' said Katherine.

She did better than that, she began reciting from memory:

> *Wrætlic is þes wealstan, wyrde gebræcon;*
> *burgstede burston, brosnað enta geweorc.*
> *Hrofas sind . . .*

'Sounds really powerful,' said Jack.

'It's a warrior language and so is meant to. Anyway that particular poem is strong stuff in its own right. It tells of a city in ruins, its well-built walls destroyed by fate, the work of "giants" and stone-smiths. It says the city's now nothing more than mouldering dust, its citizens' lives over, caught in "earthgrip" and "gravesgrasp" for more than fifty generations.'

'"Earthgrip",' repeated Katherine slowly.

'"Gravesgrasp",' murmured Jack.

'Scholars call that particular poem *The Ruin*. The buildings the poet describes were impressive, bright with colour and light, with busy people and the flow of clear water. "Wyrd changed all that!" he declares, and destruction descended and decay came, and death too.

'The poem's incomplete because it got badly burnt. The last lines are lost. Most scholars tend to believe it describes the ancient city of Bath, which was built by the Romans but abandoned after they left in the fifth century. Needless to say, Arthur disagreed with that theory.'

'So what did he think the poem was about?' asked Katherine.

Margaret hesitated and then sighed. 'It was one of his more

outlandish notions I'm afraid, but he thought it described the future rather than the past. He thought the poet had somehow travelled forward in time, and then come back to leave a warning to future generations.'

'Did he have any particular city in mind?'

'As a matter of fact he did. He interpreted it as a description of the ruins of Birmingham after some kind of extreme weather event crisis in the future.'

'A holocaust happening right in the middle of England?' said Jack. 'That seems a bit unlikely.'

'It happened before, as a matter of fact, in the middle of the seventh century AD, at the time of a legendary craftsman called Beornamund. There occurred then one of the most severe climate events ever to hit the British Isles, far, far worse than any of the local hurricanes you hear of today. It seemed like the beginning of the end of things, and Arthur believes *The Ruin* is intended as a warning to us that it might all happen again.'

Jack felt a chill run up his spine, a prickling at the back of his neck.

He stood up suddenly, Arthur's chair spinning behind him.

'Is Birmingham the same place as Brum?' he asked.

Margaret said nothing.

'That's where he's gone, isn't it? He's gone off to the Hyddenworld equivalent of Birmingham, and he can't get back!'

'Jack . . .'

'Hasn't he, Margaret?'

She looked suddenly bereft and helpless.

'*Hasn't he?*'

'I . . . don't know. He was trying . . . he wanted . . . Jack, I just don't know.'

'He needs help, doesn't he?'

'I didn't want . . . I can't ask . . .'

'Jack!'

It was Katherine protesting. She hadn't yet made the connections Jack had. All she knew was that she didn't want Margaret crying, or Jack ever again getting drawn into something that might involve him risking his life. That would be a grief too far.

'We're tired now,' she said, 'and we need some sleep before

tomorrow. And, yes, a holiday at the cottage in Northumberland after that would be great.'

'Just a few more days then,' said Jack, not sure if he meant before they would be going away, or the time he had in which to do something about Arthur.

In one way it seemed a very long time; in another, not nearly time enough.

39

FAREWELL

On the day of Clare's funeral, nature itself honoured the dead woman's passing with a display of changing moods that mirrored the feelings of those who loved her.

The day began with the clouds and cold winds that matched the sense of grief that pervaded the little congregation taking part in the service at Oxford Crematorium.

Sudden violent showers thudded on to the roof of the chapel as the service proceeded, until, with the committal of Clare's body to the flames, the most violent shower of all drove hard into the windows and darkened the entire building.

Then, moments later, as Katherine rose to say a few words in celebration of her mother's life and to speak of her lack of any fear of death, the rain stopped, the gloom lifted, and the sun came out. It projected a mosaic of colour onto the floor before the altar which, now bright, now less so, then bright again, was as alive as the memories that Katherine tearfully created for them all.

Her final words were simple: 'Mum was there when I needed her, right through the years of growing up. She taught me many, many things which will stay with me always, like the memory of her smile and her touch. Mum loved me all the harder because she knew Dad wasn't there to share it with her, so she did it for both of them.'

Katherine could say no more after that, though she wanted to and stood alone there weeping until Jack got up and guided her back to her place.

When the service was over, and all Clare's favourite music had been played, they came out into sunshine so bright it was already drying up the puddles left behind by the rainstorm.

The sun, like the puddles, reflected the mood of Clare's mourners, and turned out to be the start of a week of those lovely bright days and soft evenings that make for an old-fashioned late Spring. It was perfect for the building of the great bonfire which Jack, Katherine and Mrs Foale assembled slowly but steadily just outside the wood henge, by the two great conifers that marked its entrance.

This bonfire, they hoped, would be like a fiery herald before the henge itself, serving the twin purposes of sending Clare's ashes up into the sky over its great mystic circle as well as serving as a vivid closure to her life on earth.

The temperature now rose with each passing day, and even old things that had been left rotting for years in the many dark, dank corners of the house, or in outbuildings and the garden, rapidly turned tinder-dry and therefore suitable for burning.

Jack did most of the physical work, using a wheelbarrow to carry combustibles from various places all over the property. Old boxes, piles of papers and unwanted things from inside the house, an old kitchen table that had ended up discarded in the vegetable garden, apple-tree branches pruned by Mrs Foale, all of these were going to be burnt.

These were good days, happy days, in which Jack and Katherine experienced a rebirth of that strange confusion of feeling and desire for each other that had faltered with the onset of Clare's final hours of life. They were like two young planets whose influence on each other was as yet uncertain in its nature and power, and whose universe was, for the time being, confined here to Woolstone.

But Mrs Foale, while sitting on the cracked old terrace at night and listening to their chatter nearby, understood better than they that it was in the nature of things they would soon be gone out into the wide world.

'You all right?'

It was Katherine, followed by Jack, arriving to slump into some garden chairs nearby.

'You could have some wine,' said Mrs Foale, helping herself to another glass.

The nights now felt safer and more relaxed, as if the malevolent spirits of the previous weeks had fled. Jack thus felt confident that nothing sinister would or could happen before they departed for Northumberland.

40

ON WASELEY HILL

Three days before the night chosen for the bonfire, Margaret announced at breakfast, 'I was thinking of driving over to have another look at Waseley Hill. Anybody want to come along and keep me company?'

It was a bright, warm day and they were feeling lazy. They looked at each other both thinking the same thing: that it would be good to have the day alone together, without chores.

'Any special reason for going there?' Katherine wondered indifferently. 'It's up near Birmingham isn't it?'

'It was where we took you out for a walk soon after the accident, and where we sort of decided to have you come and stay with us.'

Katherine's interest was piqued.

'But the main reason is that I have to go to see the farmer on whose land Arthur was once thinking of doing a dig before he saw another way to search for what he wanted. Arthur used to spend a lot of time up there, so the farmer's naturally been wondering where Arthur is.' She stared for a moment at the table. 'Waseley's where Beornamund is meant to have lived.'

Whatever Jack and Katherine's previous inclinations, they now agreed a day out would be good.

The drive north was easy, and fortunately the farmer wasn't too worried about Arthur's long absence from the site.

'He's a busy man I dare say and the site's well away from the public path. Do you want to take these young folk over there now, Mrs Foale? It's dry underfoot, as there's been so little rain this last week.'

The river itself was not much more than a stream, but it had carved out its own steep little channel over the years. This was filled with gorse and brambles, and the exploratory trench Arthur had dug and then refilled was already growing weeds.

'So this is what exactly?' Jack wondered aloud.

'Probably nothing, but Arthur supposes that if Beornamund really did have his workshop right beside the river, it would have been up here somewhere rather than down in the Deritend area which historians reckon is the oldest part of the city. Whichever is right, at least we'll get a better view up here.'

They climbed on up through sheep pastures to the source itself: a spring of clear water running from a muddy scar in the hill to flatter ground below, which was strewn with reeds wherever it was not churned up by livestock.

Though there was nothing much else to see, they stood staring in delight at the clear bright water bubbling straight out of the ground.

'It's easy to see why a spring so often became a place of worship in pagan times,' observed Margaret. 'It's the beginning of things, a source of life, which is why explorers have always been obsessed with tracing the source of great rivers. It's like returning to the original home. Many such locations are associated with deities, but this one is best known for an ordinary craftsman who actually lived here, creating items you can still find in our greatest museums.'

She then recounted the legend of Beornamund to her silent audience.

'How near to the truth it is, we'll never know, but he certainly lived somewhere along the banks of the Rea, between here and the broader stream it runs into.'

'So that lost piece of the pendant called Spring is still here somewhere,' said Katherine dreamily.

'Maybe,' said Margaret. 'I like to think so.'

Jack had walked a little way off and now stood looking across the city of Birmingham, though he could see little more than a blue haze of pollution, above which rose a few towers and some cranes, signifying yet more urban development.

He thought back to his meeting with the Peace-Weaver on White Horse Hill, and realized that as she was wearing a long dark cloak which completely covered her neck he wouldn't have seen the pendant, even if she was wearing it.

'Jack?'

He didn't turn round but carried on staring across the city.

'So it was Beornamund who gave his name to the place,' said Margaret, finishing her discourse. 'It's really Beornamund's *Ham* or settlement, which through time became corrupted into Beornmundin-gaham, and sometimes even Brummagem . . .'

Jack shivered uneasily to think of what degree of cataclysm could reduce so vast a city to ruin.

There had been times back at Woolstone when his premonitions of terrible things had been bad enough, but here they felt a thousand times worse.

It felt like the sun had suddenly gone in and everything turned cold.

Like the bad spirits were following them, even here.

'Let's go,' he said. 'Okay?'

They headed back to the car in silence.

41
OLD SCARS

Katherine grew more relaxed each day that passed, becoming more talkative and less prickly. One afternoon, the bonfire nearly complete, the pair of them lay in the grass talking.

'My mum loved bonfires, but so did my dad before . . . you know.'

As Jack lay on his back, he had found his mind drifting, though he wasn't sure to where. Then suddenly he realized what Katherine had said that was so unusual: she had mentioned her father.

'You hardly ever talk about your dad,' he observed quietly.

'I . . . well, no. But since Mum died I often think about him.'

'Can you remember him much?' he asked, sitting up.

Katherine stared at him blankly.

Jack thought of an image he could never forget: a man on fire, desperately trying to get the car door open on Katherine's side. Failing to do so, and slowly, so slowly, curling up into the fire of which he had become part, the last view of him just a dying man, lost to Jack's sight behind the burning vehicle. The memory still haunted him.

'No,' said Katherine, 'I can't remember him too well, but . . .'

'But what?'

'But I do know what he looked like, from photographs at least; and sometimes . . . I think I can remember the . . .'

'The what?'

Katherine half-shrugged and looked away for a moment.

Then she said, 'The feel of being picked up by him, his arms around me. I'm *sure* I can remember him often doing that.'

They looked into each other's eyes and Jack knew she wasn't telling the whole truth, not exactly. It was his own arms she remembered most, and him pulling her from the car. She had subverted that recall into a final memory of her dad, because she needed to have at least something about him to hold on to. It was all she really had.

'But *you* remember him clearly?' asked Katherine.

'Yes,' said Jack firmly. 'Yes, I do.' He then fell silent, and they both felt it better to say no more on the subject right then.

'Better finish the bonfire,' he muttered finally.

'Okay,' she said, glancing over at it. 'But I think it's pretty well finished already.'

'I've lost track of the days,' Jack admitted. 'When are we actually lighting it?'

'Tomorrow night.'

He sat up and turned to face her, his expression deadly serious. 'I want you to stay close by me, Katherine, tonight and tomorrow night. The day after that we'll be gone, and it'll be all right.'

'It'll be all right anyway,' she replied, puzzled.

'I don't want anything bad to happen to you,' said Jack.

'Nor me you,' she said, daring to reach out a hand to ruffle his hair. 'Nor me you, Jack.'

It was the nearest they got to saying what they really felt about each other. The truth was they had already begun to say it without words.

The following morning, they found themselves meeting in the conservatory, which they had avoided since Clare's bed had been removed. Things had been getting back to normal, so far as they ever could, but the house now felt as if – for the time being – it had given them all the protection it could.

There, Jack felt a sudden tremor of doubt, as if the bad spirits were hovering again.

'It's time to leave here,' he said, staring around, and then back into the garden. 'We ought to go today. It's not safe here any more for any of us. But especially you.'

'Why me?'

He didn't answer but his expression showed his fears for her.

'I'm not a little girl any more, Jack,' she said, echoing just what he had told Clare and Mrs Foale.

'I know and maybe . . .'

'What?'

A new thought had come into his head, he was not sure where from.

No you're not, and maybe that's what they've been waiting for. Sure the chimes and Clare and all that has protected you, but could it be that now you're a woman they want you like the Peace-Weaver said? But what difference does that make? Maybe just that they knew the two of us would have a different feeling for each other when we became adult.

Katherine was shaking her head, unimpressed by his belief they should leave at once.

'It'll be time to go the day after tomorrow,' she replied. 'By then, we'll have done all we can and all we should. Anyway the bonfire's a good end and a good beginning, and we can't leave it smouldering when we go.'

Jack grunted doubtfully.

'According to the Foales, pagans have ritualistic fires at the beginning of each of the four seasons, which is when we're meant to get closest to the Otherworld. We're doing it at a different time because of when Mum has died. But death also opens unseen doors . . .'

'If you're hoping to intrigue me you're failing, Katherine! All you're making me want to do is get you both out of here.'

Jack liked none of it. Since his meeting with Imbolc, he believed anything possible.

'What we're talking about isn't some mystical joke but something real. It's portals to the Hyddenworld. Arthur must have found out how they work. But I can't imagine it.'

'Nor me.'

It was her turn to look nervous and he put his arms around her.

'We're freaking each other out!' she said. 'But I still want the bonfire.'

'All right. By this time on Friday we'll be on our way to the cottage in Northumberland. We'll be away from it all.'

He wished he felt as confident as he tried to sound. Also, the conviction was growing inside of him that he was going to have to find a way to track down Arthur Foale. How, he had no idea as yet. First he would make sure that Katherine and Mrs Foale left Woolstone safely, and then try to make his own way into the Hyddenworld.

He held her closer still.

'It is all kind of intriguing, isn't it?' she said.

Her fingers could feel the bumps and ridges of the twelve-year-old burns through his cotton shirt.

Sensing this, he wanted to pull away, but she held him closer. She let her fingers linger where they were before sliding one hand to his neck.

Jack tensed.

'It's all right,' she said gently.

He tried to pull away again, but still she wouldn't let him go.

'Supposing Mrs Foale finds us?' he said.

'Let her,' said Katherine, suddenly kissing him on the mouth.

Katherine finally pulled away, blushing and embarrassed at her forwardness. Jack's pulled her back to him.

He looked into her eyes, grinned and kissed her again, gently but quite firmly.

She closed her eyes, her lips moist to his.

Their bodies moved closer still, their arms around each other before Jack moved his right hand up her back, over her neck and then to the back of her head, his fingers in her hair.

They kissed some more, moved their hands to a hug. She whispered with a smile, 'So . . . do you want tea?'

His answer was another kiss and so was hers.

They held each other, beginning to relax, feeling their bodies close, feeling good.

As if on cue, Mrs Foale's voice sounded from the kitchen. 'Are you two there? Would you like a cup of tea?'

They both smothered a laugh, separated and went to join her.

42

SHADOWS

The sky had cleared completely by late afternoon, and a pale sliver of moon appeared early, then a slight north-easterly breeze set in and the temperature started to fall. By six o'clock it was quite cool, with the moon showing ever clearer.

Katherine and Mrs Foale began putting out a row of old jam jars with nightlights in them, which they ceremoniously lit at seven, making a meandering path of light in the twilight, all the way from the house and on either side of the bonfire, right to the entrance to the henge itself. It was meant to light the spirits on their way back and forth from the Otherworld. Once Jack might have doubted it but now he didn't. He wished he could believe that all the spirits would be benign.

They had supper at eight – thick parsnip soup made by Mrs Foale, mopped up with chunks of homemade bread.

At half past nine Jack went out with a torch to check that everything was in place. It wasn't quite dark but the air felt unnaturally cold. Fortunately the earlier breeze that had lowered its temperature had subsided.

He had matches in his pocket and had earlier put a bunch of scrunched-up newspaper and firelighters right at the centre of the bonfire, with a tunnel into it to make it easier to light, and then quickly retreat. He had put to one side a pile of wood and cardboard ready to fill the gap left behind once he had lit the tinder. It was a trick that Arthur Foale had taught them and which they had now shown Jack.

'It was Arthur's father taught *him*,' explained Mrs Foale, 'and so do the simple but important things of life travel down through the generations. As for fire, why, that connects us with the beginnings of life itself.'

Now, standing in the darkness, Jack thought of such things, and might have thought of others too, if he had not, for the first time since the day of the funeral, again felt wary here in the garden, the gathering chill of the night seeming alien, the slightest sound in the undergrowth magnified by the still air.

He moved very cautiously, looking right and left, and even over his shoulder, and then headed back towards the house for safety. Annoyed with himself, he went back beyond the bonfire, into the shadows on the far side of the henge. He shone his torch directly into the open space of the henge itself, but there was nothing to be seen there but grass. Nothing at all . . .

Then a sudden movement inside the henge to his right, and after playing his torch there and finding nothing, he turned it off and stopped still, listening with his head to one side. He could hear something all right, movement as quiet as fingers sliding over the bark of a tree.

He aimed his torch at the source of the sound again and turned it on, to find two eyes staring back at him.

'A fox!' he said aloud, and in disgust, and stamped his foot slightly to send it scampering away into the shadows.

Then more movement, this time up by the house.

'Jack? Are you there?' It was Mrs Foale.

He chose not to reply at first, not wishing to disturb the quiet of the night, but retreated instead into the shadow of the bonfire, and from there slipped away into the trees.

To his alarm, she left the house and came straight towards him along the dark path between the nightlights. He didn't move, feeling that, having not replied to her summons, he would now look an idiot if he made his presence known. But then he changed his mind and was about to call out, but stopped just in time. He might only frighten her.

Caught up in his own hesitations, Jack could only stand still and see what would happen.

Mrs Foale reached the bonfire, paused briefly, then moved on to stand between the two conifers and stare ahead into the henge.

She stood there a long time, the night darkening around her, before she suddenly gave a loud sigh and said clearly, 'Oh, Arthur.'

Then, a moment later, she added more quietly, 'You should never have gone back. It was never your world . . .'

Gone back . . . ?

This was the confirmation Jack needed that it was possible to go back and forth to the Hyddenworld. He just had to find out how.

Mrs Foale sighed again and bowed her head. As Jack stood listening in the darkness, he wished he could be anywhere else but here as an unwilling witness to this private moment. Yet, even so, he had learned something that might be important.

'May the spirit bless you this night, my dear,' she continued in a whisper, 'and guide your soul safely home.'

Then she turned around suddenly and went back into the house.

Jack was about to follow her, when he heard movement again. Definite and purposeful, it was off to one side of the henge and it felt in some way malevolent.

He realized that Mrs Foale's unexpected arrival might have served to mask the sound of his own movement towards the far side of the henge.

There was a sharp, thin utterance – a call of sorts. Very slowly he moved his head to the right, and peered through the trees into the dark interior of the henge.

A black figure, quite small? Or just an animal? A shadow? As he stared, trying to fix its shape on his retina, it shimmered away into nothing. Jack stayed just where he was, concentrating so hard that his eyes began to water. Still he did not move a fraction.

Movement again, on the far side of the henge this time. But there he could see nothing. Another call sounded and then movement much nearer, *very* near. He had the feeling, sudden and absolute, that someone was so close he could have touched him. Someone who *knew* he was here.

Unable to hold still any longer he turned sharply, a twig cracking beneath his feet, and stared hard into the gloom over to his left. He saw nothing but a shimmer of dark light darting among the trees. The chimes sounded frantically as if something had brushed against them, and that sense of a presence bled instantly away into the night.

Jack came out of the shadows, headed back around the bonfire, and up to the house, feeling very uneasy.

When he looked back from the terrace there was nothing to see at all, but the pathway of candles leading to . . . what?

The bonfire?

Something waiting to happen?

Jack cocked his head to one side, listening hard. But there was nothing to hear but the chimes' occasional stirring, the last flapping of a pigeon in the trees, and a squirrel or two, awake nearly too late, hurrying across the woodland floor.

He went inside.

43

BONFIRE

They finally set the bonfire alight at eleven.

Mrs Foale had produced some sausage rolls and mince pies in memory of Arthur, washed down with the sweet sherry he also liked.

'It's what we always have at bonfires,' whispered Katherine, making a face.

The fire took easily, and within twenty minutes was giving out enough heat to combat the chill night air. By a quarter to midnight the heat was so great that it forced them to step back.

'We don't have need for chants or incantations tonight,' said Mrs Foale, mysteriously. 'The spirits are present without them. What will be, will be.'

No, indeed they didn't. The fire and the roaring sound of it, the nearby tinkling of the chimes on the restless air, and the sparks shooting up through the branches towards the sky, they combined to say it all.

Katherine quietly slipped away from them and went up to the house to fetch the gold plastic urn containing her mother's ashes. She carried it back down the candlelit path, approaching the fire as close as the heat would allow, and then began scattering its contents into the flames.

'Ashes to ashes,' she murmured.

The fierce heat almost sucked them out of the urn, and they dispersed like a stream of tiny, red-orange stars, twisting and turning upwards with the flames, up towards the treetops now clearly lit by the blaze, and then beyond, till one by one each tiny particle was lost among the bright stars in the sky.

'Goodbye, Mum,' whispered Katherine after the last spark was gone and the real stars were all that was left. 'You're one of them yourself now.'

'Goodbye, Clare,' said Mrs Foale.

Jack just stared at the night sky, the warmth of the fire on his face and chin, the cold air of the night on the back of his neck, glad to be alive, glad to be in Katherine's company, but still wary of the shadows all about.

Somewhere, distantly, a church clock struck midnight.

'It is the end of one day and the beginning of the next,' said Mrs Foale softly. 'Wherever you are, Arthur, and whatever's happened to you, I pray you're safe and will soon come home.'

She went over to the entrance of the henge, as she had done earlier, perhaps to say another quiet prayer. She stood there, a lonely figure against the darkness, the firelight flickering over her.

'She's missing him so much today,' remarked Katherine, 'and it's getting worse for her all the time. Mum's death has simply opened the floodgates of her own loss.'

'Then,' said Jack, so quietly she hardly heard him, 'we'd better get him back.'

He went and fetched some garden chairs, to make things more comfortable. Soon Mrs Foale rejoined them, and they had another glass of sherry each.

They began to talk then, sharing memories, revealing their hopes.

Gradually they all fell silent, the firelight flickering in their eyes, each in different ways fearful of the future, which felt ever more uncertain the more they thought about it.

Mrs Foale got up. 'I'm beginning to feel cold, so I think I'll go inside,' she announced. 'Why don't you two stay here and enjoy the last of the flames.'

They sat there in silence in the dark, Jack finally allowing himself to relax, his earlier wariness dying away with the bonfire and the guttering candles. All was warm and mellow, and quiet, the occasional final flame and stirring ember seeming as soft and muted as the darkness had become.

The night was now alluring, deep and shining dark, with only the sharp call of a tawny owl to break the silence. They felt content then, the ritual of farewell to Clare performed, the Summer come, all three of them safe here, their beds awaiting them. The spirits of the night were now benign.

'Jack,' began Katherine suddenly.

He turned away from the fire to look at her, and reached out a hand instinctively.

She took it, her mouth opening to speak . . .

But suddenly there was a stirring in among the trees to one side of the henge. It was the movement of a person, swift and alien.

'Jack . . . !'

Katherine was suddenly frightened, Jack tense. It was the same quick tread he had sensed earlier.

'Did you hear that?' she whispered, moving nearer to him.

He nodded. 'I'll check it out.'

'No, don't. Stay with me. Please—'

But Jack was already up and heading towards the pair of conifers. There he pulled out his torch and shone it around.

There was nothing to be seen, yet something . . . something was wrong.

Jack's heart began to thump.

Then unexpected movement to one side.

'Jack!'

Katherine had now heard it too, and was pointing into the trees nearby.

Lowering his torch so as to allow his eyes to readjust to the darkness, he set off in the direction she had pointed in.

'No, Jack, don't go . . .' whispered Katherine urgently.

But it was too late. He was in among the trees and out of sight.

She stood up, uncertain whether to follow after him or to stay in the light of the dying fire.

Jack paused to look back.

'I won't be long,' he called out, not registering how still she had suddenly become.

'I'll be right back. Just stay there.'

Jack headed further in among the trees, his eyes keenly searching the flickering shadows.

'I'll just check it out,' he murmured, leaving her further behind.

44

LOST

The moment Jack was gone, icy shadows began to encircle Katherine.

The fire seemed to dim, as if she saw it through a veil. The cold deepened until suddenly any warmth that remained in the air was sucked right out of it, so that she began to shiver and feel deeply afraid.

The shadows grew thicker, closer and colder, continually shifting so that she could not quite make them out. She turned this way and that to try to escape them, and found herself stumbling away from the bonfire towards a tree, which she bumped into painfully.

Though her feet scuffled through dry leaves, they made no sound.

Jack! she tried to say, but no sound came.

Then the shadows began re-forming into something more solid, something malevolent.

But her voice just would not work and she could not call for help.

The cold felt like fingers digging into her, grasping and gripping at her clothes and flesh, pulling her in a direction she did not want to go.

Their cold presence shivered inside her, swirled through her head, pulled harder and harder at her to make her go the way they wanted.

'No!' she tried to shout. 'Jack!'

But the icy shadows had frozen her mouth and tongue until, unable to make a sound, she had not even strength to turn his way any more.

✳

Jack heard nothing of Katherine's muted cries, though her silence was ominous.

All he could do was stand totally still among the trees, where he thought he had heard a sound, trying to stop his staccato breathing being heard.

He was certain he sensed someone nearby, just as he had earlier. Now, whoever or whatever it was, the feeling was much stronger and more malevolent.

Jack circled around, pushing his hands up against the icy shadows that seemed to surround him as if to get them out of his way, tugging at them to dislodge them from his head, eyes wide open on a night that had changed to a nightmare he could not understand and which put fear deep inside him.

Another sound of cracking twigs followed by a brief caressing movement slithering across his face, like fingers that meant to harm; a swirl of chilling air sliding past him.

Jack focused and his mind became his own again.

Sensing something, he turned sharply, saw a shimmer of blackness before him. The shadow slowly shifted, and then darted suddenly across at eye level. He tried to follow its further movement between the trees, but lost sight of it almost instantly. He stepped forward in an effort to catch sight of it again, hoping his feet would not cause the snapping of twigs or rustle of dry leaves, but the shadow moved faster still and was gone.

He grabbed the moment to reorientate himself and it was the acrid scent of the bonfire on the breeze that finally pointed him in the right direction. He turned his head further and spotted the lights of the house off to his left and, having recovered his bearings fully once more, he realized that each step he was now taking took him ever further away from Katherine.

When another shadow stopped in front of him, Jack lunged at it angrily, but found it was nothing of substance, though the air it occupied felt bitterly cold.

'*Jack!*'

As he finally heard Katherine desperately calling his name, he immediately turned back, regretting at once that he had left her. But just then he felt a shudder in the air, saw a vibration of light, then a definite movement right across his line of vision that left him blinking.

He stopped, momentarily disorientated once more, feeling as if a sleight of hand had taken place, a trick of some kind: a clever stunt by a stage magician who, by waving his hands, makes an object disappear though those watching know it must surely still be somewhere near.

'Katherine?' he called out, uncertain in which direction now to turn.

He sniffed for the direction of the fire, turned again to check where the house was, and then, ignoring the trickster shadows, he ran back through the trees towards the bonfire.

'Katherine . . . ?' he shouted.

But there was no reply.

Jack got back to the bonfire and stared in bewilderment at the spot where he had left her, finding it impossible at first to take in the fact that she had disappeared. He had been gone only moments. Surely he would have noticed any movement away from the bonfire. This was inexplicable.

'Katherine!' he called again, running over to her chair as if, by just touching it, he could magically bring her back.

Still she did not appear.

'Where are you?!' he yelled.

He paused again and focused, then realized that something made the situation a thousand times worse. He could *feel* her presence somewhere nearby, so near that if only he could see where she was, he could easily reach out and touch her.

It wasn't so much that she had disappeared. Instead, she seemed to have become invisible to him.

He turned a full circle but still she wasn't there. All he could see were the same shifting shadows he had noticed earlier, circling him constantly but never quite within reach.

His breath came painfully now in fits and starts. He called out her name yet again, resisting for the moment all temptation to run back to the house and find Mrs Foale, because he was sure Katherine was still here, nearby, somewhere close. If he went back inside, the chance of finding her might be gone for good.

He forced himself to stand still and focus.

He had heard her call his name once, so maybe she would again.

He heard nothing.

Finally he ran back to the house, quickly, checked she wasn't in the kitchen or up in her own room, then looked in on Mrs Foale who was sitting in the library. Before she could say anything he was off again, back into the garden.

Katherine was still nowhere to be seen.

Mrs Foale had been surprised when Jack appeared fleetingly in the library and then darted away again.

She shook her head in puzzlement, stood up and went to the library door.

'Jack?' she called after him, but he was already gone.

'Katherine?' she tried.

No reply. Her eyes widened.

She reached the conservatory doors in time to see Jack running back towards the bonfire.

'Jack!'

He didn't hear her.

Something was wrong, very wrong, and it was something Arthur had warned her might happen. But not yet, not now, surely not tonight . . .

When Jack reached the fire again, he knew at once that something had changed. The chill he had felt before had begun to disperse and the shadows were clearing in the direction of the henge.

High above the trees, the moon was a glaring crescent so bright that the one remaining candle still alight on the ground between the trees was dull and listless by comparison.

Yet it caught Jack's eye as it feebly flickered and guttered, seeming to want to keep itself alive but now struggling to do so. Jack had the terrifying sense that Katherine, like this candle, was now reluctantly fading away and would soon be gone.

A tiny, vicious little breeze swirled at his feet, stirring the ashes of the near-dead bonfire, catching at an ember or two to make them glow again and send up a swirl of smoke which, as if carried by a spirit of ill-intent, billowed up into his eyes, shot up his nose and stung the back of his throat.

It was then, as he backed away, dabbing at his eyes, and wondering what he could still do to find Katherine, certain she was not yet so far away that he could no longer help her, that he thought he saw something definite again.

The smoke that the breeze on the embers had created turned into black, shimmering shadows, which tore away from him towards the two tallest trees, causing the final candle in its jar to burn more brightly.

He looked harder and thought he saw shadows rise up between the trees, whirling thick and more substantial, shaping into something, pulling at something, straining to get it into the henge.

Then he distinctly heard her voice again, a cry of distress receding from him.

'J . . . a . . . c . . . k . . . help . . . me . . .'

'Katherine?' he called out urgently, taking a few steps towards the sentinel trees. 'Where are you? I can hear you but I don't know where you are. *Katherine!*'

He ran towards the trees leading into the henge, sure now that was where Katherine must be – certain, too, that the time to reach her was running out.

Before the last candle goes out, he told himself, because its guttering flame seemed to symbolize that she was still there, alive and needing his help.

It's going out, like Katherine is, he told himself wildly. *The flame's abandoning this place, and she's going too, she's being taken now. They . . .*

Everything slowed down.

Four steps, three steps, his hands reaching towards the rushing, swirling shadows, as they pulled away at last from his world and withdrew into the henge beyond.

Two steps more, Jack straining, reaching out, shouting her name again, knowing she was there almost within his grasp.

Just one more step . . .

But then it was too late.

The last candle suddenly extinguished, the swirling shadows were finally gone, and all that remained were the last embers of the fire behind him and, ahead, the shimmer of moonlight across the open space within the henge, the silence of the cold night air. Where he was sure Katherine had been there was now impenetrable dark.

IV

INTO THE HYDDENWORLD

45

INTO THE HENGE

When Katherine found herself finally overwhelmed by the shadows and pulled into the henge, her yielding to them on the one hand gave her new strength on the other.

For one moment she found the strength to cry out again for Jack's help, and that was the single cry he heard. Then she realized she must not call his name again, because if he heard, and followed her, he might be taken also.

She decided to kick out at the very last of the burning candles as a way of warning him of the danger of following her inside the henge.

Seeming to sense her intent, the shadows began pulling at her yet more urgently. *No ... you ... won't ... stop ... me!* she screamed silently, and with a final effort made them falter and her foot connected with the jar and, as the candle went out, hot wax spattered her ankle, which made her more angry still.

But on her own behalf she could no longer act at all.

They had her now and she was drawn inexorably on, only able to look back passively and watch the last part of Jack's search for her as he reached that same dead candle, stared down at it, then back at the bonfire, and then back again in her direction, though seeming to look right through her and not knowing which way to go.

I'm here, Jack. You're looking right at me ...

Things began to slow, the sounds of the world she knew started to fade, and her anger to be replaced by a mounting sense of despair, of helplessness and finally of a grief worse than any she had ever felt before, including even that for her dead mother.

They held her firmly, but ceased dragging her onwards, keeping her there in the henge gateway from where she had to witness Jack's bewilderment. They seemed to want her to watch these last moments as if, now that they had her in their control, they wished her to suffer.

By then, it was not of herself she thought, but Jack. The first time these dark forces had tried to kill him he had only been hurt because he tried to rescue her. Now history threatened to repeat itself and this time he would surely die, because it was *him* they wanted, not her at all. She was no better than bait, and he the fish.

She felt herself pulled further and further away from where he stood hesitating at the entrance.

Go back! she wanted to shout at him as they led her deeper into the labyrinth of their dark intent and towards the trees on the sinister side of the henge. *Go back!*

She wanted to scream out her grief for what she was now losing, which was *everything* – her life with Jack, and their future, and everything that meant.

It was only now she allowed herself to admit to her thoughts of love for Jack. *Jack, I wanted to tell you but . . .*

Even that very morning, when they had talked and laughed, and she finally had her chance to say something more . . . she had said none of what she was thinking now.

It felt as if only hours before she had been a girl.

Now, as she felt herself losing him, her grief was a woman's, and her whole body ached with what she wanted to do but could not, which was reach back in time and tell him *everything*; tell him what she had never been able to; tell him everything right up to this moment now. To cleave to all he was with all she herself was.

Oh, Jack, I couldn't find a way because I was too scared and I didn't know what it was I really felt, then and now and for ever, and now I never will be able to tell you, not ever, not even at the end of time . . .

Such thoughts coursed through Katherine Shore's mind and racked her heart as she watched Jack struggling to work out what had happened, where she had gone, and to find a way to reach her.

She saw him look at the candle she had kicked over and begged him over and over in her mind to understand this was her way of warning him to go back.

But her warning was having the opposite effect on him, because it was not the warning he responded to but his desire to rescue her.

It was merely giving him the strength to carry on – to cross into the henge and so put himself under the Sinistral's control.

'I'm sorry,' she whispered aloud, her voice now no more than a breeze in the dry grass, a sorrow in the branches of the trees. '*I never wanted you to suffer, I never wanted any of this at all but . . . oh Jack, go back now while you still can. Please . . .*'

Still he hesitated, seeking what to do.

'I'm sorry,' she whispered again as, unable to watch any more what she had lost all power to prevent, she turned away from him all leftward and sinister, the direction in which no human or decent hydden should ever depart a henge, for it leads to dark places and makes any returning much, much harder.

So Katherine turned, and spoke to the shadows that held her. She told them what they wanted to hear because it meant they had won her, and that she was now lost in their darkness.

'Take me,' she told them, 'but not him, never him, *please.*'

The shadows re-formed a final time, clear now, terrifying, overwhelming.

'Welcome,' they said. 'Welcome!'

As one of them led her out of the moonlight, into the darkness beyond, the others separated again and lingered, laughing and cruel, watching Jack's struggle to find a way of reaching her.

'*Please, no,*' she whispered.

But they ignored her and stood waiting for him, dark shimmers among the shadows of the trees.

46

SINISTER

When Jack saw the candle go out, and the strange shadows that were blacker than night pulling and weaving, stirring and sliding across the open space of the henge towards its left-hand side, he knew he had all but lost track of Katherine.

They had got her and they had won because he knew he must follow her, which was what they wanted. If he did that he knew that he probably would not survive.

So he hesitated as he remembered the warning he had received from the Peace-Weaver.

Then he heard Katherine's voice, clear as anything: '*Go back!*'

Her voice was a pleading in his mind, for his own sake, but he knew that for hers he must ignore it.

He took a few steps forward between the two great conifers, then further still. He saw the shadows stirring, mounting, coming towards him, and he knew he had neither the skill nor weapons enough to defeat them and save Katherine.

'Master Jack!'

It was a voice he did not recognize, older and male, and it pulled him from the confusion and doubt that had beset him, and stopped him going further forward.

Then again, from off to his right on the far side of the henge, 'Master Jack . . . ! Do not engage them!'

The hulking shadows already forming around him came no nearer, as if they too had heard the voice. Instead they began to encircle him as if to stop the voice reaching him. He saw the staves which glinted darkly and seemed huge in the night. Their feet moved slowly and silently, their movements were subtle but their force and power self-evident.

He could not quite make out their forms, as if there were many and one, separating and intertwining in shadows of which they themselves were the creators.

He turned to where he had heard the voice, but slowly. He was losing control of his own body.

The shadows turned death-grey in colour, large and ugly in shape, clever in the slow choreography of their moves as they once more began advancing warily towards him.

His slow turn continued as his eyes scanned the far part of the henge from where the voice had come.

What he saw coming from that direction made no sense at all. It was an arcing, turning, flying stave which grew as it came, catching the light of the moon and stars as it twisted, and taking to itself the dull red glow of the last embers of the distant bonfire.

As it came he began to hear it, swish-swish-swishing through the night, ever louder, the light it cast ever brighter.

'Catch it, Master Jack!' came the voice again. 'Raise it to them boldly! Destroy them with its light!'

The shadows took form as the light from the whirling, twisting stave shot across them.

The stave took form as well as Jack reached his right hand for it and he saw it was ancient and made of wood and that the light that came from it was reflections from the intricate carvings that ran down its length.

The shadows briefly broke before the light left them and they formed again.

He caught the stave, or maybe the stave found him. It felt good.

He gripped it, turned it so he could grab its other end with his left hand, and moved towards them.

Yet even then, such was the icy impact of their assault on his mind, breaking through its defensiveness to engender fear. It was a fear compounded by strange confusion as he became aware of shifts and changes in the perspectives of his own world. The dark trees about him grew suddenly taller, the distance across the grass greater, the moon and the stars were shifting in relation to one another and him, as if he were changing position though remaining in the same spot.

Focus!

That was the first and oldest skill needed for survival. It meant forgetting all else but the reality of the present moment.

Focus!

One thing only seemed solid and certain, and that was the feel of the stave grasped firmly in his two hands, held loosely but ready for action.

Jack now took time – the kind of paradoxical time that is at once both infinite and instant – to examine the stave he held. The carvings in its time-worn wood caught the faint glimmer of his opponents, focusing it, clarifying it, so that it was dark and fearsome no longer. The stave became his third eye, and his fourth, and then his fifth . . . and so on into infinity. As if what he held in his hand was less a stave than a mirror which caught what it saw as simply reflections throughout time and place and made sense of them.

He turned it so that its light, if such it was, finally reflected back on themselves. It was only then that he knew he had been tricked. He was focused on the wrong thing.

For he saw to his horror that the shadows were no more than an illusion, some trick of the light, some projection of the other, more solid, forms that stood watching on the henge's periphery. Of these there were far fewer than he had first thought: three or four at most, but one of them dominant.

Katherine was held in their midst, shouting silently. The one who restrained her was taller than the others but not so broad. His eyes glittered in the dark and it seemed to Jack, still struggling as he was to make sense of things, that somewhere in their depth they caught the distant glow of fire, hot and burning. Jack felt a sensation like cold ice trickling down his scarred back.

He understood at last that they had not attacked him directly because he was already doing what they wished him to. They were already leading him cunningly to where they wished him to go.

For the moment they were stronger, faster, far more powerful than he was, and they were laughing as they fanned out around him and finally began to approach him from too many directions for him to defend himself.

Yet still his instinct was to press forward and save her.

He raised the stave and struck at them but to no great effect. It was as if the stave was fighting itself.

'Master Jack, give it to me!'

A shadow became solid at his side, the stave was grabbed from his hands, a solid body pushed between him and the shadows.

'*Keep back,*' this new person warned him. '*Leave them to us!*'

Whatever this new trickery might be, Jack tried to ignore it and push past the stranger who was blocking his way. But he could not and suddenly he did not need to.

As the stave was raised again Jack saw – or seemed to – a thousand fractured slivers of the moon, the moon reflected in mirrors, a moon that seemed more luminously powerful than the real moon itself. And they – the shards that were the moon – were moving straight in the direction of the shadows, like a deadly shower of glass fragments, an overwhelming cascade of light, as if Clare Shore's chimes had detached themselves from the myriad threads from which they hung amid the bushes and trees to come to his rescue.

'Keep *back!*' the voice repeated just in front of him, a strong arm and hand holding him where he was.

It was definitely male, and a clear command so authoritative that Jack finally took a half step backwards.

As he did so, those strange lights into which the moon had fragmented twisted and turned as one, changing into a new shape, as a massed flock of starlings does across an evening sky – twisting and turning and morphing so fast it was impossible for the eye to catch up with them long enough to describe their form.

The shadows, which witnessed this light force too, retreated quickly to regroup around Katherine. Then Jack, himself retreating even further, finally saw the one who had ordered him to move back.

He was grey-haired, with a lined face that was both strong and purposeful, as was his posture and movement. He wielded the stave and stood between Katherine's captors and Jack.

'Jack!'

The voice was Katherine's now and he was near enough to see her shout again, 'Jack!'

'No! You must not go to her!'

But even then his instinct to answer Katherine's call was greater than the one that told him to obey the man's repeated instruction. He tried to run forward once again.

The figure with the stave came closer and from his stave shot a great cascade of light, which, as it fractured into a hundred thousand pieces, stopped Jack in his tracks.

Helpless now, he could only watch the Fyrd finally take Katherine into their shadows, and with a harsh cacophony that was their fragmented cry of anger and frustration that they had not caught Jack as well, they turned sinister and were gone between the trees out into the darkness of the night.

Then as suddenly as all had been light, all was darkness, a slivering of cold, a sense of final loss, of departure, and Jack knew that he had failed to save Katherine and that she was gone beyond his power to save her.

He sank to knees on the grass and cried out from the depths of his being, *'Katherine!'*

But no answer came.

47

DEPARTURE

A terse voice spoke out, different from that of the man with the stave of light.

'They've gone, now, and we're not about to follow them. Nor are we going to stay here longer than we have to. So cast some light upon the situation and see who it is exactly we've come to help.'

This new person, shorter than the first but stockier, held something up in the air from which, a shutter being opened, a shaft of yellow light fell on them all.

It was a storm lantern, and Jack looked up from the ground and found two figures standing looking down at him.

He recognized the one who had commanded him to stop and wielded the stave.

His face wore a half smile of relief. A red cloak hung over his shoulders. It was held together by a magnificent golden buckle. His boots, which Jack could see best of all since he was on a level with them, were worn and muddy with travelling.

'Master Jack . . .' he began.

Jack found the strength to rise.

'Arthur?' he said. '*Arthur Foale?*'

The man shook his head his head at once and said, 'Unfortunately no.'

Jack took a step back, confused. He was sure it had to be Arthur.

'Who are you then?' he asked.

Jack saw that as well as these two there was a third in the shadows.

'My name is Brief,' said the taller one, 'and I am Master Scrivener of Brum. My friends here are, respectively, Messrs Pike and, in the shadows, Stort, who, in such a dangerous predicament as the one we have found ourselves in this night, are, believe me, the right people to have along.'

Jack stared at them dumbly, his body and mind suddenly so tired that neither wanted to function.

'Gentlemen,' said Brief, 'here is somebody you have long wanted to meet again. I think you will agree that from his extraordinary and courageous performance against the nearly overwhelming odds he faced we may take it he is ready now to play his part in the great task that lies ahead of us all.'

They came forward and shook the bewildered Jack by the hand.

'Well done,' said Pike.

'Welcome!' said Bedwyn Stort.

'Um . . . who *are* you?' said Jack, looking around. They were dressed very oddly and everything looked and felt very different indeed.

The one called Brief began making some sort of reply but Jack was unable to take more in. He listened without hearing.

His head began to feel as if it was spinning, while the circle of trees above spun too, but in the opposite direction. Then his legs felt wobbly.

All he could think of was that his actions had been far from 'well done'. He had failed to save Katherine and now . . . *now* . . .

'Watch it,' said Pike, 'the lad's having a turn! Catch 'im!'

He felt two arms go around him and his head thump into someone's chest before he was lowered gently onto the ground. He lost consciousness.

When, not much later as he guessed, he found he had been moved to the edge of the henge and then just outside it, it was the one called Stort who was with him. There was a delicious smell in the air.

Then reality set in.

'They got Katherine!' cried Jack wildly, trying to rise but failing to because Stort was holding him firmly down.

Pike's face appeared in range of Jack's confused and limited vision and he was smiling.

'You saved her life, lad. You did well, very well.'

'But . . . I . . .'

A third head appeared. It was Brief again.

'You're safe with us, Master Jack, and for the time being, once we get you away from here, which we need to right away, you'll need a great deal of rest and sleep.'

Darkness of a kind descended again and the roaring in the sky he had heard before grew a little louder.

An arm went round his shoulder and he was raised more upright.

'Drink this,' said Bedwyn Stort, adding, 'It'll help keep you awake, for we can't linger here much longer.'

'What is it?'

'Hot mead with certain additional, er, substances, to a recipe of my own invention,' said Stort. 'Let's say it's medicinal.'

Jack drank and it was good, very. His mind immediately began swimming, but this time pleasantly. Life returned to his limbs. He sat up straight, a beatific smile on his face.

He felt strong as an ox.

He got up and the smile was still there.

He felt ready for anything.

48

CAPTIVE

The Fyrd led Katherine out of the henge, across the garden, past the side of the house to the front drive, and from there out onto the road.

There were four of them, all dressed in their severe uniform of trews and tunics with gathered sleeves made of a heavy fabric that shimmered in blacks and greys, as if pale light was playing across it. This made them hard to delineate individually by day or night and next to impossible when standing beside each other.

From time to time this play of light, which seemed internal to their tunics, jumped between them as electricity does between two poles, to form shapes quite separate from their own. These, then, were the shadows that had first overtaken Katherine in the garden.

All wore portersacs of the same style as Jack's backpack and made of leather. They were armed variously with dirks, crossbows and staves. Stones on thongs linked to each other hung from their belts.

The group stopped briefly on the road to look back into the garden, checking to see if they were being followed, which they were not. Their mood seemed dour and frustrated.

One of them, a squat, humourless individual called Streik, kept rough hold of Katherine. She was swaying about and he pushed her to the ground.

He scowled and then rasped, 'We should have stayed and got the lad and we wouldn't be having to concern ourselves with this girl. It wouldn't have taken much, Meyor Feld, sir.'

Two of the others nodded, but the last, to whom these remarks were addressed, remained calm and composed.

Feld, their leader, was in his mid-thirties, clean-shaven with short dark hair. He had grey, intelligent eyes and sallow skin.

Ignoring the implied criticism he said quietly, 'The moment I saw that the boy was prepared to follow this girl into our shadows it was obvious he would do anything to get her back. Which is what Sub-Quentor Brunte predicted. The boy's . . .'

'Hardly a boy,' said Streik, 'not even a lad. He's got courage and strength even if he has yet much to learn of the fighting arts! But for the help he received we would have had him.'

Feld had to agree.

Streik was both insubordinate and insolent, but he had brains and had uses, and more important, Sub-Quentor Brunte favoured him. Feld had him on a leash, but a long one.

'There was no point in risking his life, or ours, by fighting any harder than we did,' he said patiently. 'He's bound to follow us to Brum and try to get her back. He'll be easy enough to take when he gets there – and we don't have the trouble of getting him there and trouble he would be. So, no heroics, no reprisals. We take the girl and we continue to allow ourselves to be seen to be doing so. We instruct our other patrols to harry him and the others but not to kill them. The same goes for us if the boy's headstrong enough to attack us. Understood?'

The others nodded, but reluctantly. Fyrd do not take kindly to resistance.

'And when we've got the girl to Brum and the boy's taken, what then?' one of the others asked.

Feld frowned. It was a reasonable question but he did not want to answer it.

Streik answered it for him matter-of-factly.

'The Sub-Quentor will kill her,' he said, 'or command *me* to . . .'

Streik was Brunte's executioner and he was good at his job. This trip beyond the confines of Brum was something of a vacation for him, a reward.

Feld did not respond to his comment about the girl's fate, which was not quite as certain as Streik seemed to think. It was true enough that Fyrd did not generally take prisoners unless there was a good reason. For one thing, killing in all its forms was part of their training, a routine so that each time made it easier the next. For another, prisoners often spelt trouble and cost.

But the girl was different and Feld knew it. The hydden in Brum, led by Brief, had tried to give the impression that Katherine was of no consequence, but Brunte, and now Feld too, thought the opposite might be true. There were rumours that she might be the Shield Maiden herself, though having met her Feld rather doubted it. A spirited young woman, of course, but an immortal? Feld doubted it.

Jack was a different matter. In Feld's memory no one had ever resisted four trained Fyrd and their shadows as he had, even if, in the end, it had been Brief and his stave that had rescued him. Jack was something extraordinary, and Feld could see very well why Igor Brunte would wish to take and control him before the Sinistral hierarchy did.

'What concerns me more,' he said, moving the subject to safer ground, 'is that the boy has the support of a Brummish staverman like Pike, who is nobody's fool when it comes to a fight. We will do well to avoid clashing with him anyway, even if there were not these other considerations, because he'll have back-up in one form or another.'

Streik nodded. Pike's reputation was well known, and in any other occupied Fyrd city in the Hyddenworld one such as he would be taken into the Fyrd command, or eliminated as being too dangerous. But Brum was different and there he was allowed his freedom under the titular leadership of the Hydden's High Ealdor.

'Then there was the unexpected presence of Master Brief...' continued Feld, obviously surprised that what had seemed a simple assignment to find a boy had turned into something more complex, with wider implications than he could possibly have expected when the Sub-Quentor gave him the task. 'Like Pike he is a formidable adversary, though in a different way.'

'*That* was the Master Scrivener?' one of the others said, looking both impressed and surprised.

'I cannot think of another hydden likely to wield such a stave as that, though...'

He fell silent, pondering.

The others waited.

'Did any of you get a good look at how the boy himself caught it even if his use of it was still juvenile!? My Lords Sinistral are right to be fearful of this giant-born, if he truly be so!'

The others shook their heads and Streik said, 'Couldn't see much because of the stave's confusing light, sir. It stopped me seeing anything else clearly.'

'Quite so,' said Feld. 'The old ways of fighting have much to be said for them, even if our own weapons are more reliable, but . . . this assignment is about capture, not death. I have a feeling that we were not meant to see the boy's prowess at all. Very interesting! Meanwhile we know what our task is! Understood?'

They nodded.

The boy would have a use, just as the girl now had – for a time. All this was easy enough for Feld to work out, as was the fact that this simple-seeming assignment was a test and Streik little more than the insolent eyes and ears of the far cleverer Sub-Quentor.

Katherine stirred and then stood up unsteadily. She looked dazed and her clothes hung on her in an untidy mess.

'Change her into the garments we brought for her,' ordered Feld.

One of them did so, there and then, shrugging her into a uniform just like their own, roughly pinning up her hair with the help of a metal clasp brought along for that purpose. Her discarded clothes were abandoned in a hedge. By the time they finished, Katherine was nearly unconscious.

Streik reached out a hand to touch her hair.

'Thick and horrible,' he said dismissively.

Katherine's eyes opened slowly and she tried to focus.

'She is regaining her composure,' observed Feld. 'Enshadow her once more and let us get on our way.'

They formed shadows around themselves and Katherine, and began walking along the road towards the village of Uffington. Once or twice, seeming to have some sense that she was being abducted, she tried to attract the attention of people in passing cars, but she hardly had strength to even raise a hand and the Fyrd laughed heartily at her efforts.

'They cannot see us,' explained Feld.

Streik angrily grabbed her hand and pushed it back to her side. 'Don't do that,' he ordered, not liking resistance of any kind.

They turned off the road just before reaching the village, and then cut across the fields to the embankment that carried the railway line between Swindon and Didcot.

They climbed up to the line itself, and squatted down with their backs against a pile of old wooden sleepers, then finally released Katherine from the shadows. She felt very cold and tired, but was soon able to think clearly again.

White Horse Hill was a silhouetted wall of darkness against the starry sky, but she recognized it at once and she knew that meant she was facing south.

She searched the darkened vale below and saw the lights of a village and what looked like a square church tower among its trees, and another one further off to the left.

Uffington and Childrey, she told herself.

She turned to the Fyrd. 'Who *are* you?' she asked the one who looked like their leader.

'He's Meyor Feld, *sir* to you,' said Streik, hauling her up and pushing her on towards the lights of Wantage.

When she tried to protest she was shoved all the harder.

'Come on, sister, we've got some walking to do yet, if we're to get to where we need to before sunrise.'

Katherine decided that, since she seemed in no immediate danger, it was best to go along with them until she could make more sense of where she was and what was happening. She did not want them to envelop her with shadows again. Maybe, too, when the sun rose, she might see someone who could help.

'Stop dawdling!' snarled Streik.

'There's no need to push,' she snapped over her shoulder.

'Sister, show some respect to elders, betters – and males.'

'I'm nobody's sister and you're mad,' said Katherine quietly. She was beginning to feel more like her old self by the moment.

But this sense of confidence did not last long because, whenever she was better able to catch a glimpse in the darkness of something with whose size she was familiar – a plant, a fence, the railway sleepers – they looked twice as big as they should be.

This didn't make sense, so she told herself she must be simply exhausted, or else the shadows had confused her mind.

But then they passed under a road bridge she was sure she had seen only weeks before during one of her walks with Jack. Then it had seemed normal, but now it towered above her into the darkness, far higher than she could possibly remember it being. A horrible thought occured to her.

It can't be, she told herself. *It just can't be.*

But it was, she knew it was.

She was smaller now. The shadows had dragged her into the henge and pulled her out of its sinister side, and that had somehow taken her into the same world that Arthur had tried to enter. The world was different but she felt the same.

She plodded on through the night trying to control the waves of panic that regularly gripped her.

'Where am I?' she asked aloud at one point.

No one bothered to answer.

What's happening?

They walked on and on along the railway line, until she grew tired again, each step becoming an effort.

Then she took the decision to stop.

Streik tried to push her forward again but she resisted.

'Where are we going?' she demanded.

Feld came forward and stared at her. 'Sister, you've done well to keep up with us, but keep your voice down.'

It was the first positive thing any of them had said and she could sense the respect in his voice.

'Where are you taking me?' she asked more quietly.

'To the city.'

'Which one? London?'

'Brum,' he said.

'I've never heard of it.'

'Humans call it Birmingham.'

'Why Birmingham?'

The question was as much for her as for him. It seemed a strange place to be going and a long way to walk.

She tried another question. 'How?' she asked.

The rails at their feet began to vibrate and whine. Seconds later they heard a train coming and they retreated to the edge of the embankment as it roared past, a blast of air rushing at their faces and ruffling through their hair.

'By train,' replied Feld. 'Not far to go now.'

But it seemed a long way to her and soon she found herself only able to walk by being supported on either side.

When dawn came, she was wandering blurrily among stationary goods trains, their wheels rising huge about her. They had reached the complex rail junction of Didcot.

'This is the one for Brum,' she heard someone say. 'Here, help pull her up . . .'

Then she was inside a wagon being deposited on some sacking, more being laid on top of her, all dusty and smelling of grain.

'You can sleep now,' Feld said.

She closed her eyes and slept.

49

CAMP

Jack woke to the sound of an approaching car. It seemed so nearly on top of him that he opened his eyes in alarm, ready to jump out of the way.

He was lying on bare ground, only some dry leaves protecting him from the damp beneath. Someone had placed a rough plaid blanket over him. His pillow was the exposed root of a tree whose trunk rose above him, its leafless branches whispering in the cold breeze.

Jack's head throbbed, his body was tired and aching, his mind a confusion of jumbled memories whose clarity ended with Katherine's disappearance into shadows. After that, nothing.

He could hear some people talking cheerfully nearby, and decided to stay still and try to make sense of things.

What had happened in the henge came back to him. He had been saved from the same shadows that took Katherine by three strangers, hydden as he now realized.

When he had talked with the Peace-Weaver on White Horse Hill, she had said that people were on their way to help him. These must be the ones she meant.

Another car passed by, leaving the surrounding vegetation shifting and rustling in its wake.

That he was now in the Hyddenworld he had no doubt, and it felt good to be so, as if, after a long time away, he had finally come home.

The root on which his head rested smelt mossy, earthy, and good.

In fact it was surprisingly comfortable. Then he became aware that, along with the conversation, there was the aroma of food cooking, and it smelt delicious.

Tempted though he was to turn over and thus indicate he was awake, he decided to stay just as he was while he tried to work out what he was going to do next. For finding Katherine had to be his first priority.

The names of the three people who had stopped him going into the shadows began to come back to him.

Master Brief, Pike and . . . Bedwyn Stort – the one named by the Peace-Weaver.

Stort was younger than the others but nearly as tall and that's all he could remember.

Jack gradually rolled over, keeping his eyes carefully closed in case the strangers were near enough to see him, hoping they would assume he was merely turning over in his sleep. The talking continued without a pause, so his change of position had not been noticed.

He opened his eyes and found himself looking towards a small clearing in a scrubby copse. Brief and Pike were sitting cross-legged by a small fire, while Stort was nowhere to be seen.

They were eating and drinking from rough wooden bowls. A curious contraption hung over the fire supported at its four corners by straps tied to a framework of sticks. From the fact that something inside it steamed, and it had a bulbous balloon-like shape, he decided it must be filled with liquid. The steam carried the subtle scents of . . . He sniffed a bit more, his mouth watering.

A mushroomy, herby, stewy sort of thing . . .

He licked his lips.

Pike took a large pebble from inside the fire, using two sticks tied together at one end. He then carefully dropped the hot stone into the bag-thing which Jack now decided was made of leather, which was why it was hung high enough above the flames not to catch fire. He therefore concluded that the leather bag was nothing more or less than a flexible stew pot.

Weird but clever Jack admitted himself.

He studied the pair of them more closely.

The one called Brief had used a stave that seemed to hold the light of a hundred thousand fragments of the moon, and he now saw the same stave lying nearby on the ground.

Pike, who was doing most of the talking, was aged about thirty-five, with short grizzled hair and a tough, intimidating air. He wore a grey-green tunic, loose black tights and strange leather shoes that were more boots than shoes, with soles made of . . .

Jack squinted to see them better. The soles had been cut out of car tyre, carefully shaped and then crudely stitched to the leather uppers. A stave lay by his side, too.

Pike picked up the small, blackened kettle propped at the edge of the fire and filled both their cups with some liquid whose scent had such sweet allure that to Jack's mounting hunger was now added a growing thirst.

'We can't just stay here any more waiting for him to wake up,' Pike remarked. 'It's too dangerous, Master Brief. We *have* to make a decision soon about where to go and what to do. The Fyrd can't be far behind us now.'

Jack closed his eyes. He had no real desire to get up at all. In fact he wanted to shut out all that had happened and the very world itself because . . . His eyes snapped open. *Why?* Why in the hour of Katherine's greatest need did he want to have nothing to do with it and go back to sleep?

Because something had happened that he found impossible to conceive of, let alone accept.

He had been in denial. Now he must face it. His inkling of what 'it' was had come to him in the wood henge as the trees seemed to grow taller and the gaps between them to widen. Then, as he left the Woolstone garden with the help of Stort, the wire of the fence seemed to be above his head.

No, it didn't 'seem'. It was! he told himself now.

He looked around the place where he lay and spotted what is always found by roadsides – debris from cars. It was a can of Diet Coke that confirmed what he already knew: it was twice the size it should be. So was a wrapper of a Mars bar. So, finally, was an old shoe – monstrous in size, a giant's.

It must be that his passage through the henge had not only transported him into the Hyddenworld but, in some strange way, made him a hydden too.

But if this realization horrified him, he had no time to dwell on the fact. The hydden had continued talking but now he heard sly movement down on the road below. First some steps, then whispering, and finally the sound of somebody creeping up the verge towards him.

He turned slowly back to his earlier position and saw four figures beneath, two right down on the road itself, two more climbing furtively up the embankment towards him.

Enemies, obviously!

They were dressed in black and armed with staves, crossbows and knives which looked very sharp indeed. The one in front was no more than twenty feet from where Jack lay, and he was getting nearer all the time.

50

FIGHT AND FLIGHT

J ack's brain cleared at once.

He stayed just as he was, so far unseen, hidden amid the vegetation. He knew well that while surprise was of the essence, effective action was even more crucial.

He had no doubt that he was looking at some of the Fyrd that Brief and the others had been fleeing from, with himself groggily in tow. He examined the two in front carefully, and noted the course they were on, which was very slightly off-track from himself. They would reach the top of the verge just beyond his feet, which would put them out of reach of a well-delivered kick.

On the other hand, once they were up on level ground he would have lost any advantage his position slightly higher up might give him. But he could not take them on by himself and decided to take an immediate risk. He rolled over and away from them, and raised his hand silently in the hope that one of the hydden would see it.

One of them did: the ever-watchful Pike.

Jack pointed behind himself silently, and indicated the number of them with four fingers. Pike nodded and then whispered to Brief, who remained seated by the fire.

Pike then coolly picked up a couple of staves, crossed the clearing and came and quietly squatted down beside Jack, peering down the embankment to appraise the situation. His absolute calm quelled Jack's anxiety.

He whispered, 'Stay still, lad, but listen carefully. When I step over you to take the one in front, you follow on behind me and deal with the one further down who's slightly over to the right. Use my bulk to hide yourself until the last moment, then go in hard. And I mean *hard*. You get no second chances with the Fyrd, understand?'

Jack nodded and eased himself into a better position, bringing a leg closer under his body so he could rise faster and more surely.

'And then,' continued Pike coolly, his hand lightly patting Jack's shoulder as if to reassure him, 'go straight on down and take the one still on the road over to the right. Got it?'

Jack nodded again.

'Do you know how to use a stave?'

Jack shook his head.

Pike smiled. 'You did well enough in the henge and here we have the element of surprise. He handed Jack a plain wooden stave. Then he said, 'Just poke the end into their head, neck or privates hard as you can and they'll not get up for a while!' With that Pike rose up and lunged forward hard and fast at the Fyrd immediately below him.

Jack threw off his plaid, jumped up and swooped down on the second, driving the end of his stave hard at his opponent's head.

There was no time to look back and check how effective his strike had been. All that mattered was that the Fyrd fell in front of him, and that he was able to take advantage of the momentum the slope allowed him and head straight on down towards one of the Fyrd still standing on the road.

That one's view was obscured by the vegetation, and the sudden sound of fighting offered him no clue as to what was happening upslope. Like his colleague, he was waiting for a further command from above.

What they each got instead was a sudden, devastating assault, from straight out of the obscurity of the undergrowth, by Jack and Pike respectively.

Moments later both Fyrd were lying moaning on the ground, while the ones above had already been laid out cold.

'Know how to restrain 'im?' called out Pike urgently, there being little time before the first two started to come round.

He had done some martial arts so he could hold his own in the institutions he lived in in London, and knew how to hold the Fyrd in a neck lock, his head hauled back to spine-breaking point. But that wasn't easy, because the Fyrd was a lot bulkier and stronger than himself, and began struggling at once.

Pike swiftly cuffed the other with a cord and hauled him out of sight up on to the verge.

'All right?' he called again to Jack.

It was not a propitious moment to intervene, since Jack merely lost concentration, and the next thing he knew the Fyrd was twisting into a better position to heave Jack off him and gain the ascendancy.

As Pike climbed back up the verge to the other two, and roped them together, Jack had all but lost the fight below.

Which he might well have done – and suffered grievous injury too, for the Fyrd was pulling out his knife in a very murderous way – had he not let his instinct take over.

He twisted the stave around and brought it down about the Fyrd's head and whacked his knife hand hard, sending the weapon flying.

As the Fyrd grasped his hand, Jack poked him in the throat, winding him with such effect that the Fyrd collapsed back onto the ground, just as Pike came crashing back down onto the road to Jack's assistance.

'Well done!' cried Pike, seeing the state of things. 'You're a natural born fighter, that's for sure.'

Two minutes later all four Fyrd were safely out of sight amid the thick vegetation, cuffed and tethered, the first two still groaning, the others silent. None was likely to cause any trouble for a while.

Pike turned to Jack and reached out a hand.

'You've a cool head, lad,' he said, 'but we guessed that already. If you hadn't signalled to us that you'd seen 'em, I might not have known until too late. It's good to have you with us, because I have need of another strong stave at my side for what's ahead of us.'

They climbed back up the embankment and emerged into the clearing where Master Brief waited, stave in hand and relief on his face.

'I think the lad's finally woken up,' said Pike drolly, patting Jack on the back with a smile of respect on his face. 'But for his quick thinking, I doubt we'd have broken loose from that lot without injury. Now we need to get away from here soon.'

'How long have we got?' asked Brief.

'It'll be no more than an hour before that patrol's missed.'

Brief looked at Jack. 'I dare say there are a lot of questions going round in your head – there certainly would be in mine. But you can't set off on the road until you've eaten something. So, Mister Pike, I suggest you make a new brew, and fix some food for Master Jack while I tell him what he needs to know.'

'A briefing from Brief!' said Jack with a goofy grin.

Master Brief did not smile. 'If I had a groat for every time *that* little joke's been made, I'd have enough to buy ten new cloaks and change left for purchasing several more staves.'

'But none of them as interesting as that one,' murmured Jack, eyeing the carvings on Brief's stave and then comparing them with his own.

'Indeed not,' exclaimed Brief.

Jack wanted to find out more about the carved stave but Pike interrupted them with food and drink. Jack started digging in, hungrier than he'd realized.

Pike gave Jack a mug of something like sweet herb tea, then handed him a bowl of mushrooms stewed in a light, yellow-green sauce. It smelt good but he had nothing to sup it with.

'Have some brot,' said Pike, handing him a chunk of what look like rye bread, baked in a square shape.

'Easier to pack in your portersac,' observed Brief, by way of explanation. It was clear that hydden were practical by nature.

'Brot,' repeated Jack, and immediately began enjoying it.

'We have a lot of ground to cover if we're to make our rendezvous with Stort in good time, Master Brief, but we need to put Jack more in the picture.'

'Stort's the name of the other one of you, isn't it?' said Jack.

'That's right, Bedwyn Stort is my former pupil and now a junior scrivener in his own right,' said Brief. 'But in truth his real talents and passion lie in invention and cosmology. There's none quite like him in the Hyddenworld. Anyway, back to the point . . . You just eat now while we tell you so you know what's afoot – and, more important, what the Hyddenworld expects of you. But where to begin, Mister Pike? That's always the question!'

'What do you know of your origins, lad?' asked Pike.

Jack told them that he knew he was brought to England from somewhere in Germany when he was only six, to protect him from the fate suffered by anyone who might be thought a 'giant'.

'There's no ifs and buts about that, Jack. You most definitely are what we hydden call a giant.'

'But I'm no bigger than you, Master Brief, or Mister Pike here.'

'That's true, for now. But it's because you've come back to us through the henge portal, but there's no knowing what the long-term effect of you entering into the Hyddenworld like this might be. Stort is of the opinion that it has no effect at all on a giant, because you possess the special ability to live in *both* worlds. But it may be that you'll prefer the Hyddenworld because, after all, you're a hydden deep down.'

Jack told them he indeed felt sometimes as if the human world was not his own.

'The trouble is,' said Brief, 'that we doubt Mistress Katherine will feel the same, seeing as she's human. So if you want to be with her, you may have a choice to make. But that's always the challenge of life itself, having to make such difficult choices.'

Pike pulled out his chronometer and studied it ostentatiously. 'Time is limited,' he said, 'so let's keep to the point.'

'What did you mean about the Hyddenworld *expecting* something of me?' asked Jack. 'I mean how can the Hyddenworld know anything about me?'

Brief and Pike exchange a glance and laughed.

'You're probably the best-known hydden alive who no one's ever met, until now!' said Pike. 'Explain it to him, Master Brief.'

Brief then explained how Jack's coming from Germany into the human world of Englalond had long since leaked out. Great things were expected of him, especially by the hydden of Brum who had a special interest in the prophecies of Beornamund concerning the gems of the seasons and danger to the world.

'Naturally that means you're seen as a leader against the power of the Sinistral and their Fyrd army but it is early days to be thinking of that,' said Brief. 'It was a pity – a tragedy in truth – that someone in Germany revealed your existence to the Sinistral. They pursued you and were aware of your arrival here as soon as we were – hence the attack on you when you were six. It was as well that the elder of your village took you into the Harz Mountains, a region that still respects the old mysteries and has a long tradition of protecting the weak and vulnerable and those who are in any way different. Those misty heights are the home of the Modor and Wita – the Wise Ones – who took you in, and trained you in the mysteries. And when you had grown too big even for them to keep you safe, they invoked their powers and summoned the White Horse and its rider, the Peace-Weaver.'

Jack shook his head. 'Some of that may be true, and I certainly met the Peace-Weaver on White Horse Hill, but I don't know of any so-called mysteries.'

'You do,' said Brief, 'and we know you do. It's just that you have forgotten you know them. They'll come back to you when you need them as they did when you were faced by the Fyrd shadows. Few could have survived them as long as you did without the use of a stave such as mine. Of course, you have your own waiting for you . . . but that is something you must find and win for yourself when the time is right.

'Now, what exactly did the Peace-Weaver say when you met her? In my own encounters she usually warns me the world, as we know it, is coming to an end through mortal folly, and that there's nothing we can do about it but pick up the pieces and reassemble them in a better way.'

Jack nodded his agreement with that account. 'She warned me to watch over Katherine, and then said you might come, soon. She did not say why.' He paused. 'She also said you were witnesses to the car crash.'

'We were,' said Brief, 'thanks to Stort's special sense of such things. We decided that the accident gave us an opportunity to let other people think you were dead, and thus give you time to recover and grow into your natural size, so we put it about that you had been killed. Fortunately, there was only one surviving Fyrd who realized the significance of what has happened – Igor Brunte, of whom more later. Your 'death' suited his needs and, in fact, for many years he himself believed you *were* dead, so that was all right.'

Jack's questions were piling up but he decided to continue just listening.

Brief continued. 'Only when you were summoned to Woolstone by Clare Shore did the news reach him that you were alive after all. Since then matters have moved fast – and faster still since Clare Shore died. Now the whole of the Hyddenworld knows that a giant has survived into adulthood, and there is excitement and trepidation.'

'About what?'

'Things *happen* when giants are about, and most folk think it's no coincidence that your arrival coincides with the imminent end of the present Peace-Weaver's reign. She has served mortals for the best part of fifteen hundred years, and our records show that's longer than most. Of course everyone knows that this Peace-Weaver is Imbolc, and tradition has it that she will only depart when her sister the Shield Maiden discovers the lost part of the Sphere which Beornamund never recovered, which represents Spring.'

'I don't see where Katherine comes into all this. All I want to do is to find her and get her back to the world we know, and then . . . well . . . you know . . .'

'Then what, Jack?'

Jack shifted uncomfortably. He didn't actually know what. He knew only he wanted to be with Katherine and that he was worried about her, because he . . .

I miss her, he told himself. But he wasn't going to tell anyone else that fact, maybe not even Katherine herself.

'Things aren't as simple as they seem, Jack,' said Brief. 'Unfortunately. Hydden, like humans, have a habit of making things complicated. Who do you think sent the Fyrd to capture Katherine and why?'

Jack said he had no idea.

'It was Brunte, the Fyrd I mentioned earlier, and he was acting without the knowledge of his superiors. His plan is – and it's working – to abduct Mistress Katherine so that you will follow. It's both of you he wants. He thinks, as do I, that Katherine is the Shield Maiden, whether she knows it yet or not, and together with you her first task will be to find the missing Spring gem.'

'So Katherine' said Jack, 'is both bait and something more, and I'm merely a way of him getting what he wants.'

'Yes. But, unfortunately for you, there's a good few folk in the Hyddenworld who want you to come into their lives for an entirely different reason. As I said before, they think you're going lead them against the Fyrd.'

'Me?!'

'You,' said Pike.

'Who thinks this?' said Jack, genuinely astonished. The rest he could almost believe, but the idea of him leading people he had never met against an enemy he barely understood seemed just ridiculous.

'I do, for one,' said Pike. 'And most of the honest citizens of Brum think the same. It's not going to happen for a few years yet, though we're working on it, but it'll help push things forward if you show your face in the city, even for a few days.'

Jack thought for a bit and then said indignantly, 'So, Brunte wants me in Brum so he can grab me, and you want me there to drum up support for a revolution. What about the needs of Katherine and me, then?'

Brief smiled. 'You want to be in Brum and find Katherine, so you and she can fulfil your quest to find the Spring gem.'

'No,' said Jack. 'I want to be there so she and I can leave together as quickly as possible! Oh, and also to find out what we can about Arthur Foale, who went missing about three months ago.'

'Never heard of him,' said Brief, rather too quickly. 'Not ever.'

'Me neither,' said Pike, averting his gaze.

Jack studied their faces, decided they were useless at telling untruths.

'You help me find Arthur Foale and get him home, and I might then help you with your revolution. By the way, when's it starting? Have you fixed a date?'

He was joking but Brief took him seriously.

'Yes, we have. But, as Pike said, you won't be needed at the beginning, except that it'll help if we make your existence known to a few people who will matter for a few years. Remember, these things take time to get going.'

'So when does this supposed revolution begin?

Pike and Brief exchanged glances again.

'Tell him,' said Pike, 'and he might begin to take this more seriously.'

'The opening move will be made very soon,' replied Brief matter-of-factly, 'which is why this is not the safest of times for Katherine herself to be in Brum. All hell is about to break loose in that city.'

A spatter of rain fell out of the dull sky.

Pike muttered, 'And things will be worse still if it rains. We need to go.'

They left Jack to finish eating while they struck camp, packing everything in their portersacs and removing all evidence they had been there. They doused the fire with water before refilling the ash pit with soil. As a final touch it was all re-covered with leaves.

'Best way to find a recent fire like this is by the scent,' observed Pike. 'You've a lot to learn if you're going to get through the next few days in one piece, so you might as well start right away.'

Jack got up and circled around, until the place where the fire had been lit was upwind of him. He sniffed and quickly picked up the scent.

'A natural pupil,' said Brief approvingly.

Jack had finished his meal, second helping and all, when the other two, ready now to move, joined him to finish off the warm mead.

'So where's Mister Stort?' Jack inquired.

'He's gone on ahead to meet Mister Barklice, a hyddener of very great renown whose help we'll need.'

'He'll help us to find Katherine?' said Jack, hopefully.

'Something like that,' replied Pike rather evasively.

Jack looked at him but decided this was not the best time to ask more questions.

There came an angry shout from where they had left the four Fyrd tied up.

Pike headed over to the top of the embankment, stave at the ready. He studied the situation for a moment and came back.

'They are still secure but getting restive. It's now just a matter of time before more Fyrd arrive, so we need to leave. Our job is done here.'

Then they had a final clear-up, pulled on their portersacs and were gone.

5I
ARRIVAL

As Jack began his journey to Brum, Katherine ended hers inside the wagon of a freight train.

She was woken by the squeal of wheels on steel as the wagon passed over some points, jolted a few times and came to an abrupt halt.

Streik and the others heaved at one of the doors and slid it open sufficiently for them to drop to the track below. Meyor Feld made Katherine follow them and they held her fast until he too joined them.

Katherine stood on the track looking around as the train shunted forward and then pulled back the way it had come and disappeared from sight.

It was only mid-afternoon but the light was already dull, the air heavy with rain. The rail track lay deep between towering dirty yellow brick walls which rose so high she had to strain right back to glimpse a sliver of the sky between them. The clouds were dark and angry, the air heavy and thundery. Rain was on the way.

Two hundred yards ahead of them was another cliff-face of a brick wall containing an arched steel gate. It was chained up.

Cutting across to one side, also high above, was a segment of a road bridge where street lights were already on, their distant light reflected in the rails by which she stood. In the other direction, the one the train had taken, a footbridge crossed between the walls of the deep cutting they were in. It was busy with humans going back and forth, many holding umbrellas. There was the sound of trains, the drumming of pedestrians' feet, and, more distantly, an intermingling of the sound of a busy city. Close-to, the continuous rain poured down about them until they went to stand by one of the walls to gain shelter. From underfoot came the sound of drains filling with rushing water.

'Where are we?' Katherine asked.

Feld pointed at the gate and its arch.

'That's the East Gate into Brum.'

One of the Fyrd began pushing her towards it.

Her sense of isolation and danger increased and a feeling of panic overtook her.

She realized that what they were approaching was one of the basal brick arches rising from the track level to support offices, warehouses and somewhere a roadway along which she could hear but not see the traffic moving. She looked back at the people on the footbridge and felt a nearly overpowering urge to run in their direction, even though they were many tens of feet above her head.

Feld read her mind.

He said, 'They can't see you and they can't hear you, because they have lost the habit of looking. We learned that many decades ago. Humans are almost blind to everything but that which directly concerns them.'

Katherine tried to work out how far away the footbridge was.

Streik moved forward to stop her but Feld shook his head.

'It's all right,' he said. 'Let her try! The sooner she realizes there's no escape the better.'

She thought he was bluffing and ran from them, shouting and waving her arms to attract the attention of the people on the bridge above.

'Down here! I'm here. Here! I'm Katherine Shore! Can't you see me! Down *here*!'

No one above looked down her way, no one even paused in their hurry to get wherever they were going. She continued until she was hoarse and weak with shouting and something in her began to give up.

Feld watched her with sympathy, the others with impatience. Streik went over, took her arm and led her back to them. She did not resist.

'Trust me,' said Feld, 'they can't hear you and they can't see you, and even if they began to do so they would not believe their own senses. They would dismiss you as a creature of the night, or a shadow, or some inanimate object. Humans see only what they want to see, expect to see or believe they can see. To all the rest they are blind. So please stop making a fool of yourself and come with us.'

The gate itself was massive, a good example of late-nineteenth-century ironwork. But it was poorly maintained, its rust having broken through the old paintwork and one of the hinges having loosened sufficiently for that part of the gate to tilt forward dangerously.

A notice was attached to it which read NO ENTRY TO UNAUTHORIZED PERSONNEL. *Danger of Deep Water.*

A second sign, in yellow on black, said HIGH VOLTAGE with a lightning-bolt symbol.

Two shadowy forms peered through the bars from the other side of the gate. They pointed at Katherine, whispered to each other doubtfully, but at Feld's command opened the gate sufficiently for the party to slip through, one by one.

'Welcome to Brum, brothers, welcome sister,' they said, their mouths opening into smiles of yellowed, rotting teeth and breath that stank of sewers. 'Yer all most welc'm.'

52

BY THE DEVIL'S QUOITS

At that same hour of that same day Master Bedwyn Stort, Assistant-in-Ordinary to Brief, Master Scrivener of Brum, was holding forth to an audience of one on the subject of the Devil's Quoits, a half-forgotten henge in Oxfordshire.

'The records show they tried to destroy this place,' he said with all the excitement of an academic field researcher passionate about his work, 'but fortunately, as we can clearly see, they did not quite succeed.'

'Who did?' asked Barklice, his companion and audience of the moment.

'Who did what?' asked Stort, his mind rather ahead of his words.

'Who did not succeed? Who tried to destroy the Quoits?'

They made a strikingly contrasting pair.

Barklice had bow legs and was thin, his lined and weather-beaten face carrying a restless, watchful look as he glanced about the ruined landscape of what had once been the finest and most powerful henge in all Englalond.

Stort was much taller and thinner than Barklice. That afternoon he looked even odder than usual. Having decided that the air was too sultry for his usual trews he had discarded them in favour of shorts which he had made to his own eccentric design.

They were self-made, of Harris tweed, his favourite fabric, and had so many pockets and pouches, hooks and loops, buttons and zips, all utilitarian for the many items he liked to carry about his person – from bin-bags to brot, from string to balloons – that he looked like a plucked chicken moving home.

The Quoits now consisted of a single standing stone, placed centrally, and a couple more at some distance but thrown on their side. These occupied what remained of a barely visible double-ring henge, dug over, cut in half, partially flooded by nearby gravel working. It looked of no use to anybody. But Stort was not so sure.

'The Romans were the first to desecrate this site,' he explained, 'then the Anglo-Saxons and then various different invaders and migrants down the centuries until in modern times they dug through half of it for gravel and caused this nearby lake to flood a good part of it.'

Barklice studied this 'evidence' doubtfully.

'Master Stort, it's almost impossible to see any sign of a henge at all except for this great stone we're standing by!'

Stort reached a hand up and touched the stone with affection. He got nowhere near halfway to the top. Even a full-grown human male would have been dwarfed by it.

'To give 'em such a strange name as the Devil's Quoits,' mused Barklice, 'seems an odd thing to do.'

'Ah! I'm glad you asked . . .'

'I didn't actually ask, Master Stort, I merely observed and I rather think we have better things to do than . . .'

But it was too late. Stort was off again.

'. . . because quoits are flat round metal rings used in a game in which they're thrown onto spikes to score points, which of course you know.'

'Errumm,' murmured Barklice ambiguously.

'Now according to the records I've seen in the Brum archives, there were two henges, one inside the other, which were the "quoits". There were standing stones too, which were the spikes over which the Devil was meant to throw the quoits, but only one stone remains in place as you can see.'

Barklice nodded vaguely.

'Of course, early Christians liked to suggest that anything in the landscape they didn't understand was the Devil's work, just to warn folk away from their old beliefs and practices, something which started around great Beornamund's time. But I believe that, however much a site may be destroyed, it still retains something of its original powers.'

'I see,' said Barklice, now marginally more interested. 'Such as?'

'Telling the time. Communal gatherings. Executing criminals and in former times, before the art was lost, for humans and hydden to travel between each other's worlds.'

Barklice looked yet more interested in that, but after a moment of looking around again was forced to observe, 'So they say, but not much chance of that here, I think. In any case, Stort, I'm happy with being hydden. What would I do if I suddenly grew to human size? For a start all my clothes would be ripped apart by my sudden growth!'

Barklice thought this funny but Stort did not.

'I'm working on it,' said Stort. 'If people could travel twixtandbetween once they can do it again!'

He fell silent and Barklice decided it was best to do the same, though not before adding, with a twinkle in his eyes, 'Master Stort, you're a veritable walking encyclopedia, I'm surprised Master Brief does not do away with all those dusty tomes and just put you on a shelf, ready to be consulted whenever needed. But to practicalities now. This is where Master Brief wanted us all to meet, and here we are! All we have to do is sit down and wait.'

'Are you sure they'll find all the markers you left behind for them?'

Barklice had spent a good deal of time carefully leaving markers which he hoped would lead Brief and his party more easily to this place, it being otherwise hard to find.

'Messrs Pike and Brief know perfectly well how to read my signs,' replied Barklice, 'so I shall make us a brew while we wait!'

Barklice generally made a brew to mark good moments and ill, to settle a troubled mind or to renew his purpose and intent. This particular brew would be in aid of all of those.

Later, an hour or two before dusk, Stort having poked about and made what sense he could of the jumbled site, they sat together talking about matters of the heart, as bachelors will who have learned to like each other and now unexpectedly find space to air those emotional aches and pains experienced by such as they, two shy solitaries with little experience of the mysteries of love and seemingly small chance of gaining any.

Mister Barklice was now in his early forties, a verderer of very great renown, and probably the greatest hyddener then living. In fact he looked a good deal older than his years, so wind-hardened was his face, so rangy his hard-used body. He had no wyfkin, no family at all, mainly because from boyhood he had been constantly on the move in and about Brum, and latterly far beyond it, dealing with matters, often legal and disputatious, to do with woodland and forest lands controlled by that hydden city.

Though his superiors were Fyrd who had charge of all matters of city governance, they had the good sense to leave such a difficult job to a hydden who had spent his entire life learning it.

Barklice, like Brief, was one of the few honest hydden still working as part of the administration of Brum, which was now under the corrupt governance of the foul Festoon, obese appointee of the Fyrd whose headquarters in Englalond were in London – or, as it was generally known, the City. Festoon only tolerated the free speech and bold independence of both Barklice and Brief because they were by far the most competent in their different fields.

In his capacity of verderer, Barklice had travelled over more ground between Brum and the City than any other living hydden. He enjoyed free passage wherever he went and carried with him a twin-headed Verderer's Staff to prove it.

Lacking a partner or soulmate, he preferred to travel alone unless a particular assignment required the security of force of arms, in which case Pike was his preferred companion. Failing him, one of Pike's friends would do. Of these there were many, mostly unsavoury, but dependable to death for any they escorted.

But a lone traveller Barklice generally preferred to be, even when venturing to the more dangerous territories lying to the far west of Brum, which humans apparently called Wales. It was rightly said that no one excelled in the art of hyddening more than he did. If he chose, so the story went, he could travel anywhere in the land without being seen or detected by either hydden or Fyrd, and do it blindfold into the bargain.

So naturally hydden and Fyrd alike treated Barklice with respect and he could expect a welcome, though sometimes a guarded one, at any humble home in the land. But he never abused this considerable perk, nor often availed himself of it at all, preferring, like any traditional travelling hydden, to camp out under the stars and enjoy nature's considerable bounty which, to those who know where to look, is available in abundance at any time of year.

But so it was that sometimes, alone for too long and sleeping under the stars, the verderer felt his natural solitariness a painful thing, and allowed himself a regret or two. Solitude was good, but it could be lonesome and there were occasions, especially around the four great festivals of the year, when he would have liked to share his experiences with another.

So it was, in that early evening, that Barklice freely admitted to his youthful friend that if he knew a way to find a wyfkin who might become a partner in his travels and a soulmate for his musings, then he would most certainly act upon it.

'Ah!' cried Stort sadly, having obviously had similar thoughts, 'It's indeed a difficult thing to find a mate!'

'You have found that so yourself?' Barklice wondered, looking at the gawky, red-haired hydden who, many said, had the touch of genius about him.

'Myself?' Stort replied, pondering this matter of the heart as if for the first time. 'I am not … I do not think … in fact I think it is impossible to … to … to …'

'Love?' prompted Barklice quietly, thinking that uttering this challenging word aloud might help marshal Stort's unusually jumbled thoughts on the subject.

Stort nodded vigorously to indicate he understood the thrust of Barklice's question.

Then the young scrivener spoke words so evidently straight from his honest but innocent heart that Barklice's hand stopped still in mid-air, the new brew momentarily untasted.

'Sometimes, Mister Barklice, I have felt so alone, so isolated on this great and wonderful Earth that cares for us, that I have felt it as a pain as sharp as gut-ache, or a stab wound, or the sting of a wasp or the bite of a feral dog. Horrible. Terrible. Painful. When I have imagined a life of never finding love, it seems to me a prospect that is worse than perpetual torture. We were not made to be alone.

'But ... I have instead been given gifts and ways of thought and habits that I fear might mean I will never, can never, find love. For I am told that those of a female kind require constancy, and thus abhor the inconstant wanderings of such a restless mind as I possess.'

'I think by constancy,' suggested Barklice, 'they are referring to the heart, not the mind. They do not like to think a male hydden's heart is like a butterfly taking nectar from each beautiful flower that comes along.'

'That is a very beautiful turn of phrase!'

'It is not my own. I read it somewhere and merely remember it,' admitted the verderer.

'Well, if that be true, then it's good news indeed, for the only bit of me that's inconstant are my thoughts and the sudden impulses they drive me to. I am almost ashamed to admit that ideas are as exciting to me as people, and the practical pursuit of scientific curiosity more thrilling and real than the impractical imponderables of love. How then could I promise my heart and soul to another while knowing that truth about myself? Even if someone would accept the hand of a hydden as ... as ...'

Here he waved his strange thin hands all about himself, as if trying to indicate the most loathsome and unattractive of beings, and he even stood up and turned about as if making a parade of himself for Barklice's benefit, to confirm his lack of appeal in general and also in particular. Then Stort abruptly sat down again.

'Even if someone could love a form so odd and elongated as myself, with knobbly knees and thin chest and long fingers and a nose, as I was told when I was young, only fit for sticking a bun-brot on ...'

'That was cruel,' cried Barklice, looking at Stort's long nose, 'even if, in a manner of speaking, it is true!'

'Well, that's as may be, but even if someone could love me in spite of what I am, I fear that I could not return their love.'

'Why ever not?' Barklice rejoined at once, rather alarmed at the direction their conversation was taking them and fearing that Stort had inclinations of an unusual, perhaps unwholesome, kind.

'Because I would know they had made some kind of mistake. That they had misread what they saw and, moments after my undying acceptance of their love, they would regret what they had done. Which would be painful for them and doubly painful for me.'

'And if you met someone who you . . .'

'Who I loved?'

'Yes, yes,' said Barklice, now more uncomfortable with the idea than Stort, it seemed. 'Someone you . . . um . . . loved. If that happened, what would you do?'

'I don't know. I would think about it certainly.'

'Humph!' said Barklice. 'It's not much good just thinking about love. You have to do something about it, too.'

'Yes, but what?'

They fell silent as dusk began to fall, for the question seemed unanswerable.

Then Barklice, coming out of his reverie, remembered what time it was.

'Master Brief and friends should have arrived by now and the afternoon's grown dark. Heavy rain's on the way judging by those clouds and the heavy feel to the air. We'd better retrace our steps to be sure that the sign I left for them to follow from the main path to get here is still visible.'

'"We"?' said Bedwyn Stort. 'I fear I feel weak and weary. You have more stamina than I, though you're twice my age.'

'I am under strict instructions not to leave you on your own.'

'Oh, really! I wonder why, for I am a full-grown adult. In any case there is not much to explore around here, so how can I possibly go off and get lost?'

'Well,' said Barklice very doubtfully, 'if you promise to stay within the henge . . .'

Stort looked mightily relieved and sat down again. 'I will not stir myself outside this henge until you are back.'

'You could make us a new brew,' suggested Barklice.

'I can and I shall,' replied Stort, still not stirring.

Barklice, who was an excellent traveller, took tinder and steel from his pack once more and had a new fire going in no time, and then he reassembled the sticks to support the leathern kettle he next threw at Stort's weary feet.

'The lake water will be good . . . but no moving outside the henge, promise?'

'By all that this standing stone has seen, I do!' exclaimed Stort earnestly. 'And a perfect brew will be yours upon your return.'

'Humph!' said Barklice, setting off into the dusk to make sure that Brief and the others would not lose their way at the very last, for it was hillocky and confusing thereabouts, and leaving a few more signs would not go amiss.

When Barklice was gone, Master Stort picked up the flexible kettle and made his way towards the lake.

But finding himself alone for the first time in the Devil's Quoits, it suddenly occurred to him that it might be a good use of his time, before darkness fell, to try to work out again exactly how the two circular henges ran, and especially where their north-eastern entrance would have been. For all scholars know that was always the place of greatest change and power in a henge: the true portal.

'Hmmm!' he mused, as he ascertained the north-easterly point, and saw that it must lie some way out under the lake that had partially flooded the site.

Making a brew seemed suddenly unimportant, so he put the flexible kettle on the ground so that he was free to pursue his thoughts without its further encumbrance.

'Hmmm,' he murmured again, his mind becoming dangerously active.

There was a good deal of rubbish scattered about, such as jagged bits of wood, pieces of rusting metal, thick plastic worn ragged by the wind, a rusty bicycle wheel, and much else.

He impulsively picked up a piece of oily polystyrene, and his humming grew even more urgent.

He looked at the subtle ridge of the henge, much cut into by diggings, and followed it as best he could towards the lake. He next found a tube of metal but, shaking his head, he threw it aside. Then some string, which he kept.

Hum-hum-hum he went, bending down to pick up a coil of plastic tube, the kettle now completely forgotten.

'Yes, most certainly!' he cried out with sudden excitement, some new purpose having taken root in his mind. 'I do believe I could, and before Mister Barklice returns. I should think he'll be none the wiser!'

With an expertise born of more than twenty years making contraptions, he went to work on the bits and pieces he had found. Then he did what he always did when a new idea for an invention came into his mind, and the wherewithal to achieve it was immediately at hand: he turned a full circle, as happy as a child at play.

A few minutes later, his new invention completed, he advanced towards the water. He placed his contraption on the ground and removed all his clothes, down to his all-in-one undergarment, and laid them on a plastic bin-bag to keep them clean and dry.

He then picked up the contraption and advanced into the water.

The only sign of recent activity he left behind was the fire Barklice had made, which now smouldered and sparked, and the kettle support sticks, from which no kettle hung.

It was as well that Barklice went back because Brief, Pike and Jack had stopped, tired from their journey and puzzling about exactly how to find the Quoits.

'Ah, my dear Barklice!' cried Brief with relief, when he saw him. 'We were just debating which way to turn . . .'

He suddenly stopped speaking, his friendly expression turning to extreme alarm.

'*Where's Stort?*' he continued in a lower tone.

'Safe and well and making a brew for us all,' said Barklice hastily. 'He promised me not to leave the henge.'

'Hmph!' muttered Pike.

'Make haste, make haste,' said Brief, 'for if we lose Stort in this terrain, it'll be a long time before we'll find him.'

Barklice quickly led them back to the standing stone, already regretting that he had left the young scrivener to his own devices.

'He'll be there, I'm sure of it,' he kept saying, but with a growing doubt.

'How much further, Barklice? Hurry, hurry!'

'Over this hummock and you'll see him . . .'

The top of the standing stone came into view.

'Mister Stort,' he cried out, 'we're here!'

Which was true, they were, right in the centre of the Devil's Quoits.

But the fire had gone out and the kettle, for some strange reason, lay abandoned upon the ground near the lake.

Of Stort there was no sign at all.

53

INTO THE CITY

These two keepers of the East Gate, who gave Katherine and the Fyrd with her such an intimidating welcome, were Bilgesnipe. They had the pale, greasy look of subterranean waterfolk who get too little sun, but it was their burly size and ironic good cheer that set them apart from the humourless rule-bound Fyrd.

Gatekeeping was not their preferred occupation, but the watery dangers onto which the East Gate led were such that it had been decided by the community of Old Brum that they must, from time to time, do their duty and make sure that newcomers were properly briefed on how to conduct themselves safely through the tunnels.

Streik and the other Fyrd made a show of pushing the protesting Katherine through East Gate very roughly. The Bilgesnipe were not impressed.

One of them loomed near and said, 'Yer'll kindly treat that wyfkin with respect, gennelmen, or we're going to have a falling out.'

Streik was not easily intimidated, but he could see Feld disapproved of his roughness and was not going to start a fight on someone else's ground. He fell silent at once, and Katherine thought it wise to do the same.

The gates were locked and chained behind them and she knew it was now going to be even harder to escape but that she must still try. But how? She did not know where she was, or where she could go. She knew only that, tired though she was, she must stay alert, learn as much as she could about where they had brought her, and choose her opportunity to escape carefully.

The gate itself led into a high-arched vault which ran beneath the railway lines. The Fyrd stood about for a while waiting for one of the gatekeepers to get something from a room nearby. She couldn't see what was inside this room, but she felt a blast of fresh air from it, and a strange twittering sound.

The far end of the vault was blocked by a roughly made brick wall about ten feet high, with a gap between its highest part and the ceiling. From over the top of this came deep reverberant sounds of machinery that were painful to the ears. There was a human-scale grey door which had a danger warning in red on it, and a skull and crossbones symbol.

When the gatekeeper reappeared, he was carrying three strange lanterns, from which came the same twittering sound she had heard earlier.

These lanterns were divided into two halves: the top part holding a thick candle surrounded by hinged shutters to block off its light if necessary, while beneath it was a little cage in which, to her amazement, she saw a yellow canary which sang and twittered constantly.

He eyed the group appraisingly and eventually gave one lamp to Feld, with the words, 'You lead, brother!' and another to Streik saying, 'And, brother, you follow!' The third he gave to the one guarding Katherine and said, 'Whoever this sister be and though she has prying eyes, she walks free for herself through the tunnels, all else being a danger to herself and everyone. Understood?'

The lantern holders nodded silently. The grip of the one holding Katherine briefly grew tighter on her arm, from nerves she guessed, and then quite slack. Obeying the Bilgesnipe's direction he eventually let go altogether.

The Bilgesnipe's eyes were puffy and piglike and his looming presence powerful, but Katherine decided that his occasional glances in her direction were not unkind, as if he was trying to convey to her personally through his words something which was quite different from their actual meaning.

'Listen you all to my briefing,' he began, 'for I am Tirrikh, boatman and temporary gatekeeper, but that don't mean I don't know what I should, so you'd do good to remember that, understand?'

As he said this, his eyes caught Katherine's, and by the way he said 'understand' she guessed he wanted her to remember his name and to pay special attention to any double meanings his words might suggest.

As if in confirmation, when she nodded very slightly, he returned the compliment with the faintest of smiles, though by then his eyes were moving elsewhere.

'The East side tunnels are the most dangerous in Brum, and yer got to go through 'em to get to the new city. It be raining and that means the water's on the rise and that puts the spirits of the water in mischievous mood, so don't you dally, brothers and sister, don't you dawdle. When you get going you get fast and you look sideways and anon but you don't look back.

'You stay between the white lines, as Meyor Feld here knows only too well, eh!?'

Feld had got too confident on one occasion and deviated from the lines to peer into a side-tunnel and in no time he was lost. It was Tirrikh who had rescued him ten hours later, very cold, very hungry and utterly disorientated.

'Now, if one of you is fool enough to fall behind and get separated the rest of you do *not* go looking for him. That brother's thenceforth on his own and will deserve what he gets for his foolishness. Yer all got that?'

The Fyrd grunted in assent.

'Mind you, that's not to say help's not at hand because it may be. But then it may not. So don't go missing in the first place and yer'll not have to worry about it, will yer?'

The Fyrd shifted about like naughty schoolboys; Katherine grinned to herself. She was beginning to like the Bilgesnipe.

'Now to creatures in the tunnels. They're about, trust me, and it's not good at the moment, for rain makes 'em wild and panicky and therefore dangerous. Rats of course and feral cats and dogs all abound on this side of Deritend, so watch it. Light and noise is good as it scares 'em off afore you ever see 'em. Sticking together is good too because they think you're one big animal, that's the way to work it, but if you find yourselves alone, brothers, and you too, sister, come to that . . .'

Again he glanced at her, again she sensed his words were special for her.

'. . . if yer'n do stray enough to wander, then beware especially of tomters. Very fast, very savage, very nasty. They'll have yer protuberances for breakfast if yer fool enough to stare 'em in the eye, so don't.'

Katherine looked mystified.

'You've not heard of 'em, then, that's evident! Creeper jipers, that's bad! Our oriental brothers breed 'em out of ginger toms and bull terriers. You'll know them by their rank odour. Move quick but not jerkily, sing a song and, I repeat, never look a tomter in the eye, and they'll not harm you. They'll sniff about, they might gnaw a bit but . . . well, just go careful with 'em. Half a ton of tomter hanging on to yer tallycans is no joke.'

Tirrikh grinned and winked a piggy eye.

'Next, watch out for the water, 'cos it's cold and fierce and unpredictable in these parts. Only us bilgyboys truly understand it, because it's a thing supped in mother's milk and learned in youth, and by the time you touch my age yer losing touch. Know this: it's alive that water and it wants you. It'll rise up and try and topple you; it'll send waves higher than the bridge you're standing on, to try to sweep you off; and sometimes it'll flood a place so fast that all you can do is grab one of the stirrups we set in the walls, at regular intervals, and hold your breath. We call those flash floods upanddowners. Take a deep breath, don't let go, just wait for the down, and hope for the best.'

The canaries twittered loudly as if they had been forgotten.

'And finally, the air. Flooding clears the system of the usual gases but if the birds stop singing it means oxygen's low. When that happens get out of there quick 'cos yer judgement's soon going ter be suspect. If yer can smell the gas go high; if you can't, go low. Right, Meyor Feld, that's my briefing about done, yer can take 'em on through!'

He went to the other door, unlocked it and opened it just a crack, letting them slip through one by one, shaking their hands as they went, Feld passing some money to him as he himself went through.

'Oh, yes, yes, yer really most welcome brothers!' Tirrikh rasped, 'And you too, sister!'

He held her hand tight in one of his, and covered it with the other and came closer. It was not his fishy breath she remembered after but the way his hands were protective of her, and affirmed by touch his now whispered words: 'We're watching yer, sister Katherine, 'cos it's good they got yer here, very good, and my name be Tirrikh and my mate be Maqluba, and those names count for more than groats in these festy parts! It's an honour to be the first Bilgesnipe to welcome yer to Brum! We'll get word to yer and hope yer find what yer looking for.'

'Word about what?' asked Katherine, greatly cheered by his words.

But the Fyrd behind shoved her forward before Tirrikh could say more and she found herself in a dank and echoing place, its walls covered in dirty cream-coloured tiles. She could almost smell the Fyrd's nervousness.

'They're a funny lot, they be,' said Streik, mocking Tirrikh's accent. 'As for tomters, lads, don't you believe it. They put that about to scare the shit out of you. I've never met anyone who's ever seen one, let alone had his tallycans toddled!'

'That's enough, Streik,' said Feld, cutting their nervous laughter short. 'Right . . . we do this last part of the journey quickly, efficiently and with no messing.'

'Aye, aye, sir!' they shouted.

'We're tasked to get this female bundle through in one piece and that's what we're going to do without stopping for one second, so don't fall behind.'

'Aye, sir!'

They proceeded slowly, along dripping tunnels, over slimy puddles and doing their best to stay within the white lines which in places were barely visible, it was so dark and they so obscure. They heard rushing water ahead but there was none, echoing steps ran past them but they saw no one making them, and right and left turns came at them so frequently they soon lost all sense of direction.

But for the lines, and Feld's confidence in leading them, they might easily have lost the way, for the candles guttered constantly from the poor air and the sudden and sometimes violent blasts of wind from side tunnels, conduits above their heads and the rusting grilles over tunnels that seemed abandoned and unused.

But from all entrances, and whichever way they turned, there came the sound of running, rushing water and the sense of turbulence and danger.

More than once they came across carcasses of animals long dead and unidentifiable, their fur clotted and mangy, their feathers greasy and dull. From these the odours were thick and cloying, and Katherine covered her mouth and nose, gagging as she passed them by.

The occasional show of light, usually from vents that reached high above into what the Fyrd called the Upperworld or toppermost, played strange tricks which, combined with constant shifts in directions of tunnels and angled walls, created illusions of scale. The most striking of these was when they saw what they took to be hundreds of rats on a pile of rags at the entrance to one of the side-tunnels, brought there by flood water.

When they got close Katherine saw it was the body of a white cat over whose body cockroaches roamed.

Then as suddenly as the journey began it ended. The tunnel sloped up and became drier and there was what looked like artificial light ahead where it split into two. She could hear the sound of voices and of echoing footsteps, hundreds of them.

Perhaps all of them felt a sense of relief and euphoria to have got through the tunnels, because the Fyrd, including Meyor Feld, pushed forward eagerly, taking the tunnel to the left and leaving Katherine and the one deputed to watch her at the point where the tunnel forked.

Katherine did not hesitate. She pushed him forward and tripped him with her foot and grabbed the lantern out of his hand.

Then she ran up the other tunnel towards the lights and the sound of people. She had no plan and had lost all sense of where she was, but felt certain that anything was likely to be better than where they were taking her.

But in that she was mistaken.

She had thought the tunnel led to the lights she could see, but it did not. It came to an end, and dangerously, at a wide conduit along which water came rushing. It seemed to run for some yards before turning to the right again through an unlit entrance.

She heard the Fyrd shout behind her and ran the only way she could, holding the lantern up so she could see and realizing very quickly that it was taking her back into the kind of tunnels she had just left behind so thankfully.

She stopped, turned back, and saw she had come through not one but two intersections and no longer knew what the way back was.

She tried one of them, heard voices further down and ran on willing more energy into her legs, and found herself yet more confused in a tunnel that was dark and low and old. Whatever she heard was not there. All was illusion; all confusion.

The canary in the lantern twittered briefly and then fell silent. She saw to her horror that it was dead. The candle guttered and suddenly went out, casting her into total darkness.

She moved forward, hands on the tunnel walls, and as she went she heard the unmistakable sound of something following her which from the sounds it made, and the lolloping slither of its feet, was neither hydden nor human but something worse by far.

54

UNOBTAINABLE

I t was pitch dark before Master Brief, Jack and the others finally gave up their search for Bedwyn Stort.

'He's done this kind of thing too often before,' muttered Brief, calling a halt. 'I swear by the Mirror itself that when he gets back here I'm going to punish him like the worst kind of young apprentice and give him a drubbing with my stave!'

But Brief's anger hid his genuine concern, for the ground around the Quoits was difficult enough to negotiate by day, filled as it was with loose waste from dredging, and shallow pools dangerous with quicksand, into which each of them had already slipped while looking for the youngster. By night it became totally treacherous.

The area to the south of the Quoits, which Pike took upon himself to investigate, was judged especially dangerous and the search that way had to be cut short when the light began to fade. Since then their searching to the north and shouting of his name had produced nothing.

Having found the leather kettle discarded with no sign of water in it, they guessed he had got distracted by something before he even reached the lake's edge. Now they had searched everywhere and still found nothing.

'More than likely he wandered off, and got lost and has had the good sense to lie low until daylight before coming to find us,' suggested Barklice contritely.

'Common sense is not one of Stort's virtues,' growled Pike.

'What was he doing just before you left?' Jack asked Barklice after they had reconvened by the stone, and were warming themselves with a sip of brew and trying not to think the worst.

'He had explored the henge, told me something about it, and then we sat here and talked.'

'Had he seen anything that specially interested him?'

'He told me this was once one of the largest and most important henges in Englalond,' said Barklice. 'He couldn't keep his eyes off the bits that remain, trying to work how one part related to another. He's like that, isn't he, Master Brief? Ever curious, his mind always active.'

The Master Scrivener nodded. 'He'd find anything interesting and worth exploring . . . which is why, Barklice, which is *why* . . .'

Barklice looked stricken with guilt at having broken his undertaking and left the absent-minded Stort alone in such a place.

Jack got up. 'The sky's cleared a bit and there's light now from moon and stars . . . so I'll go and have a last look around.'

Brief sighed with frustration. 'We were meant to be briefing you on our coming journey into Brum, and why the Fyrd have abducted Katherine and much else besides, but what with Stort not being here to add his views and the worry of him going missing, well . . . we've told you only half of it yet.'

'I'll go and stretch my legs anyway,' said Jack, 'and maybe we can talk later.'

The night was clear enough for the ground nearby to be quite visible, except that, as they had all discovered, it was difficult to differentiate between shadows and pools of water.

But Jack kept the stone clearly in view, and went carefully down to the lake edge, using the sound of lapping water as his guide. This was one of the areas he himself had not searched in any detail, it being plainly visible from the higher ground at the centre of the henge, and there being no obvious sign of Stort.

The ground was certainly difficult here, for all kinds of detritus had been washed ashore, presumably having been dumped into the lake and been blown across it, or carried up the shore when the water level rose with heavy rain.

So he stumbled against things a couple of times before reaching the water's edge and then, staring across the silent blackness of the lake itself, turned to his right to see if he could make out where the raised rim of the henge ran into the water. Even by this bad light it wasn't hard, not least because the ground was slightly raised and less muddy there.

As he turned to go back the other way, he noticed a black shape in the shadows and went over to check it out. It wasn't easy to see as more than an outline, but squatting down and feeling forward he was able to make out what felt like some soft dry materials resting on plastic.

He called for a light and they all came running. As Barklice opened the shutter of his lantern, they recognized Stort's outer garments laid carefully on a black bin-bag.

Before even discussing the grim implications of this very strange discovery, they began shouting Stort's name simultaneously out into the impenetrable darkness of the lake. Then, one by one, they fell silent as the grim realization came upon them that he wasn't replying and, if that was so, it was unlikely that he was ever going to.

At first they could not face the inevitable conclusion.

'But *why* did he venture into the lake?' said Brief in bewilderment. 'He couldn't even swim!'

There seemed no rational explanation for what was beginning to feel like a tragedy, and in the end it was Brief who expressed in words what they all now feared: 'Gentlemen, I very much suspect that our good friend, our much loved friend but alas our very foolish friend, has accidentally drowned himself!'

'Aye,' muttered Pike, who turned his back on them and, his voice breaking with grief, added, 'It's certain that he's gone under the water and not come up again.'

'I can only think,' continued Brief very sombrely, 'that Master Stort, who is – no, was! – one of the greatest natural scholars the Hyddenworld has ever known, was gripped by an idea so powerful, an investigation so alluring, that he entered into the water having forgotten utterly that he could not actually swim!'

Barklice had taken a few steps away from the group and stood now clutching his chest and gasping, his mouth opening and closing a few times like a fish out of water.

Then suddenly, and very shockingly, he broke into paroxysms of grief, his cries pitiful to hear and his broken posture tragic to behold as he fell to his knees by the light of the stars.

'This is no accident!' he cried. 'It is ... it is ... He has killed himself!'

The others waited for him to say what was on his mind, but he could not do so until Brief knelt beside him in the mud, put an arm around his shoulder and said, 'Try to tell us, Barklice, what it is you know or suspect. What terrible thing has happened to Stort?'

It was a little while before Barklice could reply.

But with a blowing of his nose and a dabbing at his eyes, and a good deal of breathing heavily in and out and staring at the stars, he finally began to unburden himself.

'This is not accident, nor is it suicide!'

'But what else could it be?' cried Pike.

'It is murder,' said Barklice in a ghastly way, 'murder most cruel and foul!'

'But who or why ... ?' said Brief and Pike almost as one, the latter pulling out a knife as if to protect them all from danger.

'It is I!' moaned Barklice, 'It is I who killed him. It is my fault! I might as well have taken a crossbow and shot a bolt through his heart, as leave him alone after ... after ...'

'After what!?' said Brief sharply.

Barklice grasped Brief's arm and looked up at him with terrible appeal.

'After that conversation we had ...'

A strange, mad light came to the verderer's eyes, enhanced by the steady strengthening of the moon, whose rays transmuted his state of mind into a lunatic glare which frightened them all.

'I can never forgive myself – not now, not ever! How can I? Therefore I am not worthy to live a moment more! I ... I ...'

With that he thrust Brief to one side as if he were the lightest of feathers, barged past the stolid Pike as easily as thrusting aside a wet reed, and charged straight into the water of the lake.

Only Jack's quick thinking saved a double tragedy. He ran straight at Barklice and brought him down in the shallows, from where, with Pike's help, they dragged him back to dry land.

Then, holding him down by all four limbs, until his suicidal struggle had spent itself and he had barely strength to sit up, they made him some strong, hot mead to calm his nerves.

He drank this almost at one gulp and at once took another mugful.

'Yes, one and all,' he suddenly confessed, his voice sounding a little stronger, his spirit improving fast, 'it was my fault for allowing our conversation to go in the direction it did.'

'Which was?' asked Brief, beginning now to lose patience with the verderer's maddening vagueness, for he felt it important to understand what had happened sooner rather than later in case there was still time to act on it.

'I'll tell you – no doubt about it – though it'll be difficult to confess to such thoughts, but I . . . I don't suppose . . .'

'Yes, Mister Barklice?' said Pike soothingly.

'Could you possibly allow me a further quaff or two of that excellent me-mea-meadth-thath me . . . You know . . . the me-mea-to give me courage to speak free-freth . . . feelree?'

Pike glanced at Brief, who nodded at Jack, who poured Barklice more of the intoxicating brew.

He gulped it down so fast that it spilt down both sides of his chin and induced, even before he had quite finished it, a giggle which became a hollow laugh reverberating into the wooden beaker from which he had just drunk.

'Oh yes!' he cried suddenly, throwing the beaker aside with abandon. 'I understand all too well why Stort, excellent fellow though he was, might have wished to end his days and indeed did so. It was not an act of despair but of courage! A bold recognition that the interminable pain of . . . of . . .'

'Of what, for goodness sake?' demanded Pike, now just as exasperated as Brief.

'Come c-clo . . . clother,' Barklice said conspiratorially, as if what he had to impart was something that could only be whispered, lest there were dark creatures, lurking outside the range of the light of their fire, who might hear. 'Clother thtill . . .'

They all came very close indeed.

'You ask of what!?' he roared, so loud that they started back, and then, nearly silent again, and still shedding more tears, 'Talk of *what*?

That sad state that sensitive souls such as he and I suffer but never complain of . . .'

They looked at each other blankly.

'What state?' asked Brief, glowering.

'Loneliness,' pronounced Barklice sonorously. 'The deep, existential, ghastly, never-ending loneliness of feeling as he did, as I do – for this is what we were talking of before you came – that hydden such as us are endlessly alone in this vast Universe of Earth and stars, moon and planets, without hope of ever finding the companionship, the solace and the love – I say the love – of one of the unobtainables.'

He stopped, a strange hopeless yet serene grin on his face, as in one who has faced his fate and finally accepted it.

'What exactly,' Brief whispered softly to Pike, 'is he talking about?'

'What is it, Master Brief, that we all seek but so rarely find? Yet how would you, who moves in the rarefied world of pollar . . . of pollarshiss . . . of . . . sko . . .'

'Of scholarship?'

'That's right, of pollarsick. How could *you* possibly know?'

They waited for him to answer his own question.

Barklice rolled his head, and also his eyes within his head. 'It seems no one but I knew the depth of poor Stort's desire for that which is unobtainable to the likes of us!'

'Enlighten us,' said Brief, now genuinely curious as to what his companion was trying to say.

'More brew and I'll tell you!'

'No,' growled Pike. 'Tell us right away or I'll throttle you with my bare hands.'

Barklice took this threat seriously, breathed deeply and finally explained, 'The love of one of the female gender, that is what is unobtainable. That is why Stort took his life so nobly. He knew he could never be loved.'

'But, Barklice . . .'

But it was too late, for the verderer's head slumped onto his chest and he fell asleep. Even when they pinched his cheeks and poured cold water over his head, all he could do was mumble idiotically of love and the Universe and of females, before falling asleep again.

✳

'All I know,' said Pike much later, after some further searching and constant shouting of Stort's name, 'is that if he went down into the lake – and it looks like he did – he's not coming back now.'

'He was one of the most creative and inventive hydden I ever knew,' Brief said finally. 'So it is hard to believe he's dead and gone!'

After due pause, Brief turned to the rest of them and continued, 'I suggest, with heavy heart, that we sleep now, for we have a long journey tomorrow.'

But Jack was not happy with that. 'Master Brief, you were going to answer some of my questions and tell me about the Hyddenworld, and about . . . well, everything I need to know.'

'Need to know for what?' replied Brief testily as he opened his portersac and took out his bedroll, the others soon following suit.

'About . . . what's happening. Who exactly has taken Katherine?'

Brief raised his eyebrows mysteriously and began bedding down.

'And how did you know to come and get me?' Jack persevered.

'Humph!' murmured Brief as he folded his cloak up, to make a pillow of it.

'And what exactly is . . . I mean where is . . . Brum? What's that all about? And your carved stave and how it works, I wouldn't mind you explaining that as well.'

'Ah!' said Brief noncommittally.

Pike was already lying snug on the ground and well covered, his eyes closing.

'Hmmm!' murmured Brief sleepily.

Jack undid his own bedroll, took off his tunic to provide something serviceable on which to rest his head, and said, 'And another thing, Master Brief . . . who exactly am I?'

Brief sat up again.

Pike's eyes shot open.

'Well?' demanded Jack.

'Now that's the sort of question you *should* be asking!' said Brief. 'Shouldn't he, Pike?'

'That's always the one,' replied Pike. '"Who am I?" is always a good question to ask.'

'So what's the answer?'

'Aher ghah!' said Brief which seemed to indicate, if this utterance meant anything, that he had no immediate answer.

Pike simply shook his head and closed his eyes again.

'Tomorrow,' murmured Brief, lying back. 'Let's talk about these thorny issues tomorrow, yes?'

'Well, I really wanted . . .

But Brief's breathing deepened, his limbs jerked, he snorted and snored a bit, and then he was fast asleep.

'Mister Pike? Are you awake?'

'No,' said Pike, 'I'm not.'

Jack lay down and turned on his side, facing Barklice, the only one still wide awake.

'I don't suppose *you* know who I am?' asked Jack very sleepily.

'Me?' replied Barklice. 'Of course I do – everyone does. Master Brief was just being difficult.'

But Jack, not expecting a sensible answer, was listening no more and Barklice, feeling he had said enough for one evening, spoke no more on that subject just then, for he saw that Jack eyes were closing, his body relaxing, and that he too was falling asleep.

So Barklice mumbled about love and the stars instead.

Then he fell silent and just grinned at the night.

Then he had another turn and said, 'Gesheshmen . . . ge . . . gents, I wish to make an . . . an . . . an . . . annnouncementyment! I have seen a great light!'

But no one was listening.

He fell silent, shaking his head and striving no more to make them listen.

Which was a pity because in a way he was quite right. He *had* seen a light, though it came not from the stars but the far side of the lake. The light flashed again, and then once more.

'Stort?' he murmured sleepily. 'Could that possibly be you?'

Then he too fell asleep.

55

CROSSING

T he night had gone badly for Bedwyn Stort, but not as badly as for his bewildered friends, who given the overwhelming circumstantial evidence of his death, were presuming him lost for ever.

Like so many of his schemes, it had begun with the best of intentions and most logical of ideas.

He'd used the string, tube and polystyrene he had collected and, in a trice, turned them into a breathing apparatus, using the string to affix the tube to his person in such a way that it stayed adjacent to his mouth.

His purpose was to swim with his head under the water and attempt to plot those parts of the Quoits which were now submerged, just to satisfy himself of their location and scale.

The fact that he could not swim did not deter him.

He reasoned that all he needed was buoyancy, and there were plenty of lumps of polystyrene floating about the place to provide that. All that was necessary was to attach bits to his various limbs with the pieces of string and tape so liberally washed up on the shore, and then all would be well.

Thus attired he had lumbered through the shallows and entered the water. It was rather colder than he expected but to one such as Stort, on a new quest for knowledge, this was just a trivial inconvenience. The chilly phase passed and, having got himself in order, and his limbs more or less functioning as paddles, he submerged his head and found to his delight that his latest invention worked very well indeed.

He could propel himself about, see reasonably well and float well enough to stay alive. He swam about like this, getting used to his equipment for a little while, before beginning to focus on his study.

The water being so still and clear he was able to follow the line of the sunken henge for some way out into the lake. He was rather surprised to see, as he swam along, a great deal of discarded machinery, several bicycles, a perfect cardboard box which swayed slightly in its waterlogged state at his passing, and a few fish rather larger and more toothy than he would have liked.

Stort had an aversion to animals, whatever genus they were, especially those with teeth. And that particular evening, it seemed to him that the fishy creatures below eyed him not with the welcoming warmth due a fellow traveller in Earth's waters, but with the lustful stare of predators in search of their next meal.

But his continuing interest in the henge overcame this fear and he pressed on, finding much of interest. When the water below him grew too deep and murky for him to see further, he decided to make a left turn and seek out the other arm of the sunken relic.

It was at this point that he momentarily lost his sense of direction and turned round not once nor twice but three times in all. The moment he did so, and as he reached the far north-easterly limit of the henge, something very strange began to happen. The strings and suchlike that held his buoyancy aid unaccountably tightened very painfully and then, before he was able to loosen them with his hand, they all snapped of one accord. The result was that he began to sink towards the bottom very rapidly.

In such circumstances, scientific curiosity rather than personal survival overtook him. True, it was an unhappy way to end his days . . .

Yet he told himself, *at least I shall have the rare benefit of observing my own death, which should be interesting to say the least.*

Moments later, his chest already beginning to cause him pain as he realized he could not involuntarily hold his breath for ever, a new thought occurred to him.

Ah! he reasoned. *I spy another opportunity. Most certainly death is of interest, but I cannot say I am enjoying the process of drowning. Let me therefore work out how to swim from first principles. Now . . .*

He might well have done so there and then – though not in time to save his life, seconds only remaining – when, hitting the bottom of the lake, his eardrums hurting, his lungs feeling as they were about to explode, his mind beginning to spin, he found himself staring into the eyes and then mouth of a creature of the deep, the kind of which nightmares are made.

Its eyes were a luminescent yellow, its mouth set in a gaping grin of welcome and its teeth sharp, long and rather evilly curved.

Reason deserted him, replaced by fear. All interest in the study of his own death gave way at last to the instinct for survival. The fish he had fallen upon was a pike. As it swished its tail and wiggled its spiked dorsal fin Stort's feet sought the lake floor, found purchase and he launched himself upward like a shooting star. So hard did he push that he shot straight to the surface, and upward a good way after that, before landing back on the surface with a splash.

Even as he did so he realized that, if he was not to sink back into the welcoming mouth of the pike, he had indeed better learn to swim, and *fast*. He therefore thrashed his arms in the water like the wheels of a cart, and pushed his legs back and forth like the pistons of a steam train. It was a cumbersome manoeuvre but it worked.

He moved through the water with remarkable speed, continuing until his strength began to fail. As he weakened, he discovered he was still as afloat as before, yet quite free of that difficulty of movement he had suffered when he still possessed his buoyancy aids.

In short, Stort had taught himself to swim!

Euphoria set in and he gadded about the surface for quite a time until he realized two things: first, that the evening had become night and he was utterly lost, and second that he had lost his combinations and all else and was now in a state of nature.

It was then that he heard his friends frantically shouting his name, and shortly after, the water carrying the sound all too clearly, he heard raised voices and suspected that Brief and Pike were angry with him.

That, and his desire not to be discovered naked, made him turn tail and swim as quietly as he could in the opposite direction. Matters, he trusted, could be sorted out in the morning. And, anyway, the wind was with him and it seemed the current too, for he felt himself being carried along without much effort.

However progress to the shore – any shore – proved slow, and he gradually became unpleasantly aware that a luminous shadow was swimming along just beneath him. He put his head under the water and saw the clear outline of what seemed a fish, but a monstrous one, and not the one he had seen before, which was a tiddler by comparison. This was its father, or possibly grandfather, and it looked vast and terrifying.

When his fears were realized and he felt the clamp of the new predator's teeth on his right calf, he let out a terrible cry and tried to pull his leg free. But the fish sank his teeth in deeper, and Stort felt himself beginning to be pulled under the water. Reason, logic and even curiosity once more gave way to blind panic.

He reached down to rid himself of the fish, if he could, felt the thick waterlogged trunk of a tree, and realized that what had seemed to be teeth were but branches and twigs.

Strangely a new and worse panic immediately set in, as if, though this monster fish was but a chimera, a true monster of the deep, disturbed by the commotion, might now lazily emerge from the darkness below and swallow him whole.

Kicking free of the tree, he threshed on through the water until his knees and then his hands and finally his chest hit mud and gravel. Despite the sharpness of the stones he crawled ashore, a cold and broken shadow of what he had been but an hour or two before.

There he lay, beached, like a dying whale, gasping and utterly spent.

56

EPIPHANY

When Stort finally found the energy to restore himself to full consciousness, rather hoping that what had happened was only a bad dream from which he might awaken to find himself somewhere comfortable, warm and dry, he understood at once the harsh reality of his situation.

He was very cold, very lost and very alone.

He struggled upright and shouted out across the dark waters of the lake, which now shone coldly under the risen moon, 'Help! I . . . I . . . I'm-m-m-m . . . here! *Help!*'

No one heard him and so no answer came.

He knew he needed to move and find warmth, something to wear and shelter as quickly as he could, so he decided to make his way along the shore. The gravel underfoot was sharp and the mud squelched between his toes like icy worms.

The exercise brought feeling back to his limbs and torso, and with it came a heightened sense of the bitter cold and the reminder that he had lost his underwear. But Stort was a hydden whose natural curiosity and engagement with all about him and eager interest in the challenge of a new idea meant that he was never long downhearted or much affected by personal discomfort.

So it was that as he roamed in the dark in a state of nudity it occurred to him that it was impossible for his combinations to have removed themselves from his body of their own accord. Impossible but intriguing as an idea, so much so that he paused for a few moments and he made a mental note that, should he survive the night, he might try and design and build some mechanical combinations which would have the power to divest themselves of their owner, then launder, iron and fold themselves and put themselves away until they were needed again.

But then, finding his thighs shivering and his teeth chattering, he muttered, 'N . . . n . . . not one of my better ideas,' and turned his attention instead to the mystery of where they now were, so that he might quickly put them on again.

He knew for certain he had not removed them, and he doubted that the fishes of the deep had done so either, for they would have removed some of his flesh at the same time and an earlier examination had shown that he was unwounded and all his parts present and correct.

He therefore retraced his steps and scrabbled about the shoreline looking for the lost apparel, certain it must be somewhere nearby and gratified there was enough light from stars and moon to see, if only murkily.

What he found were various items of rubbish cast up on the shore, which together presented him with a deepening puzzle that put into him a growing sense of deep unease. A tiny cola bottle, a minute and soggy box of matches, a cracked ballpoint pen such as dwarves might use, and then a plastic yellow hard hat of the kind that humans use on building sites, which looked a lot smaller than the ones he had on occasion found discarded there.

Except there was something very odd about it, which put his mind into a spin. Knowing that body heat is lost most rapidly through the head, he casually tried the hard hat on and was surprised to find that far from it being too big it fitted perfectly. He kept it on, some covering being better than none, and continued his perambulation as a hard-hatted nocturnal naturist, striving as he went to put to the back of his mind the horrible thought that was now right at the front of it.

'No!' he kept muttering. 'Absolutely not! No, no, and no again!'

His right foot connected with something soft, clammy and familiar. He sank to the ground, happy again. He had found his missing combinations.

'Bad!' he said, addressing them as if they were animate and capable of thought, 'Very bad of you to sneak off like that.'

He stood, held them up in the moonlight, and saw to his regret that they were in tatters and unwearable, as if ripped apart by a monster. Unhappily, like everything else around him, they too seemed to have shrunk to half their size.

No mortal alive was more wedded to the pursuit of truth and a desire for learning and understanding than Bedwyn Stort. But what he now had to confront was a truth beyond imagining, and a horrible one too: if his combinations were half the size they had been but an hour or two before, he needed to ask the reason why.

He knelt upon the ground again, spread them out and reassembled them, so that he could see which parts were missing.

Nothing was missing. They were in tatters but complete.

He stood up again and threw his luckless combinations back into the lake, thinking that if he could not see them he at least would not have to think about them.

But they fell in such a way that they ballooned up on the surface and the fickle breeze shifted, billowed into them, and set them on a course back across the lake like a ghost ship in the night.

Stort realized that there were only two conclusions, both impossible, to be drawn from what he had so far seen. Either his combinations and the other objects he had come across had shrunk . . . or . . .

'No, it cannot be!'

. . . or he had grown.

He frantically retraced the previous evening's events in his mind, searching for clues as to what had happened.

It took only moments to get to the heart of the matter: what he had done was to swim out of the henge specifically on its north-east side, which all students of henges knew very well could be, in certain circumstances, its portal to the human world. But that ancient art of travelling had been lost to Englalond for many centuries.

Was it possible that he had rediscovered it by accident and in doing so had unwittingly morphed into something bigger than he was before?

'No, no! Too horrible!'

Stort began walking in ever-increasing circles, as if in search of his former self.

He then retraced his steps to find the matchbox and the cola bottle. Compared with his hand they were indeed half the size they ought to be, and therefore confirmed the possibility that there had been a relative change in his own size.

Still unwilling to be convinced by this evidence, he rushed hither and thither on the lonely shore, in search of absolute proof. The means was unfortunately readily available.

The area was prone to flooding, so the humans had erected a white post a yard or two out into the water on which gradations marked in feet and inches had been placed to show changes in the level of the lake.

The moon was bright, the gradations clearly visible.

Stort stared at the post in horror, reluctant to put his theory to the test. Eventually, he waded into the water and stood next to the measuring post.

The post was eight feet high – it clearly said so.

His head reached up to the six-foot mark, leaving only two feet above.

He peered more closely at the gradations, but there was no doubt, for they were clearly marked in the imperial measure humans used and that the hydden themselves had adopted a century before.

'I have grown in the course of my passage across the lake and become . . . become . . .'

He could not easily bring himself to say what he had become, but he finally did so.

'*I have become a human being!*'

This appalling realization so shocked him that he had to clutch hold of the post itself for support, as he cried out in a strangled way, 'This is a fate worse than death! I, Stort, a hydden through and through, am now a monstrous human being. That means Bedwyn Stort as he was known is no more.'

It was at this moment of ghastly realization that he saw advancing towards him along the shore a ghostly apparition about his own size.

It was, or seemed to be, in female form and it – she – was not messing about. No, she was advancing upon the innocent and naked Stort at a considerable speed of knots.

'I shall not yield to her!' he cried out and, turning from the same apparition, began to run back the way he had come.

He ran all the faster when he heard the unmistakable sound of her subtle female feet chasing after him across the gravel and mud, and then yet faster behind him, until she reached out to touch him, even caress him, and his terror nearly froze him to the spot.

All he could do was turn to face her as she, helped by a following wind, reached her arms and legs around him, blocking out the moon and stars with her vast and confusing body, which left him breathless before tumbling him backwards as if falling to an inevitable doom.

Bang!

He hit the muddy gravel, flailed at her strange clinging form and felt himself beginning to asphyxiate for the second time that night until, his head breaking free of her clammy hair, he saw what she truly was: a large square section of abandoned bubble-wrap adorned with sticky tape which cleaved to him with annoying tenacity.

'Ah! I am mistaken,' he said with relief, his natural optimism returning at once to turn this disaster into success. 'This is not some rampant female after all, but a life saver! This excellent human-made material will keep me warm and help me survive the night!'

He gratefully draped it around himself and retreated up the hostile shore to hunker down in the grass and gorse on higher ground. Thus insulated, Stort began to get warm again. A mood of mystical content-ment came over him.

He breathed deeply, and began to meditate on the meaning of life and of what it was now to be a human being, and to have once been a hydden and much else.

It was now that Bedwyn Stort, inventor and scrivener, began a journey into his own mind and heart which resulted in the greatest epiphany of his relatively short life.

He saw that there was no difference between a human and a hydden except what the mind itself – that mischievous, uncontrollable thing mortals spend their life being deluded by . . .

'Illusion is all,' he told himself. 'I am most of all what I *think* I am. I am human, I am hydden, I am both, and I am neither.'

How long these astonishing insights occupied his mind he had no idea. The moon certainly carried on its progress across the sky during that time of discovery, and the stars shifted too.

He felt the awe of one who knows that, though he is as vulnerable and friendless as he has ever been, yet his solitary tribulations are as nothing compared with the firmament of stars and moon and planets above, which he looked at with new wonder, all feeling of cold now leaving him and in its place occurring one of warmth and oneness.

He saw the risen moon as if it were a friend.

He felt the rough, hard gravel of the Earth beneath his feet as though it were his mother.

He felt the wind as something wholesome and cleansing; and the distant sounds of the world beyond as something to love.

He saw the dawn reflected in a growing cloud and that everything was One and therefore to be seen in everything else.

It was then that he realized that using the henges as portals betwixt and between the human and hydden worlds – which he would need to do again if he was to get back to being a hydden – was not as hard as it seemed. It was all a matter of using the natural energies of a henge to make a shift in relative perception. But whether he would recover this insight in the light of a new day was a matter of some doubt.

His work for the night was done and so he fell asleep, cocooned still in bubble-wrap.

Soon after, as dawn came and the wind brought its mists around him and drifting out across the lake, there came clip-clopping along the shore the White Horse and its rider, who looked down at Bedwyn Stort and smiled.

For once Imbolc wore no guise.

She was very old now and even the soft dawn light did not make her seem less so. Perhaps even more.

The horse dropped to its knees that she might more easily dismount. She walked with pain, the horse rising when she was ready so that it could now walk at her side and she grasp its reins for support. Her feet were swollen and her fingers bent. Her teeth were almost gone, her hair thin, her face lined and lived-in.

Yet, seeing Stort all huddled up, his eyes closed, his mouth a little open, his face showing the contentment of a difficult problem solved, she smiled at him and her face lit up, all her tiredness and pain momentarily gone.

She kissed him so tenderly that he stirred, as if Love itself had come visiting and he had known it, though asleep, and he murmured words that for a few moments held no form but that of pure happiness.

The White Horse reared, suddenly impatient to be gone.

It dropped to its knees to make it easier for the Peace-Weaver to climb on its back once more. Then rider and horse turned away and raced on and were lost in the mists of the dawning sky.

57

NIGHTMARE

After her flawed escape from the Fyrd, which had left her alone in the tunnels without food, light or adequate clothing, Katherine's night had been even more fearful and isolated than Stort's had been.

That she was being followed was certain and that it was a tomter seemed likely. Its rank odour and terrifying speed and agility as it ran around her grunting and jumping up on the walls, sometimes so close to her face she could feel its hot breath, seemed to confirm it. It was able to navigate in the dark and was playing with her as a cat does with a mouse.

Until a more sinister trend emerged.

The only way she could move was by running her feet along the tunnel floor and her hands on its wall. Since the tomter did not immediately attack her and if anything seemed calmer when she moved, she did so as best she could, hoping to find light and a way to get away.

In this way she had reached a spot in the tunnel onto which street light filtered from far above and she was finally able to see the beast.

Its legs were long, its body like that of a fighting dog and it had a square head and jaws to match. But also there was about it the heavy belligerence of a confident tom cat, and the same pattern on its fur. It had a cat's eyes too and its paws were feline.

It stared at her and she at it before remembering what Tarrikh had said. She quickly looked away and the tomter stood down a little. She had moved on very carefully so as not to provoke it and, not sure if the Bilgesnipe's instruction had been for real, she obeyed it anyway and hummed a tune of sorts.

That did seem to calm it but it still followed her, now near now far, blocking her way down some tunnels, seeming to guide her towards others. It was this that now began to unnerve her, because it looked as if the tomter was herding her to a destination of its choosing – and that she did not want.

Try as she might she could not bring herself to push it out of the way, because every time she got near it growled and bared its teeth. So she resigned herself to being forced in the direction it wanted to take her. Wherever it was going felt warmer, the air ever more fetid.

She turned a corner, found herself in filtered light again in what appeared to be its den, littered with the bones and skin of animals. It stank and it crawled with rats and maggots.

But that was not the worst.

Occupying pride of place in this filthy domain was the tomter's bitch, which lay on its side feeding four young from swollen dugs each heavy with milk.

It took Katherine a moment to overcome her shock and fear of this new horror. When she did she realized she was in the open air, the tunnel having led her to a tiny courtyard in the middle of an ancient building whose windows did not start until three storeys above her head and out of reach.

Ambient light came from the night sky and from two of the windows far above. A shadow crossed one of them, a human. Katherine shouted but it felt futile and the bitch rose at once, scattering its slobbering young, and advanced on her.

She froze and waited.

The tomter female came close and she saw that it was far larger than its mate, almost as tall as herself. Huge in fact, but with power in its paws and body, and bulk too, to overwhelm her if it wished.

As it was it nudged at her, its weight sending her back.

Then it settled down, licking its hideous mouth and utterly indifferent to Katherine when she slowly turned away to try to go back the way she had come. Not a chance, with the male now firmly blocking her path.

So it was there she had to stay, obviously ready meat for the tomters when they chose to attack her, with no way out that she could see.

The calmness of someone who has met her worst nightmare fell upon her and she squatted down in the filth completely exhausted.

Astonishingly she slept, because when something jolted her awake dawn light was in the den and the square of sky above now dull grey.

It was not the tomters that woke her, nor even their pups, it was the sound of a horse's hoofs. Quite close but hard to tell exactly where. The tomters noticed it too, and looked suddenly uneasy and then strangely docile as if grown tired. Indeed the pups did sleep, entwined together in the rubbish on which their mother's legs rested.

The male pushed past Katherine, yawned and settled down to sleep with his family.

She heard the horse's hoofs back down the tunnel and took her chance to follow. They seemed very close but she never caught up with them as they led her through the labyrinth of tunnels by a route she could never have worked out for herself.

Then they faded away and as she turned a corner, she found herself staring into the eyes of Tarrikh the gatekeeper.

'Been lookin' for you,' he said, with obvious relief. 'I told 'em I'd find you and they'll be pleased at that. Won't be angry for what yer did. The Fyrd respect a fighter. You stink of tomter so you must have passed near one which missed you.'

'No, they did find me. I was in their den.'

Tarrikh's eyes widened.

'You couldn't have been, they'd have eaten you alive.'

'I think they were planning to but . . . I got away.'

'How?'

She told him about the horse's hoofs.

'Did you see 'im? Was he white?'

'It might have been a mare,' she said, teary with relief.

'You saw it?'

She shook her head.

'And 'twas a horse definite and certain what led you out of there?'

Katherine nodded.

He looked at her in awe. 'You be the Shield Maiden solid as I'm standin' here! You be!'

'I'm Katherine,' she said firmly.

He shook his great head and blinked his small eyes and grinned his friendly, yellow-toothed grin. 'And I be Tarrikh and I be Bilgesnipe and come the day me and mine can give you help, you ask for it and never fail. Understand?'

'Yes, Tarrikh.'

'Now follow me, girl, and remember that nothing about New Brum is as it seems. And don't run away, you may not be so lucky a second time.'

'You could help me now instead of leading me back to them.'

He winked a reassuring wink. 'They may not be what "they" seem, Katherine.' With this mysterious observation he turned and led her away; and with the stench of tomter in the air, she did not hesitate to follow.

58

DEPARTURE

J ack and the others woke early at the Devil's Quoits, despite their fatigue after the long search for Stort the night before. They quickly erected a tarpaulin to protect both themselves and their fire from the rain while they had breakfast.

Jack was given the menial task of collecting water and firewood, while Pike and Barklice, expert campers, arranged things so that the rain poured off their temporary cover first as a shower to wash themselves, about which they were meticulous, and then to fill their water bottles.

In the wake of Stort's likely death the mood was sombre: Brief said little, Pike nothing at all. The practical Barklice, apparently unaware of the lunatic state he had got into the night before, now wanted to strike camp as fast as he could and get back to Brum.

But, unlike the other two, he did not now believe for one moment that Stort was dead.

'He'll pop up soon enough, you see if he doesn't!' he assured Jack more than once.

Nevertheless they decided to wrap Stort's clothes in the bin-liner he had left behind and place them conspicuously by the standing stone, along with his portersac. By way of a memorial, Pike gruffly stuck a piece of dried driftwood in the ground nearby. Brief said a few last words of farewell, his voice shaky and his eyes hollow.

'Terrible, most terrible . . .' he muttered, before finally turning away, the sad ritual barely over, 'but, gentlemen, if we linger much longer, despair will take hold and we will lose the desire to press on along the way to Brum, where we have much work to do – and, if we are not already too late, a young woman to rescue, eh, Jack?'

Jack could only agree yet reflect that, like Barklice, he too could not really believe Stort was no more. He got to his feet to set about clearing the camp, as he had seen the others do the day before. No one else moved.

'If you all help,' he said, realizing that they needed encouragement, 'then the job will be done all the sooner. Mister Barklice, please bury the fire. Mister Pike, kindly wash these pots and utensils. Master Brief . . . you've forgotten to pack your plaid.'

In this way Jack got them organized, ready for the off.

Even so, when this was done they stood around staring at each other with nothing left to do but leave, yet none of them wanting to.

Again, it was Jack who broke this impasse.

'Gentlemen,' he said, adopting their own style of addressing one another, 'maybe we'd feel better if we made one last effort to search for clues as to what happened to Mister Stort. I want to get on with the journey to Brum and find Katherine, but I'd travel easier if I knew we had searched that area we were not able to investigate yesterday because of the failing light.'

'That's well said, Jack,' said Brief. 'And this last gesture to the memory of Stort will help get us away from this now doleful place.'

The wind and rain was driving hard off the water into their eyes making them struggle to see across the lake.

Various water birds huddled on the shore, and they heard the miserable calls of some of them carried by the wind over the water.

'A heron I believe, Master Brief,' said Barklice, pointing at a grey-white mass that bobbed on the water in the distance.

'Seagulls, I suggest!' said Brief.

Pike's eyesight was better than his older friends'.

'Human refuse, plastic probably,' he growled.

'Come on gentlemen,' Brief commanded them, tired of this point-less diversion, 'let's search the shore as Jack has suggested.'

Very soon they saw how wise Pike's decision had been not to search much of the area to the south during the night. It was hummocky, difficult ground, filled with treacherous pools of mud, obstructions of wire and shattered lumps of concrete. The rain drove off the lake straight into their eyes, and made the going slippery. It was not long before they lost sight of the stone and almost of each other, floundering around in search of signs of Stort that might give them hope he had somehow survived, or at least a clue as to the nature of his death.

One thing soon became clear. The rain had brought a rise in water levels such that the route they had first taken into the Quoits was now too flooded to risk leaving by the same way. They therefore decided to go back to the Stone and depart by way of the higher, drier ground to the north-east.

This gave them opportunity to search along the lapping, rising waters of the lake shore one final time. It was then that Pike pointed out something that had come to rest in the rocky shallows and let out a terrible cry.

It was Stort's combinations, filthy with mud, and torn to shreds, looking as if they had been lying there for days rather than just hours.

'He was taken by a great fish of the deep,' said Pike, unable to name the most likely culprit after which he himself had been named.

'Yes,' said Brief, holding up the bedraggled garment with a stick. 'This is proof positive, gentlemen. Stort is most certainly dead. We must therefore be gone at once, and put this episode behind us . . .'

They were brutal words but true ones.

'Aye,' said Pike, 'it isn't often I admit defeat, but now . . . I do. I have failed to protect my young friend Stort, and for that I shall never forgive myself.'

With heavy hearts they turned as one back towards the standing stone, but it was hard going for the wind was now against them, the terrain more confusing still.

Meanwhile, and long since, Bedwyn Stort had awoken to his state of nudity and insight and the dread fact he was now of human size.

His insight was as revolutionary as it was simple and it concerned the way in which henges, whether made of trees as at Woolstone, or half-submerged and ruined ones like the Devil's Quoits across the water, actually worked. He had leapt up with the dawn, ignored the cold and the fact that bubble-wrap is not much of a covering against a chill wind, and set about putting his new theory to the test.

What he had realized was that by some lucky chance his odd passage with flotation aids out of the henge, even though its remnants were lost in the mud at the bottom of the lake, had described a pattern that triggered a shift in his perception of things. The secret lay in the dance of movement which created a state that felt like waking from one state of being into another, from being a hydden to becoming a human.

'All I have to do, semi-nude though I am, is to do backwards what I did forwards yesterday and I shall trick my mind to a renewed perception of old self and become hydden once again. Easy! In theory . . .'

The question was how to get back across the lake and position himself in the water above the submerged north-eastern entrance to the ruined henge.

The answer in the end was given to him by the wind. It was blowing hard across the lake towards the distant Quoits. Committing himself once more to the deep, confident that the bubble-wrap would act as both new flotation aid and sail, he began to journey back across the water.

It went well, though he was sorry to spy as he went that his friends had given up waiting for him and were going. He tried to attract their attention but it was to no avail, so that as he reached the submerged henge again they were gone. He gyrated in obverse manner through the water, hoping he would not disturb the fishes of the deep, closed his eyes to lose touch with reality and allow his head to go into a spin, and was gratified when all of a sudden he found himself slipping out of the bubble-wrap as if – which was indeed the case – he was becoming hydden-size again.

He sank below the water, broke free of the plastic and doggy-paddled ashore, an action he could not have managed the day before.

'We live and we learn!' he told himself.

Then, naked, cold and hungry, but as usual quite undaunted, he strode ashore and headed for the stone in the centre of the Quoits, where he ascertained that relative to the stone he had indeed returned to hydden size – a welcome fact confirmed by finding his clothes as the others hoped he might. They fitted him perfectly. Very much relieved, yet excited by all that had happened, he found shelter from the rain, lit a fire and made a brew and found time to muse briefly on what had happened.

'Was it a horrible reality that I became a human for a few hours or the lunatic dream of a budding hydden philosopher?' he asked himself. 'Without evidence or witnesses I shall never know! But I owe it to myself and the world to attempt to repeat the experiment some time in the future under more auspicious circumstances.'

He knew that it is one thing for a hydden to make a scientific discovery, quite another to prove how it works and that he can make it do so again and again.

A short time later, dry, warm, and victualled, he left in a different direction to the others. He left no note, since he naturally assumed they had already left.

A short time after he had gone, and not much further along the shore, the others came to a halt.

'Are you sure this is the way back?' Brief wondered aloud, not for the first time.

'It's not my habit to get lost,' said Barklice, rather irritably. He sniffed at the air as if to show he could almost smell the right direction, and Jack affected to do the same. The moment they did so, they both frowned and stared at each other.

'That's strange,' said Jack. 'I can still smell our spent fire even in these damp conditions!'

'Strange?' said Barklice in a low voice. 'It's serious more like. Perhaps strangers have turned up, made a brew without realizing we're still about or, worse, they are lying in wait for us. Mister Pike, what do you suggest we do?'

'Leave this to me,' said he, the fire of purpose returning to him at last. He raised his stave into fighting mode and looked suddenly very ferocious.

'I swear to you, gentlemen, if there are Fyrd here I will give them a drubbing to remember!'

He moved forward fast and silently, the rest of them keeping low and following a little way behind. When he was in sight of the Stone, Pike stopped and beckoned them nearer.

'They are out of sight on its far side,' he whispered urgently, 'and there may be too many for me to handle.'

He turned to Jack. 'You proved yourself before,' he said, 'and now's your chance to do so again. I'll go round the left side of the stone, and you take the right. Barklice, you follow Jack – and, Master Brief, you follow me. Ready?'

The rain swept down but they were not daunted.

They turned, readied themselves and, without further ado, proceeded in the way Pike had ordered, uttering various roars and cries as they advanced, by way of adding to the Fyrd's confusion and surprise.

'Charge!' cried Pike at the final moment. 'And kill!'

Which they might indeed have done, had anyone been there. But no one was visible, and they stood about breathing heavily and feeling slightly foolish.

Yet there was the distinct smell of fire and the strong feeling that someone else had departed this place, other than themselves, only shortly before.

It was Jack who spotted that something else had disappeared. Of Stort's portersac and clothes, there was no trace at all.

Nor were there any useful footprints which might have helped them work out in which direction the thief or thieves had gone who had so casually desecrated Stort's modest memorial.

They uncovered the fire they had earlier buried and, sure enough, the steam that came off its suspiciously hot ashes, as the rain made contact, suggested it had been put out again only a short time before.

'It's an old trick,' observed Barklice. 'Whoever stole Stort's things guessed we had just left, and they found where our fire had been by touch or smell and then used it as the basis of their own fire to speed things up for a quick brew.'

'But who could it have been?' asked Jack.

'Fyrd almost certainly,' said Pike. 'One of the patrols under Meyor Feld's command, sent to keep an eye on us. It's as well we did not surprise them here and force a confrontation. All that is needed is for them to know we are here, and that we are following them. That's the game we're playing, so let us play it.'

'More than likely they had already been watching us,' said Pike morosely, 'and snatched their opportunity to grab poor Stort's garments.'

'Whatever,' said Jack, fearing that another extended and pointless debate might slow down still further their pursuit of Katherine and her abductors. 'Could we now please move on?'

59
SISTERS CHASTE

Katherine lost count of the twists and turns in their route after Tarrikh found her and followed him blindly, but eventually they reached an echoing space where the murk gave way to light once more. Only then, when Katherine caught a glimpse of the sky through a vent of some kind far above her head, did she realize that a whole night had passed and it was morning again.

To one side were arches through which Katherine could see people coming and going, some dressed in the same dark uniforms she wore, others in what looked like medieval clothes of fine cloth but subdued colour.

Very few of these people looked their way, but when they did, sometimes inadvertently, they quickly turned their heads as if afraid of being seen even to look at one dressed in the Fyrd uniform.

Katherine was now so tired she no longer felt anything but a desire to sleep.

Meyor Feld appeared, looking very relieved. He said nothing about her running off at all, but instead told her she looked tired and he knew just the people to look after her. He knocked on a door in which a metal grille was set at chest-height. It snapped open immediately and two suspicious eyes peered out. There was a hurried whispered conversation before the grille snapped shut again.

A few moments later it opened once more and Katherine was hauled to her feet.

Her protests and questions were ignored.

The door opened, a hand came out of the darkness within, grasped her arm and pulled her in.

She had no time to say anything before the door was slammed shut behind her and she found herself face to face with a woman dressed like a nun in white robes, her hair covered.

It was difficult to tell her age because her face was caked with white make-up and her lips painted red. But Katherine could see her eyes were wrinkled and bloodshot, and when she spoke that her teeth were yellow.

'Welcome, Sister Katherine,' she said, her smile quite warm.

'Who are you? Where am I and what . . . ?'

'One thing at a time, child. I am Sister Supreme and you are safe now, very safe. We will do you no harm and with us you will learn how to lead a better, happier life . . .'

'But . . .'

'Follow me!'

Two similarly dressed younger women appeared behind her and, giggling and chattering in a friendly way, eased her forward. Katherine had no option but to do what they wanted and soon found herself passing through a series of spacious rooms whose air was light and held intoxicating scents of oils and perfumes, where exquisite females, with long thick dark hair and pale complexions, greeted her, one after the other. Some with handshakes, some with caresses to her arms and cheeks, some with kisses; all with smiles and laughter.

No sooner had she begun to think she was in some kind of dreamscape, from which no good could come, than someone gave her a gold flagon of a drink that smelt delicious.

She asked what it was.

'It is a harmless elixir such as our order has always made, most beneficial to mind and body,' Sister Supreme declared. 'Drink it, my dear and you will feel better.'

'I'd prefer water,' said Katherine cautiously.

'Of course, of course my dear . . . why not lie here in comfort while one of the sisters fetches some for you?'

The air swirled sleepily about her, its warmth inviting after the uncomfortable journey, and the cushiony, silky, shadowy bower they led her to was too tempting to refuse.

'Well . . .' she said, weakening, 'but I don't know who . . . or what you . . . ?'

Their hands were firm on her shoulders, their smiles winning, the laughter and strange music of the place easy on the ear and reassuring.

'Just for a moment then,' she heard herself say, her voice seeming almost harsh and rude in such a place, 'because I am tired and I . . .'

She sat down and gentle hands eased her back into plumped-up cushions which supported her back and shoulders while others were put ready for her neck and head.

'I don't want . . . I don't know . . .'

Across the room, through some arches, on a tray of gold, a crystal glass seeming to float on the air towards her, the hand that carried it, and the person whose hand it was, seeming much less important than the water itself, which sparkled with light so clearly that her thirst increased the moment she saw it.

When they put it to her lips it felt so wonderfully cool and refreshing she could not stop herself drinking.

'Who are you exactly?' she said, as they refilled her glass from the crystal ewer, the water tinkling slowly down and swirling around in the glass, hypnotic in its light and clarity.

They came closer, their red mouths smiling, their eyes sparkling, and the hair of each of them the same perfect shiny black. She noticed abstractedly that they wore identical wigs.

'We are the Sisters of Charity,' they said, 'and once you gain Lord Festoon's approval we're going to make you one of us.'

Katherine tried to protest, but she was so tired and the women so charmingly firm that she was lulled into thinking they couldn't possibly mean any harm. She did not want to go with them but for the time being the fight had gone out of her.

'Come on, my dear . . .' one of them said, and Katherine found herself half carried along until she was riding the wave of dreamless sleep.

60

RESURRECTION

Barklice led them northward, their destination a railway cutting near the obscure human village of Worton where, he explained vaguely, 'we'll pick up our transport for Brum'.

What this conveyance was he didn't explain and, given the general sense of despondency and unwillingness to talk, Jack did not ask.

Their route lay parallel with the River Thames, which meandered to their right across fields already waterlogged, between which the drainage dykes were filling almost before their eyes under the heavy and persistent rain.

The going got steadily more heavy and difficult, but since the area was prone to such regular flooding it was devoid of human habitation and therefore an ideal hydden route during the daylight hours.

Pike took up the rear with Jack, instructing him in the necessary skills of observation and lookout which that important position entailed.

'Keep a sharp eye either side, and ahead as well, since you'll get a different viewpoint than the leader, and you'll often spot things he does not. Watch behind you, too, for it is surprisingly easy for enemies to come upon you from behind before you know it.

'Woodland presents special problems, as do walled fields and high hedges, but you'll soon get a feel for it and develop a sense of what to do. It doesn't hurt to linger behind once in a while, but not for too long and preferably where you can still be easily seen and heard by those going in front.'

Once he saw that Jack was comfortable with this new responsibility, and as strong a walker as Barklice himself, he left Jack to it so that he might head up front and discuss with Brief several matters to do with their approach to Brum that same evening.

'It's a city liable to flooding,' he told Jack before he went, 'and what with all that's afoot there in the coming hours and days, we need to consider carefully how best to find Mistress Katherine and get her away to a place of safety.'

They did not stop until they reached the outskirts of Eynsham, and there picked up the green route presented by the track of the long-abandoned Witney and East Gloucestershire Railway.

There, fortified by an excellent ginger and blackcurrant cordial of Brief's making, and dried flesh of red perch that was Pike's speciality, they shared convivial reminiscences of Master Stort, his death now accepted, his memory already a source of pleasure and instruction.

'Of course, Stort was the master of old transport systems,' declared Barklice, his companions nodding their heads vigorously, for their late companion's expertise in that arcane field was well known. 'It is an incredible fact that he had committed to memory every main and branch line in Englalond, and their associated stations and halts, along with their current timetables – and, of course, that of 1908.'

'Are you serious?' asked Jack.

'Oh indeed it is true,' explained Brief. 'Memory was Stort's curse, as he himself put it. The poor fellow had only to glance at a page of print to know it for all time, however much he might try to dispel it from his mind. Due to an unfortunate accident three years ago, when he got stuck in a forgotten lift shaft in Brum, beneath New Street Station, he was able to tell you the times of any train from one station to another, and all the changes in-between, for the year 1908.'

'Why that year in particular?'

'Apparently the only object of any use in that lift shaft, apart from himself, was a Bradshaw Railway Gazette for that same year, which had somehow tumbled down it decades before he did. He memorized each and every page before he ate it.'

'He ate a timetable?' said Jack faintly.

'A very sensible thing,' said Brief, 'for it was his only form of sustenance. I believe he was rescued just before reaching the pages for North-West Scotland, an area far beyond the ken of any hydden I know, so that remains a regrettable gap in his knowledge.'

It was soon after they resumed their trek along the old railway track, and things were going easier, when Jack had his first sense that they were being followed. The rain had not eased at all and visibility was poor, the looming presence of Wytham Hill, beyond the Thames to their right, being shrouded in mist.

He told Pike what he suspected but his companion seemed unworried by this possibility.

'Probably the Fyrd,' Pike replied, 'just watching us. They want to be sure we're well on the way, and we want them to know as much, so they'll think we are taking you straight into the trap they have already set.'

This seemed reasonable enough, but Jack felt rather exposed at the rear and therefore apprehensive, remembering as he did those cold shadows in the henge at Woolstone, to which he had so nearly succumbed.

He decided therefore to try to spot them if he could. He lingered, he turned suddenly, he speeded up, or hid by a tree, but to no avail. They were certainly nearby, but too well camouflaged and quick for him to see.

Tired of this game, he began speeding his pace again to catch up the others. As he did so, he was astonished to hear someone call out his name from some scrubby bushes on his left-hand side.

'Jack!'

He peered into them, gripped his stave tightly and approached.

'Jack, my dear fellow, it's me, Stort. Over here!'

To Jack's amazement and delight, it was indeed their lost companion hiding there in shadows, his Harris tweed suit the perfect camouflage.

'But how did you . . . ?'

Stort ignored the question utterly, stayed where he was and, glancing nervously after the others, whispered, 'A drink, Jack, that's what I need.'

Jack handed him his water bottle.

Stort gulped its contents down.

'There's plenty of water around,' remarked Jack, 'I can't see why you're so thirsty.'

'I have made a close study of the lipper fly,' said Stort, 'whose hatchlings invade flood waters in conditions such as these. They are not pleasant parasites to have in one's gut. Now, got any brot?'

Jack produced some, which Stort stuffed rapidly into his mouth.

'I am tired and wan,' he said, offering no explanation as to what he was doing there, or how he'd got there, 'but excited all the same. Last night I had a miraculous epiphany, and I saw myself as part of the Universe. Today, as you might expect after such a vast experience, I feel a mite anticlimactic.'

'But they all think you're dead, Stort. You'd better now go and tell them you're alive.'

Stort retreated further into the bushes.

'No, no, they'll be cross with me, and I cannot bear it when Master Brief is angry with me. As for Mister Pike, I have let him down and his displeasure will become my misery.'

But it was too late.

The culprit had been spotted and the party came to a grinding halt, and then retraced its steps to where he hid.

'Is this wretched object really Stort?' growled Brief, his face turning a strange puce colour as of someone struggling with conflicting emotions of relief and irritation so extreme that words failed them.

'Master Brief,' cried out his protégé, hoping to mollify his mentor's mood, 'I have had a very interesting and enlightening experience which I may say . . .'

'*Stort, come here at once!*' thundered Pike, his eyes bulging, his mouth opening and shutting, his emotions so topsy-turvy that he seemed almost unable to move.

Stort emerged fully into the light of day.

'Yes, indeed, gentlemen,' he continued with false merriment, 'it was an experience worth the telling . . . I have discovered what it is to be human.'

But this near-revelation of his accidental discovery about how to use henges to travel between the hydden and human world and back again passed Brief and Pike by, so great was their anger at him. Seeing which, Barklice quickly intervened.

'Tell them later, Master Stort,' he advised in a whisper, winking at Jack, and stepping quickly between Stort and the other two, 'while I make a brew. Jack, give more of the cordial to Pike. It will soothe him.'

Stort could not at all understand the impact his disappearance had caused, and the raging emotions his reappearance invoked.

Ignoring the advice of Barklice, he persisted, 'My latest discoveries will indeed interest you all and . . .'

'You'll discover what it is to be really dead in a moment,' warned Barklice again. 'Right now, Master Stort, silence is golden.'

But he did not stop, for nervousness made him garrulous. He talked on, oblivious of the trouble and heartache he had caused them.

Yet, watching it all, Jack could not help noticing that not one of them held on to his anger for long. The most that was said was said by Brief, and that offered with all the conciseness of simple truth: 'Master Stort, you are one of the most irritating people I have ever met, and yet nothing could have made me happier this day than to have you among us once again!'

While Pike, his anger overwhelmed by his relief, and along with that a realization that something in him would have died had he never seen Stort again, went and stood by himself for a little, his back turned to them all, while he surreptitiously wiped a tear of relief from his eyes.

But it was Jack alone who understood that behind Stort's words lay an experience as yet unspoken.

'Master Stort,' he said, when they got on their way again, 'something important happened out there, didn't it? Something that you're not really mentioning?'

Stort fell silent for a while

'Something did happen,' he said eventually, gripping Jack's arm. 'I have inadvertently rediscovered the forgotten art and science of how our hydden and human forebears used the henges to travel between each other's worlds.'

Stort had wonder and excitement in his eyes, and Jack recognized the importance of this discovery, to himself especially, at once.

'How did you do it?'

'By going in the right direction with an open mind,' said Stort. 'That's the beginning and the end of it.'

'Which direction?'

'North-east one way, and back-to-front the other, that's half the trick you see! It's all illusion and reflection, but you know what the secret really is?'

Jack waited.

'It's never to try to go back to the past, or strive to get into the future before you're ready to. The henge is about the here and now, and about the passage from one form of it to another. Is that not most beautiful?'

'I think it might be,' said Jack, 'though I don't understand it exactly.'

'Understand? *Understand!?*' exclaimed Stort. 'My dear Jack, you don't have to *understand* to do it. Understanding doesn't help at all. It merely gets in the way.'

'But how can I do it if I don't understand?'

Stort came close. 'Have you ever been in love with a . . . you know, like . . . a *female*? That sort of thing?'

'I . . . I'm not sure. I think maybe I have. Well . . .'

Jack thought of Katherine and something unaccountable happened. His heart begun thumping, his mind whirling, his breathing became erratic and his brow felt clammy.

'In love?' he said vaguely.

'Well, have you?'

'I think maybe . . . maybe I have. I mean I *am* in love, I think.'

'You think but you don't know?'

'Yes. I mean no. No, I mean yes. I am . . . in love.'

'And do you *understand* how it happened?'

'No,' admitted Jack, coming to his senses again but feeling utterly different than he had before as, despite the rain, the mud, the tiredness and the weirdness of the new world he was in, everything seemed suddenly wonderful.

'I *am* in love,' he said, 'and I think she's in love with me.'

'Putting that to one side,' said Stort, who had no comprehension of the drama that had just taken place in Jack's heart, or mind, body and spirit, 'my point is that you do not need to understand the ineffable nature of love in order to experience it.'

'You don't have to understand it?' said Jack.

'Exactly. By the same token you do not need to understand how to use the henge to travel between the worlds. We just do it.'

'But how?'

'By stopping *trying* and by keeping an open heart and mind to the possibility.'

'Of what?'

'Of what we can become and who we really are,' Stort said simply.

Soon after this exchange, over which Jack continued to puzzle, they skirted around Worton, ducked under a fence and climbed down into the nearby railway cutting, where they readied themselves for what Barklice described as the most difficult part of the journey.

They retrieved some oily planks rather longer than themselves from a hidey-hole behind a small signal box, and then settled down very near the railway track.

'It is already dusk and, if my memory serves, this particular train arrives just after half past the hour. Correct, Stort?'

'Correct. Being a goods train, it is more likely to be on time.'

'But there's no station or halt here,' said Jack,

Barklice tapped his nose and winked.

'It's what we in the Hyddenworld with an interest in human transport systems call a Pausing Point. Other trains, unseen from here, must pass by on other lines, so this train pauses until the signal ahead, which will soon go red, goes green again. Upon such opportunities, and many others of different kinds, rests the vast edifice that is the network of hydden travel upon human rail tracks.'

'What's with the planks?' asked Jacks.

'Easier to show than tell,' said Pike. 'Eh, Master Brief?'

'But remember to be quick about it, for pausing trains are not patient trains and they'll cut your legs off if they can.'

The train was pretty much on time, the signal turning red before it appeared from the south and heaved to a halt right where they stood.

'How do we get aboard?' asked Jack, as they all got up and walked over the track towards the train whose wheels towered above them.

'We don't,' said Barklice. 'We travel underneath.'

'Underneath?' Jack eyed the narrow gap between the bottom of the train and railway track itself. 'Are you joking?'

'No, he's not,' said Pike, already crawling under the train. 'Show him how, Barklice.'

Jack followed the verderer beneath the train, crawling with some difficulty and discomfort over the stones, for in addition to his portersac and stave he was now encumbered by the board. The train itself vibrated ominously above their heads.

'About here,' said Barklice, stopping. 'Now, roll on to your back . . . for the train's creaking means it's about to move. Put your plank up . . . so . . .'

He put one end over a metal bar by his head and then, raising the other end of the plank, slid it back so that end was resting on yet another rod. There was a narrow gap between the plank and the wagon floor above.

'Now for the difficult bit . . .' said Barklice, grasping a metal fixture above his head, and heaving his portersac onto one end of the plank. 'Now we place a foot onto the plank and . . . we heave a bit and . . . we twist a bit . . . and with a final . . . pull . . . here we are. Now it's your turn.'

Barklice had disappeared into the oily, metal-bound shadows above, and was now resting safely on his plank.

The train creaked and shifted.

'You'd better get a move on, lad. The train's about to leave!' called Pike.

Jack got his plank in place with difficulty, then his portersac, which rolled off twice before he got it secured. Then grasping the rod, he tried to heave himself up into the grubby, metallic place above.

It was not easy.

The train creaked and rolled forward a foot or two, dragging the struggling Jack with it. Then it eased back again, pushing his back painfully into the track below.

'Watch your foot, lad!'

Jack had swung one leg onto the line. A huge wheel began rolling towards it.

'Hurry!' came Brief's urgent voice.

Jack got his foot in place on the plank, heaved himself up, twisted and rolled and was prevented from falling off the other side by the timely intervention of Pike's foot stretching over from his own plank. Then, secure at last, he found himself perched gasping on the plank, staring back down at the track which now began moving away beneath him.

'Time for a rest,' called out Barklice as the train gathered speed and the noise level increased. 'Keep yourself wedged in so you don't fall off if there's sway or jolt, and if you lie on your back put your portersac over your privates to protect them from . . .'

The noise level increased and Barklice's voice grew indistinct.

'From what?!' cried out Jack nervously.

'. . . the clinkers!' yelled Barklice. 'They can play havoc with your dingalongs!'

But more Jack could not discover, because the noise became too great to hear another word. All he could do was shift about to get comfortable, the best position in the end being on his back, place his portersac protectively on the lower half of his body and wonder how on earth anyone could hope to sleep in such a place and position. Yet Jack soon got used to the constant racket of train and track, till the rhythm and the warmth of his situation made him feel as if he was being rocked to sleep in a cot.

He closed his eyes and gave himself up to the next part of his journey.

61

HAIS

When Katherine finally awoke, it felt that a long time had passed, and that she was in serious trouble.

She had been moved into a small cell, its walls composed of rough grey concrete, with dim light filtering through a tiny grille set high up in one corner. She was lying on unvarnished wood set into a simple wooden frame, and her covering was merely a thin blue sheet. The room itself was warm, almost stifling, and the floor was bare concrete painted green, with a drain in the centre. A line of three thick pipes, each covered in a different colour of thermal insulation, snaked across the ceiling.

Her clothes had been replaced with a simple gown. There was a throbbing pain behind her eyes.

But when she put both her palms and all her fingers to her head to try to soothe away the pain, she discovered something that seemed far worse. Her hair had been cut short. She looked around for a mirror but there was none, nor even a window where she might see her reflection. She felt her hair again and it felt horrible, and she knew what she had known from the moment she arrived in Brum – that she had to escape from here and get away.

She lay where she was until her head began to clear. She guessed she had been somehow drugged the night before, which meant her instinct not to accept any drink except water had been basically right. She would not make that mistake again.

Katherine thought through all that had happened and how, when the shadows had finally encircled her in the henge, it was Jack she had first thought of. It was of him she thought now.

'I never told him what I felt about him, not really – not *really*.'

Where are you? she asked in the frightening silence of her mind. *What are you doing? Are you safe there in Woolstone? Tell me you didn't come after me to this horrible place, where they cut off your hair and you lose all sense of direction and nothing feels right. Tell me that, Jack.*

A tear coursed down her cheek.

I need you she admitted to herself. *I need you to ... to share this with to ... to make me laugh.*

More tears came.

Then Katherine heard the sound of people approaching her door, and she dabbed at her eyes and nose and sat up, listening. The door also had a grille at eye height, but it had a wood panel on the far side to shut it off. The people immediately outside were females, she could hear. They chatted and laughed and then went on by, without anyone trying to enter. A short while later they returned, and went back the way they had come.

She looked around the room and found a pair of leather shoes placed neatly under the bed. They had pointed, curly toes and gold-thread decorations, like something from a Middle Eastern bazaar. They fitted her perfectly, however.

She heard approaching voices again, and the clatter of footsteps heading downstairs, and she impulsively got up, went over to the grille and found she could easily tweak open the flap on the other side. She peered through into the corridor just outside in time to see the passers-by.

They were so close that she would not have made sense of them, but for seeing their like during the evening before. They were two women dressed in white gowns, with the same wigs of flowing black hair.

Behind them walked – almost ran – a girl with a yellow blouse and a skirt of flowing coloured silk, full and multi-layered. Her hair was real, however, beautifully coiffed, and pinned up with shining combs. The taller women preceding her gave the impression of being elegant but ill-tempered, while the one behind looked plump and cheerfully at ease.

Katherine was tempted to call out, but they had passed before that idea fully formed itself.

She idly turned the handle of the door. To her surprise it opened easily, so that she fell forward into the corridor beyond.

As she did so, she heard a cry followed by what sounded like two hard slaps being administered. Then an angry shout and a third slap followed by sobbing. Moments later came the sound of steps returning.

Katherine looked wildly to right and left, then decided it best to scurry quickly back into her cell, close the door and let them pass. She peered through the peephole in time to see passing the same two taller women as before. The girl with dark hair was not with them but Katherine could still hear sobbing, and guessed it came from her.

Then the steps stopped and began heading back again.

Katherine instinctively took her slippers off, put them neatly where they had been before, and dived back onto the bed, pulling the sheet over herself.

It was as well she did. The door opened suddenly, and someone entered. Katherine kept her eyes firmly closed but guessed that from her strong perfume, musky and soporific, it was one of the same women she'd just seen.

Some Sister of Charity! Katherine told herself, as the girl's sobbing continued down the corridor.

The second woman now joined the first, and they stood quietly while Katherine, eyes shut, tried to keep her breathing slow and regular.

'She's the lanky one who arrived last night,' remarked one voice.

'Horrible thick hair . . .' replied the other.

'. . . and a rough complexion, all red and raw.'

'She's been in the Upperworld I expect, working out in the sun. If that Bilgesnipe doesn't stop snivelling, I'll have to punish her again!'

'Shall we wake this one up?'

'Uh-uh, no point. She'll be useless and drowsy and I'm not going to waste time trying to revive her yet. Give her an hour or two, and then douse her with cold water. It works faster than anything else I know.'

'Look at those feet, so big and horrible.'

'She'll scrub up well enough. They all do in the end.'

'Should this door now stay unlocked?'

'We lock them up only if they're difficult. This girl's easy so far, and leaving their doors open gives them the feeling they've nothing to fear.'

'Well, they haven't, really. Not exactly.'

'No, not if they're sensible. They'd never get past the guards, and even if they got that far they'd be punished, so it's not worth it. And anyway . . .'

The door began to close.

Anyway what?

Katherine heard no more.

She sat up at once, not sure whether to feel frightened or furious.

Big feet, indeed.

She was only size seven.

Rough complexion?

Her Mum and Mrs Foale always said the opposite.

Lanky?

Well, all right, but she was fast filling out . . .

Katherine grinned suddenly, knowing how Jack would have laughed.

Bilgesnipe?

She wondered if they had been describing the girl she'd seen who had the same dark skin as Tirrikh.

Upperworld?

That took a moment's thought before she reckoned it must mean outside, in the real human world above them.

It was the last bit of their conversation that worried her most.

'Only if they're difficult. This girl's easy . . . the feeling they've nothing to fear . . . Well they haven't . . . *exactly* . . .'

Katherine didn't like the sound of any of it, at all.

The moment their footsteps had died away completely, she got up again to open the door, and immediately turned in the opposite direction to the one the two Sisters seemed to have taken.

The corridor was about thirty feet long, with doors just like hers, which also had peepholes. All but one were dark. She peered inside that one and saw a girl asleep on a bed, as she herself had been until a few minutes ago.

She moved on further and reached a T-junction. The corridor leading off to the right was dark, that to the left was lit up. She turned left towards the light.

The dark-haired girl was in a side-room, folding clothes and straightening boxes on the many shelves. It smelt good, like a laundry but without steam or irons.

The moment Katherine reached the door, she turned around. The moment she saw it was Katherine she looked relieved.

'I didn't hear you,' she said. Her voice was softly accented.

'What is this place?' asked Katherine.

'It's a house of the Sisters of Charity.'

'Who are they?'

'They do good works. You'll soon become one of them.' There was a sense of pity in the way she said that, and there was defiance too.

'Why were you crying?'

'Sister Chalice hit me – like she always does. She's horrible.'

Katherine could believe it. Chalice was obviously the tall one with the sharp voice.

Katherine fired questions ever more rapidly. She was now afraid the Sisters would come back and she wanted to find out as much as she could before they returned.

'Are you what they call a Bilgesnipe?'

The girl hesitated, her eyes showing a kind of hurt.

'I am,' she said, looking down, as if ashamed.

All Katherine could see was that she was beautiful, her dark eyes subtly made up, her mouth full, her skin dark and smooth, her bust full, the cleavage showing above a silk blouse. The dark jacket she had been wearing was folded neatly over a box nearby.

'Meaning?' said Katherine.

The girl looked puzzled, and repeated again, 'We're a different race and they despise us.'

There were centuries of exile, rejection and isolation in that word.

Somewhere Katherine heard footsteps but they didn't come nearer.

'What does that word mean exactly?'

'They don't like us. We're different. We live by rivers and canals. They think we're dirty, that our skin is dark because of the filth of things there.'

Katherine look astonished, so much so that the girl grinned.

'We're not really,' she ventured.

'They claimed my skin was rough and raw,' said Katherine.

The girl came nearer, instinctively wishing to reassure her.

'It's not. It's lovely but . . .'

'But what?'

'They'll ruin it and make you look old and pale. Then you'll have to always wear powder, until they're caking it on.'

'I'm called Katherine.'

The girl said nothing.

'What your name?'

Again a hesitation, then: 'Number eleven.'

Katherine gaped. 'That's not a name, it's a number. What's your real name?'

'Hais.'

Footsteps again, somewhere above them.

'So why did they hit you, Hais?'

'Because I said I think all this rain means there's going to be flooding, and so I need to get back to Deritend while I can. I'm to be Bride for the Day, and that only happens once in a lifetime!'

'What's "Bride for the Day"?'

'Most areas and a lot of streets in Brum celebrate the High Ealdor's birthday tomorrow. The Deritend celebration is the most famous apart from the High Ealdor's party itself, but it's only people from the rich families in New Brum who get invited to that! And unusual visitors like you. In Deritend what happens is that the Bride finds her groom and gets trothed . . .'

'You mean you go round the streets looking for someone to marry?'

Hais laughed.

'No, we fix it so that the Bride gets the right groom. In my case it's a boy I've known all my life, and so it's a public way of saying we're likely to get wed.'

'Sounds great,' said Katherine.

'Yes, I suppose it is,' replied Hais rather soberly.

Katherine picked up what she was thinking at once.

'You mean you like the idea of being the Bride but the boy concerned isn't the right one?'

'I suppose so.'

'Do you have to marry him?'

'No, but done this way and with the Deritend families involved it will be a bit harder to get out of! It would be fine if the choice was made by me, but unfortunately it's decided with the Cunning Knot.'

Katherine looked puzzled.

'It's the Bilgesnipe way of deciding certain things where emotions get in the way of reason, to quote my father. I think it's a lot of nonsense but you know what older people are like. They believe these superstitions!'

But Katherine was thinking of something Hais said earlier which struck too close to home for comfort. Her friend Sam had always said Katherine let her mind rule her emotions. She wished she'd been more honest with Jack about what she really felt for him while she still had the chance.

'I don't understand why the Sisters are angry with you,' said Katherine.

'It's not about me going to the celebration in Deritend. Sister Chalice is just being mean about it because she's jealous I've been chosen to be Bride for the Day, which *she* was never chosen to be! They know I have to go because they know my father, his brothers and our extended family, which means half of Deritend, would come and get me and drag me down there! The revolution some of our people talk about would finally happen and all because of me!'

She laughed again and it was infectious, because Katherine laughed too and felt better than she had in days.

Hais got serious.

'But you shouldn't be here. You must go back to your room before they find you're missing.'

Katherine shook her head. 'I'm trying to get away, not go back.'

The footsteps sounded louder again, and this time they heard voices too. Katherine could hear the unpleasant laughter of Sister Chalice, and Hais's eyes widened in fear.

'They're still upstairs but she'll be coming down soon.'

'Is there any way out of here?' asked Katherine urgently.

Hais shook her head. 'Not without going past the guards, and you don't look at all like a Sister of Charity. You look too much of a mess.'

Katherine giggled, not offended. 'What will they do to me?'

'Make you into a Sister, so you can serve him.'

'Serve who exactly?'

'The High Ealdor, of course.'

'Who's he?'

'He's like . . . in charge of things, I think. His Bride of the Day will be chosen tomorrow too, so be warned. It might be you!'

'What's he like? Very old? Wise? Cruel? His title makes him sound he might be one of those things.'

'I've never met him but they say he's large, very.'

'I like tall men,' said Katherine playfully.

'I didn't say tall, I said large. But I mean he's fat. Very. You had better go before they come . . . If you run and they catch you, they'll probably give you over to the Sub-Quentor for punishment. Not recommended!'

The sound of the footsteps sharpened and now became metallic. Someone was descending some metal stairs.

'Will you help me get away?'

Hais shook her head. 'If I do and they find out, I most certainly won't get back to Deritend in time for my big day.' There was fear in her voice now. 'You've got to go. If they even think I've been talking to you . . .'

The footsteps got louder and nearer.

'Run, Sister Katherine!' said Hais desperately. 'Run back to your room!'

Katherine did, reaching the door to her cell just in time to slip back through it, put the shoes back where they were and dive onto the bed.

She did not have to pretend to be asleep for long. In moments the long hours of her journey and the changes during it caught up with her once more and she slept again.

62

AT THE WEST GATE

The clinkers were advancing horribly over Jack's body down from his head and up from his feet and he realized that, if he did not break free of the paralysis that had gripped him, they would soon reach his privates, and then . . . then . . .

'No!'

He woke up, regained movement and brushing them off his body he sat up and – bang! – fell back on to his plank again.

'Jack, wake up! We're here now!'

It was Barklice tugging at one end and Pike at the other, trying to get him to roll off the plank.

'I thought the clinkers were getting me,' he muttered, reality breaking in.

They laughed. 'Hurry, the train only waits here a minute or two.'

Sleepily Jack did as he was told, his head feeling thick and his body stiff. He pushed his portersac and stave down onto the track below and followed them.

'Bring your plank as well,' called Barklice. 'It must be stored ready for someone else to use.'

He found Brief and Pike standing together in the convenient shelter of a huge, empty, wooden cable reel which lay on its side beside the track. The rain thundered down all around them.

'Let's have the planks then,' said Barklice who, without any complaint about getting himself even wetter, took them one by one and secreted them under some concrete slabs nearby. He then wandered off to see how things were looking beyond the track.

'You'll know where they are hidden by the broken ragwort and rosebay willow herb,' explained Pike, 'should you have need of them in the future. That's our tradition. Failing which, shove 'em anywhere convenient but use your common sense!'

'The planks you mean?'

'That's right, so other travellers can find and use 'em. I take it you do know what ragwort looks like?'

Jack nodded, and the willow herb too. He had identified both with Katherine, during some stage of their wanderings.

His head was now clearing. 'Where are we exactly?'

'On the approach to Brum's West Gate. It's only three hundred yards further along the track, down the embankment and on the right-hand side,' said Pike. 'But, of course, we can't just stroll up and ask the Fyrd to let us in. We may well have to find some other way, but that's Barklice's job.'

Jack peered along the track towards the city and then through the tall metal fence separating it from a road below. Heavy traffic was sloshing along, with headlights switched on early, windscreen wipers struggling furiously. Over the right-hand side he could see a water course, the water risen so high it was lapping at the edges, the wind catching the wavelets and turning them to spray.

Barklice now rejoined them, his cloak streaming wet.

'The river's very high, but it's not backing up yet. If the weather's been like this all day, then the Bilgesnipe are doing a good job controlling it. But getting into the city unseen with Jack was never going to be easy, gentlemen, which is why I arranged for some back-up before we left.'

Brief, a bit too tall for the sheltered space they were huddling under, stood leaning forward on his stave and seemed preoccupied. The others said nothing either, while they waited for him to speak. Stort had sat down and, having slipped a green plastic shopping bag over each of his feet, was securing them tightly with string just below the knees.

There was, Jack was beginning to realize, an old-world courtesy about them all – evident in the way that, having sensed that Brief was about to say something important, they let him do so in his own time; and also in the easy acceptance they showed for Stort and his eccentricities.

'Who are these Bilgesnipe, Mister Stort?' whispered Jack, squatting down beside him.

'"Stort" will do, so drop the honorific. They're water folk primarily. They live and breathe water, and keep Brum working at times like this when flooding becomes a danger. Be warned, Jack, they're very inventive but inclined to passion, and they sing a lot, which can sometimes be annoying. But don't ever accept the help of such hovellers if you're not ready to pay in cash or kind for their services.'

Just then, Brief finally spoke.

'Gentlemen, I suggest we go carefully from now on. Clearly the city will be flooding, but there may be greater danger than that – to ourselves in particular and therefore to our mission.' He spoke slowly and cautiously.

'What aren't you telling us, Master Brief?' said Barklice.

Brief's face still gave nothing away. 'I have an inkling that things – great things – may be afoot in Brum today. It may be wiser that I say no more than that for now. However, let us observe the gate and see what we can deduce about the state of things within, from there. It may be, Mister Barklice, that we will need your special knowledge of the routes into Deritend.'

They moved off cautiously, keeping to the shadows under the wall that edged the embankment on its watery side.

Jack, fully recovered from his bone-rattling rail journey, felt good in himself and excited too. He was nearer to finding Katherine now, and more comfortable in this new world in which he found himself.

Despite the remorseless rain and the lash of water all about, he was glad to be back within a city. Its sounds were those same ones he had grown up with, and familiar too were its broken shapes and silhouettes in the murky afternoon, its chiaroscuro of light and shadow, its very smell, its ordered chaos, its busyness, its sheer life.

He felt alive and strong and ready for anything.

'We cross the track here,' Pike turned to him, pointing at a run of shadow from a tall building which loomed over the track. 'Go one at a time . . . and be very alert on the other side. This is a favourite spot for Fyrd to try to catch us out.'

'Not on a night like this,' said Barklice with confidence.

They crossed the line and were soon at a vantage point that allowed them to easily survey the West Gate, though at first Jack could not see what they meant by that. Eventually he worked out that what they were all focusing on was a rectangular hole in a wall halfway down the embankment towards the river. It was blocked off by a gate but, as his eyes grew used to the dark, he could see dim lights moving back and forth there.

Pike produced a bulky monocular from his pack and examined the scene carefully.

Barklice was doing the same, using his circled hands as if they were binoculars.

'Try it, Jack,' he murmured.

Jack did and it worked, cutting out ambient light and drawing the eye to the scene they needed to focus on.

Pike took his time and eventually said, 'Something's up, eh, Barklice? Something's definitely not right. There's no guards on the gates and they're . . . damn me if they're not ajar! There's even folk coming out!'

It was true.

There were people emerging through the great gates, some carrying bundles, a couple holding their children's hands, hurrying down through the undergrowth to the river's edge where they became impossible to see, it being so dark.

'Eight o'clock left!' said Barklice grimly. 'By the guard door . . .'

Jack spotted it at once: someone lying face down on the ground.

'It's a guard! And there's another one at two o'clock. Got it?'

Pike sat back and lowered his monocular. 'The revolution's started and I've missed it!' he said.

'You've missed very little, Mister Pike,' Brief murmured, 'since what's going on here began less than an hour ago.'

Barklice pulled back into the shadows and silently led them closer. The open gate and the motionless bodies were now easy to see, but for the moment there was no one else in sight.

'You were saying, Master Brief?' said Pike in a low voice.

'I wasn't going to say anything yet, but now I see I need to. This is not a revolution that you're witnessing,' said Brief slowly, 'it's an insurrection. Which is to say a revolt against the Fyrd from within their ranks.'

'Led by who?' asked Pike.

'I have no idea,' said Brief unconvincingly.

'Against who?'

'That I do not know either.' He was plainly lying.

'Who is your informant?'

'I cannot say – yet.'

Pike looked furious. 'And I am meant to be your chief staverman.' he said ironically.

'Mister Pike,' said Brief carefully, 'I was told of the possibility of this happening on condition I revealed it to no one, and only because the person who informed me was aware all this might happen before we got back from our mission. In which case we might be walking blind, as it were, into a very dangerous and unsettled situation. We could not have known in advance that Mistress Katherine would be abducted and brought here. What we do know is that powerful wyrd is abroad that affects all of us, and that these two young strangers are now in our care – and in Brum's too.'

He brought his great stave of office diagonally across his chest, and held it there with both hands. It seemed to Jack that it glimmered in the half-light of this rainy afternoon.

'This is not *your* fight, Jack,' Brief went on, laying a hand on his shoulder, 'nor is it your dear friend's. But, with each moment that has passed since I met you and we began our journey here, I have become more and more convinced that your joint mission is to fulfil that ancient prophecy from Beornamund's time and, in some way as yet unknown, to find the Shield Maiden and deliver to her the gem of Spring. How Brum is involved, or this present trouble, or even ourselves, or this ceaseless strange rain, I know not!'

He turned then to Pike, who had calmed down a little. 'As for this insurrection I know only that no citizen of Brum is better placed in terms of experience, or knowledge of the city, and the trust others place in him, than yourself, Mister Pike, to see to matters of fighting and the like as they affect the good of our community.

'What I also know is that the experience of history, on which I myself can speak with some authority, shows that nothing is predict-able and much now depends upon our individual and collective strength. We must act right, trust in each other, recognize our true friends, know our real enemies, and then hope that courage, common sense and determination will see us through.'

'Aye,' said Pike, mollified, 'I'll second that. And there's something else which history tells us, and even if I'm not much of a reader, I know it's true. Fights and battles, like wars, are rarely over quickly. What's happening here in Brum today may take weeks, months or years to reach a conclusion, eh, Master Brief?'

'It may, Master Pike. It may.'

'But you still won't tell us the name of your informant, Master Brief?' prompted Barklice. Like Pike, he did not appreciate being excluded from such secrets.

'I will only tell you this. The person who gave me this information is cleverer than any of us in some respects, and when the time comes he will need our support to see him through. Now, Barklice, how are we going to get Jack and ourselves into Brum without running into trouble with the Fyrd?'

'Deritend's the place to go,' said Barklice, 'and unfortunately there's only one way to get there quickly and still avoid the Fyrd.'

He looked at the surging canal. 'All we need is the professional services of one of the Mallarkhi, the Bilgesnipe family that covers this side of Brum.'

'You are having me on, Mister Barklice,' said Pike, shaking his head. 'You can see from here that the canal's dodgy in this wind and rain. Once we turn off it into one of the sewers that lead to Deritend, you can start searching for our bodies, for we'll never come out alive.'

Barklice ignored him and clambered down the embankment. They worked their way through a metal fence, repaired with barbed wire, and crossed carefully through rough and muddy ground to the canal's edge.

Here they found a small huddle of shivering folk taking shelter among dripping bushes. Pike called a greeting, and several peered at them from the shadows, staves ready in some hands, dirks in other. Then one ventured nearer, had a good look at them, and turned to cry out to the others, 'It's Master Brief himself. And Mister Pike with him! Mercy be, but we're saved at last!'

Others came running from the damp shadows and soon a gaggle of hydden, clutching their possessions and children, had gathered around them hopefully. Some nursed injuries, while a few seemed too infirm to be still on their feet.

To Jack they looked poor and downtrodden. The light of the hope that kindled in their eye on seeing Master Brief was the brightest thing about them.

'Please lead us away from the city to safety!' one implored. Others began to weep and wail.

Brief calmed them sufficiently to ask what had happened.

'Nobody rightly knows,' one of them replied. 'We got word the Fyrd were coming to seal the gate, and that set up a panic and there was fighting when Fyrd actually arrived. We're the lucky ones because we live near the gate and were able to get out . . . Please, it's not safe for you to go into Brum, so stay with us, for nobody would dare harm you.'

Pike inquired, 'You actually heard they were going to *seal the gate*?'

'Everyone was running and shouting . . .'

'It does sound like there's a sealing order,' said Pike grimly, 'and you know what that means! It means blocking off certain of the tunnels, which will cause flooding and likely deaths as well if places can't be evacuated. Work to do, Master Brief! We can't dawdle here.'

Brief turned to the group of refugees and said, 'My friends here and I have urgent business in Brum, but the safest place for you people to go is up-canal, not back down it with us. Lie low a few days and Pike here will send word up Northfield way to tell you when it's safe to return. Good luck, my friends, but we must go now.'

'You're never venturing into the sewers, Master Brief?!' insisted one of them, alarm rising in his voice. 'The level's so high on the canal itself that you'll not get safely through into them. And if there's backing up from the river to the east, you're all going to be drowned!'

'We must try,' said Brief calmly.

They left the refugees to the mercy of the elements, and pushed on through towards the canal. They heard its uneasy, angry sucking sound before they finally saw it on the verge of breaking over its banks.

'Barklice,' growled Pike, 'this does not feel good. Anyway, who's going to be acting ferryman on a night like this?'

'Old Mallarkhi is a personal friend of mine, and very reliable. As I said before, I left him clear instructions that I would be needing transport this afternoon, and he's never let me down, just as I have never let *him* down!'

Barklice let out a soft call, like that of a female coot in season.

No response.

He tried again, a little louder.

Again no response.

'Just as well,' said Pike with relief. 'We'll now have to walk it, which is going to be a lot safer.'

There was a further horrible sucking sound from the canal below.

'She's regurgitating,' said Barklice in a low voice, 'and that means we'll just have to wait but be ready. Our boat'll be along once she spits back down. Be ready one and all, be ready, for the boat won't be able to linger on a backing river!'

The canal sucked yet again, like water going down a vast plughole, and dragging everything in its wake.

'Barklice, are you really sure this is a good idea?' It was Brief expressing doubts this time.

'Am I still alive after all these years of journeying, Master Brief?' cried out Barklice, annoyed at being doubted. 'Clearly, I am. Have we got back to Brum in good time? We have indeed. Do I try and do your job, Master Brief, or yours, Mister Pike? I do not! So, yes, I think it's a good idea. Therefore you shall now sit and you shall wait, and you shall trust in my ability to get you where you wish to go in one piece, just as I shall trust in your common sense and co-operation in the final stage of our journey to Deritend – which will not be easy, and certainly involves risks, but is not helped one bit by your moaning, groaning and constant doubts. Do I make myself clear?'

With that, Barklice sat down with his back to them, and everyone else sat down too, suitably chastened and daring to complain no more.

BRUM

63

OLD AND NEW

The hydden city of Brum lay just below the centre of modern Birmingham, whose human inhabitants went about their business in ignorance of the fact that one of the most historic cities in the Hyddenworld existed right under their noses.

Some parts of Brum were actually in the open air, visible to any human who cared to look, though not without great difficulty. These places were buried away in shadows, cut off by the projections and overhangs of buildings, or located around nearly inaccessible corners.

However, the main parts of the hydden city – its accommodation and religious institutions, its places of business, its residential areas and its places of delight and leisure – lay underground and out of sight.

That is not to say that the hydden did not make use of the human part of Birmingham – or the Upperworld.

During the day there were many parts of Birmingham – the lower half of the River Rea, for example, which runs largely unnoticed right through the city, abandoned canals and old rail tracks, also many of the interstices between the motorways, factories and tower blocks – that were safely accessible to those hydden who knew the routes. At night the opportunities were greater still, and included the roofs and sills of most of the buildings in the city centre and the shadowed parts of many streets and pavements.

In short, Brum and often The Upperworld were as busy with hydden as any metropolis in the mortal world.

The hydden city proper was divided into two parts, Old and New.

The older part dated back to Beornamund's time and lived out its busy, murky, semi-secret life in the dank places that lie below and either side of the bridge that was the first medieval crossing of the River Rea. Here, in the north-west corner of Europe, developed one of the greatest pilgrim cities of the Hyddenworld. Drawn by the legends of Beornamund were seekers after truth, journeyers in search of peace, personal wisdom and – let it be honestly said – drawn in the hope that *they* would be the ones to find the secret of the lost gem, which was Spring. They came in their thousands like bees to a spiritual honeypot and the Brummers were not slow to satisfy their need.

Immediately on its west side rises Digbeth, where rich hydden traders once made their residences under the shadow of human ones, enjoying the ample space, fresh air and views across the city which are now lost beneath the inexorable vertical rise of the human city.

To the east of the bridge lies Deritend. Down there, in among the sewers and conduits which constantly discharge their contents into the Rea, poor folk with nowhere better to go eke out an unhealthy living.

A hundred and fifty years ago this simple pattern of the centuries changed for ever with the coming of the railways and the building of several passenger and goods termini, and associated building, to the north and east of Old Brum.

The deep, crypt-like footings, or underwalls, of these great new structures formed the necessary base for what was built on top. Once built, they were often soon buried and blocked off to further access by humans.

However, for the enterprising hydden of nearby Digbeth, these brand-new, partially underground structures offered an open invitation to take up residence.

Set among new canals and railway lines, culverted streams, sewers and conduits, these offices and homes (or 'humbles' as the hydden called them) formed the foundations for New Brum. In fact, this adoption of railway systems as the basis for new hydden enterprise and cities occurred simultaneously in all the great metropolitan railway centres at that time – not just in Englalond but across Europe too.

But in Brum – New and Old included – something extraordinary then happened.

While the economies and societies of the Hyddenworld were transformed within a few decades, and with them the basis of global power, the essentials of Brum's spirit of independence and creative originality remained the same. It was a bastion of free thinking, of rude licence, of subversive humour, with a rich cosmopolitan culture unlike any other in the Hyddenworld. Though occupied by the Fyrd for many decades before the coming of Jack and Katherine to the city, it remained free of most of the stricter Fyrd observances and laws, a place in which thinkers, artists and the like could do their work with little fear of reprisal or repression.

The reason for this was entirely the result of a whim of Slaeke Sinistral I, founding father of the Fyrd, and himself born in Brum. He stated more than once that it was his wish that Brum should remain free of all censorship and petty rules until, as he put it, 'my Winter's End'. This was taken to mean until his death.

However since Slaeke Sinistral's final act, before disappearing for ever from public view, was to declare himself immortal, the Fyrd hierarchy, whose headquarters were in the Rhenish lands of Germany, could not suppress Brum's unique freedoms without calling into question the godlike status of their own founder.

In practice what this meant was that real power in Brum was vested in the hands of an unobtrusive Fyrd executive, routinely appointed from Germany, whilst titular authority remained with the city's High Ealdor, always chosen from one of the remaining five of Brum's great families – the Gopsals, the Deans, the Warwicks, the Briefs and the Avons – whose members, households and employees were readily distinguishable by the different colours and patterns of their liveries. The sixth of these families had been the Sinistral but they had decamped across the North Sea in the wake of Slaeke Sinistral I's establishment of his stronghold in the Rhineland.

The Fyrd in charge of things when Katherine and Jack arrived in Brum was General Elon, a veteran of the Empire who regarded his posting to the easy position of administrator of Brum as just reward for his many years in the service of the Sinistrals throughout the Hyddenworld.

The High Ealdor of the time was Lord Festoon, unmarried last scion of the once-great Avon family, lover of food and exotic entertainment, who had no interest in politics or his own succession, which made him an ideal puppet of the Fyrd.

As it happened, there were a few hydden in Brum who still bore the name Sinistral, but this was a very minor branch of the Imperial dynasty and was now tolerated more from sentiment than any notion that it had hereditary right to power or respect in Brum.

The consequence of this strange history was that, although New Brum was well placed to exploit the myriad opportunities offered by the burgeoning Upperworld of humans, its riches were invested in what might be called cultural pursuits, while its innovations in all else – and there were many, especially in industry, finance, and the sciences – were routinely exported to Germany or otherwise placed under Sinistral control.

The city thus became a magnet for the oppressed, the artistic and the disaffected which, cynics said, was exactly the Sinistrals' intention. It meant that they had in one place, and under their control, many of their most outspoken critics and enemies while still being able to pay lip-service to freedom.

But while New Brum became a vibrant youthful city throughout the nineteenth century, renowned for its cosmopolitan culture in the twentieth, what happened in Old Brum was very different.

There only the poor, the exploited, the diseased and the criminal elements remained, and that already decayed area went into deep decline with the coming of the railways, its people becoming no more than sad providers of labour for their better-off neighbours.

Poverty and lack of education breed an indifference to the past. The medieval libraries, the public altars and private temples that grew from Beornamund's foundation, the graceful art and architecture of old times, the nooks and crannies which had been hives of hydden craft and in which so much had been created and achieved, gradually fell to rack and ruin.

Soon many such places, some holy, a few truly historic, but all of interest to the antiquary who loves such things, were raided for their artefacts and materials – or bricked up, sidelined, and forgotten.

Yet not quite all.

History is the story of great trends swayed by unforeseen events. It is full of ironies, twists of wyrd, and of strange and unpredictable confluences which produce things new and turn former cul de-sacs into lively new thoroughfares.

Old Brum – and in some respects the human city of Birmingham – was saved by just such an eddy in the stream of history.

For this filthy, watery, labyrinthine place, fifteen feet or more below the surface of the human city, had always been the natural home of the Bilgesnipe: a nomadic hydden folk of a Middle Eastern ethnicity whose natural element is not dry land but water. On which and with which they thrive.

Their homes were abandoned hulks and barges of one kind or another, or areas of cleverly constructed waste material, which to humans look like nothing more than flotsam thrown up by the ever-flowing waters of river, stream, canal or sewer.

These tough but good-humoured folk are fiercely protective of their culture, which came originally from Araby along with their trader ancestors and then spread, over long centuries, throughout the Western world and beyond, reaching to anywhere there were commodities to trade and money to be made on the turn, out of one transaction or many.

The Bilgesnipe have a way of life famously rich in music that is strange and sublime to other ears, and their folk costumes are colourful, often made of silk and satin; a culture perfumed by scents that seduce the mind and body, in which all is intertwined with philosophies deep and marvellous, theories extraordinary, sciences forgotten, poetry elusive, and it is also one protected by martial arts more spiritual than physical, which are therefore cunning, secret, fearsome and most deadly.

It is unfortunately the case that other ethnic groups have always feared and despised the Bilgesnipe, so that in all areas of the Hyddenworld – including Old Brum's Deritend and Digbeth districts – they were frequently ghettoized, and sometimes violently suppressed.

In consequence of such prejudice, their numbers became few and their living precarious, depending as they did on that one special occupation which no other ethnic group had the skills or traditions to take up: the control and safe evacuation of water, be it clean or dirty, sweet-smelling or fetid.

So it was that Brummies, Old and New, had always tolerated a few Bilgesnipe to live among them as water-folk, cleaners of sewers, repairers of conduits and drains, checkers of locks, engineers of ebb and flow, and expert predictors of spring flood and summer drought.

Then, several decades ago, one of history's great tidal eddies came into play and, as it were, washed up on to the shore of liberty-loving Englalond a wave of migrant Bilgesnipe seeking sanctuary from an assault, right across the greater world, upon their culture, their supposed wealth and their very persons.

This occurred in the wake of the expansive imperialism of the Sinistral's Fyrd armies. The irony was that one of the few urban places where any migrant could find permanent sanctuary was Brum, particularly Old Brum, because of the freedoms still allowed there.

The arrival of a wave of Bilgesnipe immigrants through the first part of the twentieth century may have brought with it many pathetic sights of poverty and stories of tragedy but, in the longer term, the timing could not have been better.

For over these same decades the humans had added to the city's waterways of stream and river, notably the Rea, many canals, and a vast increasing of the culverts and pipes needed to carry water to the city and its manufactories, and also away from it.

The ancient skills of the Bilgesnipe were needed in Brum to control the effects of this perceived human development. At the same time, changes in climate and local weather began to bring to Brum, as to so many places in the world, different patterns of rainfall. The Bilgesnipe came to the right place at just the right time, and from being a tiny, despised minority in Old Brum they became a much-needed group who in Deritend were soon even a majority.

Their skills, their habit of cleanliness, and their cultural sophistication brought a new renaissance to an area of Brum that had fallen into decline, though largely unseen or recognized by the rich hydden and their Fyrd masters in New Brum.

Out of gratitude for their salvation, and to make the place safer and more healthy for their families, they put to rights the watery wrongs that indifferent humans had committed, and which the few Bilgesnipe already in residence had so far been unable to rectify.

They made the city safe again, reduced flooding to a minimum, and made a life for themselves where no one noticed them – which they much preferred.

Along with this came a new will, unusual among an immigrant people, to preserve Old Brum's masterful heritage, which in the years of decline had so nearly been destroyed. The very ethnic group so long despised in Old Brum thus became its conservators and experts, investing their time and money not in empty displays of wealth, as their hydden neighbours in New Brum did, but in secret collections of artefacts, in museums barely known, and above all in the library, that great and extraordinary library, in charge of which they appointed not one of their kind, as the hydden might have done, but the scrivener who by common consent was most suited to that task of collection, conservation and scholarship – namely Master Brief, a member of one of the oldest of the hydden families of Brum.

To him the Bilgesnipe gave continuing support, both moral and financial, and in him they invested their trust and therefore – it may be said – their love of free scholarship. Through them, as well, because of the bursaries and funding they allowed him as the most promising of Brief's protégés, Master Bedwyn Stort found support and sanctuary which, without their presence and their great culture, it is highly unlikely someone as eccentric as him, and so errant in his ways, would ever have enjoyed.

Such was Old Brum.

But there was something more, and it concerned the city both old and new.

For, in more recent years, another of history's eddies had brought two individuals together in Brum who believed they had a part to play in the future of the city and in the fulfilment of the Beornamund prophecy concerning the lost gem of Spring. The bloodline and heritage of one was rich and cultured, of the other lowly, brutish and obscure. But though they were chalk-and-cheese different from each other, they shared an ambition that had its oldest roots in the legend of Beornamund, and its newest in the car accident which ten years ago had devastated the Shore family and nearly killed Jack himself.

For each was obsessed with the idea of finding the lost part of the great CraftLord's Sphere, which was also one of its most important, that exquisite gem that was said to hold all the colours of the Spring and which they believed lay waiting to be found even now, some fifteen hundred years later, somewhere within Brum's bounds.

The first of these individuals was Lord Festoon, High Ealdor of Brum, and in a titular sense its first citizen. He saw the gem as a heritage to protect and to honour.

The second was Igor Brunte, a Fyrd who had risen through the ranks much slower than he would have wished since the day of the Shore vehicle accident, when he had murdered Brum's Quentor-elect and another Fyrd so that he might keep to himself the secret of the Peace-Weaver's appearance that day, and any knowledge that the boy called Jack had survived the crash.

For Igor knew that this was no human child but a giant sought by the Sinistral himself, who suspected that in his wyrd, or destiny, lay the power to reconstruct Beornamund's Sphere and thus hold sway over the future of both the Earth and the Universe. It was power Brunte dreamed of gaining for himself.

Those same days and nights of rain when Katherine was being brought to Brum against her will, and Jack was setting forth to save her in the company of new friends, these two dreamers of the legacy of Beornamund were plotting change – great change indeed, and plotting it together.

64

LORD FESTOON

There are times when even the sturdy, enterprising folk of New Brum, so widely known and respected for their commercial enterprise, creative endeavour and spirit of freedom, can look morose and glum. For if there is one thing that discomfits them more than any other it is rain, and the rain that had been falling on the city for the past fourteen hours, and looked set to continue for many hours yet, had that inexorable quality that usually leads to flooding. Every surface was streaming with water, every drain roaring, every tiny stream emptying into the Rea itself soon turning into a gushing river and then into a rout.

Look upwards and it lashed down into eyes, nose and mouth; look down and it trickled coldly down the back of one's neck; tread incautiously in deep puddles and at once shoes and boots would fill with icy water. While the Bilgesnipe might now be in their element, all were aware that on such a day even they would have their work cut out to keep the waters flowing and the floods at bay.

For good reason, too. Few cities have so many canals as Brum, and though the city's River Rea is not particularly sizeable in breadth or length, it adds considerably to the problem. When heavy rains descend, it fills up so rapidly that, without the culverts humans have built to transport it secretly beneath their feet through the heart of the city, it would break its banks and overwhelm the nearby houses, factories and roads on either side of it.

In normal conditions that system is effective. But the capacity of the Rea and its artificial conduit is limited, and sometimes it overfills to become a hazard, not an aid to rapid drainage. Instead of the waters flowing naturally downhill towards north and east, or sideways into the streams that feed it, they begin to back up and reverse for, unable to continue forward or sideways, they try to go back the way they have come.

As the hours progressed from dawn into mid-morning that day worried citizens watched the levels rise with growing concern. Levels were not yet near the point where the river would run back on itself, but if the rain continued this way it was only a matter of time before serious flooding would begin, probably sometime in the course of the afternoon.

So it was that as Katherine succumbed to the soporific enticements of the Sisters of Charity, and thus slept off her fatigue, the state of things among Brum's normal citizens was bordering on collective panic.

Yet strangely, as another night advanced with no let-up in the rain and a mounting sense of imminent calamity, many of the richest and most influential members of the New Brum community, who ought to have been worried by the rising waters, were concerning themselves with something else entirely. They were pampering their sleek and well-fed bodies in fragrantly oiled baths, and debating how best to adorn and bejewel themselves ahead of one of the biggest social events of the year – the birthday celebration of their High Ealdor, Festoon Avon or Lord Festoon, as he grandly styled himself – on the morrow. This was not a fixture in the social calendar they could easily get out of.

Yet the truth was that in all its long history, Brum had never witnessed such a sorry, corrupt, perverse individual in that great and historic office, nor one apparently less capable of guiding the helm of a great commercial hydden city. In the view of his many critics, there was no surer sign of Brum's final descent into decadence during the years since the Fyrd had taken over its administration than the awful fact that he was now this great city's figurehead.

This was a tragedy all the greater because of the six great families who had most put their stamp on the city, two stood out head and shoulders above the others: the Avons for good, the Sinistrals for ill. Now the Sinistrals ruled the Hyddenworld and Brum from Germany, while their puppet Festoon shamed his own family name in Brum and was the laughing stock of the Fyrd worldwide, a figure of fun and japery, the joke of comics and the sorry butt of ribald songs and tawdry theatricals in every language known to hydden.

His first sin was gluttony.

He had started young and it was said that he had abandoned the nourishment of his mother's breast at the age of only five months in favour of sweetmeats, which he had consumed on a massive scale ever since.

He was so vast in bulk that he had trouble rising from his chair without help; so unfit he could barely climb three steps without running out of breath; so indolent that he spent vast sums on servants to do everything for him, or on machines to perform functions that required exertion. The Sisters of Charity were effectively his servants and his chairs were made to be wheeled so he might avoid unnecessary exercise.

He covered his rotund frame with shapeless perfumed silks, voiles and damasks, soft fabrics from the east, as if he was – which he sometimes imagined himself to be – an emperor from Araby.

But clothes and sweet scents were not the only thing on which he had wasted his vast inheritance since he had taken possession of the ancestral estate and the Fyrd had made him their puppet and amiable plaything.

He had spent his fortune in spectacularly self-indulgent ways – with endless expensive fripperies, vast quantities of rich food, exotic entertainments, as well as priceless lotions, manicures, pedicures and massages, along with musicians and entertainments of every kind – and anything else that his sudden whims and appetites might desire.

It was truly said that what had taken his careful ancestors two hundred and fifty years to steal from Brum, and the world beyond, he had given back in twenty-five, the number of his living years.

That he had survived the vicissitudes of fortune under the Fyrd, who had brought down so many other members of the leading Brum families, he owed to two things.

First was the very obvious fact that one so young and seemingly naïve was a threat to no one at all, and therefore an ideal figurehead, easy to control and manipulate.

Second was his indisputable charm and ability to flatter the humourless Fyrd without appearing in any way deceitful. He pleased easily and was easy to please, and the Fyrd generals who took over the city's administration, one after another, since his appointment as High Ealdor at the age of just fifteen, ten years before, had found him the perfect partner. He was indeed clever and well-connected enough to know who was who among the hydden, how to flatter each of them, whose palm to grease, whom to exert his charm upon, and when to employ the stark threat of a visit from one of the Quentors, the inquisitors whose job it was to execute the orders of the Fyrd high command.

The contract was simple: in return for allowing Festoon to indulge himself with his own dwindling fortune, the Fyrd got all the benefit of his local expertise.

There was however one aspect of this comfortable arrangement that puzzled the Fyrd as much as it did the rich and the notable of Brum, who regarded Festoon with a mixture of embarrassment, shame and contempt. This was the fact that, for all his excess and wasteful extravagance, he enjoyed huge popularity among the ordinary folk of the city, whether they lived in New Brum or Old.

For them he embodied a quality which had never been satisfactorily defined, least of all by the denizens of that city themselves. It might be called 'Brummishness', which is the ability to poke fun, more or less with impunity, at whomsoever they pleased in a witty, droll and often unspoken way.

There was the sneaking suspicion among Brum folk, never spoken aloud nor even hinted at, that Festoon's excesses and grotesqueries were aimed in some subtle way at the Fyrd themselves who, being what they were and coming from the culture that they did, could never quite get the joke.

It was a possibility bolstered by a very simple practical fact: while his forebears in the Avon clan had built their vast wealth at the expense of the poor folk of Brum, and in particular those who lived in lower Digbeth and the slums of Deritend, their last scion, the inheritor of their ill-gotten gains, seemed intent, through his extravagance, on giving them back in one single generation all the wealth that had been stolen from them throughout many.

For who grew fat on Festoon's spending, apart from himself? The butchers, the bakers and the candlestick makers, and all such traders and artisans he continuously employed – all of them hydden, all from Brum, all those folk whose arts and crafts, under the direct domination of the Fyrd in any other city in the Hyddenworld, would have died away to nothing and been replaced by the dull uniformity that characterized their alien breed.

But in Brum they flourished like never before, and by them, and the families they supported, Lord Festoon was seen as a much-favoured and popular lord and master of them all.

So most certainly, though Festoon might merely be a puppet, a fool he was not. That was a fact he disguised very well as he downplayed his considerable intelligence and learning on matters cultural and historical, and his willingness to spend his wealth not just on himself but on the arts and sciences as well, for it pleased him to patronize any whose skills and creative talents might bring a return of glory to his fading city.

But those few who knew him well, and whom he trusted, understood something else. He had an obsession, and one he self-deprecatingly claimed he would climb a mountain for, even in his obese condition, just to satisfy. He would, indeed, have relinquished his position and his remaining wealth for it, perhaps even his life.

The thing Lord Festoon most wished in all the world was to gaze upon Beornamund's unrecovered piece of the Sphere, which held the colours of Spring.

To this end he had formed a collection of artefacts, archives, and much else besides, of items from all over the Hyddenworld which had anything to do with Beornamund, or the Peace-Weaver, or the legendary pendant of gold, inset with three of the four gems of the seasons, that she was said to wear.

In this he was given a start by the modest collection begun by his great-great-grandfather, Raster Avon, who had possessed the wisdom and foresight to bring to Brum, in the heyday of its development, the greatest architect of Araby, and a wise philosopher, namely ā Faroün of blessed memory.

It is well known that among the most extraordinary of that sage's creations in Brum was the elusive Chamber of Seasons, to which very few apart from Lord Festoon and his chef, Parlance, enjoyed access. Festoon himself, when he was well enough and had sufficient strength to climb the steps and negotiate the complex corridors necessary to reach the Chamber, would go there to indulge in reverie and to meditate; and Parlance would arrive simply because he had been summoned to take instruction from his master.

It was Festoon's genius to order his extraordinary collection so that its different items were housed according to the season they represented within the Chamber – or, more accurately, in the sequence of chambers, each of which represented one of the different seasons.

Festoon believed that he himself was a direct descendant of Beornamund, and it was this fancied connection which drove him endlessly in pursuit of the lost and last piece of the fabled Sphere.

So it was that very often, when he was not indulging in public entertainment and feasting, he spent much time and effort in reading ancient tomes brought to him from the city archive, which might help him pursue this quest. As a result he was both friend and supporter of Messrs Brief and Stort; and when news of some discovered text or artefact came to their ears, it was Festoon's habit to send the dependable Pike and Verderer Barklice off in search of that item, since clearly he himself was in no condition to go.

Festoon lived in – or rather beneath – a landmark building that was very well known to hydden and human alike – a building so prominent in Brum, in fact, that it offered proof of the original business genius of his ancestor Raster Avon to have grabbed it for a home when it first became available for hydden occupation.

The London and Birmingham Railway Company and its partner the Grand Junction Railway could never have imagined when they built the Curzon Street Station in grand neoclassical style in 1838, that within a few months of its opening the latest scion of the Avon family would be moving in. And that there, after importing leading architects and artists from Araby, he would create one of the greatest hydden buildings of all time which, apart from the mysterious and private Chamber of Seasons, included amongst its many glorious spaces the extraordinary Orangery whose warmth and humidity, so necessary for cultivating citrus fruits, was brilliantly engineered by a subversion of the city's early steam boiler systems and daringly restored in the 1930s by the dour genius Archibald Troop, a designer famed for having entrapped the venting systems of nearby New Street Station and thus saved the Orangery and its rare specimens in the nick of time.

By Festoon's generation, all that remained of what had once been the most elegant rail depot in Englalond – whose railway lines once fanned out eastward across a vast acreage – was its colonnaded entrance building.

Raster's infamous bully boys had secured as much of the footings of this building as was possible, thus gaining control of miles of already half-forgotten conduits, drains, access ways and culverts in and around New Brum. In this way was created not just the base of the Avon business empire, but also room for its steady expansion under Raster's successors.

Such was the foundation of the glory days of the Avon family.

But the strong seed of the past had turned to something impotent and sterile: the branches and shoots from the mighty trunk that had once been were now withered and dry, and all that was left of the trunk itself was the vast but seemingly rotten bulk that was Lord Festoon.

During those long days of rain when Katherine and Jack arrived in his city, Festoon was in no way exercised by the dire threat of the rising levels of river and canals. It was the eve of his birthday and, though every watercourse in Brum was overfull and rushing to discharge its load and flooding was imminent, he did not intend to lose sleep over the fact.

True, he listened briefly to the drumming of the rain and the sluicing of the pipes, considering matters carefully, but then, throwing all that aside with the careless comment, 'It is out of my hands now and I shall not let it spoil my feast!'

He had long since decided to break with tradition that year and hold his fest in one of his inner sanctums, the splendid Orangery created in Arabesque style back in Raster Avon's time by the lute-playing genius ã Faroün.

This extraordinary architectural fantasy, whose drapes shimmered exquisitely according to the cleverly directed winds and draughts of passing human traffic far above, and whose strange glass-and-metal panels, designed to reverberate to the shunt and hiss of steam trains overhead, were now responding subtly to unseen human cooling systems and Festoon's private band of percussionists, was one of the glories of modern Brum.

Festoon loved it and sometimes, in the privacy of the night, it was his habit to go there alone, lock the doors and jump and pirouette elephant-like to the rhythms of the music in the place, imagining himself to be a delicate nymph rather than the grotesque obesity he actually was.

An invitation to celebrate his birthday in this rarely viewed Orangery was Brum's must-accept ticket of the year, and everybody that mattered was coming, bar a few misogynists.

He had all but retired to his vast, soft bed when it occured to him that a conversation with Parlance, his personal chef and Master of Cuisine, might be sensible, to check all was in order for the day to come.

With much huffing and puffing Festoon raised a hand and tugged at the velvet bell-pull that hung ever-ready for his convenience. A short while later Parlance appeared. He was thin and tiny but made up for his minute stature by wearing built-up shoes and a very tall chef's hat.

Parlance handed his lord the day's menus and they were studied in reverential silence. There was considerable mutual respect between these two, and a strong sense that the gastronomic efforts of the day were an exciting joint enterprise.

Festoon gave his verdict at last. 'More crayfish, Parlance, stewed in lime,' he whispered weakly, 'and we can never have enough of your slivered *Apfelkuchen*, but powdered today, I think, with grain of cinnamon.'

'*Grain*, my lord?' said Parlance in some surprise. This was indeed a departure from tradition.

'Yes, I mean a grain. In the structural sense, as if it *were* a grain, which it is not, as I am perfectly well aware. Shall we say instead that it is cinnamon reduced to fragments which are smaller than granules, yet not so fine as powder?'

Parlance gazed at Festoon with admiration. No employer he had ever heard of had such startling originality as Festoon in matters of gourmandy, or was capable of such delicate precision in his instructions.

'I fancy,' said Festoon, after indulging in a sweetmeat or two and wiping his sugar-shiny lips with the damask that was his preferred material for napkins, 'that those marinated bleakfish you roasted in mustard last week are a tad on the murky side for our guests today, though I myself prefer them thus served. Was it English or French, the mustard?'

'French.'

'A mistake perhaps. Try the more piquant English, and less of it, with a hint of vaporized lemon – lemon, I say, not lime, for we are using that already – which, I believe, will excite any hydden palate worthy of the name. Agreed?'

'Yes, my lord,' said Parlance most cheerfully, for great though his own skills were, he knew that Festoon's instinct added a touch so complementary to his own that the result was, on occasion, near-genius.

'And the wines, Parlance, what of them?'

They talked their way similarly through the wines, the beers, and small-beers, the fruit elixirs and the meads, adding and discarding until the balance was absolutely correct.

'Our work is now done,' said Festoon at last, 'and I must away.' Parlance discreetly withdrew and Festoon fell into a happy reverie about his special day.

65

JIGGERED

It was only when Barklice called out for his boatman a third time into the gathering gloom by the West Gate that he got a response.

There was a sudden rustling in the vegetation further along the canal, the knock and rattle of wood on solid wood, and someone called out, 'Ho there! Mister Barklice and party?'

'That's right,' replied Barklice.

A figure then appeared along the bank, holding a lantern in one hand and clutching a sturdy oar in the other.

Jack gazed at the newcomer, mightily impressed. His face was in shadow but he seemed to be dark-skinned, and his garb looked vaguely Indian, with a touch of the far Orient. He wore only a dark vest and a loincloth, beneath which his muscular legs and feet were bare. He had thrown a thick red cloak over his shoulders, while round his head was rakishly swathed a band of material of the same colour.

He approached with a swagger and stopped directly before them, parking one end of his oar on the ground so that it towered above him vertically. His face opened up into a wide, white-toothed smile.

Jack stared at him in astonishment, for 'Old Mallarkhi' seemed a strange name to have given someone so young. Strong he might be, but this was a boy of no more than twelve.

Pike swore and growled, 'There's no way I get in any boat with a luggerbill boy in this foul weather!'

'Where's your grandfather, Arnold?' asked Barklice uneasily.

'Busy as a dozen rats, Mister Barklice. Our own patch was set to back up half an hour ago, and that's got to take priority, so he left off waiting here and sent me up instead. The luggerbill's waiting below in the dark, and it's the best craft to use in these conditions.'

'Most dangerous craft ever invented!' snarled Pike, pushing past him through the bushes to the canal's edge, from where came a horrible slurping sound as the water swelled and billowed against the bank.

He stared down and shook his head at the craft below. 'He's not old enough to have passed his apprenticeship, let alone handle one of the trickiest craft on the water. I tell you, Barklice—'

'Tell him what you like, Mister Pike,' reported Arnold Mallarkhi, 'but if we don't get off now, and that means *now*, we'll not just be jiggered but we'll be gargled as well. The back-up's beginning to merge. I can feel it in my bones.'

Arnold, the most junior of the Mallarkhi boating clan, smiled again. Ignoring Pike he nodded respectfully at Brief, and then stuck a finger in Jack's chest.

'You ever been in a luggerbill?'

'Well, I . . .' For some reason Jack's mouth went dry.

'You paddled a canoe?'

'Well, I did once. I . . .'

'Good! Your name?'

'Jack.'

'Jackboy, jump in, helm end, and stay centred, help this cargo down one by one, do as I say, and *move it*! Minutes is turnin' to seconds, and once seconds run out we'll be worse than gargled – we'll be spewed!'

'By the Mirror, Barklice, I'll—' cried out Pike.

'Shove 'im in, Jackboy!

Jack found himself obeying these sudden commands. He pushed past Pike and surveyed the craft below, which was long, narrow, clinker-built and very unstable-looking, rocking about on the troubled, nasty-looking water like a cork.

He eased a leg into it, towards its prow end, got himself central and without more ado, sensing that time was of the essence, pulled Pike in after him.

He stowed his portersac and stave, took Pike's as he climbed aboard, and then reached a hand up for Barklice, the luggerbill now rocking around very dangerously. Barklice as good as fell into the small craft, as the young boatman helped Brief in at the stern end with a respectful, 'That's right, Master Brief, you just sit down and think nice thoughts!'

Stort got in last of all and clumsily, only saved from slipping into the water by Arnold reaching down and quickly grabbing the seat of his trews, then effortlessly heaving him in so that he lay, a jumbled heap of limbs and possessions, in the bilges.

The wind blew hard, spray spattering their faces, and Jack nearly slid into the water on the far side of the craft before he managed to squat tidily and regain his balance.

Somehow, such was Arnold's ability to command them all, in no time at all they were huddled down ready for their boat trip.

Jack had always thought that canal water did not flow, but this particular waterway was flowing all right, first one way and then the other. Worse still, now they were all onboard, Jack could see why Arnold had earlier mentioned canoes. This vessel felt just like one, bobbing up and down, and side to side, with each wave that went under it and every little movement inside.

Worse still, their combined weight was such that the luggerbill's sides were only inches above the water at their central point.

'Jack, loose that lanyard!' called out Arnold.

Jack guessed this must mean the rope which was precariously tied to the slender branch of an alder growing on the bank, which whipped back and forth and was slippery and hard to get hold of. His fingers were cold and they fumbled feebly to get the rope undone.

'Jackboy, we're out o' time! Just snap the bugger off and be ready with your paddle.'

Finally freeing the lanyard, Jack stowed it under the prow, then scrabbled around till he found a wooden paddle. His knees were sticking painfully into something hard and knobbly, but he ignored that discomfort, such was his sense of imminent disaster.

The moment he released the rope, the canoe started bucking about, but was held fast to the bank at its other end by Arnold's oar, whose handle end sported a hook which he had attached to a thick root protruding from the bank.

'You others, get ready to bail. You'll find *tamoons* stowed under the seats, and, lads, when I say bail I mean *bail*, 'cos our lives'll depend on it. Ready, Jack?'

'Ready,' he said grimly, turning to face the watery darkness ahead.

Then they were off, Jack using his paddle instinctively on one side and then the other, exerting all his strength into the water, with no idea at all where they were heading.

Behind him, at the stern, Arnold Mallarkhi whistled cheerfully, and at one point called out, 'Nice and easy, Jackboy, don't overdo it. Save your strength till later. This is just the easy bit!'

Stort began humming in a very desperate way, his most recent experience of water not having been a good one.

Barklice stared goggled-eyed into the dark on one side of the canoe; Pike, swearing quietly under his breath, was staring out on the other side.

Beard ruffling in the wind and rain, Brief sat erect, his eyes firmly closed.

The only available light came from the wild sky above them, and occasionally the orange lights illuminating the bridges under which they passed.

Ahead lay only darkness.

But Arnold seemed to know exactly what he was doing, his cheerful whistling giving them confidence, but his occasional whooping and hollering, whenever the canoe banged and bucked, encouraged them rather less.

'Jack, keep yer fingers well inside the boat, if yer after holding on to 'em! We're about to start a jigger here.'

The sides of the canal narrowed to become vertical walls of slimy brick, and the water was suddenly so powerful in its surge that it lifted and banged them hard from side to side.

'It's jiggering!' called out Arnold. 'Get ready to bail, my boys! Jack, you got to lean harder into the paddle one way when she's going the other, else you'll sink us!'

It was just as well that Arnold had instructed them to be ready with the *tamoons* – which resembled small woks – because moments later a wall of water cascaded into the canoe from one side and then the other, and gradually they began to sink.

'Backs into it now, including you, Master Brief! Jack, lean a bit harder, but yer doing good.'

For a few seconds which felt like hours, they battled to keep the craft afloat and even the right way up. Jack, who had turned his head just as the water gushed over him, faced forward over the prow again. To his horror all he could see there was a wall of dark brick, green with weed, and with a few rusting chains dangling down into the water.

He looked back at Arnold, who was leaning hard into his oar to bring the boat about – the vessel suddenly slow and still, while monstrous suckings and slurpings emerged from the darkness towards which they were steering.

'Ready now, boys!' shouted Arnold. 'And listen good. We're turning about and backing into the sewer, before it backs-up into us. Lie low, hold on, and hold yer breath. Jack, grab that lanyard and wrap it round yer wrist. If yer get swept off, just hold on till she's through, and we'll fish you out the other end!'

The walls he had seen with such alarm only moments before slid slowly past until, to Jack's amazement, he saw that Arnold had somehow managed to bring the stern of the boat round to face a small arched tunnel that looked too low in the water for their craft to enter. Worse, they were going in backwards, and worse still they were being greedily sucked in.

It looked as if Arnold, and his oar, would be swept right off by the rim of the arch as the luggerbill shot into the tunnel beyond, but at the last moment he ducked down into the stern bilge and lowered the oar along the length of the craft.

As it gathered speed, Jack realized that he was confronting the same threat if he did not get down quickly. At that point he noticed that Pike, looking totally terrified, had clenched the fingers of both hands across the sides of the boat.

Jack dived forward to pull Pike's hands out of harm's way, before himself crouching down as low as he could.

Bang! And they were in, the tunnel's ceiling now just inches above their heads, jiggering from side to side, pitch blackness descending, water rushing at them from all directions. Jack's right hand clung instinctively to the lanyard, and that was just as well, for several times, as the tunnel ceiling rose, he felt himself being pushed or even sucked out of the boat.

But he held fast, kept down, and hoped his friends had managed to do the same.

Then, as suddenly as it started, it all came to an end, and they were through the tunnel into a great and mysterious underground pool lit only by a solitary shaft of light angling down from some distant opening above.

Slowly their eyes adjusted to the murk and they saw that their craft was silently circling on some unseen current in the dark deep water immediately below them, with no apparent way out of the cavern they were in.

'Well, that was a jigger and a half,' crowed Arnold cheerfully, his voice echoing about that lofty, cathedral-like space from all sides of which came the constant whisper of wild water.

'It's backing down now, so we've still got a wait of two or three minutes. Then hold fast again, especially you, Jack, because this time we're going the right way through, so you'll not want to come off or you'll be dragged under the keel and get crushed on the rollers. Understood?'

'Um . . . I do,' said Jack, anxiously.

'When we take off, we'll take off fast, so listen out for the gargling – because that's the . . . clue . . . Jackboy . . . *Jack! Doooown!*'

It was too late.

Deadly and powerful, the water's currents, acting in silence, had brought the craft out of the gloom towards another sewer entrance. The others had seen it, but Jack was still curious about this place they were in, and therefore turned to face the sewer entrance so late that he instinctively raised his left arm to protect himself and it was caught on some sharp obstruction at the apex of the arch, while his left was still holding on to the lanyard as the boat slipped forward beneath him.

'Lift 'im!' commanded Arnold as Pike and then the others, one by one, tried dragging Jack back into the boat. 'Lift him!' he yelled again.

Only Brief understood but, powerful though he was for his age, he was unable to raise Jack high or quickly enough to get him off whatever had snagged him.

But Arnold himself knew what to do.

He thrust the hook end of his oar at Jack, and caught the fabric of his jacket in it, while setting the other end firmly against a rib in the stern. As the boat swept under the arch, its own momentum pushed against the oar, which lifted Jack right off the unseen obstruction, briefly up the wall, and then out over the water beyond the arch before, the boat continuing on underneath and the oar now falling flat behind the craft, he tumbled down along with it.

'Grab this rope, Jackboy!' yelled Arnold, and a length of rope came shooting out of the dark hole of the sewer mouth, straight into Jack's outstretched hand.

He grabbed it, quickly, looped it tight around his hand, and clenched his fist firmly over it.

Then all was chill darkness and cold submersion as he was dragged along underwater, glad that instinct had made him gulp some air immediately before he was submerged.

His lungs bursting, he found enough purchase on the bottom of the sewer to push himself upward, only to find himself in a space full of water.

I'm going to die . . .

He felt as if his arm was being half wrenched off, his body repeatedly bashed into brick projections and sills, felt himself move faster, his chest suffering a ferment of pain, and suddenly he was up and out of the water and into spinning light, spluttering and choking as willing hands grabbed him and pulled him back into the luggerbill.

'You can let go the lanyard, Jack, and get back to your station, there's still work to do!'

Half-drowned, gasping, shoved roughly along the length of the boat and back to the prow, Jack was astonished to now see Pike holding the paddle.

'Grabbed it,' he rasped by way of explanation, 'but *you're* the expert!'

He thrust it back into Jack's hands just as Arnold called, 'We're off again!'

'Couldn't someone else have a go?' said Jack.

'You're doing just fine,' growled Pike, to which Arnold added, 'He's a natural!'

Sopping wet and still grumbling, Jack took his position once more at the prow.

It was only then he noticed they were outside now, in a concrete canyon it seemed, and on a watercourse of some kind, and moving faster and faster yet again.

Above loomed the same dark sky of a stormy afternoon, while ahead lay the glow of a city lighting up for evening.

'Gentlemen,' called out Arnold Mallarkhi, with the confidence of one who knows the end is in sight, 'bail out the bilges and hold on tight, for there's rapids ahead!'

Of the rest of it, Jack afterwards could never remember very much. Except he felt good, his hands strong on the paddle as he heaved and pulled it, pushed and slid it through the water to either side of their craft, responding to one obstacle or change in direction after another, and to the occasional shouted instructions of his youthful captain.

The culvert they travelled in narrowed, the blank walls on either side changed to those of buildings, and occasional lights in human habitations appeared. As they went under one bridge, then another, the buildings alongside them changed again, this time to old warehouses and abandoned factories. At which point Arnold steered them at speed into a side channel, and the boat slid under a final arch to reach a wharf that rose some distance above their heads.

There were shouts, the scent of food, other craft coming and going nearby, derricks and all manner of equipment. And finally Arnold's voice again: 'Tie her up, Jackboy. Your job's well done.'

They had arrived at some kind of harbour which, as they got out of the craft and climbed some slippery stone steps, Jack found was as busy a place as ever he had seen.

Lanterns lit the cobbled ways, signs hung above shop fronts, and candle-lit stalls sold roast chestnuts, crayfish steaks and jellied eel.

'Welcome to Brum, welcome to Deritend,' said Arnold. 'But we need towels and a hot toddy, so follow me, lads!'

Shaken, wet, bruised and truly battered, Jack silently followed the others, feeling so tired that he could hardly put one foot in front of the other.

But he had survived, and he felt as alive as he had ever done, though there was no one at the moment he would rather have seen than Katherine.

But it seemed that before all else, there was important business to attend to.

Arnold turned to them and said, 'That'll be a groat and a half each, gentlemen!'

'Or five for the whole group,' replied Barklice firmly. 'And Master Brief and myself get a special rate, seeing who we are, which makes it four. Agreed?'

Arnold put on a pained expression. 'You drive a hard bargain, Mister Barklice, but a fair one, because I knows it be true that you always give a generous tip. Agreed?'

It seemed to be so.

The money was paid over without further ado, but for one thing.

'Jack,' said Arnold, 'this is for you!'

He put a coin in Jack's hand.

'Prowman always gets a share and, by the Mirror itself, I swear I've never had a better one for a beginner! Now listen good, for we luggerbill-boys do things certain ways. If this is your first payment on any craft, you don't spend it for a year, maybe many more. You keep it safe against the day when there's true reason and need for that groat. It ain't much but it was well and fairly earned, so when the time comes you spend it wise and good, agreed?'

'Agreed,' said Jack.

66

BRUNTE

It was midnight and the level of the watercourses in and around Brum had continued to rise.

So far there were no reports of flooding, and the Bilgesnipe still had things under control, but further heavy rain was forecast and the strong wind was shifting in a westerly direction, making it almost certain that the River Rea would soon back up.

The Council of Ten, the ruling body of the city, was therefore holding an emergency session. Such a meeting was never going to be welcome on the night before the High Ealdor's birthday, when most of those now forced to attend would have preferred to get eight hours' sleep ahead of readying themselves for his reception during the coming afternoon.

But needs must, and Councillor Hrap Dowty, whose remit was Transport and Thoroughfares, had introduced a complication. He was a pale, taciturn transport specialist with an obsession for detail and time schedules, and he had put on the table a once-in-a-decade proposal that New Brum should be sealed off from Old Brum. The reason offered was compelling.

Major road works undertaken in the centre of the city by the humans had resulted in a diversion of certain sewers, which made it much more likely in the present conditions, he said, that unpredictable flash flooding would occur in Deritend, and probably Digbeth too, which had the potential to spread north and east into the privileged areas of New Brum occupied by . . . most of the members of the Ten.

However, a sealing-off would cause much greater damage to Old

Brum than would be the case if the rising waters were allowed to flow more naturally. It would almost certainly result in loss of life as well, for sealing off always meant that folk got trapped.

Dowty finished his report and sat down. Anyone closely observing him might have noticed how he cast a momentary and involuntary glance in the direction of the least important executive attending this meeting, namely Sub-Quentor Brunte.

Brunte himself noticed it, as he noticed all else.

Like some feral beast whose survival depends upon its ability to smell what its rivals are thinking, Brunte had a preternatural ability to work out others' motives and thoughts.

He was sniffing now, and what he got was the usual conflicting odours of self-interest among the assembled members of the Ten.

All wanted to protect their grand residences and their businesses, and on those grounds they would vote for a Seal.

But each one knew that this move would be unpopular, because it would cause destruction and death to the most vulnerable and weakest members of Brum society. The city had ever been a restive, radical kind of place, where revolution seethed not far below the surface, and such a Seal therefore risked giving life to that grim spectre which had always been the Sinistrals', and through them the Fyrd's, greatest fear concerning Brum: revolt.

An empire, like a bank, depends for its survival upon a combination of credit and might. Each must seem to be invulnerable; though neither ever is.

So the Ten, with the Administrator, the elderly General Elon, in the chair, debated the issue, while their three Quentors, or executives, and Brunte as Sub-Quentor, none of whom had any right to speak unless invited to do so, sat listening impassively.

Brunte attended to this debate with all the fascination and self-interest of one who had spent his still-young life wholeheartedly studying survival and the gaining of further power. He heard – in fact he smelt, almost tasted – the thundering rain outside, and it was becoming increasingly sweet. It represented *opportunity*. It signalled a change long time in the making, ever since as a nineteen-year-old he had witnessed the abortive attempt to kill the giant-born.

But the debate was diffuse, the Ten uncertain, their tendency towards deferral. Brunte sensed that an intervention was necessary, but without a direct invitation he could not speak. If he tried, it would be a step too far; if he remained silent, the decision would go against the Seal and the moment would be lost.

Brunte did the only thing he could.

Waiting for a pause in the discussion, he leaned forward, beyond the subservient line of his superiors, the three Quentors; he exhaled deeply and audibly, and tapped his fingers on the table very lightly – not enough to appear in any way impatient, yet just sufficient to be noticed. Which it was likely he would be, for Brunte possessed that indefinable quality of all great conspirators, who are able to make others believe the impossible is possible, that dreams can come true, and that they are the ones to turn the weak into the strong and then lead them to the promised land. In short, a sense of potency and power, charisma and self-belief.

Having made his presence thus felt, he said nothing but waited calmly and reflected with secret pleasure on three things that were very relevant indeed to the way he must steer the Ten, but which he had no intention of revealing to them.

The first thing was that the report from Hrap Dowty which had provoked this debate was false. The sewers had certainly been diverted by the humans, but the Bilgesnipe had already forestalled any extra danger by making diversions of their own. Dowty must surely know that, just as Brunte did.

The second thing was that Festoon Avon, High Ealdor of Brum, was a fraud. The pose of innocence and weak irrelevance which he had fostered among the Fyrd, through every hour and every day for the fifteen years since his appointment, was bogus. He was in fact intelligent, calculating, manipulative and a true leader of his people, and Brunte knew that. The question was who else did. Not any of the Ten, that was for sure.

Thirdly Brunte knew that if the Ten voted for a Seal, then two of their number at least would be dead before four by the clock the following afternoon. Within an hour of that, the three Quentors seated at his side and seven more of the Ten would be also be dead, leaving just one alive to take over as Administrator.

By then, as well, he would have promoted himself from the lowly rank he now held to something impressive – he had not yet decided his title.

He relaxed. He could *smell* the chairman's acquiescence to his unspoken desire to speak.

'I think,' began Elon, 'it might be prudent on this particular occasion to ask the views of the Sub-Quentor with respect to the present state of law and order in our city, and thus any implications that it should have for the decision we are about to make.'

'Agreed,' murmured several of the Ten.

They turned to Brunte and, as if surprised by the invitation and sensible of the honour it accorded him, he smiled modestly and began speaking, with murder in his heart.

It was twelve years since Brunte, then only nineteen years old, had witnessed the car crash that destroyed the Shore family and nearly killed Jack, driving Brunte to murder a junior member of the Sinistral dynasty and the Fyrd officer accompanying him. He had done this to keep to himself – and for his future use – the secrets of that night.

More than a decade on he was broader, his face fleshier, his bright intelligent eyes always jovial as a convenient cover to his inner thoughts, his brows bushier, the fingers of his hands hairier, his forearms stronger, and his presence powerful and capable of being menacing in one still so young.

On his arrival in Brum, Brunte had quickly spotted that the best opportunities for a Fyrd with no connections, and therefore little prospect of fair promotion, were in the service of the Sub-Quentor.

It was a lucrative post, open to bribery and corruption, and Brunte watched how those serving in it acquired both wealth and power. But it was also a dangerous post, and most occupied it for only a year or two before they were sidelined, killed or exiled on ever-justifiable charges of corruption.

Brunte himself had gained his position a year before in the time-honoured way, by eliminating his predecessor, one Finial Fane. In Brunte's case he had done this in collusion with General Elon, to whom he had passed over considerable income from various of Fane's more profitable activities.

His position being at least temporarily secure with the hierarchy, Brunte moved quickly to eliminate any potential rivals in positions under him, and put in their places a team of people who combined brains with brawn and on whom he knew he could rely. Elon could not have imagined his underling's ambitions went higher, but then nor could most Fyrd who had encountered the seemingly friendly and sociable Brunte.

'Sub-Quentor,' said Elon haughtily, 'is there really an issue of law and order with respect to effecting a Seal, or is this mere bureaucracy?'

'It is not, General, at least not in the sense you mean. Dissent in Deritend is always mostly hot air, for the place is now in the hands of the Bilgesnipe, and you know their strong loyalty to the Fyrd who have given them sanctuary here for so many years.

'As for Digbeth High, you have my personal word on it that any dissent can be contained. I would add only this: there is a certain advantage in organizing a Seal, for it will certainly bring out the disaffected and, particularly if there are deaths, then there will be a mood of rebellion and, even better, public talk of it.'

'"Even better" – why do you say that?'

Brunte squared himself to the table and to the Ten, giving a small glimpse of his real power. He chuckled. 'If we apply emergency powers, it will give us the opportunity to stamp out any rebellion for another generation. Which, with the Ten's permission, we will do . . . thoroughly and in a way that will not easily be forgotten.'

No one doubted it.

'In short, Councillors, I believe that the situation gives us a rare opportunity to impose ourselves anew, and if there are a few dozen drownings of the lower orders in the process, it will serve to remove from Brum some of its more troublesome elements.'

It was enough for them.

The Seal was agreed and, immediately after, a state of emergency declared. The Sub-Quentor was instructed to see that both were enforced, and the three Quentors charged to be ready for summary hearings.

'Leave it until after the High Ealdor's feste,' said Elon drolly. 'We wouldn't wish to spoil things . . .'

The Council broke up minutes later, Elon giving a nod of approval in Brunte's direction as he left.

The Sub-Quentor gathered up his papers and headed back to his chambers, where his brutish minions awaited him, despite the late hour.

'We have a decision,' he announced triumphantly. 'It's to be a Seal. Be back here tomorrow afternoon at half past two. Be armed and ready, for finally we have work to do.'

Left to his own devices, Brunte was not idle. He sat thinking through his plans for the next day and when he was satisfied summoned Feld.

'You found the girl, and the boy followed?' asked Brunte brusquely.

Feld smiled grimly.

'The "girl" Katherine is now fully adult, Sub-Quentor. As for the "boy" Jack, he's already a formidable fighter and had the courage to hold us at bay in the henge for long enough to get back-up in the form of Master Brief and Mister Pike. So we took Katherine and she is safely lodged with the Sisters.'

'And the boy?'

'As we planned, well on his way to Brum in pursuit of her according to my information. One of our patrols made an abortive attempt to capture him and were left trussed up for their pains. Since then we have left well alone and waited for Jack to deliver himself to us, which inevitably he will do.'

Brunte considered this, and then glanced at his chronometer.

'Well, well, you have done your job. In other circumstances I would have gone at once to talk with this ... Katherine, but events here have been brought forward by the threat of flooding. We cannot afford to give the Fyrd hierarchy time or opportunity to counterattack. Now is the hour and I intend to grasp it.'

Feld eyed him and smiled both conspiratorially and with respect.

He might in theory be Brunte's senior but he knew he lagged a long way behind him in his ruthless ability to take the right action to seize the moment.

There was something Brunte did not know about him, and it had changed everything. Feld had seen the reports about Lavin Sinistral's shocking death in Englalond twelve years before. Reviewing the evidence he had little doubt that Brunte, then only nineteen, had had the nerve and skill to kill the junior Sinistral and the senior Fyrd officer with him.

Nor did Feld doubt that Brunte had killed his predecessor to gain the post of Sub-Quentor – one which most senior Fyrd would never believe might offer any useful base from which to gain power.

Feld had been sent to investigate Brunte, and possibly arrest him as a danger to the state. What had happened was almost the opposite: Brunte's charm, strength of purpose and ambition against the power of the Sinistral dynasty had found an echo in Feld's own thinking. Now he was his ally in revolt.

'Meyor Feld,' said Brunte, 'you have done well. *We* have done well. But on this day of days there is much more to do – *much* more – and I shall defer my meeting with Katherine until our primary work is done. Stay close, keep me informed when you learn the whereabouts of Jack, be here at half past two tomorrow, and be ready.'

Feld nodded grimly.

'If I understand you right, Sub-Quentor . . .'

Brunte spoke plainly.

'What we are about to do will be the first clear and public challenge to the Sinistral for many years, since some of my own people in Poland, including my family, revolted and were crushed with a cruelty beyond reason. If I succeed here it will offer the potential of changing the course of the history of the Hyddenworld – and succeed is what I intend to do.'

Feld dared to look doubtful.

'I still think – and fear – that the first thing the Sinistral will do is to send a Fyrd force to crush you as they crushed your people in Poland.'

Brunte shrugged coolly.

'I think they will not because they have overextended themselves elsewhere in the Hyddenworld. Either way, Meyor Feld, I shall expect your continuing loyalty.'

Feld smiled.

'Either way, Sub-Quentor Brunte, you have it.'

67

THE HANDS OF MODOR

Imbolc was having a busy time of it and the time of day, or rather night, made no difference.

Having visited the sleeping Stort on the shore of the lake near the Devil's Quoits two days before, and then sent her horse to guide Katherine through the tunnels to safety, of a kind, she had paid a call on old friends in Thüringia, Germany.

This was the Modor or Wise Woman and her consort the Wita. Imbolc persuaded the Modor that she was needed and had to travel.

There are some who say that Peace-Weavers hold special sway with the Modor because she herself was once a Shield Maiden and so is one of the Peace-Weaver's previous sisters. Be that as it may, much though the Modor hated travel she agreed to go with Imbolc.

'Where's the Wita gone?' Imbolc asked, curious.

She knew the two to be not unlike a long-married couple whose grouses and grumbles about each other hid abiding love.

'Not here, that much is certain,' came the ambiguous reply.

A comment, thought Imbolc, which like most of those made by the Modor appeared vague but probably got straight to the heart of things if only she could work out what those things were.

'I would have liked him to accompany us, Modor.'

'So would I but, for now, as for some time past, and perhaps some time to come, that will not be possible.'

It seemed to Imbolc that the Modor looked troubled and that was a matter of concern to her, for it was of concern to the whole world. A troubled Modor meant a troubled world.

The Modor smiled wanly. 'Sometimes, Imbolc, we must dare lose hope – all hope – if we are to find what we need. You, who have waited so long to see your beloved Beornamund again, know that better than most.'

Imbolc stared at her with alarm and compassion. 'There's something you're not telling me.'

'There is, my dear, because I do not know it myself. Now, you want me to travel. Where to?'

'Brum,' announced Imbolc.

The Modor's face lightened and her eyes seemed brighter. 'Now that,' she said, 'is music to my ears.'

Then, like two old witches, they mounted the White Horse and were gone.

It was well past midnight before Arnold finally led Jack and the others to their accommodation for the night. It was, he explained, his grandfather's establishment, an ancient looking waterside tavern.

It overlooked a dry dock which ran back from another that fronted the river. It was so far lower than the street level of the human city, and so hidden by juts and overhangs of buildings, or inaccessible across fenced-off ground, that its comings and goings and the lights on at that dark hour were a long way lost to view to humans.

As for the hydden, all they could see toppermost were the occasional lights of cars reflected from one angled tower-block window across an open space to another like silent faded ghosts, red and white and sometimes flashing blue. Of the humans themselves, there was no sign at all.

Jack now had the opportunity to examine his first hydden hostelry. It had a long, rotting black-painted board that stretched from one side of it to another above two doors and three windows. On it, in dirty white lettering, was written its name, *The Muggy Duck*. The origin of this hung vertically from one corner of the building. It was a sign on a rusting wrought-iron bracket on which was painted an image of a pure white swan gliding on the blue waters of a clean river, a vestigial memory of what Brum's River Rea might once have been before the human city, and the hydden one within it, buried it so deep.

The hostelry's windows were ablaze with welcoming light. When they entered, Old Mallarkhi himself was nowhere to be seen, but no matter, the Duck, which was full to overflowing with customers, was under the iron command of his daughter, Arnold's mother, Ma'Shuqa, the best-known and best-loved Bilgesnipe in Brum.

She took her son warmly to her ample bosom and smothered him with kisses, from which he emerged gasping for air. Then she welcomed the others, who she evidently knew very well. She surveyed Jack with interest and delight, holding him with a strong hand on either shoulder as she did so, before taking him to herself as she had her son but stopping short of the kisses.

'Welcome one and all,' she said, 'but my, you're sopping! Arnold, take 'em to be steamed and soothed afore they're fed and tell Jellybee it's two for the price of one for these important customers, massage thrown in!'

She turned to Brief and said, 'That'll keep you all occupied until things ease up in our kitchens, this being a busy night as you can see, what with the birthday parade outside tomorrow and folk sheltering in from the rain.'

She moved off to deal with other things but turned back again to call out, '. . . and don't forget to give up your staves and other weaponry for safety's sake to Mister Klim in the armoury.'

Jack handed in his stave through the bars of a window behind which sat a very thin gentleman upon whose forehead, disconcertingly, was tattooed in Gothic lettering the word 'KLIM'. He took it without expression and asked for Jack's name, which he mouthed silently to memorize it, hopefully correctly since he gave no token or receipt in return.

Jack watched his stave disappear into an elongated pigeonhole which had no numbering or lettering that he could see and which was one of hundreds, some empty, many filled, and some so full of dust and cobwebs it looked like their owners had never reclaimed them.

While he waited for the others to hand over their weapons he glanced about the great, beamy place, at either end of which there was an inglenook in which great logs blazed.

The Duck's clientele, male and female, were drinking from narrow, single-handled flagons. There were three refectory tables, long and wide, where others ate from platters piled high with vittles and dived into bowls of steaming pottage, laughing, talking, shouting, and mopping their mouths and brows with red napkins provided, like the food, by busty, beribboned, Bilgesnipe girls.

'. . . and Master Brief,' called Ma'Shuqa, eyeing Jack meaningfully as they were led by Arnold through back rooms to where they were to clean themselves up, 'someone hove in a short while ago and is waiting for young Jack by the baths. He's in for a massage he won't forget!' Not for the first time, Jack told himself, a great deal seemed to go on which affected him without him being told about it.

The bathing establishment lay behind the hostelry, set among a tangle of huge pipes, some insulated, which came down from the human city above. From the fact that some steamed, and others had spewed calcareous deposits down the walls to which they were fixed, Jack guessed these were part of a water-heating system and boilers which fed human needs above.

They came to a door, marked Mallarkhi Steam and Bathing Company Limited, above which shone a dim red light behind a piece of glass on which were written the words 'Open always saving Holy Days and April 10th'.

'Ma's birthday,' said Arnold by way of explanation. 'Her special treat. With the girls.'

They entered a humid foyer where a large muscular attendant clad in a sarong and white vest welcomed them and took money provided by Mister Pike, who seemed well known. They were given a loincloth and thin towels.

The danger of imminent flooding elsewhere had emptied this normally busy and always profitable establishment of its normal clientele and Jack and the others had its steam rooms to themselves. They luxuriated on wooden benches at ever-increasing temperatures, massaged by dark-skinned silent male attendants whose large hands and elbows and feet, but most of all fingers, found out their many aches and pains and soothed them.

The series of treatments came to an end with a vertical plunge into a pool so cold and deep that it made Jack feel for a moment that he had leapt into the void of a pleasant death and glorious afterlife.

It was only as he dried himself off that he realized that for the first time in his life he had exposed to general view the savage burns to his back and neck from the car accident in his youth.

If he expected no comment to be made or attention given he was mistaken.

'By the Mirror itself,' cried Brief, who cut a more solid and muscular figure in a loincloth than Jack had expected, 'I had no idea . . .'

Stort, too, was curious, and even Pike, while the masseur who had earlier attended Jack but said nothing now reappeared and declared there was to be a special treatment for Jack.

He was led into a different room, the others following. It was warm and quietly lit, and an old woman awaited him. She was a healer of some kind, with a face so lined with age but eyes so bright with intelligence and youth that it was impossible to guess her age. She told Jack to lie on his stomach, his scars exposed to the others, while she examined him.

Towels were placed over his head and the lower part of his body, and on the less injured side of his back as well. The couch he lay on had a V-shaped hole in it which allowed him to breathe, but the position and towels made their voices muffled.

She played her fingers over him lightly as a feather, until finding some bump or knot, they paused, grew firm and pressed in to release tension beneath. As she did so she sang a soft song which at first seemed dirge-like, but before long, and because someone unseen played flute-like music, it seemed to him the most beautifully sad thing he had ever heard.

Except he *had* heard it, long ago and he knew that at any moment . . .

He was right.

The beat shifted to something fantastic, rhythmic and exotic.

'I know that tune,' he murmured. 'I heard it when I was very young and I . . . it reminds me . . .'

Her hands were firm on his back, her voice soft in his ear.

'You know the music, the music knows you. It'll welcome you back one day no doubt, for it is the tune of all your clan . . .'

'What do you mean?' he mumbled, unable to turn his head to look at her.

But his desire to know, though it naturally ran deep, was no match for the lassitude he felt as her touch continued.

Was she massaging him? He was not quite sure.

Was she weeping his own ancient tears? He certainly began to think it felt like it.

Did her touch reach through his hurt body to his heart? He was sure it did.

Did he sleep for a time? He did not stay entirely in the mortal world.

When he finally did awaken, it was Brief himself who said softly in his ear, a hand firmly on his shoulder to keep him still and quiet, 'Jack, our clothes have been washed and pressed and yours are here. You shall join us for late supper shortly but first the Modor wishes to talk with you. She says to rise gently and slowly, then to dress. Stort will stay with you.'

Jack heaved himself cautiously off the couch, his state of mind so relaxed that he did not much mind that the old woman watched his every move. Stort was his usual self, indifferent to his surroundings and uninterested in whether Jack was putting on his clothes or taking them off.

When he was fully clothed, the woman signalled for Jack to sit. He was glad to do so.

The Modor looked at him and spoke quietly: 'You'll feel very tired for a few hours, so you must sleep. When you wake you'll feel you've been bashed all over with staves. Then you'll feel wonderful for twenty-four hours and then . . .'

Jack nodded and was about to ask what she'd done to him when she continued.

'You've reached a crisis, so expect a rough time. Your old injuries run deep and may never be cured.'

Jack thought for a moment and raised his eyes to meet the piercing stare of the Modor.

'You said I *may* never be cured. Does that mean I *might* be cured: that my skin and burnt muscles could recover?'

The Modor sighed and bowed her head, eyes half shut. Then she stood suddenly and with a speed belying her age came over to Jack and took his hand in hers. Her eyes were black pools around which a thousand dark wrinkles gathered.

'Most things can be cured,' she said, 'even such injuries as yours. It will take courage and cause pain, more than you can imagine, and who can tell if the healing is worth the cure for all the changes it will bring? But that is the journey of a giant and I can feel his spirit in you and that your wyrd is too strong to be easily swayed. And anyway . . .'

Jack shook his head with frustration and interrupted her. 'People keeping saying I'm a giant but I don't even know what that means.'

The Modor chuckled. 'None of us know for certain what it means,' she said. 'But one thing is for certain – you're a wyrd's fool at the very beginning of your journey, so don't linger in Brum at all, or in the Hyddenworld too long, you're not ready for either yet. And neither is the Hyddenworld.'

Jack wanted to ask questions, about what she was saying, about the tune he had heard being played earlier, about who the Modor was herself, but he felt dazed and very tired. And what did it mean to be a 'wyrd's fool'?

'When you do know what being a giant means – then you'll find your cure,' she told him gently.

Jack looked across at her as she moved towards the door.

'I have other questions . . .' he said, reaching towards her.

But she was gone, eyes lost in shadows, a smile retreating to memory, an absence as palpable as loss.

'Who was she?' Jack asked Stort.

'Everything,' said Stort, mysteriously, 'but most of all . . .'

He murmured a word Jack hardly heard; certainly it seemed to make no sense.

The word was 'love'.

Jack and Stort rejoined the others in the Muggy Duck where the crowd had thinned to make preparations, Jack was told, for the Chaste Parade next day.

'Local to Deritend, the way we do it,' he was told. 'Forget the nobs up New Brum way, and the roughs in Digbeth, we do it like it should be done!'

'Do what?' asked Jack.

But answers were there none, people being too inebriated for lengthy explanations, or their thoughts elsewhere. He was so tired from travelling and the treatments that he couldn't follow their discussions about floods and insurrection, the mixed arguments about tradition and parades, and Birthday Brides and Knots.

'Knots,' he asked her. 'What knots?'

'Only one,' came the reply. 'You'll see'.

Much later, after two in the morning, members of the Mallarkhi clan began to arrive, bent on enjoying the day to come.

Ma'Shuqa Mallarkhi reappeared, declared them ready for bed, and cheerfully steered them into the small room with a long palliasse across the floor which they had to share. They lay down, blew out the candles, listened to the rain outside, and fell blissfully asleep.

68

CAUGHT AGAIN

It was the thump! thump! thump! of the steps on metal that woke Katherine from her nightmare to a real-life one.

She knew they were coming for her so she leapt out of bed, ran out of the cell and realized almost at once that when she turned right she was running straight towards them. Too late. She came face to face with Sister Chalice, who grabbed her arm and snapped at her as if she were a child, 'I *thought* I heard someone being naughty!'

Sister Supreme was there also, along with two even larger Sisters.

'Ah, good morning Sister Katherine,' said Supreme, with a fixed smile. 'I am glad you have been able to stretch your legs a little. Glad, too, that no foolish thoughts about escape came to your mind, for you can be assured that if you were to venture into the dark and dangerous corridors hereabouts we would not be able to rescue you from certain ruination. Aren't you glad, therefore, that we found you before it was too late?'

Katherine opened her mouth to protest, but decided against it.

She pretended instead to be sleepy and confused. The Sisters surrounded her and led her on up the corridor, the way they themselves had come, and then up some old, cast-iron stairs. From above she could detect the sound of laughter and the smell of perfume.

'Where are you taking me?' she managed uncertainly.

'We're going to a party, my dear, but first we must prepare you. You look so hideous as you are. Your hair is naturally too wild, of course, but that is easily fixed. Your body is also too thin for your height, but a little padding will soon put that right.'

'Padding?' exclaimed Katherine.

'Padding and other such female artifices may help you get chosen. You would not wish not to be chosen, believe me, for you are too delicate, too spirited, to endure the base attentions of some of the lower Fyrd. Worry not, Sister, for before long you will look exactly like one of us. Aren't you pleased at the thought?'

'No,' protested Katherine, 'you all look so artificial and horrible.'

This only made them laugh more.

'Come on, my dears, let us have some fun turning this duckling into a swan!'

She found herself ushered into the same softly lit chambers she had arrived in the night before. It was full of Sisters in various stages of applying make-up and adorning themselves for some special occasion.

'What are they getting ready for?' she asked.

'Lord Festoon's birthday party, of course. Just think, each one of us here might become the Chosen One.'

'Chosen for what?' said Katherine uneasily.

'Drink this my love.'

'No!'

'But yes.'

Someone grabbed her shoulders, another her arms, and a third clasped her head tight. A glass of fragrant liquid was put to her mouth, then her nose was pinched tight. She held her breath as long as she could, but eventually was forced to open her mouth just to gasp for air. The moment she did so, they tipped the liquid down her throat, and the next thing she knew she was swallowing it.

They held her tight until, against her will, she felt herself relax and even begin to smile.

'Time now to attend to your hair, my dear,' said Chalice, turning to someone else. 'Sister Mary, what can you and your scissors do with this atrocity!?'

Katherine heard herself laughing helplessly as she watched a pair of scissors come snapping through the air towards her, held in a hand most beautifully manicured.

'Relax,' soothed a voice gently. 'The worst was over yesterday, this is just a final trim.'

Katherine laughed again, a strange, wild, giggly kind of laugh.

'*Relax*,' the voice purred.

'I already am,' she was horrified to hear herself say.

69

MAKE IT PLAIN

J ack woke in the dark, fuggy room provided by Ma'Shuqa Mallar-khi feeling disorientated. He had lost all sense of time and for a moment had the disconcerting feeling that he had lost something else as well. The silence beyond the heavy drape tacked across the window told him what it was.

'The rain's stopped,' he murmured, painfully aware that there was not an inch of his body, from head to toe, that did not feel bruised, battered, strained and weak.

He was very surprised to find his arms wrapped tight around the snoring form of Bedwyn Stort who, hearing his voice, stirred a little before snuggling deeper into the straw-filled palliasse they were sharing with Master Brief. Pike and Barklice were nowhere to be seen.

Jack sat up gingerly, each movement bringing pain to some new bruise or injury from the boat journey. He stretched, winced a bit and finally got up, pulled open a rickety door and found himself in a panelled corridor that smelt deliciously of roasting meat.

He followed its scent and turned finally into the inglenook room that served as the Muggy Duck's main place of entertainment. The tables had been rearranged in a large square, the chairs around the edges, as for a feast.

There was a general hum of activity about the place, as of a well oiled machine, but no sign of it in the room, There, it seemed, the preparations had long since been made.

Ma'Shuqa, her plaited hair now gaily ribboned in reds and greens, sat under the inglenook at the far end, humming quietly to herself. She was basting a great haunch of venison, using a wooden ladle to scoop clarified butter from a bowl on the hearth before her. It was this that smelt so good.

Outside the rain had stopped and doors and windows were open to let in fresh air and sunshine. From the feel of things Jack guessed it had gone midday.

He picked his way towards his hostess and greeted her.

She gave him a warm smile, murmured a welcome to the day, took a steaming jug from a special holder by the fire where it was keeping warm and poured him a generous cannikin of the brew.

It smelt coffee-like and almost tasted like it too.

'Colomby bean mixed with smoked Charn acorn,' she said by way of explanation. 'You'll not find a better pick-me-up after a night before in all the Hyddenworld. Sup well, lad, and dunk this corncrake in it for sustenance. Big meal's on the way.'

She saw his hesitation and showed him what to do.

She nodded first at some round, soft, yellow figgyways on a plate, one of which she picked up, rolled into a tube, dunked in the colomby and then proffered towards his mouth as if she was feeding someone young or an invalid.

That lesson learnt he dunked the rest himself, watching as she tended the meat, its juices dripping to a bubbling tray below from which she scooped more liquid to continue basting it. Obviously the venison was to be the centrepiece of a communal feast later that day.

Jack sat by the fire recovering his strength in companionable silence as memories of the long night before came back to him.

The fire crackled and so did the surface of the venison.

'Smells good,' he said.

'Roadkill,' she murmured by way of explanation. 'Barklice nabbled this one before he jaunted off long days since with Pike and Master Brief to find you, so it's been well hung and goodly matured. Arnold told me you did good and earned your first groat. That's put the good word out about you.'

Jack nodded, liking the praise.

He glanced at her a little shyly, for all he could remember of their meeting the night before was the way she had enveloped him in her arms by way of greeting and saying goodnight, as she did the others. That seemed the Bilgesnipe way.

She was large and bosomy, the coloured ribbons in her hair matched by the colours of her striped silk dress, which though almost down to her ankles was not quite long enough to hide the full yellow petticoats beneath, and the matching lacy camisole that peeped above her bodice.

Her plump fingers were adorned with rings and her wrists with golden bracelets which jangled as she worked at the venison, which as well as basting she routinely poked with a skewer.

From all Brief and the others had said, and from the dark shiny colour of her skin, Jack guessed he was in the presence of his first genuine, full-blown, Bilgesnipe and he liked what he saw. She breathed life and good cheer and a kind of energetic contentment which engaged with him, as with all else about her.

'That's 'im coming!' she announced, 'So it's rousting time.'

She stood up and went and opened a door into the kitchens.

Jack heard feet on the wooden floor above his head and a wheezing coughing followed by the sudden explosive sound of someone spitting followed by what seemed a long silence before he heard the metallic clang of a spittoon in receipt of the lump of phlegm.

'He's spat, he's on form and he's coming!' roared Ma'Shuqa into the kitchen, 'so look about folks! You know the where and the why so all you've to do is the what. Meal in an hour when the Chosen One and her party turns up.'

'Not you then this year, my dear!' sang someone from within.

'Nor any day to come from now to eternity!' replied Ma'Shuqa good-humouredly. 'I had my day as Bride and won the swainiest of 'em all.'

'You did, Mirror rest his soul!' said someone else sympathetically.

From this exchange, and the sudden sad look in her eye, Jack guessed they were talking about her husband, Arnold's father, and that tragically he was no more.

'That be so!' she said, guessing Jack's thought. 'Pa'Shuqa they called him, though he were never no Bilgesnipe. That be his stave above the inglenook waiting for the day he's able to come back, for come back he will. The Fyrd got 'im but I doubt they killed him because he's not the dying kind.'

The stave was huge and was attached to the wall with hooped nails covered in soot.

Women came in from the kitchen carrying ewers of water and some large round brots on wooden platters.

Brief and the others appeared looking half asleep and out of things as Jack had earlier.

At the same moment Old Mallarkhi himself appeared, having wheezed his way from above down some unseen stairs, and through a door from the rear of the property.

'They chosen yet?' he said, eyeing Jack briefly before offering himself up to his daughter for a loving and respectful hug and kiss on both cheeks.

' 'Tis nearly gone one and a half, Pa, so I 'spect they have. But the rain's stopped and the flood paused ready to fall back and a watery sun showing its arms and legs. So they'll not be shading our door a while yet!'

'Time enough,' announced Old Mallarhki, 'for us to have our natter with Jack.'

He offered his hand with a wrinkled smile and Jack took it, surprised how strong his grip was.

'We'll take our vittles in the Big Parlour, my love,' he said, leading them back the way he had just come to a room almost as large as the main one, but not beamed. It was a talking shop and rest-place and had chairs plenty enough for them to sit down in comfort.

While the others had colomby and dunked corncrake Jack looked around. There were some rickety shelves, a few tatty ledgers, an out-of-date calendar from a manufacturer of gas lighting for the year 1912. There was a fire which burned cheerfully in a cast-iron grate set into the wall raised off the floor. Wood was stacked on one side, coal in a scuttle on the other, and safely out of the way was a small box of tinder and a larger one of kindling.

Mallarkhi was of average height but very thin, with a face grey and cadaverous, but from illness rather than any defect in humour or personality. He looked as he was, a hydden whose days were numbered.

Yet he exuded such strength and life, such overwhelming warmth and purpose, and obvious courage in the face of illness, that the initial alarm that Jack felt at his sorry outer appearance was replaced at once by a desire to see him right in every way.

His clothes were of very mixed quality, his trews being of thick, high-quality stuff, dark and well cut. But they were hauled in around his waist by a piece of green twine, of the kind used for tying up bales. His shirt was of delicate white cotton, very clean, but its collar was far too big for him and his painfully thin shoulders did not fill it any more. Jack knew he was looking at clothes once made and worn for a man who was no more, except in spirit, and that still fighting for life every inch of the way.

The air in the room held the pleasant scent of sweet, aromatic tobacco which Mallarkhi obviously enjoyed because he raised his head back and smelt the air as if smelling the perfume on a woman. A shelf above the fire had a rack of pipes and a tin box labelled *The Fabled 'Dammer* in raised but chipped and faded red-lettering, against several images, external and internal, of a foreign hostelry very like Mallarkhi's own.

He opened it and the rich, moist scent of fresh tobacco emerged most deliciously. The substance itself was inside a yellow pouch, made of a flexible opaque material that looked like a cross between rubber and plastic.

Mallarkhi opened it, sniffed it long enough to close his eyes and seem to dream for a few moments, and then took a pinch and placed it on an iron plate that hinged out horizontally from the fire, where it curled in the heat, blackened slowly and began to smoke and so add its scent to the room.

'One and all,' said Mallarkhi, whose authority in his own domain took precedence over Brief's, ''tis safe to say that Jack here's accepted. We know what he did, how he's come, and the scars on his poor body which I have heard some of you espied yesternight in the baths confirm the tale that Master Brief was long since personal witness to, as were you Mister Pike and you Master Stort, though but a lad then.

That tale being that he saved the life of the girl Katherine and thereby fulfilled certain prophecies and the like upon which Master Brief be the expert not me. Which being so means that the main purpose of his coming to Brum has been served and satisfied.'

They all nodded enthusiastically except for Jack.

'I thought I came to Brum to find Katherine,' said Jack.

'Ah!' said Brief ambiguously.

'Hmmm!' murmered Stort.

Pike breathed in heavily but said nothing.

Jack waited.

Old Mallarkhi broke the silence and said, 'I can't say I be mightily surprised at his confusion, seeing as the brains of Master Brief and Stort combinate into a labyrinth of cleverness filled with spidery webs of mystery which often leaves ordinary mortals like me here puzzled, as it now has Jack. He don't understand the web you weave, so you better disentangle it for him. Make it plain, Master Brief, make it plain.'

'All I want to do is find Katherine,' Jack repeated.

'My dear fellow,' said Brief, 'that is not the issue, not the issue at all.'

'Well I think it is,' replied Jack angrily. 'You don't seem to understand . . .'

'We *know* where she is, *that's* not the problem.'

Jack looked astonished.

'Where is she then?'

Pike pulled out his chronometer.

'Right now? She's being made up to look like a Sister of Charity and already she's enjoying herself getting ready for the birthday party of the High Ealdor.'

'Oh,' said Jack, not understanding much of this.

'It won't be too hard to get her out when we need to, but the problem is getting you both out of Brum *without* you getting taken by the Fyrd or by Sub-Quentor Brunte,' said Brief, 'which is the tangled web Mister Mallarkhi is talking about . . .'

Jack stood up. He wanted to get going.

'Take me to her!' he demanded.

'Sit down if you please, Jack,' said Old Mallarkhi, taking command again. 'It disturbs me when folk stand over me and I'm liable to stab 'em in the giblets.' His right hand wandered menacingly towards the sturdy-looking dirk that hung from his belt. 'Old habits die hard among us Deritenders. Tell the lad the truth gennelmen and we can all rest easy. It's time he knew.'

It seemed to Jack that everyone in the Hyddenworld knew what was going on but him.

'But you're sure she's safe?'

Only when they had all confirmed that much did he sit down again. Brief began to talk.

'In the next few hours Igor Brunte will take control of Brum. It will be the first serious insurrection against the Fyrd in a major city in the Hyddenworld for nearly twenty years. The last one resulted in the execution of over two thousand people and the public flaying of the instigators, so Brunte is doing something very risky.

'Strictly speaking he's not a Fyrd at all. He's a Pole who has been brought up a Fyrd after they wiped his family and village out. He hates the Fyrd and he hates the Sinistral who rule them. He'd kill the whole dynasty if he could.

'So he's got something in common with the free-thinking peoples of Brum and Englalond, a fact of which our High Ealdor Lord Festoon is well aware and which we wish to turn to our advantage. So we support what he's doing when it comes to ridding us of Sinistral control of our city.

'Now this is where you come in, Jack. Brunte's known of your existence and that of Katherine, and the bond between you – and the fact that the Peace-Weaver watches over you – ever since the night of that terrible crash . . .'

'How can he possibly know that?'

'He was there, Jack, he saw it happen. As were myself, Stort and Pike. We were none of us there by chance. You could say our wyrds brought us there but that's too simple an explanation, true though it be. Stort led myself and Pike there because he had a notion, as he sometimes does, that something was going to happen.

'The Peace-Weaver was there because it's her job to be where she needs to be and anyway she was looking for her successor the Shield Maiden, who of course she found, but more of that in a moment.

Brunte was there because he was accompanying one of the Sinistral clan and it was they who caused the accident under cover of violent weather. But you know some of that already . . . ?'

Jack nodded grimly.

'Things didn't go according to plan. They were trying to kill you but you didn't die and what's more you saved Katherine which, strangely or not as the case may be, fulfilled a prophecy about a giant and a maid, or seemed to, that Beornamund is said to have made. Brunte did not know any of that then, but he did glimpse the Peace-Weaver and he saw the pendant of Beornamund and, in that moment, to his hatred of the Sinistral was added a desire to one day possess the Sphere, a desire shared by Slaeke Sinistral the Second, head of the dynasty.'

'Why did they want to kill me?'

'They feared that you would find a way of stopping them recreating the Sphere.'

'You mentioned the Shield Maiden . . .'

'Yes, Katherine . . .'

'That's ridiculous, she's just Katherine. There's nothing special about Katherine except that I . . .'

'Except that you what?'

He coloured but said nothing. He did not need to. His love for Katherine was obvious enough.

'One way or another the High Ealdor and Igor Brunte, though hardly bosom friends, colluded to keep your continuing existence a secret. The Sinistral assumed you were dead because Brunte had the sense to tell them so. As for Katherine, no one knew her importance and it was best left that way. The one human who knew for certain about the Hyddenworld was Katherine's mother, because she remembered us being at the crash and the help we gave.

'Most of us have made the journey to Woolstone through the years to place mirrors and chimes in her garden to protect Katherine from the Fyrd. They confuse them.

'We guessed, as did Brunte, that the Sinistral had finally worked out about you and Katherine being alive and that when Clare was gone Katherine would be vulnerable and through her you would be too. Slaeke Sinistral sent Meyor Feld, one of his more experienced

Fyrd, and some colleagues to investigate Brunte and take you – though for what reason we can only guess.

'Probably he thought that one way or another you would lead them towards finding the lost pieces of the Sphere. Brunte succeeded in winning Feld to his point of view about the Sinistral. If he had not done so you would probably be back in Germany by now.

'We were not sure he would keep his word to Brunte, so we came to Woolstone to keep an eye on things and offer what protection we could. One of the reasons we wanted you to make an appearance in Brum was so that people would know for certain that you exist. Brunte's takeover of the city is only the beginning of what is likely to be years of revolt against the Sinistral dynasty.

'You, Jack, are a giant-born and, we think, born to be leader of a global revolution against the Sinistral.'

Jack shook his head in disbelief.

'Sounds like Brunte's the leader, not me,' he said. 'All I want to do is get Katherine to safety and normality.'

'That's all we want for now, and for Brum folk to know you exist. Once they know something about you, it's up to you to do the rest. But that will not be for a few years yet.'

'Like what?' said Jack doubtfully.

'It's in your wyrd that something will happen.'

'Humph!' said Jack.

'It's also in a giant's wyrd that a great deal that is unpredictable will happen,' observed Bedwyn Stort.

'Which is where we come in,' said Pike. 'We're here to keep an eye on things.'

'When you say the problem is getting us out of Brum, what's wrong with the way we came in?'

'Brunte will not let that happen. He's imposed what's called a Seal, claiming it's against the floods. There won't be floods, not this year. But the Seal'll remain in place until he gets you.'

'What will he do with me and Katherine if he does?'

'We don't know. Keep you close-guarded until you lead him to Beornamund's artefacts – and we don't want him to get his hands on those. Or maybe he's curious about Katherine being the Shield Maiden. We don't know for certain. But what happens in Brum this week, next week, next year, is not your concern. The prophecy says . . .'

'What exactly?' said Jack dismissively.

'That you'll be back in no time at all,' said Stort.

'Back to do what?'

They shrugged.

'Have to wait and see,' said Stort.

'Just so,' agreed Brief.

'Now . . .' said Stort, getting up, 'I have to go and work on Jack and Katherine's exit strategy . . .'

'I've only just got here.'

'As Mister Pike explained, that's all we ever wanted for this first visit, that you're seen,' said Brief. 'Ideally you'd actually do something as well, but that's not something we have any real control over. Eh, Mister Mallarkhi?'

'That be how it always is,' came the reply. 'But time to end this good talk, the Bride's Feast be nigh!'

70

PARTY TIME

L ord Festoon's twenty-fifth birthday party officially started at noon, but did not get going until a little later because of delays to arrangements and guests caused by the floods.

Two hundred of Brum's great and good, along with the not-so-great and the definitely bad, were now crammed into the Orangery, enjoying food and drink, the conversation, and watching the myriad entertainments their host had so lavishly provided.

Subterranean though it was, and without benefit of direct sunlight, the great architect ã Faroün, composer and lute player, blessed be his name, had succeeded in directing light into the huge chamber by way of mirrors and reflective tubes energized by a simboul, or sounding board, composed of vibrating rods of timla wood, so that oranges could grow there in abundance, their fragrance delicious in the sweet-flowing air.

A good time after things had started, the Master of Ceremonies clapped his hands and the guests fell quiet, waiting now for the procession of musicians, acrobats, clowns, circus acts, japery, jesters and dancers which traditionally preceded the presentation of the birthday cake. This was the moment when the citizens of Brum honoured its High Ealdor with a gift of the supreme art of one of the many patissiers employed in the kitchen of Parlance, Master of Cuisine.

The procession wove snakelike among the guests, so that they could feast their eyes and ears on all that was on display while helping themselves to delicacies, both sweet and savoury, offered by the

Sisters Chaste, as the younger members of the Order of Sisters of Charity were known. On this special occasion these girls were dressed in the alluring diaphanous garments of Chastity in order to signify their untouched and unblemished state – to the delight of all, including themselves.

Among them was Katherine herself, looking just like a dozen others.

Her face was caked in bleached chalk, her eyes lined with mascara, her mouth turned into a sugared cherry by the expert application of bright red lipstick, her cropped hair now hidden under a black wig, her pale robe of floaty silk suggestive but not actually revealing.

From the beatific smile on her face it might have seemed she was thoroughly enjoying herself, and in a way she was. The anointing of her body with seductive oils and potions by the Sisters had proved a very pleasant and relaxing experience, her mood already carelessly dreamy as a result of the mildly hallucinogenic elixirs with which she had been plied since her capture.

There was also an infectious excitement about the occasion and a sense of camaraderie among the younger Sisters which made it very tempting for Katherine to enjoy the present and not worry about the future. Finding the will to fight back and clear her brain for the second time that day was proving difficult. But even so she had already begun looking for a way to escape.

71

ADMONISHMENT

Lord Festoon's birthday party was the one annual function in Brum which it was obligatory for the entire Council of Ten and their senior staff to attend. Any absences were taken as an insult to the office of High Ealdor, and therefore to the city as well. There was even a city statute, going back nearly two hundred years, which decreed that such non-attendance should incur an 'Admonishment' by the Sub-Quentor, subject to the Quentors' say-so, the nature of that Admonishment being 'at the discretion of the Sub-Quentor' himself.

But Brum being a free and easy sort of place, there had been no Admonishment for more than a century. The Statute had continued to be ignored ever since the Fyrd took over the city, because their senior hierarchy, especially those who were also Councillors, had as little interest in festivities as they had in old statutes.

Sub-Quentor Brunte, however, like so many power-seekers before him, recognized that old and half-forgotten statutes could serve their purpose for those who knew how to exploit them to legitimize actions that others might otherwise object to. All he needed therefore was an 'Order of Admonishment' from the Quentors.

Brunte had three habitual offenders regarding this statute to attend.

The first and most important on the list was General Elon, the city's Administrator, who was responsible for maintaining the civilian and material security of Brum. He had no time for Festoon and his self-indulgences, and he was adept at finding excuses not to attend, some better and more plausible than others.

The rain and rising waters of the past days and the previous night's decision by the Ten to impose a Seal provided the perfect excuse for the apology he had given. He was more than content to stay in his quarters, where he could get on with some work, receive reports, and keep a general eye on things with the help of junior staff, while his senior people attended the illustrious celebrations.

The only one of these high-rankers who elected not to go was Lieutenant Backhaus, a taciturn officer who Elon liked to keep near by him because of his great efficiency and ability to make logical decisions quickly.

A second habitual stay-away was Freddy Wick, commodity trader and the richest hydden in all Englalond, who, having genuinely ricked his back twenty years before, had ever since found it the perfect excuse to avoid doing anything he did not wish to.

The afternoon of Festoon's party had become the occasion for a little tradition of his own: having an athletic time in the arms of his mistress in his nuptial bed. It was a secret ritual which gave him strength to put up with his loathsome and self-centred wife, who would not have missed Festoon's celebrations for anything.

The third and last stay-away among the Ten was Transport Director Dowty, whose lack of personal skills and nitpicking obsession for rules had caused his demotion from the same job in Berlin three years before. It was a slight he had taken badly at the time, yet he had ended up happier. For Brum had worked its magic on him and, thirty-six months later, he knew how to control things to enhance the traffic flow of this complex city better than anyone, including even his human counterparts in the Upperworld. A sworn enemy of Elon, and indeed of most of the other Fyrd hierarchy, because he so much disliked their general air of superiority, he had never been once to the High Ealdor's party – and would never go, even if it became a sacking offence.

His usual excuse was that his timetable did not allow it. Which was the absolute truth, for he was obsessed by time-keeping, so that every minute of his day was scheduled and prioritized, with the result that he never wasted time on what he considered unimportant matters. In fact his life was an arid desert, devoid of any of the pleasures that delight others, whether of the spirit, the mind or the flesh.

Dowty lived alone because that meant he was not subject to others' domestic inefficiency. He preferred simple food, generally eaten raw, because cooking and washing-up absorbed valuable time. He had no leisure activities, because he thought they served no purpose. He would never use two words if one would do, and often he used none at all. Though not totally devoid of normal mortal impulses where matters of the heart and flesh were concerned, he suppressed them as being mere time-wasters.

Yet Dowty had friends, though not many, mainly people like himself who were wedded only to efficiency and finding strategies to improve it. One such soul mate had been Brunte's late predecessor, Finial Fane, who had shared with the transport manager an obsessive love of numbers and efficiency. It was through him that Brunte had met Dowty and learned that he possessed an extraordinary, perhaps unique, natural gift: he could tell the time without reference to a chronometer. In fact he could *count* the time with an accuracy greater than any chronometer.

It happened that Fane, before his death, had asked his friend about the source of this gift in Brunte's presence. Dowty could only suggest that it was like tuning in to a universal clock, though not one which possessed a tick or any mechanism. Rather, he said, it was an inner rhythm, as if by some freak chance his body had been aligned or attuned to the rhythms of the Universe itself.

It was that word 'Universe' which had struck a chord in Brunte's mind, and that association, along with the fact that Dowty was by far the most efficient and reliable of the ten Councillors, decided Brunte that this was someone who might have his uses.

Brunte summoned a meeting of the Quentors, timing it deliberately to coincide with the start of Festoon's party at midday, insisting that this meeting would not take long but was crucially important.

The elderly Quentors, who habitually left no doubt in Brunte's mind that they regarded him as their minion, protested at having to delay their arrival at the festivities, but they were persuaded to do so by his urgency. Brunte arranged a meeting place just two floors below the Orangery itself, and the chamber chosen was ill-lit and damp, a rough desk and chairs hurriedly assembled. The Quentors were rather surprised to see several of Brunte's guards posted outside, under the command of Meyor Feld. 'Sub-Quentor,' one of them asked impatiently, the moment they sat down, 'what exactly is this about?'

Brunte explained to them about the ancient statute of admonishment and argued that it was his duty, and theirs, to enforce it.

They were reluctant to do so, not understanding why it was an issue, or why he was being so tiresomely formal about this matter, since his predecessors had turned a blind eye to Council members' absence from the birthday party.

'We need to keep our books in order, gentlemen, in case we undergo an Inspection,' he explained. An Inspection, conducted by Fyrd sent over from the heartland, was a matter of dread for the administrators of all hydden cities.

'Is one imminent?' one asked anxiously. 'I myself have not heard of it!'

'There has not been one for so long here in Brum that I fear one may be impending,' replied Brunte, his smile wide and warm, as if he was merely doing them a favour by raising the issue. 'So do I have your permission to visit these three Councillors who intend not to attend the High Ealdor's feste and formally admonish them on your behalf?'

The Quentors prevaricated.

Two of the people concerned – Elon and Wick – wielded considerable power. The third, Dowty, was an obsessive who nobody would miss anyway.

One of them heard the shuffling of feet outside.

'Are those guards out there really necessary, Brunte?' one of them inquired dismissively.

Brunte's eyes glinted, for he liked neither the tone nor the manner of delivery. In silence he got up and summoned Feld.

'The Quentors want to know why you're here, Meyor.'

Feld replied smoothly, 'There has been general unrest, gentlemen, in the wake of word unfortunately getting out that the Council of Ten has ordered a Seal. We are only here for your safety. On this particular day of the year things can sometimes get out of hand.'

Considering the possibility of danger to their own persons, this was not something they could argue with.

'Well, then,' one of them began, 'we don't want to spend all afternoon on this business, so let's at least talk about it.'

They conferred among themselves for a minute or two.

'You may certainly visit Councillors Wick and Dowty, if you must,' Brunte was told, 'but you must leave General Elon strictly alone. It would hardly be politic to admonish *him*!'

They even laughed, as if the idea was absurd.

'And anyway, Sub-Quentor,' added one of the others, using a tone of cold, superior irony that was not lost on Brunte, 'even someone as persuasive as yourself would hardly find the right words to reprimand such a superior officer.'

'You could be right!' replied Brunte, with such seeming good humour that they all laughed. 'Yet you would agree, as would surely the General himself, that under the rules he too needs admonishing?'

They shifted about a bit, more interested now in getting to the festivity than in a mere technical wrongdoing by one of the most powerful Fyrd in the city.

'We might think that, but it would be unwise to declare it officially.'

'Unofficially?'

'Statutorily, yes, he should be here too, but, well . . .'

'Well, he has very good reason for absence during a time of potential floods, a fact I suggest we officially minute,' said Igor Brunte, adding jovially, 'but he *should* be here, and he isn't, and that's a fact as well.'

'It *is* a fact, Mister Brunte! Now, can we . . . ?'

'Of course, but let us at least also minute your . . . shall, we say *dismay* at his absence. That word will amply cover the situation should any Inspection ever be made and this matter raised – should it not?'

Uneasily they supposed it might.

Brunte signalled his clerk, Doam, to minute this 'decision' and then got the unwilling Quentors to initial it.

The moment it was done, Doam handed up the book to Brunte for examination. The Sub-Quentor looked at it closely, smiled with satisfaction, tucked the book under his arm and stood up, his smile fading.

'Thank you gentlemen. Feld, see the Quentors now to a place of safety, and return here immediately!'

The room quickly filled with guards who surrounded the Quentors and led them protesting from the room, and from there down the metal stairs leading into the darkness of the corridors below.

'Where are you . . . ?'

'This is not . . . '

'You cannot do this . . .'

But Feld did, with the willing help of the guards.

Brunte sat back down at the table, listening to the fading footsteps of the Quentors below and the growing sounds of revelry above. There was silence where he was, and peace.

Doam meanwhile said nothing.

Brunte stared at the Minute Book.

Only when Feld returned with two of his guards did Brunte rise.

'It is done,' said Feld grimly. 'They will be a problem to you no longer.'

'Good,' said Brunte. 'Now, gentlemen, we have very important work to do.'

They reached General Elon's well-guarded residence twenty minutes later, and demanded to see him in the name of the Quentors.

Lieutenant Backhaus appeared.

'I am here to administer an Admonishment,' announced Brunte formally, holding out a copy of the Quentors' minute prepared by Doam.

Backhaus read it quickly and shook his head in surprise and disbelief: 'I don't think this is wise, do you?'

'Are you refusing us entrance?'

'No, Sub-Quentor, I am not.'

Brunte smiled and followed Backhaus inside. There was already an unspoken understanding between them. Backhaus's conflicts with Elon were well-known.

'Your men can stay outside,' said Backhaus.

'They could, but I need witnesses.'

'Brunte, this is ridiculous.'

'Let's get it over with,' said Brunte, pushing past him.

They found Elon in his private quarters, flanked by an orderly. He was still in uniform.

'Sub-Quentor?' he said formally, with evident surprise and annoyance.

Brunte looked apologetic and explained that, much against his own advice and judgement, the Quentors had decided that in view of Elon's absence from the festivities he should be admonished.

Elon's response was frank: 'I have better things to attend to than Festoon's foolery, so now you've done your duty, I stand admonished and you can leave.'

'But we have not,' replied Brunte with a dangerous smile, 'yet done our duty.'

Elon's eyes widened in surprise, and then in alarm, as the smiling Brunte stepped forward and pulled out his knife.

Then, in one well-practised movement, he clasped one large hand firmly behind Elon's neck, and with the other thrust the point hard and fast into the General's right lung.

Elon half-screamed, half-grunted and raised one hand in protest. Brunte brushed it aside and thrust the blade into him again, this time piercing his stomach.

The orderly stared open-mouthed as his superior officer fell sideways. Letting out short, deep gasps, he hit the floor and his legs began shaking uncontrollably.

Brunte turned to Backhaus. 'Finish him off,' he ordered.

It was his way of getting the young officer to become party to the 'Admonishment'. It was also the best possible way of testing him.

Backhaus looked from the fallen Elon to Brunte, and back again.

Elon was immobile but still conscious, his eyes filled with pain, fear and bewilderment. He watched as the young officer unsheathed his own knife. Backhaus bent down to his stricken commanding officer, stared briefly into his eyes without compassion, and thrust the knife into his heart. Elon shivered briefly and died.

'It is done,' said Backhaus, pulling away and turning round. He stared unflinchingly into Brunte's eyes.

Opportunity comes only once – that is a basic message in the training of Fyrd fighters. It is not necessarily true, but is as good a four-word mantra as any.

Backhaus said, 'There'll be no need not to trust me, sir. I am with you. Elon was not a worthy commanding officer. Nor are any of his personal staff worth much either, or even to be trusted.'

'You know who needs to be dealt with?' inquired Brunte.

Backhaus nodded.

'Then do it, and wait here for my further instructions. You'll follow that order carefully?'

'To the letter, Sub-Quentor. There are many junior Fyrd under Elon's command ready to support an insurrection against the Sinistral. It will not be hard.'

'Many, Lieutenant Backhaus?'

'Not yet a majority, but they are well placed and after today . . .'

'It is today that matters in terms of who I shall trust, not those who join us after it. Be watchful, Backhaus. Survive this day and you will have my favour. Understood?'

Backhaus was not entirely sure he did but he nodded all the same.

Brunte strode out of Elon's quarters as calmly as he had walked in. Backhaus began herding Elon's frightened staff together with the help of Elon's shocked adjutant, in preparation for eliminating those he decided he could not rely on.

Brunte now looked different, almost smelt different: he had that aura of command and power about him that comes to one who has assumed it forcibly. He glanced at his chronometer, and his waiting men gathered close.

'We shall now admonish Mr Wick,' he said. 'That need not take us long.'

Nor did it. They found Wick naked in bed with his long-term mistress. They killed them both, right where they lay, leaving them obscenely entwined together for Wick's wife to find in her marriage bed.

Brunte knew well enough the note of fear this would instil in the cosy world of Brum's upper echelons. He fully understood the value of a reputation, and that, on this day of days, his own was in the making.

His last visit was to Hrap Dowty, whose operation room – from which Brum's complex transport system was supervised – lay within a stone's throw of the Warwick and Birmingham Canal's aqueduct, beneath the River Rea side of the old Corporation Wharf.

All the walls but one were just bare, dirty-yellow brick. The exception was a steel wall, painted dull grey, which sloped steeply upwards at the same angle as an attic room built into the eaves.

But this, Brunte knew, was no attic wall.

Blue light filtered down onto shiny tables whose upper surfaces were in fact exquisitely drawn maps of the city.

Over the impressive room, which was a hive of constant activity, Dowty presided from a simple wooden chair placed before a simple wooden desk. His clothes were simple too, tailored of brown fustian without any ostentation or ornament, except for a solitary dark red flash on his right shoulder, the distinctive mark of a Councillor.

'Sub-Quentor,' he said by way of greeting, when Brunte arrived flanked by his people. A wave of fear swept across the faces of Dowty's assistants, but his own remained impassive.

'Councillor,' replied Brunte with a slight smile. 'Your report this morning was well received, I think. *Will* there indeed be flooding?'

'Unlikely, on the scale implied,' said Dowty, 'but nevertheless some. Organizing the Seal was a wise precaution anyway, quite apart from its usefulness in your own enterprise. But I suggest we begin to undo it soon. Has the party begun?'

'Well under way. However, if word gets to Festoon's residence before my work is done, it is possible there will be some escapes and even counter-attacks. You yourself will be targeted no doubt, therefore I am leaving three guards here with you. You are not to leave until summoned by one of my people, and all your staff should remain here as well. If anyone visits, they are not to be allowed to leave, but my own people will see to that.'

Shivering slightly, Dowty stood up and shut his eyes, then opened them again.

'You are three minutes and four seconds ahead of the schedule, Sub-Quentor. That is good, but you had better leave now, for the River Rea is rising fast at Montague III.'

He pressed a button on his desk. The steel wall immediately behind him began to rise.

'Which is where exactly?' wondered Brunte. He realized he liked Dowty – liked his precision and his jargon. It gave him a feeling of security.

'It is *here*,' replied Dowty. 'Montague III is our own section here.'

Watery, racing, mottled light replaced the steel wall as it disappeared somewhere above them. For what it now revealed was a second wall, this one of thick plate glass, across part of which the river flowed, the higher section being spray and sky and not much else. The river's constant roar sounded loud.

'Do not take the lower route to Curzon Street,' advised Dowty. 'Instead take the upper one by Proof House Lane. Do you know it?'

Brunte confirmed that he did.

'Until later then,' he continued, 'when all will become clearer than it is now. You had better get your replacement ready, Councillor.'

'That I have done long since,' said Dowty. 'Now, if you will forgive me, we have reports from Deritend.' He turned away to attend to them.

But Brunte stayed where he was, his eyes glinting suddenly red and flinty.

'Councillor!' he said sharply.

Dowty turned back, slight alarm in his expression.

'Never turn your back on me again,' said Brunte, 'not ever. It is . . . impolite.'

Dowty stared at him, processing this new information.

'I never will,' he promised.

72

PARTY OVER

The climax of Festoon's party was the parade of the Sisters Chaste before his mock throne so that amidst much jollity he might choose one of them to be his Birthday Bride.

This ritual was an ancient one, dating back to medieval times when the question of succession was an important one for cities such as Brum. For without a successor there was no continuity and without more than one heir there was insecurity. The Chaste Sisters were the young virgins among the Sisters of Charity, and the selection of one of them each year by the High Ealdor was a means to that end.

The Chosen One was allowed to spend a single night in the High Ealdor's bed, after which she was sequestered for nine lonely months, watched over by the most senior Sisters of Charity. Many produced no heir and were returned to ordinary sisterhood; a few bore young, and these became heirs to the throne of Brum. On them the future relied.

By Raster Avon's time the ritual had lost this traditional significance and was simply an occasion for japery and fun – the Chosen One being a mere symbolic bride for the day whose reward was not a night in the bed of a ruler but a pendant disc of gold-plated base metal, fashioned and bejewelled in the imagined guise of the mythic pendant that Beornamund had made for Imbolc and with which, it was still hoped, she travelled down the years.

Under Festoon the ritual had an edge that was bitter-sweet, for how could it ever be that one such as he, so obscenely obese, so evidently the last in the now corrupted Avon line, should have need of a bride, or the interest or even the competence to father a child upon her?

So while most folk clapped and laughed, those of them who knew the history of the tradition and understood its importance could hardly bear to look.

With a roll of great tibla drums of the Russian steppe and a fanfare of tuble horns the crowd was marshalled around the edges of the Orangery and an expectant hush fell.

For a brief moment total darkness descended, until one by one spotlights shone onto the floor into which red-silked tumblers somersaulted and held still. Then they began tumbling in and out of the orange trees, plucking fruit as they went which they hurled high above everyone's head such that they arced into final descent to the hands of jugglers who threw them back up again to arch back and forth across the room, caught in light and an endless stream of colour.

'Splendid!' cried the delighted Festoon, so taken with the clever display that he half rose from his throne, clapping his fat hands together, his face beaming, his stomach swaying from side to side before, tired from this unplanned exercise, he slumped back down again.

Then, with a further fanfare, and drum rolls on the tibla, the crowd began clapping as the first Sister Chaste was led in on the arm of a grey-haired military man, his uniform in the bright, dashing style of Burmese dacoits.

Katherine had been having a great time. She had never been much of a party-goer but this, by far, was the best she had ever known, her normal reservations having been left behind when Sister Mary chopped more off her hair, drugged her and then fitted her with a black wig.

She had somehow teamed up with Sister Mary at the party and the two, realizing more fun was to be had in company, had stuck together and joined the dance which brought the Chaste Sisters together in the centre of the gallery before Lord Festoon as the central attraction.

At first Katherine hardly cared.

The music was as intoxicating as the costumes, the decorations, the astonishing feats of acrobatics all about her and the amazing way in which one of the jugglers, having reached one end of the gallery, was now somersaulting back and juggling oranges at the same time.

When the Sisters Chaste drew level with the throne Katherine said, 'So that's Lord Festoon! He looks truly awful!'

'There is no other like him!' giggled Sister Mary.

'What do I do if he asks me ... well ... you know ... I mean I don't really have to ...'

They laughed some more at that even more awful thought.

'It is an honour you cannot refuse ... but nothing actually happens except you get given a golden pendant you can keep and you have to sit on his knee.'

'Yuk!' said Katherine. 'I wouldn't go anywhere near him.'

'Well you won't get chosen anyway, because he prefers us short ones apparently, so relax.'

'I am relaxed,' said Katherine, adjusting her wig and praying that Jack was a million miles away but safe. 'More or less.'

'Same, same,' replied Mary. 'My family won't like it if I get chosen though, they'd prefer to continue thinking of me as pure.'

'Quite right! You're meant to be chaste.'

Mary grinned knowingly.

'I am,' she said, '... more or less.'

They laughed again, as everyone else was doing, and cheered and joked and linked arms with other Sisters, aware now that everyone's eyes were on them and that the men in the crowd, especially those up around the High Ealdor, were pointing to various of them and assessing which was the worthiest to be chosen.

But then as the music swelled and things got wilder still Katherine felt her head begin to clear and reality to set in.

She was here against her better judgement, they had criticized her body shape, they'd cut her hair, and she had on more make-up than she thought was possible for a single face to wear.

'Time to get out of here,' she told herself, trying to turn the mounting anger she felt to good effect.

But she knew she had to keep up the pretence that she was enjoying herself, so she laughed and clapped and linked arms with Sister Mary and danced about while her eyes darted in every direction looking for ways to escape.

The Master of Ceremonies announced, 'Ladies and Gentlemen, the High Ealdor is making his choice!'

This moment was part of the fun of the ritual as the more senior members of Festoon's court gathered about him looking conspiratorial while they whispered among themselves, pointed at various of the Chaste Sisters, nodded or shook their heads in exaggerated approval or not as the case might be, and generally made a comic meal of it.

It was made all the funnier by the costumes that these supposed courtiers had been dressed in, which were exquisite in their over-the-top detail – brocaded silken jackets with puffed sleeves, silks and dark blue stockings beneath flowery breeches, silk slippers with salmon-pink tassels, and magnificent turbans of loose purple silk which looked like vulgar decorations on a cake – as in a way they were, for they echoed the iced-sugar confections on Festoon's huge birthday cake.

They conferred, Festoon frowned and stroked his chubby hairless chin, they pointed at one or two of the Sisters very ambiguously, nodded their heads and pulled back from their lord. Festoon now smiled and nodded towards one of the courtiers, who came near and consulted.

'Ladies and Gentlemen, the High Ealdor has chosen his Birthday Bride and is now advising the equerries who the lucky Sister will be.'

Katherine watched carefully but with only detached interest, hoping that the chosen one would be Sister Mary but also thinking with a beating heart that if she was going to get away from the Sisters the near-chaos of the party was going to be her best bet. She began looking around the huge room for different entrances to the one she had come in by.

She saw that Sister Supreme and her arrogant assistant Sister Chalice were close nearby, watching them it seemed. Beyond them were all sorts of distinguished-looking people, while at the only entrances she could see folk were more subdued, perhaps because there were Fyrd guards there, their numbers increasing all the time.

Getting away was not going to be easy.

Sister Mary touched her arms and said, 'Uh, uh! He's coming our way.'

An equerry had detached himself from Festoon's side and was slowly crossing the Orangery floor and heading in their general direction.

His turban was even more monstrously woven up above his head than the others, and his impressive beard waxed so much that it shone in the light, as did his red cheeks. The trouble was, Katherine saw, that his eye was not on Sister Mary, but on herself.

'You'd better duck!' said Mary, grabbing Katherine's arm. 'Otherwise he might choose you!'

Katherine looked at Lord Festoon and he was smiling and looking straight at her, confirmation that she might have, unfortunately, caught his eye.

'I'm not going to allow that to happen,' she said to Mary, trying to sink towards the floor.

The horrible equerry was almost upon her.

'He's wearing earrings,' whispered Mary, 'and his stomach's on the way to being as large as the High Ealdor's!'

The equerry stopped in front of them.

'But I don't *want* to,' Katherine whispered urgently to Mary, everything having fallen silent and with everyone crowding round to see which of the Sisters was finally going to get chosen.

The equerry reached for Katherine, and had turned dramatically towards Festoon for him to confirm that she was the one, when a curious wave of movement spread through the crowd and then came a shout from the entrance.

It was sufficiently loud and urgent for people's heads to turn, including Katherine's. Fyrd guards had entered in numbers at one end of the Orangery and seemed to be pulling someone out of the chamber against their wishes. Then they went for someone else and people began to retreat, while other more senior officials tried to go and see what was going on.

The turbaned equerry was pulled away from Katherine by the swirling, panicking crowd. But when he fought his way back quite fiercely and momentarily grabbed her arm she decided enough was enough and this was the best moment she was going to get to flee the Sisters.

Earlier, when she had looked for escape routes, she had noticed a tapestry, hanging near where the bulk of the Fyrd were, which occasionally moved as if caught in a draught. She saw her chance, stamped on the equerry's foot, snatched her arm from his grasp, ducked low and ran.

73

THE CUNNING KNOT

The Deritend Feast at the Muggy Duck was a very informal affair compared with the event at Lord Festoon's. The party consisted almost entirely of Mallarkhi's relatives and friends and started long before the Bride herself got there.

When she did there was a great commotion at the door and another crowd of people came in, leading a girl more beautiful than Jack had ever seen.

'There she be!' cried Old Mallarkhi. 'The Chosen One herself. Our Perfection! Our own Bride! And don't she look the part!?'

She was dark like Ma'Shuqa, and had the same full figure, and bright ribbons in her dark hair. Her smile was wide, her eyes sparkling.

'Gentlemen and Ladies, one and all, there's not one of you that don't know Hais, the best-made Bride there ever was . . .'

Jack, who was standing next to Master Brief, grabbed his arm and said, 'How long is this going on for? I want to go and find Katherine, I can't stay here . . .'

But it did no good.

'It's under control, Jack. Trust us. She's at Lord Festoon's and we've people there who will get her to safety at the right moment. It would be deeply insulting to leave a Deritend party early, and give great offence. Only a life-and-death emergency will get you away from here and not have folk talk about it badly. The idea is to build your reputation, not destroy it. Relax, Jack! Enjoy yourself! Katherine will be all right.'

There being nothing else that he could do, Jack allowed himself to follow this advice.

Hais was led to the place of honour, the rest of them taking their places where they liked, Jack and Brief finding seats opposite her along with Pike.

There was no denying her great allure, from shining eyes and hair to a bodice that invited lingering stares, a hydden form tall and graceful, and a smile and voice as sweet. Old Mallarkhi, who sat next to her, stood up.

'Let's get on with it!' he called out, as Master of Ceremonies.

Jack could not help noticing that she looked remarkably happy to be the centre of this ceremony. She smiled, clapped, laughed and looked here and there, from one to other of her many relatives, with a real sense of joy.

'She's beautiful,' said Jack admiringly.

She was as different to Katherine's fairness as night to day.

Their goblets were charged with red mead and an elderly relative of Hais stood up and made a toast.

'To the Bride's Gift and whither it be bound!'

They raised their goblets, spoke out the words 'Bride's Gift' in unison and drank.

'Ma'Shuqa, bring it on!' cried her father.

She did so, carrying a long object wrapped in black silk and curiously bound with silver cord, variously knotted but with so many loose ends they were impossible to count.

Close-to it was impossible to say what was inside, or how it might be untied, and the only thing for it was to pull one of the cords and hope for the best.

The wrapped and bound gift was then taken to the person indi-cated, a cord pulled and, that failing, another person chosen.

Each time a new person had a go it was the custom to call out rather dramatically, 'This one I think!' before he or she tugged hard at it.

'It's not a gift for the bride but from the bride to her groom,' whispered Stort. 'Each pull on one of those cords tightens the knot. But in theory there's one cord to release them all, however tight the knot gets, and the gift can then be unwrapped by the lucky recipient.

Whoever pulls it and finds out what the gift is becomes the groom. But that never happens of course, and that's the joke.

'Nobody wants it to because then the bride gets to choose who she wants, and we already know who *that* is.'

Brief was right, nothing did happen when people chose and pulled a cord, and so it continued, the pleasant tension rising ahead of the moment when, the round of the gift completed among the guests, the bride herself could use the pair of golden scissors placed near her to cut the Cunning Knot, reveal the gift and give it to the groom.

The process was slow, various courses being consumed as they went and the drink much enjoyed as well, so that the event became increasingly jolly and each pull of the cord accompanied by an ever louder shout of approval and merriment.

Brief nodded to the bashful young hydden, the best friend it seemed of Arnold Mallarkhi, who sat next to the bride.

'He'll get the gift in the end,' said Pike, without much enthusiasm because he too wanted to get going after Katherine, 'but once the gift's given we can probably slip away.'

'So there's no cord that will undo it?' asked Jack.

'Ah, now *that* is a very interesting question on which some of the Hyddenworld's greatest mathematicians have worked without result,' said Brief. 'Including myself. It's called a Cunning Knot and it has not been released for over a century and a half.'

The Gift proceeded on its way, everybody taking turns to tug one or other of the loose cords, some very hard indeed to make sure the knot tightened up still further.

'But surely whoever ties it knows the secret?'

'Ma'Shuqa tied it on this occasion, it being a Bilgesnipe thing, handed down from mother to son and then father to daughter. They do it blindfold in a darkened room.'

'Does it ever get untied?'

'There's only ever been one recorded occasion when it has. A century and a half ago, in Raster Avon's time, ā Faroün, Master of Void and Lute Player, was given the Gift at this very Feast. It is said that after a moment's meditation he tugged gently at a cord and the knot opened without difficulty.'

'And what was the gift?' asked Jack.

'You are ever practical and ever-questioning, my young friend,' said Brief. 'It was a lute, of which he was of course a Master, and the strange thing was it was his own.'

'What did he do?'

'Played it, I should think!'

The Gift had all but done its round, with Brief having tried and failed and only Jack to go, when the door crashed open and Barklice almost fell in among them, dishevelled and grubby from journeying through tunnels.

With apologies to one and all he hurried over to Jack and the others.

'I know where she was,' he said, 'and where she should be, but Brunte's Fyrd moved in and all took fright and she was last seen running for it.'

'Where to?' demanded Pike, his face very grim.

'No idea, Mirror help us,' said Barklice, 'but New Brum's a very dangerous place to be for a lone female, dressed like a Sister, who doesn't know the place or the tunnels thereabouts. She hasn't got a chance. Brunte'll have her in no time and all our plans to get you out of here will be scuppered!'

A hush had fallen around the table and smiles faded.

'Your turn Master Jack!' called out Old Mallarkhi, trying to recover the event. 'Say the words and pull a cord.'

'Do it,' whispered Pike, 'and let's get out of here, offence or no offence.'

Jack took the gift, sensed that the arrival of Barklice and their long faces was in danger of spoiling the occasion, and said, 'Ladies and gentlemen, our apologies. We have news from New Brum that my close friend and companion is in danger and we shall have to leave . . .'

There was a murmur of sympathy and a look of approval from Brief for this graceful apology. He could see that the Deritenders appreciated it.

'Your friend be our friend, young Jack,' returned Old Mallarkhi, 'and you better be New Brum bound.'

Jack looked at the gift and then at the bride and smiled.

'Hais,' he said, 'I wish you and your groom every happiness you can find in the years ahead!'

'Pull the cord lad and be on your way with our blessing!'

Jack grinned, glanced at Hais again, and held the gift high for a moment before saying in the traditional way, 'This is the one I think!'

He took one of the cords and pulled it.

It did not tighten at all, but rather wound out from the complex of cords and knots like a wraith of mist sliding away before the sun.

There was a gasp of surprise and dismay.

The knots unwound of their own volition and the cord fell away from the Gift, the black silk wrapping, light as gossamer, following it. But neither cord nor silk went slowly. They shot away from it as if pulled by unseen hands and Jack was left holding what had been inside, which was a wooden box, its lid closed tight.

It was obviously a mistake and not meant for him. Hais already had her potential groom sitting right next to her, having overcome the nerves she had earlier. He was looking as surprised as he was.

Jack thought fast, smiled broadly, looked Hais and then her groom straight in the eye and said, 'Where I come from traditions are different. The bride-to-be has a champion who protects her person when her betrothed is fighting wars!'

Where this came from he was not sure but it seemed to work: the hydden, visibly shocked by the opening of the Cunning Knot, were relaxing.

'But at her marriage his role ends when he hands to her beloved her gift, which I now do!'

He presented the unopened box to the groom.

This bold piece of nonsense did the trick, even if the faces of some of the older, more conventional folks showed they were not convinced. But Old Mallarkhi had the sense to take Jack's gesture in the spirit intended and stood and clapped his words, and then encouraged the groom to open the gift at once.

It was a splendid dirk with a silver handle, with a sheath and belt of the finest leather.

The moment passed, the festivities continued, but this strange twist of fate left enough of an impression on Jack that he looked at Hais more closely than he had done previously and found that she was looking at him with equal curiosity.

He looked down from her gaze, his attention caught by the shifting colours of her dress in the sunlight. It was rich in embroidery of fields and flowers: green leaves, reeds, the blues of a river, flecks of yellow and red, exquisite eyebrights, violet bushes filled with birds, sapling trees. It was a torrent of all the colours of the Spring.

And suddenly he remembered a simple posy of flowers that had been left for him in the bedroom at Woolstone by a girl with hair the colour of wheat to welcome him home. *Katherine!* he thought suddenly, with a huge torrent of feeling – love and desire mingled with longing. *She's my Spring – my first love. I have to get her back . . .*

He looked at Pike and Brief, who both got up.

It was Old Mallarkhi who spoke for them all.

'My young friend,' he said, 'there bain't a single solitary soul at our feast who is not honoured to have you among us, a giant-born with things to do. Raise your glasses one and all, for though this be our Bride's day I swear by the Mirror that Master Jack has made it historical too.

'The Deritenders shall be his loyal followers the day he returns to Brum, assuming that is what his good friends and ours – Master Brief, Mister Pike, Mister Barklice and that gennelman we all love to laugh about but admire from the bottom of our darksome hearts, Master Stort, who is not able to be among us seeing as he's looking about some mysterious business of his own at this very minute – intend.' He tailed off to wink meaningfully at Brief, who nodded back with a slight smile. Jack guessed they had hatched a plot to help Katherine and help them both escape the Fyrd, but what it was he had no idea. He decided to find out the moment he could. Then the old hydden raised his glass and continued, 'So long as Master Jack is a friend of Brum, we shall be a friend of his!'

This was taken as the toast it was meant to be and the others all joined in and raised their glasses too.

'One and all raise your glasses to the Groom that Won't Be – yet!'

It was well done and Jack was able to leave with honour, his reputation secure and the festivity in no way dishonoured.

74

REUNION

Katherine was right, there was a small door behind the tapestry she began running for when people were diverted by the entrance of the Fyrd into the Orangery. It led to a metal spiral stairway that went both up and down. The trouble was she could see that Festoon's equerry was now following her.

She was not the only one to flee that way, but unlike the two or three ahead of her who stopped when the steps spiralled down into darkness and decided to go up, she descended into the depths below, hoping to lose her pursuer.

Heavy steps came down after her and a voice shouted, 'You must stop.'

The man had got a lantern from somewhere and its light helped her see the steps below. She hurried on down, taking steps two at a time, but she could not lose him.

Then: 'Don't go that way!' her roared at her.

She ran on and thump! she hit some unseen projection in the dark and fell forward, rolling down what turned out to be the last few steps before reaching the bottom.

She lay stunned and disorientated in the shadows, sounds of running and disturbance all around her.

There were only two ways on. The first was a large tunnel, but she could see Fyrd and their prisoners down that way. The other was a gate into a smaller tunnel.

It was locked, and by the time she turned around her pursuer had reached the bottom of the steps, his lantern raised, and was coming straight at her. With his turban and scimitar he looked like a bandit from an Oriental tale. The light from his lantern blinded her and she could not see his face.

She turned away, towards the other tunnel, but saw that some of the Fyrd had seen them and were running their way.

The scimitar flashed, the lights of the Fyrd moved nearer, the cries of their prisoners grew louder.

'I don't want to go with you,' she said, her chest painful with fear and her thumping heart; her mouth dry when she spoke, 'but I don't want them to catch me!'

He stood staring at her and dropped his weapon to his side.

'Katherine,' he said urgently. 'Katherine, don't you recognize me?'

She stared in astonishment as he pulled off his ridiculous turban, came slowly towards her and lowered the lantern so she could see his face properly.

'It's *me*, Katherine. It's Arthur Foale.'

But there was no time for explanations.

He took a key from a bunch hanging on his belt, opened the gate, shoved her bodily through, slammed it shut and locked it just in time.

'Run!' Arthur shouted. 'Run, or Brunte's Fyrd will take you.'

They ran and ran, and went faster still when they heard the gate crash back open behind them and the Fyrd in pursuit.

But when they reached a wide subterranean vault where a barge was moored they saw more Fyrd and some hostages ahead.

'Have to hide and hope for the best,' said Arthur.

A conduit ran into the tunnel at chest level from which filthy water trickled. Katherine heaved herself up and crawled in, her horrible black wig falling off as she did so. Arthur threw it in after her and, with her help, climbed in himself.

It was only just in time, as the Fyrd arrived moments later and searched about angrily. But more Fyrd and hostages were arriving by the moment and the search was soon abandoned.

Katherine and Arthur looked out at what was happening, but not for long. Hostages were being lined up by the barge, and summarily killed with crossbow bolts and knives, or clubbed to death with staves. Then their bodies were thrown into the barge.

They lowered their heads and covered their ears from the screams of the victims and the visceral grunts and occasional laughter of their executioners.

75

MASSACRE

Dawn in the old Curzon Street tunnel of Brum is no place for the living. First light yields up sights of crumbling decay and foul blockages of fetid pools of slime in tunnels unvisited by humans for decades, of corpses brought down by rain of creatures so rotten they are barely recognizable .. and the rats, streams of them, returning from a night of scavenging through the wasteful human world above.

It was the slither of their tails and the scratch of their feet across Katherine's bare legs that woke her.

She did not scream.

She simply sat up slowly in the tunnel, her eyes blank to the nearby shaft of light from the drain high above, her mind a place of bewildered devastation.

'Arthur,' she said blankly.

The rats were on him as well, or rather running over him to get to the larger tunnels from which they had climbed to escape the Fyrd the evening before. Like her, he barely reacted to them when he woke.

'Dear God,' he said and then again, shaking his head, 'Oh dear God.'

Katherine sat motionless, lacking the will even to speak.

Arthur reached out and said, 'I am sorry you had to see and hear what you did, I am really so sorry . . .'

What they had been silent witnesses to had already changed both their lives. Innocence had gone and Katherine seemed to have aged overnight.

They waited an hour, watching for signs of the Fyrd and straining to hear their movement, or the movement of anything. There was nothing, and when they emerged the barge had gone, with its terrible cargo.

'We'll go back the way we came and try to reach the place I had originally intended to take you.'

'I want to find Jack.'

'He's with people who will know where we are. Once he comes we can get away and we can talk . . .'

Katherine registered little as they went.

'I just don't want to meet any tomters,' she said.

'They don't exist,' said Arthur.

'Oh yes they do,' she replied. 'Where are we going?'

'To somewhere very few people ever get to see, somewhere extraordinary created by a genius such as even the human world has rarely seen. There's someone there I want you to meet.'

Katherine lost track of the tunnels they hurried through, steps they climbed, huge pipes and girders they clambered under and, eventually, derelict cellars lit by distant cobwebbed half-windows, into which they came.

Arthur led her towards what seemed an impenetrable and wide brick column, taking her arm the last part of the way.

'Stay close,' he said, 'there are many pitfalls here.'

They shuffled along very cautiously over the last few feet, a drop into voids on either side.

Arthur reached towards what looked like a gate, pulled it aside and opened murky doors beyond, then led her carefully onto a floor that jolted beneath her feet.

'Where are we?'

'It's a lift.'

He closed the outer and inner doors and pulled a lever. The lift began to sway and move.

'Hold tight,' he warned in the pitch darkness.

The lift moved quite fast, then slowed and finally stopped.

He pulled open the doors.

'Watch yourself as you step through,' he said. 'The levels aren't always the same.'

She stepped into a very large round chamber so filled with light and colour after the tunnels that she could hardly make sense of it. At its centre was a platform filled with all kinds of pulleys and cords, mirrors and lights, and reclining on a vast and sumptuous chaise longue, a recognizable figure nibbled lazily at a sweetmeat stuck on the end of a bejewelled silver cocktail stick.

'Ah!' he said when he saw them. 'I'm glad you made it, Foale. I rather feared when you left the party that you might have been one of those taken by the Fyrd, but it seems you live still! My hearty congratulations!'

Then, gazing in the most benign and pleasant way at Katherine, he said with lazy good humour, 'So ... *this* is the charming girl you so wished me to meet? The future Shield Maiden?'

'I believe she may be,' replied Arthur Foale.

Then Katherine found herself, despite all impulses to the contrary, shaking the limp, plump hand of the beaming Lord Festoon.

76

THE MARSHAL

That same morning Igor Brunte was listening to the very latest update from one of his new subordinates on the state of things in Brum following his swift and ruthless takeover of the governance of the city the day before.

A succession of people, in a variety of states of shock, bewilderment and awe at the scale and speed of change, and the smooth and rapid assumption of power by the Sub-Quentor, were coming and going through his makeshift office off Digbeth High with the latest information, but things were now settling down.

It had been a busy twenty-four hours and he had not slept at all. But the news was all good, and with Brum under his control he was happy to be the still but potent centre of his minions' feverish activity whilst he stood shaving his strong chin and snipping at his bushy moustache.

He had a visit to make and he was scrubbing himself up so he looked less like a revolutionary and more like the leader he now was. It was a meeting he was looking forward to. He intended to formally take power from the High Ealdor, Lord Festoon. He'd been useful for a while, but now there had to be an uncorrupted chain of command – with Brunte at its head. There was no room for a fat, useless noble who was an outdated figurehead for a system that didn't work. He didn't expect any trouble but decided to take along Feld and Streik just in case.

Brunte completed his ablutions with the application of a beeswax balm, scented with the musky oil of an ox's tail which, he believed, gave him added presence and personal potency.

Though satisfied with himself and the world, for good reason – his takeover, so meticulously planned, had gone with barely a hitch – he was not complacent. He'd asked a newly arrived aide if there were any threats to his dominion left at all and was just listening to the final part of his report.

'. . . and finally the latest reports on the floods are excellent, sir, they are subsiding as expected . . . but . . .'

The news was indeed good, all positions secured, the blood-letting more or less over, the city his.

'But . . . ?'

'Ah, yes, sir. The Rea threatened for a time to back right up, but as you know the rain has eased off south and west of the city and we believe that will be sufficient . . .'

'You meant it might back up Northfield way?'

'Beyond, sir, as far as Waseley Hill, which is always the problem since then . . .'

'Since then the water floods back down, an event that has not happened I have been told in fifteen hundred years.'

'You are well informed, Sub-Quentor.'

It was meant as flattery but it brought a frown, though not because his aide had done anything wrong. But suddenly 'Sub-Quentor' felt like a rank too low for a leader. Possible new titles and ranks whirred away in the back of his mind as he returned to present matters.

'The Bilgesnipe diverted the waters north, though not without misgivings as it meant flooding some of their own people . . . but the Seal necessitated that procedure.'

Brunte told himself that Old Mallarkhi, their not-to-be-underestimated leader, would need acknowledgement of some kind. It had been a mistake by successive regimes of Fyrd commanders to under-value Bilgesnipe support.

Brunte's eye was caught by a sudden glimmer at the dirty, broken windows of his temporary headquarters which occupied a corner of a derelict warehouse off Digbeth High. The choice had been a clever and prudent one, in case his plans had gone awry and his opponents had regained control and come in search of him. Here in the Upperworld of humans they would have found it hard to track him down and even harder to attack him.

The location had another advantage.

He had arranged for a fire to be set to one of the larger of the human tower blocks to the east of the city, which had diverted human attention from the floods and made the Bilgesnipe's task, and his own people's dispositions of their murderous work, a great deal easier.

'Nearly time to leave this place I think,' he said, sitting finally at the rough human-sized office table which, with its legs sawn off, the legs of his matching chairs likewise, they had utilized for the purpose of viewing the papers and maps used in their operation.

'They' consisted of Brunte and his chief of operations, who, for the past twenty minutes while his commander shaved, had said nothing. He still said nothing while Brunte mused further on a variety of issues and ordered the clerks to be ready to move at a moment's notice to a location better placed for continuing command of New Brum.

The distant fire had been fierce in spite of the rain but was now easing. He nodded towards it with a smile.

'Humans call it arson,' he said to his silent colleague, 'but the Fyrd call it tactics, as do I. Now, I had intended to visit Festoon at once, but on second thoughts I think it wise we attend to this matter of the River Rea backing up all the way to Waseley Hill . . . and . . .'

'We should wait to see who returns to occupy the third seat at this table, sir,' said Hrap Dowty, breaking his silence.

His voice was cool and matter-of-fact, as it had been throughout the long hours past, ever since Brunte had so suddenly elevated him to his position as Chief of Operations.

'Dowty, you're not inclined to bets or wagers I take it?' said Brunte.

Hrap Dowty thought about this, assumed that his new master was making a joke, and offered a half-smile by way of acknowledgement, though he thought it unfunny and finally shook his head.

'No,' he said, 'I'm not.'

Brunte actually liked Dowty. He did his job perfectly, he had no personal ambition beyond it, and he feared no one. He was reliable and not a threat. He would have been boring but for one thing, his obsession with time, on which subject, and that alone, he could talk endlessly, and fascinate those around him.

Dowty would never be one to go whoring with, or drink with, or joke with, or do anything much with at all.

But in an insurrection of the kind that Brunte had led, and the campaigns against the Fyrd still to come, and anything else requiring meticulous organization and timing, he was the perfect partner.

'Were you a gambler, Dowty, which I guess you are not, I would have a wager with you as to how long it would be before the third seat at our table is reoccupied.'

'Ah!' said Dowty without interest. 'Is it important?'

'Not particularly,' agreed Brunte, 'but it gives me pleasure to forecast things.'

'Too many unknown variables in this instance, sir, to make a forecast with any accuracy.'

The two were talking about the return of Doam, Brunte's dependable clerk and number two. He had sent him earlier to the late General Elon's quarters, ostensibly to see how Lieutenant Backhaus had got on. He it was who had been left to sort out things after Brunte himself eliminated Elon, it being better that Backhaus did that, since he was trusted by the survivors in the household. But it was not entirely desirable that Backhaus lived afterwards, seeing that he was witness to Elon's murder, though Brunte could see arguments in his favour. He was bright and clever, and like Brunte himself had long deserved the promotions that the hierarchy led by Elon routinely blocked.

Doam was less bright perhaps, but he commanded loyalty among those under him and Brunte could trust him. But it might be that his time of usefulness was over. Brunte debated the issue with himself and finally decided that there would be trouble between them if both survived the insurrection. He'd made his doubts about Backhaus known to Doam and suggested it would do no harm if he, too, were eliminated. How was up to Doam. Sometimes it was best for a leader to take a back seat where those beneath him are concerned and let them sort things out for themselves.

He guessed only that if Backhaus was half the Fyrd he thought he was he would expect and be prepared for the worst from Doam's visit. Which would leave him several options. Bow to the inevitable? Flee? Argue with Doam? *Kill* him.

Brunte and Dowty now awaited Doam's return to learn the outcome.

The truth was that Brunte was glad he did not have to make a bet, because he actually had no idea what the outcome of Doam's murderous quest would be. Nor did he much care.

Footsteps below, guards' voices, someone admitted down there. Then, steps up the stairs to the floor they were on.

The door opened and Backhaus entered alone.

A surprise.

'Where is Doam?' asked Brunte, very curious. The lieutenant's self-assurance was impressive, the obvious respect for Brunte very welcome, his nod towards Dowty a prudent courtesy.

His first words were perfection. They did not waste time in tedious explanation and they made very clear who Backhaus acknowledged was in charge.

'We have work to do, Field Marshal Brunte.'

Brunte nodded slowly, the wrinkles around his eyes showing his appreciation. 'Sub-Quentor' had indeed become inadequate. Backhaus had offered the solution.

'I think "Marshal" will do well enough!' he said, adding after due pause, 'Kapitan Backhaus.'

The newest Kapitan in the Hyddenworld smiled and felt it necessary to be crystal-clear about his dead rival: 'Unfortunately Doam suffered a fatal accident and will not be joining us,'

It was all that was said or ever needed to be upon the subject. Doam was a casualty of war, Backhaus one of its beneficiaries.

'I also met Meyor Feld downstairs, Marshal. He is, I take it, my immediate superior?'

Brunte nodded.

'He has been promoted to general for his recent work and much else besides. You will find him an agreeable colleague.'

Backhaus stared past his new patron at the human world behind and watched bemused as a huge building, from which smoke billowed up into the evening sky glowing with the fire beneath, collapsed slowly into itself and was no more.

He blinked and might have mentioned what he had seen and suggested that it felt like time to leave these grubby premises, but the abstracted expression on Brunte's face showed that he had moved on. As if on cue a clerk appeared.

'The girl is alive, Sub-Quentor . . .'

'Marshal,' corrected Brunte pleasantly.

'She has been observed in the company of Professor Foale heading in the direction of the High Ealdor's private quarters. But of the boy there is no sign.'

It was indeed perfection.

'The boy will follow her before long,' said Brunte simply, getting up to indicate their time toppermost was over, 'and we shall be ready for him. We must consult with the Bilgesnipe and reassure ourselves concerning the River Rea, and then I shall call upon the High Ealdor. Agreed, gentlemen?'

'Agreed,' murmured Dowty and Backhaus as one.

'Agreed,' said another voice.

It was Feld, who had appeared in the doorway and heard their talk. Brunte felt good.

He had won the city, gained the right courtiers, and all he needed now were the keys to the kingdom.

77

THE CHAMBER
OF SEASONS

Lord Festoon's interest in Katherine was real and sympathetic. 'I was very sorry, as we all were, to learn of your mother's death. It is not something that is easy to get over, I know – I too suffered that loss at your age. And I, too, had no father to help me bear the burden of it.'

'You knew she died? Even here in Brum?'

'We have kept an eye on things. And, naturally, Arthur has briefed us too. But her death, though to be expected after so many years of suffering, was upsetting.'

It was, but Katherine's grief was no longer as raw as it was and now she wanted to know about Jack. She met with a satisfactory answer when she asked about him.

'On that we cannot enlighten you except to say this: Jack is in capable hands and we have plans afoot to get you out of here safely and well away from Brum. To be frank my dear, matters such as lost gems, prophecies and Shield Maidens, important though they are, are less important than your safety and Jack's. One way or another he will be on his way here, and when he is we can act. As for those other things . . .'

He waved his hand about as if 'those other things' were of no importance at all.

But the moment he heard about the massacre they had witnessed the night before, and that the Fyrd were looking for them, he wanted to talk with Arthur alone and said she must look after herself for a time.

But first he made sure she was comfortable.

'Pray make yourself at home,' he said, pointing to a luxurious Turkish rug that was spread across the floor before his throne, which stood on a raised dais along with the paraphernalia she had noticed when she first came into the Chamber.

There were trays of succulent fruit on the thick rug, silver boxes full of chocolates and sweetmeats dusted with white and pink sugar, and a golden ewer filled with iced water sprinkled with rose petals, all set among the softest, deepest, most luxurious cushions and bolsters she had ever seen.

'Rest, eat, drink and sleep,' he suggested, 'and by all means wander about this famous chamber too, but avoid the doors, they are not as they seem. But then things rarely are. On no account attempt to open them. *That* would be folly indeed if done at the wrong moment and in the wrong way.

'Meanwhile, should you have any special need in the way of victuals I am sure my dear friend Parlance here will see to it. He is about to return to the kitchen with my orders for the coming hours.'

It was only then that she noticed the strangest of diminutive figures hovering behind Festoon's throne. He wore the starched white jacket and black and white chequered trousers of a chef. His white chef's hat was inordinately tall.

'Madam?' he said.

At first Katherine didn't understand that he was asking if she wished for anything in particular, and her immediate instinct was to say no, but there was such genuine interest in her welfare in his eyes that a sudden thought came to her.

In fact it was a memory, a powerful and unexpected one, and it was connected with Arthur, and Margaret, and her mother and many happy hours in Woolstone sitting and talking, whether in the kitchen of the old house, or the conservatory in more recent times by her mother's bed.

It felt that what she suddenly wanted was something she had not had in years, though really it was barely more than days ago.

'I wouldn't mind a cup of tea,' she said.

The moment she said it she realized that in such exotic surround-ings what she had asked for seemed ordinary, even ridiculous.

But Parlance looked delighted.

'Ah! Tea! That most excellent and, in the Hyddenworld, underrated beverage. But for Professor Foale here, who made a like request when he first came among us, I fear we might not be able to satisfy your request. But my suppliers sent forth their requests for what tea they could find and, well, my goodness me, what riches did they discover and have we tasted. Is that not so, my lord? Would you not agree, Professor?'

'It is and he does,' said Festoon enthusiastically. 'The young lady makes an intelligent request. Satisfy it at once, Parlance!'

He bowed, retreated and was suddenly gone, though exactly where to she could not work out. Nor, when she looked around her, could she see where the lift had come in, and where it too had disappeared.

Katherine decided to explore while Festoon and Arthur talked. To do so, she had to walk around Lord Festoon's dais which, being very large and the perspectives in the room made more confusing by the strongly chequered parquet floor, seemed to take a strangely long time.

But she soon realized it was difficult to work out how far off the walls were, the more so because while the centre of the room was well lit from an octagonal lantern of windows high above, the walls were in shadows.

Lord Festoon and Arthur were engaged in such a lively discussion, with occasional looks in her direction, that she delayed her exploration for a few moments in the hope of hearing something useful.

What she got instead was a diversion by the High Ealdor on the subject of his chaise longue and the clever way in which, at the touch of a button, it came upright on hinges to become a throne.

'A huge improvement, my dear Foale,' she heard the High Ealdor say as he demonstrated how the contraption worked, before adding in a helpless way, 'My weakness, my frailty, caused by my long years of illness, necessitates these easements to my daily chores.

'I fear that physical exertion of any kind is dangerous to one as delicate as I, and that there is no hope that I will ever reach the vale of years towards which those without my sad afflictions can live and hope. Eh?'

He brought himself upright again just as Parlance reappeared, again mysteriously, with a tray of tea things. He poured some for them all while Festoon helped himself to a chocolate from a plate of them which, at the touch of a button on the arm of his chair, appeared before him, held in the grip of a large articulated silver hand which concertinaed out from a fixture behind him.

'My latest *ballotin des pralines*, made yesterday for my feste by the new young chocolatier from Wallonia who Parlance recently engaged. The recipe is a refinement of Aroudel's classic of the 1790s and is, I believe, an improvement.'

He signalled for Arthur to have one, which he did, though not without a dubious look at the chocolate, his own stomach, and the very much larger one sported by Festoon.

For 'sad affliction' read 'greed', Katherine told herself, confident that Arthur was thinking the same.

The various pieces of equipment with which Lord Festoon was surrounded had an old world air. They were made of richly varnished wood with shiny brass fittings of the highest quality and craftsmanship, apparently created especially for his comfort and easy convenience. Raised together on the dais, and from a distance, he looked to Katherine like a captain on the bridge of a nineteenth-century steamship.

She turned her attention to the room again. She had first thought it to be circular, but once she had walked right round it she realized that was not so, it was octagonal.

Its eight walls were differently sized. Four were no bigger than the width of the doors set into them, while between them were the four much wider walls on which hung tapestries depicting different seasons.

Each door had the name of a season painted on it in a shimmering gold script of a Gothic design that was shadowed by the colour of its season: green for Spring, yellow-gold for Summer, red-brown for Autumn, and bleak grey for Winter. But otherwise the doors looked old, even dirty, and were in places cobwebby, with brass handles tarnished almost black. They looked as if they had not been opened in years, maybe decades.

'Perhaps even centuries!' Katherine murmured to herself.

Lord Festoon heard her and called out, 'Not quite *that* long, my dear, but certainly long enough!'

When she turned to him to ask him something more about the doors she was surprised to find that he and his dais were facing the other way entirely, even though she was sure that had not been the case moments before. She saw for the first time that the dais was able to rotate, probably at the push of a button, so that its incumbent could study the tapestries without having to move at all.

Even so she was puzzled that he had moved so far round in the time it took for him to speak and for her to look at him. The Chamber played tricks on her not only with scale and distance but with time as well.

Then something stranger still: when she went back to where she had just come from, which was the door of Summer, she found it had changed its name to Spring, and looking back she saw that Summer was where she had just come from.

Katherine gave up on the doors and began to examine the tapestries on the walls between the doors. They were exquisitely embroidered with fauna and flora, and each one depicted the different seasons according to their position relative to the doors on either side of them.

The tapestry between the doors of Spring and Summer had images of snowdrops in melting snow on its left side but moved on to the bright blues and yellows of eyebright on the right.

The next tapestry, between the doors of Summer and Autumn, continued the theme of Summer with the first soft pinks of eglantine, its leaves shiny with Summer sun, but as it reached the door marked Autumn the flora changed accordingly, becoming a bank of fading nettles, with sloes beginning to show their blue bloom and the red-orange fruits of lords and ladies nestling in moist shadows below.

'So the tapestries are sequential,' she muttered, 'and each shows the end of one season and the beginning of the following one.'

'Correct!' said Lord Festoon cheerfully.

He was now sitting facing her, while Arthur lolled on a Turkish carpet on the floor in front of the dais, drinking from a beautiful golden goblet.

'Have some,' he said amiably, pointing at a tray on which were more goblets and a matching ewer.

'Later, thanks,' she said, turning back to the tapestry.

She knew most of the flowers, but not all of the animals that gambolled among them. The sight of them put into her a sense of nostalgia and loss for days gone by in the countryside around Woolstone, when her mother was still well enough to share such things with her . . . days she knew could now never return. She felt a wave of sorrow and grief.

She saw that while the flowers of the seasons made the eye read the tapestries one way, from left to right, from Spring to Summer and on to Autumn in a circle clockwise round the room, the landscapes they depicted took the eye in the opposite direction.

At the top right of each tapestry was a mountainous landscape which sloped generally leftward and downward into foothills, on to high moors and heaths and so on down into gentler woods and valley pastures, until at the lowest and left-hand side of each tapestry there lay the sea.

In each of the four tapestries this natural course from mountain to sea was followed by a river, a raging torrent for a time, but in the end a slow winding thing of old age that passed through marshes and side waters, deltas and mudflats of its own making, and so into the waiting sea.

Seen one way therefore, the tapestries were depictions of the endless cycle of the seasons and renewal of life; seen another they showed the passage from youth to old age across Earth's face. One way was to the right and the other . . .

'Sinister,' breathed Katherine, thinking then of so many things – her mother, the shadows in the henge, her own passage through childhood, Jack's hurt body, her feelings for him, which had changed like the seasons and yet remained the same from the first day she met him, which felt as solid as the Earth.

'Except it's not solid,' she told herself, her gaze following the river from its youthful phase in the high mountains of early Summer to its place of old age, as a meandering waterway, in late Spring.

'Oh!' she whispered. 'Of course! It's obvious when you see it . . .'

The rivers in each of the four tapestries seemed also to flow into

and out of each door, or rather the place beyond the door. In seeing
which, Katherine began to think that the eight walls of the Chamber,
whether doors or tapestries, were dissolving away before her eyes into
a great world in her mind of the cycle of life's renewal through youth
to old age, of death and rebirth, as if there was an eternity in each
living moment, each connected to the next backwards and forwards,
up and down, every which way and more.

'You like the tapestries?' asked Lord Festoon, his voice saving her
from a whirling and turning in her own mind that was gathering pace
so fast that her body was beginning to do the same, and she in danger
of losing her balance and tumbling into the confusion of the dazzling
reflections and geometric illusions of the oak floor and thence into
the tapestries themselves.

'You *do*!' he exclaimed with delight, answering his own question,
though mistaking her silence for simple pleasure rather than the
kaleidoscope of feelings it really was.

He had stopped talking to Arthur and seemed to have been following
her progress around the chamber from the vantage point of his dais.
He and his throne were now facing her, while Arthur had moved,
along with the carpet he lay on, almost out of sight on the far side.

'I do like it,' began Katherine, 'but . . .'

'Sit down, my dear, for you seem quite dizzy with its pleasures and
surprises, which is how we mortals should be in our wondrous world.
It is only the limitations of our own minds, and the fear we surround
change with, that makes our lives and perceptions dull and unrealized.
I should know!'

He motioned to the floor to his far right from where, as if the
carpet was sliding over the floor, Arthur soon appeared, still happily
reclining. She frowned, shook her head and gave up trying to make
sense of anything.

'Sit on this rug,' said Festoon enticingly, 'adjust these soft cushions
to your pretty person, lie down now and enjoy the refreshments from
the master of my kitchen, as our mutual friend is himself presently
doing.'

He spoke now so mellifluously that each word seemed to nudge
Katherine's limbs softly one by one to bring her to a supine position
near Arthur.

'Will this drink make me think strange thoughts,' she asked doubtfully, 'like the so-called water your Sisters of Charity gave me?'

Festoon affected to be offended by the question, but laughed
heartily as he did so.

'The Sisters have their ways and wiles, as they always have had, but
trust me when I say that this plain water, which has merely been
caressed by the essence of rose petals, will clear your head and whet
your appetite for other pleasures to come, which is to say the later
supper which it is my habit to enjoy in the night and in which I trust
you will join me.'

'I thought it was about the middle of the day.'

'So it was,' he said ambiguously, 'when you arrived. *Tempus fugit!*
Wherever is Parlance with your tea?'

She drank the water and felt immediately refreshed, and then
drank more.

A bell suddenly tinkled and Festoon jumped as the speaking tube,
which hung to the right and above his head, dropped down conven-
iently to his right hand, where with minimum effort he took it and
applied it to his ear.

'We are ready for supper,' he said into it. 'Light but nostalgic suits
my mood.'

A whispering voice was heard and Festoon nodded and replaced
the tube.

'Supper is on the way,' he announced.

Katherine decided to keep a close watch for where Parlance
appeared so that she would know where his lift came from, but
somehow knew that wherever it was it would not be in the direction
she was looking. Nor was it. It emerged finally in the shadows of the
dais, somewhere behind the throne itself, almost silently.

One moment Parlance was absent and the next he was present,
holding aloft a vast silver tray on which their supper things were laid
out along with a teapot, milk and a cup and saucer.

Festoon, who seemed to notice everything, observed her surprise
with pleasure.

'Unlike the other *ascenseur*,' he said, affecting the French for the
more mundane 'lift', 'which has a good deal of the clackety-clack
about it, this one has need to be utterly silent, so that its coming and

going does not vex me and shatter my sleep. It offers a direct connection to the kitchen.'

'Where does the other one come up?' asked Katherine. 'I couldn't work it out.'

Festoon was delighted to be asked.

'It is all done by hydraulics which work as well as the day they were installed so many decades ago. It emerges through the floor over there . . .'

He nodded vaguely in a direction which lay between the doors to Winter and Spring.

'The floor opens, the lift emerges noisily, its occupants get out, and there you are! Simple but intrusive, but such is the nature of life – it should be simple but the world intrudes, *n'est-ce pas*? But forgive me, you are hungry as am I. Parlance, serve us if you please.'

They ate in pleasant silence until, supper nearly done, Katherine said, 'Lord Festoon?'

'My dear? You have a question? I always did appreciate an enquiring mind,' he said. 'What would you like to know?'

'Is Jack coming here? Will you help us escape from the Fyrd?'

'He is, my dear, and we will.'

'Shall we escape through one of the doors?'

'No doubt you will,' said Lord Festoon.

'But what lies beyond the four doors of the seasons?'

'Dreams,' he replied.

'Whose?'

'Our own,' he whispered, turning from her sadly, the question evidently too hard for him to think about for long.

78
DOORS

But Katherine refused to let him avoid the subject so easily. She sensed she was near a truth that had to do with her dreams as well as his.

'What's your dream?' she dared to ask.

He didn't have to think for long.

'To go to a place which . . . or rather, where . . . a place . . .'

He shook his head. The memory was too painful, the dream too hard to face.

His eyes were filled with real sadness.

'To which *what?*' persisted Katherine.

'You're very direct, just as the Shield Maiden should be.'

'I'm not the Shield Maiden or whatever, I'm Katherine.'

'Well you're direct, that's certain.'

'So . . . what's the answer? Have you been to the places beyond the doors?'

'Only one of them, which was Spring. The rest I have visited in imagination only, with the rather special help of Parlance.'

'When did you go through the door into Spring?'

'Ah!' he said very softly. 'You have asked the question I feared you would. I cannot *actually* go there again of course. Indeed, in my condition I cannot now go through any of the doors, not ever. But I suppose if I tell you about Spring I can briefly relive that time again and you will understand better why I am in the pitiful and helpless position that I am.'

'Speak of it, my lord,' murmured Parlance dreamily.

The chef had an odd ability to make himself scarce most of the time but to reappear when needed. In fact Katherine had forgotten all about him. Now here he was, bold as brass, wiping a nostalgic tear from his eye.

'It is the madeleines we have just eaten that make me weep,' he said, 'as much as my lord's sad words and the memory of a Spring gone by.'

It was Lord Festoon who told her the outline of the story and Parlance who filled in the details.

When Festoon was ten he had wandered away from the servant who looked after him and found himself outside and alone. He reached the banks of the River Rea, attracted by the noise of stones splashing in the water. It was a kitchen boy, Parlance, playing ducks and drakes with flat stones they found.

'It was that most magical of days,' recalled Festoon, 'the first day of Spring, when the sun shines lightly on the first new life and the air, so long made harsh by Winter cold, turns warm again.'

The two boys lost themselves in the wonder of the day, roamed up the river and found themselves finally on Waseley Hill, that verdant rise of ground from which the river issues forth as a tiny spring.

'We were out all day and half into the evening before my mother's servants – my father being dead – found me. My siblings had all died young and I too was a weak child and so she was more fearful for my health and safety than she should have been. I was chastised severely, but that was not the worse punishment. I was also confined within, and from that day on I was never allowed to go out more, nor to meet again the boy whose companionship was the first true friendship I had ever known.

'From that time on I knew him only from the food he secretly sent me from the kitchens, made for me by his hand as evocations of the sights and sounds of that single day of Spring we saw, or thought we saw. His food was a celebration of our friendship and my gift in return was to enjoy it and suggest new things.'

'But did you not go outside at all?' asked Katherine, astonished.

'That I did not do . . . and of course, as I grew, and grew large, and then fat and . . .'

'If only I had known what I was doing to my lord,' cried Parlance, 'but I did not and no one told me what he was until he was obese. Too late, too late. From that time on I cooked to comfort him and he ate to comfort me.'

Festoon waved his hands over his vast body and tree-trunk legs and simply said, 'It was just so, too late and I could no longer do what I had so wanted to.

'But there were compensations. Parlance's skills increased, his genius emerged, as did mine in matters of taste and ideas. Having conquered Spring in a culinary sense, we spread our clipped wings and explored the other seasons too. My weight increased still more.

'When my mother died, and I took over as High Ealdor, the first thing I did was to summon Parlance. He wept to see what I had become.'

Katherine stood up impatiently.

'But . . . but you could . . . surely between you both it would be possible to . . .'

'Pray don't tell me to stop eating as so many have before. If I do that I lose the one pleasure that remains to me. Do that and I die. And who then would Parlance, a true genius at what he does, cook for?'

'But you would still like to experience Spring for real?'

Festoon hesitated. Parlance likewise.

'More than anything but one thing, and of that I'm not even sure.'

'Which is?'

'To hold the lost gem of Spring, of fabled Beornamund's creation, in the palm of my hand. Then I could die and return to the Mirror-of-All content that my life has been fulfilled.'

'But failing that?'

'Yes,' he said, 'I would like to see again the places we so briefly saw when young.'

'Would that not happen if you went through the door marked Spring, Lord Festoon?' asked Katherine. 'You said our dreams lie beyond it.'

'I suppose it might. But for me that is but a dream, and better left that way. I cannot even rise from my throne without help, let alone cross the vast empty space that lies between it and that door . . .'

They looked over at the door, and seen from Festoon's perspective it did indeed look far.

'For you, Katherine, it is a different matter, and when Jack gets here I suggest that you take your courage in your hands and open the door into Spring. Try it. Nobody else has, though it is perfectly true that after ā Faroün, he of blessed memory, made this room, which was his last work, and had the tapestries hung, he asked to be left alone. He sat in this very throne. When his servants called for him, and finally dared enter the Chamber, he was nowhere to be found.

'It is thought that he passed through one of the doors, and since he was very old and his hair, such as was left, all white, he was in the Winter of his years, and I believe that was the door that he took.

'What stops me now? What really stops me? For it would be possible I suppose to rig up some sort of wheeled contraption to get me to the door of Spring . . . What stops me? The same thing that stops most people doing things. Fear. Just that, Katherine, and no more. So simple. So very hard to conquer.'

Katherine looked across the Chamber to the door marked Spring and paced all the way to it and back again.

'It's no distance at all, my lord. Why not try?'

Festoon laughed.

'Really,' said Katherine, 'just try to reach it. You don't have to open it or anything, just see if you can get to it. We'll help you. Arthur! Parlance!'

She was suddenly animated and determined.

It wasn't far and it wasn't impossible.

'Try to, my Lord Festoon,' said Arthur. 'Why not? We have nothing better to do while we wait for Jack and the others.'

Festoon laughed.

'You lighten my spirit, Katherine, and terrify it too. There is a great deal of the Shield Maiden about you, whatever you may say. Therefore, help me!'

He half rose from his throne, Katherine went to one side and Arthur the other, with Parlance pushing him along from behind, having thoughtfully taken off his belt lest the sharp knives he carried there damage his master.

Nor was it as difficult as he had imagined.

Not easy, not without a stumble, nor without a pause for breath, but absolutely not impossible.

Three feet from it he said suddenly, 'I had forgotten I will have to get all the way back, perhaps I should . . .'

'You're nearly there,' said Katherine firmly. 'Don't give up now! You just have to touch it . . .'

'Now *that* is a bad idea,' said Festoon, pulling up short. 'Touching dreams has a habit of turning them to dull reality. But . . .'

Even so, with their combined help he heaved himself forward one more step and reached forward as if to touch the door of Spring. It seemed to Katherine that the golden letters above it began to glow brighter, and the green shadowing around them to shine.

He stood for the briefest of moment with a look that combined the deep hope of one who has almost reached his goal in life with the despair of feeling he can never reach it.

But there was no further chance to find out. Suddenly there was a rumbling sound a little way off and, to the sound of ancient machinery and rattling parts, several of the sections of the wooden floor slid back. Then the lift in which Katherine and Arthur had earlier arrived rose up before them.

Behind its metal grille, doors slipped open, a heavy hand pulled the grilled doors open too, and out stepped Brunte, followed by Feld, Streik and another Fyrd.

'Ah! Lord Festoon, up and vertical,' said Brunte, evidently very surprised to see what was happening.

Lord Festoon sighed as if for ever defeated and said, 'I have been expecting you, Sub-Quentor Brunte . . .'

Brunte eyed him with the unwanted good humour of a new first among equals.

'Pray, say nothing more until I have returned to my throne, or I will collapse,' he gasped.

Brunte shrugged, Feld smiled coldly, Streik sneered, his right hand fingering one of the knives on his belt.

The other Fyrd walked over to the dais and took up his post by the throne as if to stand guard by it. The movement was unspoken but it said volumes. The reign of Festoon was clearly over.

'I think it better that you stand where you are for a moment, Festoon, so we can talk as equals,' said Brunte, coming closer before looking first at Foale dismissively and then at Katherine. 'Your lackey I know, and the girl is the one who some say has connections with the Shield Maiden? May even *be* her. Looking at her I rather doubt it. But if the giant-born believes it that's good enough for me.'

For the second time that day Katherine found herself looking into the eyes of someone she might reasonablely have expected to dislike but who, on the surface, seemed quite amiable. Brunte's face was warm, his smile broad, his personality obviously gregarious.

'I'm Katherine,' she said, 'and I know nothing about Shield Maidens and I think you should let Lord Festoon go and sit down because standing is hard for him. I'm sure Meyor Feld agrees.'

Feld did as it happened, because there was something disturbing about Lord Festoon's legs beginning to shake and his face to perspire with the effort of merely standing.

'Help him get back to his throne,' said Brunte, his smile fading. Feld and Streik moved towards him.

It was as they did so, and as Brunte opened his mouth to ask a question, that something very extraordinary happened on the dais, which since only Katherine was facing that direction, only she could actually see.

The Fyrd who had been standing there appeared suddenly to fall slowly backward, someone else's hand over his mouth and his eyes opening wide in shock as he was dragged to the floor. Katherine couldn't see his assailant and her mouth opened in surprise, but she had the sense to look down at the floor so that Brunte did not see where she was looking. But it was too late, the instinct that had kept him alive and moving forward through life kicked in and his right hand moved to the bigger of the two knives that he habitually kept on his belt.

He turned, as did Festoon, to look in the direction in which Katherine had been looking.

So it was that all three of them simultaneously saw the hapless Fyrd upended and thrown into the lift that Parlance normally used, which immediately began to descend with its reluctant but now unconscious cargo.

As it did so, his elimination of that danger complete, the assailant turned to face them and Katherine's heart leapt. It was Jack, looking dishevelled and bloodied as if he had been in a fight he had barely won, but with an expression on his face of such purpose and determination that it left no doubt he expected now to engage in another one.

'Streik . . . ' begun Brunte in a guttural warning voice. *'Feld!'*

It had not been his intention to cause anybody harm. But faced by this direct assault on one of his officers and what looked like Jack's imminent attack, his natural aggressiveness kicked in.

Jack might well have looked the worse for wear.

His journey from Deritend to the Chamber of Seasons had been as dramatic as it was speedy.

Barklice led him, Pike helped him, and Brief came along to lend what support he could and gain passage through places and past Fyrd guards where only his authority held sway.

Their objective had been to find the Sub-Quentor, and it was a shrewdly chosen one. They reasoned that wherever he might be when they set off, his most likely purpose that day would be to locate Festoon and formally take power from him.

That much seemed certain.

As for Katherine, they had no certain idea of her whereabouts, but what Brief was privy to was the plan for her to be chosen as Bride and so spirited away to Festoon's most inaccessible Chamber.

Inaccessible but not unknown.

Brief and latterly Stort had not studied the works of ã Faroün in vain. The drawings and plans of that ineffable architect and mechanical genius had lain untouched for many years in Brief's archive. Their measurements were encoded, their lines mysteriously misdrawn, their perspectives so odd that they rendered any who looked at them quite dizzy. As for the captions and explanations of the drawings, most particularly those for the Chamber of Seasons, Brief had got so far but no further. It had taken Stort's genius with numbers and languages to decode and make sense of them, and it was his work over the years that had given Brief his understanding of where the

Chamber was, how it worked and, most important, how to gain access to it.

Not, until that day, that he had ever tried.

Needs must, however. But when the trail led, as it finally did, to the Chamber, Brief's authority failed before the authority of the Fyrd guards Feld had earlier put in place by the main lift up to the Chamber, awaiting Marshall Brunte's arrival.

A struggle had ensued from which Jack and the others had only just managed to escape, all of them injured, Barklice more than the others.

Hurriedly putting their friend in the care of one of the kinder Sisters of Charity who was known to Brief, Brief had led them to the kitchens of the royal residence, where they had great difficulty finding the lift Parlance habitually used.

Too late they discovered they had been followed, so that once again they had to fight the Fyrd who tried to obstruct their passage to the smaller lift to the Chamber.

It was in the midst of this that Brief thrust Jack into the lift and sent him upward in the dark, with the command to do what he could. No matter how slim his chances, the message would go forth to the good folk of Brum that although the giant-born might be inexperienced, he did not lack courage.

As the door of the lift closed Brief took Jack's plain stave and thrust his own stave into Jack's hand.

'You used it successfully in the henge; do so again now. Trust it and it will do for you what it must. Fight it and it will fight you!'

Jack heard him and was gone, the stave in his hand. He felt it in the darkness as he ascended in the lift and it felt unnaturally cool, like a creature that needs the sun and warmth to awake. No light came from it as it had in Brief's strong hands.

The lift finally emerged into light once more, and to his surprise Jack found himself within inches of the back of a Fyrd on guard. There was no time to think, only act. Jack put his hand over his mouth, pulled him violently backward and shoved him into the lift, which by some volition of its own, or because he had unwittingly pressed its control, sank back at once towards the kitchens far below.

Even as this happened Jack realized he had let go of Brief's stave, which, to his astonishment, began falling one way, twisted another and then, waking up as if something animated it, shot straight back into his right hand.

It was then that he saw across the polished floor of the Chamber as strange a sight as he himself had presented seconds earlier to Katherine.

There was a sturdy and powerful-looking hydden, with a wide peasant face but sharp intelligent eyes, who Jack guessed must be Brunte.

To one side of him stood a bearded man whom he recognized from photographs he had seen at Woolstone as Arthur Foale.

Next to him and hopping about on his feet was someone who looked like the most diminutive chef Jack had ever seen, with the tallest chef's hat on his head in all the Hyddenworld and probably the human one as well.

All that was odd.

Odder still was the vast figure who stood tottering on huge legs and appeared to be dressed in silken pyjamas of pale green over which a pink silken robe had been cast.

His eyes were as wide with surprise as the others' at Jack's sudden appearance, but only momentarily. He glanced to right and to left, then at Jack, and with a slight nod of his head as if to say, 'I can do this and you can do the rest' Festoon reached both arms out and around Streik and Feld and pulled them bodily into his soft flesh, as a sow might draw two of her young piglets to her belly.

In they went, all arms and legs, one moment in control of things and the next enveloped and drowning in the silken, perfumed, fleshy folds of the High Ealdor's pampered body.

Streik felt himself suffocating first, his feet raised from the ground and unable to get a purchase on anything, his hands slipping and sliding in a world that was suddenly incomprehensible as his breath was forced out of his body by Festoon's hold, and his mouth and nose were so lost to sight that any hope of taking breath was gone.

Feld managed a yelp, aimed a kick at Festoon's thigh, and finally gave a frustrated scream, for his years of training had never prepared him for this sort of capture. Arthur and Parlance went to Festoon's aid in restraining the struggling Fyrd.

Jack watched this strange spectacle unfold as if in slow motion as Brunte took the grim scene in, realized he had suddenly lost all advantage, and drew the bigger of his two knives.

Even then it was not Jack who responded so much as Brief's stave. It seemed to see before Jack did that Brunte's hostile intent was aimed at the struggling group rather than at Jack. The stave itself dragged Jack off the dais into a run towards them. Then, somehow, catching the ground before him, it sprang from his grasp and turned slowly through the air in such a way that its end struck Brunte's hand and sent his knife flying.

It was sometime in those moments that the stave caught the lights of the chamber along its carved length and sent a show of light towards Brunte which caught him in its beam and threw him across the chamber to its far side with a sickening thump.

That done it returned to Jack's hand.

It was only then, and for the first time, that Jack was able to see Katherine properly, for she had been half hidden by Festoon's form and the protective Arthur.

The instinct of each was to reach for the other, but in those extraordinary circumstances they could not do so. Instead their eyes locked, they said in silence what they wished they had said days, even weeks before and mutely and mutually agreed to act first and say what was in their hearts later.

'Which way?' he shouted, his stave at the ready against Brunte, who had got up and was running back towards them, his other knife now drawn.

It was Festoon who spoke.

'This way,' he gestured calmly, turning back to the door he had so nearly touched. 'This will get you to safety.'

He had found new strength in the crisis and seemed almost to have forgotten that he had two weakening Fyrd in his grasp. He let go of them together and they collapsed breathless and half conscious to the floor.

Jack did not hesitate. He pushed straight past, took the handle, turned it and threw the door open.

'Come on,' he said.

'Jack . . .'

'Come on, we'll be no match for them when those two come round. There's more below as well.'

He shoved the protesting Katherine bodily through, then stared at Festoon and said, without much conviction, 'Are you coming?'

Parlance and Arthur he seemed barely to see.

He followed Katherine through.

'Come *on*,' he shouted to the others still in the Chamber, 'we can't delay longer, they'll be here.'

But Festoon was not listening. He was looking past them to the landscape beyond, the look of terrible longing and regret that had been on his face earlier now greater still.

'My lord,' said Parlance, who moved to his side and whose voice was filled with wonder, 'do you see what I see . . . ?'

'So near, so near . . .' murmured Festoon helplessly, pulling away from the door, 'but *we* cannot . . .'

Behind them Brunte had stopped, his progress momentarily halted by Arthur Foale. Feld and Streik were coming round, Streik already rising, his dirk back in his hand. Off to one side the lift was emerging from the floor again with the angry sound of Fyrd inside, who almost at once tumbled out, staves ready and crossbows cocked.

'Come *on!*' said Jack, 'or close the door, we can't wait around here . . .'

'But you can't leave them!' said Katherine. 'Help them, Jack, to find a way here. It's only a few feet. Pull them through . . .'

Jack eyed Festoon, shook his head in bemusement and pushed back into the Chamber, the stave fragmenting light and forcing the Fyrd to retreat.

'Quick!' he shouted. 'Follow Katherine while I hold them at bay.'

Arthur Foale had been thrust hard to one side and now lay on the ground out of reach and struggling to rise.

It was Parlance who made a move, darting around Festoon and out through the door. The Fyrd began to advance as from them, fragmenting in turn, came shadows, cold and icy

'Jack!' screamed Katherine. '*Jack!*'

'My lord,' Parlance said gently, the calmest of them all, 'please try to come through. If I can you can, and I do not wish to be left to wander the rest of my life alone.'

Festoon was the picture of doubt and hesitation as Parlance reached a hand for his from the world beyond and back through the door's opening. His voice was soft, his words most loving.

'You found me once when we were young, my Lord Festoon, remember that lost day and find me again, remember . . .'

Somehow then, as if Festoon was a great beast of the field nervous to pass through a gate, Parlance coaxed him trembling through.

'I cannot,' whispered Festoon at the last.

'You *have*, my lord, you're through!'

'He's the one we want,' cried Brunte, pointing at Jack. 'Get him!'

Which they might well have done but for Arthur Foale.

He rose again, dived between between Jack and Brunte, turned to face Jack, pushed him hard through the door and grabbing the handle slammed it shut so that Brunte and the others could not follow even when they tried to turn the handle. It would not open a second time.

Beyond it, Jack tried to open the door again, but there was no handle on the far side. It seemed that Spring was a door that opened in only one direction and never twice.

They stood in wonder and bewilderment at their sudden transition from the Chamber and its danger to . . . where?

They had no idea.

79

FLIGHT

Not till several moments later, when they looked back from a vantage point where they sensed they were safe, did they realize that what they had come through was not a door at all. It was more like a shifting curtain of voile through which they themselves could no longer be seen or reached, though they could see those within.

There was Marshal Brunte looking dumbfounded, Meyor Feld quite cool and Streik angry. As for Arthur Foale, guessing that they might in some way still be able to see him, he had turned towards the closed door to shout something in their direction.

But his mouth moved silently, and like the others and the chamber itself he was rapidly fading into monochrome like a photograph whose chemicals remain unfixed, whose image dies before the viewer's eyes.

'He's warning us,' said Jack. 'He's telling us we haven't much time.'

'Arthur . . .' said Katherine desperately, 'we can't just leave him, we must try to go back . . .'

Jack shook his head.

'We had to get out of there,' he told her firmly, 'whatever it cost, and he knew that.'

'But they'll punish him for what he did and hurt him because they didn't get you.'

Jack put his arms around her.

'I'm sure that Arthur knows how to look after himself in Brum better than us,' he said quietly, 'and he'll find his own way home.'

Jack held her tight until, with the vision of the Chamber finally replaced by what looked like mist, he knew it was time to heed Arthur's silent warning and make sure none of them could be found.

The mist thickened for a moment, then swirled and weakened until what remained was a view of a city stretching away below them, its lights already on against the dull and dying day.

The city's office blocks and occasional church steeples glowed red in the setting sun and the air hummed with the muted sound of a city's people going home for the night.

'It's Birmingham,' said Jack, 'and judging from the lie of the sun, we're on a hill north-west of it.'

The hill, of open grassland, sloped up quite steeply and they were on a footpath which contoured it to left and right.

Lord Festoon was slumped against the slope, Parlance standing next to him, his tall chef's hat still on his head. They were pointing with excitement at an area a little further along the path to their right.

'Look!' Lord Festoon cried out to them with delight. 'Look what we have found. Help me up at once, Parlance, help me up. We must take a closer look and see if we are right.'

What seemed to excite them was no more than a rutted, muddy, tussocky area of grass beneath what looked like a cutting in the hill.

Jack and Katherine went to his side and helped him stand while Parlance, looking as surprised and happy as his master, said, 'I never thought the day would come, my lord, when you and I . . . you . . . and . . . I am quite overwhelmed!'

Indeed he was, for tears were openly streaming down his face.

'As am I, old friend!' declared Festoon empathically.

Tears had wet his fatty cheeks as well.

'Where are we?' asked Jack.

Katherine stared at the two of them and then along the path and a look of comprehension crossed her face.

'It's Waseley Hill. This is the place you told me about, Lord Festoon, where you came that Spring day when you first met Parlance.'

'It is, my dear. Where my life began and in a sense ended, where my dreams have so long resided. It is the place to which I wished to return before I died and here I am! Dreams it seems come true.'

'No one's going to die while *I'm* around,' said Jack, 'unless we linger too long. That's Birmingham below us, meaning we're too near Brum for safety. We must get away at once.'

'And how pray do you think I can do that!?' said Festoon matter-of-factly. 'I do not move easily. It was bad enough getting to the door across a flat wooden floor, but here on this rough and dangerous ground I rather think that this is where I must make my last stand against the Fyrd, while you good people, having done your duty by me, flee. Including you, Parlance.'

'I am not leaving you, my lord.'

Festoon sighed and looked resigned.

'I suggest that we debate what to do sitting down, and I can think of no better place, if I can get there, than the source of the River Rea which I spy from here.'

It was the muddy patch of ground they had been looking at.

It wasn't easy but they got there eventually and Festoon, delighted, plumped himself down and looked longingly at the spring.

'I don't suppose, Parlance, there is any way you could help me have a drink?'

The chef had already detached a ladle from the many cooking utensils that jingled and jangled from his leather belt and dipped it deep into the bubbling water.

Jack stood impatiently by, wanting to get away and debating whether to forcibly remove Katherine and set off without the two oddest people he had ever met and leave them to their fate. But he could tell that Katherine would protest, and anyway now the pressure was off a little he could see the importance for the future of Brum of getting its High Ealdor away to safety.

Meanwhile Parlance proffered the ladleful of spring water to Lord Festoon with the words, 'Here it is, provided for us by Mother Earth. Taste it and pronounce!'

He drank the water as greedily as if it were one of Parlance's summer cordials laced with the essence of fresh-picked blackcurrants, crushed, as in the medieval recipe, between the palms of maidens and slivered with a hint of pistachio before the slightest dusting of the crystal glass rim with a blend of mace and dappled sloe. So great seemed his pleasure.

He mulled water about his mouth, briefly entered a state of ecstasy, and when he spoke it was as if his voice came out of wonderland: 'It was – it *is* – perfection, better by far than any culinary concoction that I could dream or Parlance possibly ever make. This is the elixir of life itself!'

He beamed at them all.

'Cast your worries to one side, for moments like this occur but rarely in a mortal lifetime. Drink, be merry, for in a very short time from now I die but you shall still be alive.'

'You are too mordant, my lord,' said Parlance.

'I'm realistic,' said Festoon. 'Look who's coming up the hill!'

They looked down through the dusk and saw a formidable line of Fyrd advancing towards them.

'We've got to get away,' said Jack for lack of anything better to say. The fact was they were not going to. They were outnumbered many times and one of their number could not even walk, let alone run for his life.

Parlance, who seemed that day very prone to tears, began weeping again.

'It is all my fault! I should have fed my lord more frugally and then he could escape. As it is my food, quite literally, weighs him down, like a ball and chain upon a prisoner's leg.'

'There must be a way,' muttered Jack. But he couldn't think of one.

Parlance brightened.

'My lord, should we escape from this predicament I want you to know that I, Parlance, your chef, will make it my duty to feed you a diet that will ensure that you shrink back to become the High Ealdor you can truly be.'

Festoon stared at him in considerable alarm.

'This doesn't sound too good, Parlance.'

'It isn't, my lord. If you are to live, then my recipes must change utterly. Simplicity will rule, frugality will be your lord as you are mine, and natural goodness rather than a gourmand's artifice will be our guide. This watery feast we have just enjoyed is the very first of our new meals!'

Festoon looked glum.

'The more you talk the worse it sounds, Parlance,' he said, his face hang-dog. 'Leave me, escape, I would rather die than diet!'

'It will get worse before it gets better, that's certain!' replied Parlance a touch forbiddingly.

It seemed that fresh air was giving him new life and a new direction.

'Meanwhile,' said Jack, his patience with their talk worn out, 'our only real option is to negotiate . . . unless I can persuade Katherine and Parlance . . .'

'No!' they both said together.

'That's settled then,' said Jack, 'negotiation it is . . .'

He surveyed the approaching Fyrd, who were getting harder to see by the moment, the light fading fast. There were twenty of them directly below and with more to either side. They did not look the negotiating kind.

'Anyone got a better idea?'

The fact was that someone did, but he was not there among them right then.

The first they knew of his impending arrival was the sound of a klaxon behind the line of Fyrd. It took them a moment to work out where it came from, and when they did they could scarcely believe their eyes.

For from out of the gathering gloom, like an avenging bird of prey of great and clumsy dimensions, they saw a raggedy contraption with a great basket hanging beneath it from which fire shot upwards. Against the fire they could see a familiar silhouette.

'Stort,' shouted Jack, beginning to smile, 'it's Bedwyn Stort!'

What he was flying was the most ungainly hot-air balloon ever cobbled together in a few hours. Hanging beneath from ropes, their staves at the ready, were two dozen stavermen.

Stort's achievement in arriving just when he was needed was all the greater for the fact that he had never been in command of a hot-air balloon before. For strangely, arriving at the right place at the right time was not the result of chance or coincidence. His investigation, guided by Brief, into the nature and creation of the Chamber of Seasons by ã Faroün had long since given him knowledge of where the four doors of the seasons led, which was each to a different place.

His knowledge was of course theoretical, since he had never been in the Chamber itself. But the great architect had left sufficient clues to work out the doors' destinations. The problem was which door? Stort thought he knew.

He and Brief had realized that escape might be needed and Stort, after much debate, had decided that a balloon offered the speediest escape possible.

'Much will depend on the wind direction,' he said, 'but since we can only build the balloon in one place if it is not to be seen, and we cannot control the wind, we must trust to our collective wyrds that all will be well on the day.'

Of the construction of the balloon in secret in the deep recesses of the shadow factories built by humans not far from Waseley Hill, of its firing on the day, of its bold ascent and bumping ride across the roofs of Northfield, much has been written and much made up.

The simple fact was that while Jack and their friends raced through Brum in search of Katherine, Stort had slipped away to mastermind the launching of the balloon with the help of some of Pike's staver-men. Somehow they had managed it, and he was mightily relieved when he saw that the wind was a north-easterly, for he guessed from his researches that they needed to reach the destination that ã Faroün dubbed Spring.

The timing was another matter, for the Fyrd had come to hear of the bold enterprise and where it was taking place. Pike's stavermen had to fight them off while they helped get the balloon filled and then see it safely off the ground, with themselves hanging on in the desperate hope they might be able to get off again.

So it was that the balloon flown by Stort with some of Pike's stavermen dangling beneath appeared from the north-east just when they were needed. The balloon continued its course towards them, and where the hill rose before it the stavermen dropped to the ground and ran upslope to engage the Fyrd.

In this they were helped by the basket which, hitting ground and maintaining its forward drive, cut a swathe through the Fyrd and sent many of them flying. The basket ploughed on, tearing grass and bushes before it, and throwing any Fyrd unfortunate enough to be still in its path out of the way, but for one who, like a surprised fish, was scooped inside.

Stort succeeded in kicking him straight out again as he clung and struggled to close down the flow of liquid gas from a drum purloined from humans and adapted for the purpose.

The klaxon sounded again and Jack hauled Festoon to his feet. They all pushed him to the right and then the left and as the basket swept up the hill a final few feet to reach them they tumbled him in with Parlance too.

His weight brought the balloon to a juddering halt.

'Get in!' cried Stort, and Katherine and Jack followed.

It was then that one of the Fyrd must have loosed off a crossbow shot, for it caught Jack in the back of his shoulder and drove him into Katherine's arms.

'One of the ropes is caught,' yelled Stort, leaping out to release it but keeping one hand on the basket so he could climb back in.

There was a lurch, a jolt, a shiver and a pull, the basket was yanked upright and the freed balloon shot into the air. The upward surge tumbled them all together, another bolt thudded into the basket, but harmlessly this time, and then they were aloft and away.

A great cheer rose from the stavermen on the ground, and from what they could see the Fyrd were retreating back down the hill. They saw torches lit and heard another cheer.

'What's that shouting?' wondered Festoon.

'Your subjects, my lord,' said Parlance, 'content and happy to see their High Ealdor free and safe from danger.'

'Tell 'em I'm coming back!'

'If I had the means I would, but I think you may take it they know that you will!'

There was a third cheer, fainter this time, and then they were gone up into the dark.

But Jack didn't hear it. He had slumped forward, clutching feebly at the bolt in his back, and then fallen into unconsciousness.

'Stort?' said Katherine desperately. 'I need light to look at his injury. Stort?'

The basket was large, Festoon filled most of it, it was hard to see, but it did not take them long to realize they had left Stort behind.

'But how do we fly this thing?' said Katherine, Festoon being incapable and Parlance too small to safely reach the controls of the gas cylinder. Only one thing was certain. The ground below was getting ever more distant, the houses ever smaller, as the balloon continued to ascend.

It was then they heard a shout from below, which seemed odd, for they were very high and the ground a long way off.

Parlance climbed on Festoon, leaned over the edge of the basket and peered down.

Another shout.

He cocked his ear and heard a scream of desperation and rage.

'I think,' he said, 'it is Mister Stort dangling beneath us from a rope.'

It was, and getting him back on board was impossible until Festoon suggested they loop the rope to which their pilot was attached to his own arm. Each time they heaved Stort upward a little he would loop the rope around his arm, and his weight would hold the rope in place.

In this way did they winch Stort up until he came within their grasp and he was heaved aboard.

He set to work at once reducing the flame from the gas, making the balloon descend once more and finally stabilize its flight.

Jack had come to and Stort was able to shed some light from a Lucifer on his injury. The bolt had lacerated muscle and skin on his shoulder very badly, tearing open scar tissues from his old burns.

'I'll stem the blood,' said Katherine, 'but anything more will have to wait.'

All she could do was put her arms around Jack to make him comfortable. All he wanted to do was sleep, but even then he winced and gasped in pain.

'Where are we going, Mister Stort?' she asked. 'Because the sooner we get there the better.'

'We're going westward towards the borderland between Englalond and Nordwalas, which humans call Wales. My kin live there and it's where I'm from. The Fyrd will find it hard to track us down there.'

'How do you steer this thing?' wondered Festoon.

Stort shrugged.

'Don't ask me,' he said. 'I've never flown one before.'

The air was still, their flight through the night very slow, and but for Stort they all got some sleep.

Later, the first glimmering of dawn showed in the east but the sky was still black towards the west where they were flying. Katherine said, as much to herself as in the hope that anyone else might hear, 'That door said "Spring" but we didn't find it.'

Lord Festoon opened his eyes and gazed at her and then at the restless but sleeping Jack, his head on her shoulder.

'Didn't you?' he said with a smile. 'Didn't you my dear?'

Katherine looked down at Jack and her arms around him tightened.

Later still Lord Festoon was restless.

He addressed Parlance very politely.

'I don't suppose, my dear friend, that somewhere about your person you have a sweetmeat or two? Something to keep the ravening wolves of hunger at bay?'

Parlance dug around in the pockets of his chef's jacket and produced, like a magician bringing a rabbit from a hat, a chocolate bonbon on which a cashew nut nestled as a baby to its mother's breast.

'This is a rather special one, my lord.'

'How so, Parlance?'

'It is the last you are going to get for a very long time and marks the end of an era of indulgence and the beginning of a time of austerity. Your diet is about to begin. Enjoy!'

But Festoon surprised his friend.

He offered it to Katherine and, since she did not want it, to Stort, who ate it in moments.

'Delicious,' he said.

'The best you have ever eaten I daresay?' said Festoon lazily.

Stort shook his head.

Festoon looked surprised.

'Who pray could possibly be a better chocolatier than Parlance here?' he wondered.

'My mother,' replied Stort matter-of-factly, 'as hopefully you're going to find out. If we ever get there – the fuel's running low.'

The balloon stuttered on through the dawning sky, the gas flame flaring uncertainly, a strengthening wind swinging the basket now this way, now that.

A thin, weak ray of the rising sun struck cloud behind them, the last of the moon over the Welsh hills shone faintly ahead.

'Keep your fingers crossed,' announced Stort. 'The gas has just run out.'

VI

SPRING

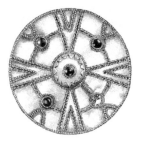

80

THE VILLAGE

It was dawn and the sun was rising brightly across the river upon one of the quietest, least changed, obscurest villages in the Hyddenworld – Wardine-on-Severn.

Wardine nestles on the west side of a great wide loop of the River Severn and has a single cobbled street which slopes down to the gravelly shore of the river. The street, and the two or three lanes that run off it, are lined with old-style humbles which to the human eye look like mere banks of river gravel and soil, their old doors, secret windows, chimneys and side entrances all equally obscure.

To hydden eyes, now more used to the modern urban world, the place has quaint beauty and an atmosphere of peace and tranquillity which derives in the main from two things: the slow, eternal flow of the river to which it owes its existence and location, and the unusual peaceableness and quiet wisdom of its inhabitants. The two might be connected.

Things are taken slowly in Wardine, but to say nothing ever happens would be untrue. Indeed it might be said that it is in such a place that the most important things of all happen – lives are well lived, truth is spoken, folk appreciate the things they have without regret for what they have not, and each helps the other as a matter of course without making a song and dance about it.

Wardine is a place of celebration – of births and birthdays, of marriages and anniversaries, and of death as a fact of life not to be feared for its finality but accepted for the new stage on the journey that it marks.

Folk laugh in Wardine and they weep; if they are angry they say so and forget it; if they do wrong they do their best to put it right; and if they leave, then when they come back their return is a matter of joy and welcome.

The street widens down by the river into a piece of common ground called The Square where public things happen – greetings, farewells, the making of trysts and all those things that form the daily and the annual life of ordinary folk.

In days gone by, there were two ways to reach the village – by road from the south-west and then across fields, or over the railway bridge to the north. The bridge has gone and now there is a ferry on that side which, inevitably, a Bilgesnipe looks after with his family, whose home is in the dank but happy confines of a half-sunken barque nearby.

That particular dawn a white horse stood for a time on the bank by the ferry and watched its mistress, Imbolc the Peace-Weaver, being carried across. Its tail swung back and forth, and when it seemed satisfied it was gone off across the surface of the Earth, up in among the galaxies of stars to bide the time until it was needed again.

For her part Imbolc was approaching the village which, in all the centuries of her travelling throughout the hydden and the human world, she most liked to visit. She was, after all, Peace-Weaver, and it had taken her many centuries to find a place so naturally peaceful that it had no special need of her skills.

She had come to witness something important and to rest awhile before the rigours yet to come of the very last years of her life. Her sister the Shield Maiden was coming and Imbolc was readying herself to finally give up the now battered pendant she wore around her neck and earn the right to return at last to the only one she ever loved, Beornamund.

Time is different for immortals, it moves now slow now fast, in fits and starts, sometimes drifting lazily and at others rushing by as on a flood.

Imbolc's journey from her own distant Spring through the seasons to Winter, and now through the borrowed years beyond, had taken fifteen hundred years, what remained was hardly anything at all.

So she sat in the ferry at leisure, enjoying the sun before she shape-changed into her usual guise thereabout, that of a female pedlar. She did not worry about the ferryman. His was an ancient calling, moving constantly between two worlds. He had seen things more dramatic than white horses and shape-changers.

. . . but this morning you may see something that may surprise even you Imbolc told herself with a smile.

A few fisher folk were already about on the Wardine shore, getting ready for a day's work, but no one else. She landed and paid off the ferryman and walked up the cobbled street past the grander humbles until she came to a lane that wound steeply off to the right before dropping down from the last few dwellings before the great floodplain of the river, a wide open expanse which at that time of year had a dry crust of mud and verdant growth of reeds and marshland flowers.

She stopped by a modest humble at its top end, from where the open fields beyond could be seen and the ruined railway bridge. Its door was rough and unpainted, its windows unclean, its curtain ragged, but for all that there was a certain comfortable atmosphere about the place. A tangle of climbing roses formed a canopy over the door and on the roof, which was thatched and overgrown with wildflowers and sward. It was the home of butterflies and a dormouse. Nuthatches and siskins searched there for food.

Part of Imbolc's pleasure was that she had come to give news and so fulfil a promise, a most happy one.

She pulled a piece of twine that served to ring a bell but it was still loose and there came no sound. It had been loose over ten years because the dweller within was waiting for the return of the boy, now a man, who made the bell – her son, Bedwyn Stort.

It could have been fixed in a few moments, but she wanted him to do it, for she knew it would give her pleasure that he did so.

'He'll come back to do it one day,' she would say, 'you'll see. And when he does he'll do it Bedwyn's way, and give us the fright of our lives!'

Imbolc knocked.

'The door's open!' called out Mrs Stort.

When she saw who her visitor was her eyes smiled and dared show hope.

'He's coming home,' said Imbolc at once. In the presence of Mrs Stort she allowed herself to be seen as she really was.

Mrs Stort hugged the ancient crone nearly to death.

'When?' she said.

Imbolc broke free as best she could, changed back into her normal guise and consulted her chronometer.

'In about eighteen minutes' time,' she said.

Stort's mother laughed for joy but she cried as well, for the years of waiting, for the loss that absence means.

'I think you should be there when he arrives,' said Imbolc.

'But he'll come here.'

'He will, but I still think you should be there to witness it. The village will not have seen its like before and never will again. He brought great honour here through his intelligence and scholarship and now on his return he brings great honour for his courage and inventiveness. Come and witness it . . .'

'But . . .'

There were no buts, nor time to do her hair or change her clothes or anything. The most famous son of Wardine was coming home and Imbolc was going to make sure his mother did not miss it.

'We must raise Mr Kipling too,' she said, as they hurried down the lane.

'The scrivener, Stort's old teacher?'

They knocked at his door and Mrs Stort called out, 'You're to come and come now, Mr Kipling. He's coming home.'

Kipling stared at her, his mild eyes surprised.

He was old but sprightly, his cheeks rosy, his face benign, his brow somewhat furrowed, as if he was in a state of active thought. Which he was.

'When? How? Where? Why? And come to think of it how do you know?'

'I just do and there's no time for dawdling or debating or looking it up in books. The pedlar says he's coming and so he will.'

'When?'

'Now!'

'Bedwyn coming home?!'

His face suffused with simple joy.

Three of them hurrying down the lane and then a fourth and a fifth, for in a village like Wardine news travels faster than light and one person's happening is everyone's event.

'Bedwyn's coming!'

'The lad's coming back!'

'Look lively, he's the most famous Wardiner there ever was and they do say, or so I've heard, that he has seen the High Ealdor of Brum himself! Imagine that! He's coming home!'

So it was that a few seconds before the eighteen minutes were up and Stort due to arrive, half the village was already waiting in The Square and the other half well on the way, all eyeing the far bank and the ferryman who had returned to his station. Not a trace of life or movement could be seen.

'Who said he was coming?'

'Mr Kipling used his orbs and sembles, his rules and pendometers to predict it to the nearest second.'

'Which was when?'

'Three minutes ago.'

'So much for science and for scriveners!'

Luckily for the sake of Kipling's shaky reputation in the predictive arts, now so unfairly maligned, Imbolc's estimated time of arrival was not far out and her guess as to where he would land would have been entirely accurate had Stort not had to change course for safety's sake.

The balloon appeared suddenly above the tree line on the far shore as if out of the risen sun, raising a great cheer.

But his intended landing site was so full of people that he sensibly changed his plan at the last moment, scraped the roofs and landed in the mud by the river beyond the village.

Stort was as eager to see his mother as she him, and she reached her hands to his face to feel it as she did when he was a child, for though seeing may be believing, touch is love.

Not that she was slow in coming forward about the bell which, as she had so long predicted, he fixed even before he entered his old home.

The village was much less interested in Jack and Katherine, and as for the fact that the High Ealdor of Brum was in their company, along with his chef, they could not quite take it in.

'Er, Parlance, have you had sight of any food?' whispered Lord
Festoon the moment they were secure on firm land and the fuss died
down, 'I am quite faint with hunger.'

'They are preparing a feast in the village square, my lord, to which
all are invited. But . . .'

'But what?' said Festoon unhappily.

'I have given very strict instructions about what you can and cannot
eat.'

'What is the main item in the feast?'

'Suckling pig and that most firmly fleshy of fish, the Severn salmon.'

'That is good, Parlance, very good. Served with Mediterranean
herbs no doubt, and slivers of parsnip roasted in avocado oil?'

'This is a village on a wild borderland, my lord, not your palace in
Brum. In any case those items are not on my list of things you can
eat.'

'What *is* on the list?' asked Festoon meekly.

'Very little, my lord. Very little indeed.'

But Katherine did not go to the feast.

It was obvious that Jack's back was a matter of grave concern.
Several of the village women took him in hand, tending to him in Mr
Kipling's front room, which for the moment was turned into a sick
ward for one.

Katherine sat with him and the Peace-Weaver too.

'He's very ill, isn't he?'

Imbolc nodded and said, 'Sicker even than he seems, my dear. This
day has been coming for very many years. He has fought for others,
now he must fight for himself and others must help.'

'How?' said Katherine. 'What can I do?'

Imbolc smiled.

'Give of yourself, my love, that is all you can ever do and it is what
one such as Jack is most in need of.'

'But I'd do anything for him.'

'It's not the intention that matters, nor even the action, it is far
deeper than that. Not in Jack's case. Give of yourself and he will be
healed.'

81

ILLNESS

But whatever Katherine did, however hard she tried, Jack did not get better. It didn't seem to be the crossbow wound, which had healed quite well, but something else.

Not even with the advice and help of the wyfkin in the village, however gifted in the healing arts. Not one of their ointments, infusions or potions, handed down from mother to daughter through the centuries, had any effect.

Jack did not get better.

If anything he got worse.

His pain was immense and though he bravely muffled his cries his suffering was plain for all to see. His formerly robust looks thinned and aged, his hair grew lank, pustules appeared on his face as if he was diseased, his joints ached.

Strangely, despite the danger of further harm through his open sores and wounds, they stayed clean and showed no infection. Yet no sooner had one wound begun to look healed than another would appear, as if beneath the hurt and damaged skin a terrible anger raged.

His condition was a mystery and its cure a puzzle beyond the community's combined skill.

Mr Kipling could do no more than play kind host, to him and to those who came visiting to help. He could read to Jack, he and Stort could talk to him, Katherine could lie by his side when he would allow it and try to sooth him, but that stratagem often caused more pain than comfort and he would grow angry and tell her to stop hurting him and leave.

Though she remembered his patience with her own moods when her mother died, and his ability to stay calm in the face of her rages, she found it was not so easy to do the same. She felt hurt by his tirades against her, angry at his unfairness, yet guilty that she felt those things.

His illness hung over Wardine like a cloud. Even on the warmest days of Summer, when families of swans drifted down the Severn as they always had, and fish rose in slow-turning pools near the reeds and yellow flag, Wardine in those days was not summery at all.

82

REGIMEN

Yet there were bright spots and other, lighter, things to talk
about.

One of them was Lord Festoon and his chef and their diet.
The two had taken up residence in premises alongside the river once
occupied by one of the village's long-established fish traders and
processors.

The business had been run from the ground floor, and these
echoing and derelict chambers were now occupied by Lord Festoon.
Parlance took over the residential suite above.

The place smelt strongly of fish, which, strangely, Festoon welcomed, because the mixed odours of tench, chub, bleak and roach,
shot through with a hint of rotten salmon, served to dampen his
appetite.

It also encouraged him to take fresh air along the property's old
wharf, which fronted the Severn. There Festoon perambulated when
he wished, propping himself up on the various fish barrels, mooring
posts and even the small hand-crane when shortness of breath and
faintness overtook him.

The all-important kitchen, a crude affair compared to the vast and
well-appointed one in Brum, was on the ground floor and accessible
from above by narrow back-stairs which Parlance used. The entrance
from Festoon's quarters was locked against his craving for snacks at
midnight, and at every other hour too.

Parlance knew of course that in the early days of his new
regime his master would be too weak to get as far as the kitchen

door, let alone bang on it for attention. But the day would come when he would have strength enough – a day the chef would welcome with all his heart – and Parlance wished for no slippage meanwhile.

So the door was locked and Festoon's now frugal but sensibly nutritious fare was carried to him by way of the street door, round the side and through what had been the boat repair shop. Or, on warm days and for luncheon, the food would be taken to a table on the wharf which Parlance created out of the dagger board of a rotten skiff, nailed rather crudely to a sawn-off post within easy reach of a rotund tar barrel of sufficient size and strength to accommodate Festoon's bottom and his weight.

Some things the chef did not let go, and one of them was his chef's hat, his white jacket and his chequered trousers. Another was the standard of his presentation and service, which remained impeccable, even if all that his master's breakfast consisted of was a solitary coddled egg sprinkled with ashes of bay leaf.

Naturally the good folk of Wardine-on-Severn had never seen such goings-on in their lives, and the thrice-daily sight of the chef emerging from the front entrance of the not-so-humble river premises was a matter of astonishment, interest and, eventually, delight.

Wardine wyfkin were not slow in coming forward when it came to matters of hearth and home. That a male should cook at all was amazing to them, but that he should plainly relish doing so, and do it well, was disturbing too.

It was not long before news of his latest dish became the village's daily fare and the question of what he cooked and the ingredients, and soon his methods too, a matter of debate and even instruction. One of his talents, as it must be for any chef, was sourcing ingredients, but the greater skill lies in recognizing the potential in new things and finding creative ways to draw out and blend flavours of one thing in new ways with another.

The need for ingredients to vary the High Ealdor's diet, and keep him on course to becoming lean yet not too hungry, brought Parlance into creative contact with the villagers and those from the wider hinterland who serviced their needs. Very soon the fact that Wardine was playing host to a demanding chef who cooked for the High Ealdor himself, and one who knew not only his onions but his wild garlic, stimulated folk in the vicinity to send him gifts of special foods to try and so, hopefully, to buy.

One day Parlance found Festoon sitting at his table eating a bonbon.

'No, my lord, you may not eat that, desist at once! If, as I fear, you have eaten several already . . .'

'Take pity, Parlance, they appeared upon my table as if sent from heaven, accompanied by the flowers of eglantine woven into a heart upon a base of rose-scented marzipan and cream . . . how could I not eat them?'

'No doubt they were sent by a maiden lady or scheming widow seeking your hand in marriage, my lord!' Parlance declared. 'How many, my lord, *how many?*'

'This the last, Parlance, and look, I hurl it away!'

'How many?'

'Eleven before it? Only eleven.'

'Eleven!!! No supper for you tonight, my lord, and it is doubtful if you deserve breakfast either, which is a pity because I had planned a special treat.'

'A treat?' said Festoon most miserably. 'What treat?'

'Brot, my lord. Brot superlative, brot magnificent.'

'Brot?' whispered Festoon. 'But I have not had even a thin slice of that for a week.'

'No, you have not. Nor may I allow you this either, though . . .'

'Parlance, explain!' said Festoon in a persuasive way, for he recognized excitement when he saw it, and a wish to share a culinary discovery.

'I have found a new source of brot which has put me in a dither, for it is very many years since I tasted brot better than my own.'

Festoon saw his opportunity at once.

'I daresay, my old friend, that you might appreciate a second opinion of this brot, but of course it would need someone who has discrimination and judgement and far as we are from Brum it is unlikely, unfortunately, that you will find such a person here. That is a pity, and though I myself would normally oblige I cannot under your regimen and so you must remain in a state of uncertainty about the quality of the brot you have discovered.'

'I must, my lord,' said Parlance, weakening. He was desperate to have his opinion confirmed by the one person in Englalond whose taste he knew to be true.

'Perhaps if you left a tiny piece of this brot . . .'

'No, my lord.'

'. . . a crumb or two, a dry crust, a . . .'

'I must not, really I must not . . .'

'Nobody would actually know . . . if you left the kitchen door open for a little, and that brot upon a board with a knife to cut it with, would not . . .'

'Breakfast, my lord,' cried Parlance giving in, 'you shall have it then, but if and only if you promise never to eat such bonbons again!'

It was agreed, and when breakfast came they tasted the brot together, with choice dripping made from roast swans' thighs to help it go down.

For the briefest of moments it was like the old days. They were in the seventh heaven of the gourmand, tasting something new and, as it turned out, something truly great.

'Parlance,' declared Festoon, 'this is a brot beyond all brots, even the one you bake upon my birthday! Who made it?'

'A lady I am told, but more I know not. This loaf was left along with others and I have no way of knowing who made it.'

'Seek out that information, dear friend, for she is a jewel.'

'I will.'

'When you find her, Parlance, whatever the circumstances, if she be free, then propose to her there and then, for trust me a wyf who makes such brot as this will be a wyf in all things and a wyf indeed.'

'Yes, my lord, but she is probably already married.'

'Probably is not certainly and I have made a command, Parlance, not a suggestion or request. You understand?'

'I do.'

Lord Festoon did not err again, less because of the strictures of his chef than because tasting that extraordinary brot, and the fact that of late he had slept better and woken feeling brighter, reminded him that good food and gluttony were poor bedfellows.

He redoubled his efforts to follow the regimen Parlance imposed on him, continuing to eat less, feeling steadily better, discovering that his clothes needed regular taking in and that his perambulations were more frequent, longer and more satisfying.

Such was his improvement that he even began to think more of others' health than his own, and so it was that following a distressing visit from Katherine concerning Jack's decline he decided to visit the patient and see what he could do to help.

Wardine had seen some strange things of late, but nothing quite so memorable as Lord Festoon, with Katherine on one side and Parlance on the other, without his hat, for this was a social call, making their slow and careful way up its cobbled main street. It was quite a hike, and at the end, as they neared Mr Kipling's house, a suddenly steep one.

Folk had gathered and indeed followed the progress, calling out encouragement, making obeisance of one kind and another and generally making it very clear to the High Ealdor that in their village at least there was much liking and support for him.

Some even cheered when he finally reached the door of Mister Kipling's house, who opened it willingly, sorry only that Stort was absent just then from the village and unable to witness the great event.

Lord Festoon was exhausted from his effort but he undoubtedly looked thinner, and that made him look the tall hydden he actually was. He had a very long way to go if he was to get back to normality, but he now looked and walked as a High Ealdor should.

Jack, however, looked wretched.

His open wounds were livid and suppurating, his muscles weak from inactivity and his eyes rather sunken. He looked pale, he was evidently in great pain and it seemed to Festoon he had given up hope of recovery.

Festoon said nothing at first, visibly shocked. But then he had an idea. As Parlance had helped him, could the chef not help Jack? Seen from a certain perspective after all, food is medicine, and as its master Parlance might be perceived as a healer.

It was a stroke of genius on Festoon's part.

Parlance took on the assignment and agreed that after due time and consultation with the patient he would attempt a diagnosis and cure.

This brought the prospect of an end to the cloud over Wardine's summer that was Jack's illness, and such new hope and excitement for a cure that Wardiners could not wait for Parlance to pronounce upon his patient.

83

SCRUMPET

Parlance finally did so at the end of July as Summer reached its height.

He would have liked to make his statement more privately, but in Wardine that was difficult, and so he did it standing on a fish barrel in The Square.

The crowd was so great that Katherine took up a place to one side in the sun, sitting on a little wall with a female carrying a large basket. The scent of brot that came from it was so delicious and alluring that it seemed to reach right inside her. It calmed her, made her close her eyes, made her almost forget why she was there.

Until she found herself saying aloud, 'The trouble is that the one person who should be here isn't here!'

'And who's that?' asked the woman with the fresh-made brot. She was a female in her forties, plain but with the strong hands of an experienced brot-maker.

'Jack,' said Katherine.

'You know him then?'

Katherine nodded and told her a little about Jack and hinted at something more about themselves.

The brot-maker's eyes were bold, her forearms formidable, her bust large, her bearing powerful.

'I loved someone once,' she declared, 'but it didn't work out.'

'I didn't say I loved him exactly.'

'But you do, don't you? I expect you won't admit it, like I didn't until it was too late.'

'But Jack knows . . .'

'Does he? Really? If ever I meet someone to love I'll tell him again and again with every loaf of brot I make, each one, every day, over and over.'

'But I . . .'

'I'd tell him, if I had my time again. Second chances don't often happen.'

Katherine thought of everything they'd been through recently and realized that though she thought her feelings had been recognized by Jack, she'd never actually told him how she felt. She was interrupted in her reverie when her neighbour tapped her on the arm.

'What's Mister Parlance look like?'

'Like that!' said Katherine, pointing at Parlance, who was on the fish barrel and trying to get everyone's attention. 'Why?'

'I'm one of those who have made him some brot it seems.'

She nodded towards a group of wyfs of various ages, sizes and bulks who were standing about with brot to show Parlance, some with but one or two to show, others, like her friend, with a basketful. 'It seems he's looking for the wyf who made a particular brot to do her the favour of asking for more for the Head Ealdor, so here I am in the hope he'll like my wares. But . . . *that's* him?'

Katherine nodded.

'He's a fine-looking gentleman but very much on the short side. Is he wed?'

'I don't think so,' said Katherine.

'In these parts eligible gentlemen do not appear often, so I must tend to my need as you must to yours. Go to!'

But Katherine did not immediately 'go to' but stayed where she was to watch what the brot-maker did.

The brot-maker promptly pushed her way through the crowd and, arriving very near Parlance as he was about to speak, she pulled aside the cloth over her basket to allow the fresh scent of her creations to waft its heady way to the chef's delicate nose.

Meanwhile the crowd hushed as Parlance finally started to speak.

'Ladies and gentlemen,' he said, 'after taking the patient's history . . .'

He paused, his nose twitching.

'. . . after, I say, examining him carefully and observing him as I might observe very carefully the basting of a joint of meat or, more to the point, the slow rising of a thrice-kneaded cake or, even, the fermentation of a plum wine, or even . . .'

His nose twitched more and a look of ecstasy crossed his face which seemed at odds with the subject matter of his speech, 'Nay, most especially, the baking of simple brot, I have come to my conclusion . . . but . . . but . . .'

The look of ecstasy was replaced by one of determination and purpose such as might settle on a great chef's countenance when he had a new dish in his sights, but that day Parlance's purpose seemed different.

'But I must interrupt myself, step down from this box and ask a question. Who baked that brot?'

But Katherine had no interest in the answer and no reason to linger more. The brot-maker had given her the answer she needed concerning Jack, and she knew now what to do.

She turned from the crowd and started back up the street towards Mr Kipling's house, where Jack lay suffering. A long time ago he had saved her life and ever since she had seemed to feel his strong arms around her, right round her, making her feel safe.

Now it was her turn to help him, and she didn't need people telling her how to do it, she needed to find that out for herself.

She knocked lightly on Mr Kipling's door and getting no reply went inside. The room where Jack lay was darkened and he was half asleep.

She went to his side and looked at him. He was so thin, so hollowed out by what had happened to him.

'Jack,' she whispered, 'Jack . . . ?'

Her voice roused him.

'I know where you want to be, but I . . .' she whispered.

She reached a hand to his and he responded for the first time since he had been in Wardine.

'. . . but I can't take you there.'

She lay on the bed next to him and he did not resist.

'You want to go home but I don't know how to show you the way. I know what's wrong with you but I don't know how to put it right.'

They were closer now, hand to hand, fingers intertwined, clinging and cleaving, hold on.

'I don't know how to repay you for rescuing me from the car when we were so young, or ever to put right the harm done to you. I feel there's nothing I can do, Jack, nothing at all.'

He felt her tears on his face and he whispered something in her ear, his voice thick as if it came out of the shadows and the vales. His hand squeezed hers.

'You're doing it,' he said, 'you're *doing* it, Katherine.'

She held him and, as best he could, he held her.

'I love you,' she whispered.

'I know,' he said, his hand slipping from her hair and face back to his chest.

They were a long time silent, then: 'They're talking about you in The Square. Parlance is saying what's wrong with you.'

Jack stirred and almost laughed. He would have done so if laughing hadn't hurt so much.

'I've guessed what's wrong with me,' he said.

She pulled back a little and looked at him.

'What?' she said.

'I'm not ill, not in the normal sense anyway. I'm *growing*, that's all. Parlance got it almost at once. He said that's why my wounds don't heal. Obvious really. I'm a giant-born and this is what one day it had to mean. It hurts so much and I've been alone here, everyone around me but alone.'

She nodded, her fair hair on his eyes and lips.

'I don't even know where home is,' he said. 'Jack isn't even my real name – and growing like this hurts like hell. Normal hydden just don't get this big.'

Katherine looked around the little room with all its hydden-sized furnishings.

'I don't think you should live in this room any more!'

He nodded and said, 'Will you find somewhere I . . . where we . . . where you can look after me while I get better?'

She nodded in return. His hand went to her face, then her cheek, and finally his fingers to her lips, feeling her.

'I'll sort it,' she said.

He was closing his eyes and his breathing growing easier than for weeks. He was letting go.

'Sleep,' she whispered so quietly she could hardly hear her own voice. *Sleep*.

He reached for her face again as if to be sure she was there. She stayed where she was and only when his breathing grew regular and deep did she leave.

But she and Jack were not the only ones in Wardine to find a healing and new purpose that day.

For Parlance, having cut short his startling diagnosis of the true cause of Jack's illness, which he later confirmed by way of a written notice posted in The Square, had pursued the scent of brot that caused him to interrupt his speech with tenacity and verve.

Much to the chagrin of the strong-armed brot-maker who had given Katherine good advice before she pushed herself forward towards Parlance, it was not her he chose. Nor any of the other brot-makers who had assembled at his bidding in the hope of finding she who made the bread that Festoon pronounced superlative.

Yet when they were dismissed and the Wardiners all dispersed, that scent lingered still, visiting Parlance's nostrils like a plague of exquisite gnats stirring him along and causing his heart to flutter as when he was a boy.

'My lord,' he announced breathlessly, having rushed to where his master sat impatiently awaiting his next meal in the open air, 'supper will be late!'

Before Festoon had time even to complain Parlance was gone, running hither and yon with his nose in the air, seeking out the elusive scent.

He was fortunate that the air was heavy and still, for it gave him time to close his eyes and follow his nose right out of Wardine onto a rutted track that led who knew where.

Upon it, her back to him, her gait rather slow, he spied a wyf most humble, poorly dressed, a small basket under her arm, her hair unkempt though not unclean. Parlance ran after her.

'Madam, pray stop!'

She stopped and turned hesitantly, her head low, her manner very shy.

'Madam . . . I wish to ask . . . I mean to say . . . let me see the brot you have made.'

She uncovered her basket and offered a loaf to him.

'When I saw those other brot-makers with their big baskets full of lovely things, and their good natures and strong bodies . . . I saw no purpose . . .'

He did not hear her words, for the scent was so evocative of life itself that no words were needed. He broke the brot open, put it to his face, and took in its scent.

'It is magnificent,' he said, 'it is perfection.'

'Sir, I . . .'

'But wait,' cried Parlance, 'what other things are you hiding in that broken basket?'

For broken it was, from use not carelessness.

'A dumpling,' she replied, 'and other things, but those other wyfkin . . .'

'A dumpling?' repeated Parlance breathlessly, 'made by your fair hand?'

'But my hand yes, but fair no. It is freckled and I . . .'

'What else Madam have you there?' said Parlance in a low and urgent voice, as if he had the feeling he was within reach of jewels in a national treasury which any moment now might be stolen and lost for ever.

'Nothing much. A tartlet or two, some flead crust, puff and plain, and Wardine scrumpet.'

'A scrumpet!' cried Parlance. 'But I thought that art was lost?'

'Not so, Mister Parlance, I have the recipe in my head and the feel of it in . . .'

'In your freckled hands,' he said, grasping them tightly, much to her surprise, and dropping to his knees.

'Sir, let me go!'

'I cannot, I am commanded by my Master to hold on to you and never let you go. Marry me! I am not much but together we may tread the road of dreams. What are yours?'

'To travel far from Wardine!'

'Granted. Utter another!'

'To be loved for what I am, which isn't much. You're mad, sir, or bad, sir, or blind. Look at me!'

He looked at her.

'I am lame,' she said, 'and plain, and my dreams are silly. Let me go.'

He looked at her.

'I feel as I see and as my nose directs: beauty pure and simple and the hydden wyf I wish to be bound to as she to me. I am not much to look at, and I am short, and I shout in the kitchen and I can offer nothing but life in the shadow of the greatest hydden on Earth, namely Lord Festoon.'

She looked at him and felt his hands on hers – strong hands as hers were, a cook's hands, rough, gentle, confident.

'Have you a father I should speak to?' he asked. 'Or brothers?'

She shook her head.

'Not even a husband,' she said with a slight smile. 'The first is dead, my brothers have fled and there never was a husband or even a swain. Look at me sir!'

'I see only flour in your hair where flowers should be,' he said, 'and that is my only note of doubt, now and for ever. Marry me! My knees are hurting but I must kneel until you give your consent.'

'I don't even know you!'

'You don't need to. Just ask yourself how many hydden are there on this Earth who would be roused to passion by the thought of scrumpet. Not many. Therefore, please marry me.'

'I will,' she said.

'What's your name?'

'Charmaine,' she replied.

Parlance's knees were so sore from this lengthy proposal that it was a struggle rising again. When he did he took off his hat.

He found there was the same height between them bar an inch or two, but which suited them both as they kissed to the scent of brot and swooned at the blissful thought of eating scrumpet together.

84

HEALING

J ack's healing began when Katherine found the courage to share her doubts and feelings of helplessness with him, for that enabled him to share his own with her.

Within a few days she found a place for him behind Festoon's residence, but out of sight of the street and with an access and view to the river which made it private.

Parlance brought him one kind of sustenance daily, Katherine brought another through her presence and her touch. Before, she had just been trying on the surface, her self-consciousness and awkwardness getting in the way. Now she was herself and that was what he needed.

That and her encouragement – as he found his confidence and strength again.

As the weather was so warm she persuaded him not to wear a shirt to get the air to his skin. He would have liked to swim, but the river was deep and filled with dangerous pools and under currents. There was a skiff in the lee of the bank, old and half-rotten.

'Why not repair it?' she suggested.

It was all he needed for him to set to, repairing it for lack of something better to do. Bending, straightening, banging, twisting, lifting and reaching . . . each little movement brought new life to his back.

At first he just sat in the skiff staring at the water flowing past, unwilling yet to test his craft and the paddle he had made against it, or himself.

Stort appeared and made a shower for him out of an old water tank set in a tree with a hand pump, a bucket and a hose. It looked crazy but the very fact of having to raise the water, adjust the bucket and move about to get under the sporadic flow was the exercise he needed.

At first Katherine came at times agreed, but gradually she came when she wanted and left when she wanted too.

Stort was their most frequent visitor, their joint companion. He too could be silent, their conversation sometimes no more than a shared listening to the river.

But mostly it was Jack and Katherine, sitting watching the flow of water, enjoying the warm nights of Summer.

Often Jack would stare across the Severn to the opposite bank, or watch the Bilgesnipe ferryman and his boy come and go. One day he waved to him and got a wave back, one side of the river acknowledging the other.

The Bilgesnipe was surprised. Wardiners were friendly folk and paid him well, but they were superstitious too, for a ferryman is a stranger between worlds and get too friendly with him and who knows if you'll wake up in the wrong place.

No matter to Jack, he liked to raise a hand once in a while, for he had been alone for a time and knew what a greeting meant.

Some nights when he and Katherine and Stort were sitting on the bank they'd see the glow of a fire on the ferryman's side and hear him play the tuble.

The water and its dangers lay between them, but when the tuble played and the fire glowed who was to say how far or near they were?

'Across there is where we're going,' Jack would say, 'when I'm better and our time here is done.'

Katherine agreed.

Stort too.

It was time for a generation to move on.

One evening when Stort wasn't there, Katherine said, 'You've been silent these last couple of days. Is anything wrong? Are your burns hurting again?'

These days she had learnt to be more direct than him.

He shook his head.

Finally: 'It's just that . . .'

'*What*, Jack?' demanded Katherine, frustrated.

'There's something I wanted to say but it's difficult . . .'

Her heart began to thump. He was looking across the river at a world they had to find a way to return to, whether as hydden or humans. It seemed he did so with longing but without her in his sight.

'You want to go back to Brum don't you?' she said, because he had said more than once that he felt at home there as he felt at home in the Hyddenworld.

Then, more hesitantly, she dared ask: 'Are you . . . I mean . . . are you trying find a way to . . .'

'To what?'

It was his turn to get frustrated.

'I've no idea what you're trying to say, Katherine.'

They were standing now, facing each other.

She had never felt so distant from him, or the fear of losing him so deeply.

'Are you trying to say goodbye?' she said finally.

He stared at her in astonishment and stepped closer.

'Goodbye?' he said. 'No, I'm not.'

'What are you saying then?'

The river stirred in the semi-darkness beyond the bank, swirling along, dark, cool, deep.

'I'm trying say hello,' he said. 'I'm trying to say, well . . . I don't want to cross the water back to whatever's over there without you. I'm trying to say I love you and . . .'

She reached a finger to his lips as she had once before on the bridge over the Thames.

'Don't say any more but what you just said, Jack.'

'I love you Katherine,' he said.

'I want to cross the river with you, only you,' she replied, 'because I love you too. And . . .'

He kissed her to stop her saying more too. There was no need for words.

They held each other tight until, not long after, Stort showed up and sat nearby, waiting.

The ferryman played his music.

The Severn flowed on by, a barrier, a link, the great unknown beneath the surface. The distant bank seemed no distance at all.

'Mr Barklice and I couldn't work love out at all,' said Stort to no one in particular.

'Nor can we,' said Katherine breaking free from Jack, 'but you'll know it when you find it!'

With each wound that healed, each new scar that did not break, they came nearer telling each other what they really thought; and strangely Stort was part of it, friend and catalyst, a good companion to them both in those slow days of Autumn.

'We've had people telling us what we are and what we're meant to be all our lives,' said Jack, 'but now we've got to find out what we want to be.'

That first real touching they explored in Mister Kipling's house had opened the doors on more. It wasn't chaste but it wasn't much more than that either, not then, not yet. It was slow as the river itself. Sometimes he slept in her arms; sometimes she in his. There was no hurry towards a goal to which they knew they were going together. It was easier to let the flow take them, as it took the river, to where they would go when the time was right.

One afternoon Jack was sitting on the bank alone when he heard a splash across the river and a shout. He looked across the water and saw the ferryman's boy's head bobbing up and down. The river flow was heavy and that boy was going to drown.

Jack did not hesitate.

He jumped into his skiff, released the lanyard and shot across the water as Arnold Mallarkhi had taught him one night. Like a bolt from a crossbow he went, arcing with the current, his eye never leaving the boy's head. But at least he could swim, which often ferrymen can't.

The shout had barely faded but he was there, heaving the boy into the gunnels, turning the boat into the flow to make it easier to steer, paddling fierce and strong to get to the ferryman's wharf, heaving to and holding fast while the boy was hauled back safe and sound onto dry land.

'He be all I got,' said the ferryman heavily. 'What shall I pay you?'

Jack stood on the bucking skiff, the water good beneath the planks, the boy sopping, the Bilgesnipe wanting to balance things out, which is natural enough.

'Teach me to play the tuble,' said Jack without thinking.

Teach me to save the world.

So the ferryman did, through the evenings that followed, real Bilgesnipe music, for which Jack discovered he had an ear.

85
FAREWELL

It was the Wardiners' tradition to light a Lammas bonfire, which they did a week or two after the first day of August when the pagan calendar said Autumn began. They liked to rest a few days before their own festivities, to enjoy the fullness of Summer in the mellowing of leaves and the slowing of the river, and to make preparations for feast and ritual.

'They want you to light the fire, Jack,' Stort told him.

'Me?'

'They asked the High Ealdor, but he refused, said you'd do it better. You're their second choice.'

'Who's building it?'

'You are.'

'*We* are,' Jack corrected him with a grin.

'We *are*?' exclaimed Stort.

Jack had been a cloud over the village when he first came. Now, as Samhain approached, he seemed to be its heart. He had suffered fire not once but twice, and each left different scars, which gave him a certain gravitas.

'We built a bonfire before and look what happened then!' said Katherine.

They built it all the same.

Then, the day before the night of its burning, when Wardiners claimed that spirits start to roam, three new spirits roamed right into Wardine, carried over on the ferryman's boat: Master Brief, Mister Pike and Barklice.

'My dear friends,' cried Festoon, 'I am delighted to see you, as are we all.'

'Tell me, Master Brief, have you ever seen this gentleman before?' said Pike, winking at Jack.

Brief eyed the trimmed-down Festoon very fiercely.

'Never, he's a stranger to me and rather gaunt. Barklice, you know him?'

'Can't say I do,' said Barklice.

'Jack,' said Brief, 'we know you, and Mistress Katherine, who's got colour in her cheeks, and Mister Stort, scrivener lately of Brum but soon to return we hope, oh and Parlance – we know him. But *this* gentleman . . .'

Brief shook his head.

'He's a stranger to us!'

Festoon looked at them magisterially.

'That's a very great shame,' he said, 'for I was planning to have a midsummer feast this very night.'

'A frugal feast, my lord?' asked Brief, eyes twinkling.

Festoon smiled in a conspiratorial way. Diets are good, but breaking them once in a while is better.

'You're welcome all,' he said, 'very welcome, and frugality be hanged. This will be a feast of feasts, of food rich to the point of nausea, refined to the limit of existence, exotic and overblown to a degree beyond the nth!'

'It is true I have prepared a little something,' admitted Parlance, who looked as happy as ever he had, 'and to whet your appetites – and with the help of my new kitchen companion . . .'

Even Festoon looked surprised, for Parlance had kept his proposal to Charmaine secret until then.

'. . . I have prepared, by way of an appetizer, bonbons of the savoury sort.'

'What companion?' wondered Festoon.

Parlance did not answer the question. The feast was imminent and there was work to do.

'*What* companion?' repeated Festoon, the suspense killing him.

'Later my lord, when the feast is done.'

But though Lord Festoon might have controlled for ever his addiction to food, to curiosity he was for ever wed.

He took time out from the feasting and crept to the kitchen to look inside.

Parlance, chef and healer, was not alone.

A wyf was helping him who, it seemed to Festoon, might be rather more than a wyf. She was small, a little lame, but from her every movement emanated love for her work and love for Parlance. Festoon knew at once exactly who she was.

'My lord!' cried out Parlance, seeing he was observed.

Festoon eyed his companion.

'The maker of brot superlative, brot supreme, I presume?' he said, bending low, which he most certainly would not have been able to do but weeks before, and kissing her on each of her floury cheeks.

'A wyf who makes Parlance happy,' he said, 'makes his friend Festoon Avon happy. Welcome!'

And welcome she *was* made by all of them, especially Katherine, who had met her soon after Parlance had proposed to her.

Such and many more good things were in the nature of the midsummer festival in Wardine-on-Severn that year.

Another was Jack signalling to the ferryman to come on over with his boy, for the first time ever, and join the fun.

A third was Brief, Pike and Barklice taking Jack aside.

'You'll come back to Brum when you're ready, Jack?'

He didn't doubt it.

'The giant-born who saved the High Ealdor is a hero indeed. Which is just what we were hoping you would be!'

'We all saved him,' said Jack, which was indeed nearer the truth.

'That's not how the good hydden of Brum will see it,' said Master Brief. 'They have their hero and will expect him to return when the time is right.'

The feast continued into the early hours until one by one the villagers returned home and only Festoon and his friends remained by the bonfire, their faces made red by its last embers but their eyes alight with the many pleasures of companionship.

In addition to Festoon and Master Brief, Pike was there and

Barklice. The feasting done and their first work together complete and declared a triumph, Parlance and his Charmaine had joined the company. Jack sat with Katherine, their love and ease together plain for all to see.

Stort, overheated by the fire, was down on the river bank watching the river's dark flow. So it was he who saw the swirl of a horse's mane in the darkness on the fair bank; and he who saw the ferryman's light and the advance of his craft across the water.

'We have a visitor,' he said, rising to go and help Imbolc ashore.

'Tell them to stay their distance,' she whispered, 'for it is too much effort for me now to adopt my guise and I need not linger long. Tell them that and . . .'

But such folk were not going to remark on the Peace-Weaver's appearance.

They brought her to the fire, sat her down, and if the fire glowed more brightly and made her seem beautiful, and the stars and moon shone in her hair and made it seem as fair as when she was young, no one was surprised.

If too a slight wind stirred through the village she loved best of all, waking its inhabitants and drawing them back into the night to pause and stare but not come too near, no one minded or said a thing.

For they were believers all, each and every one, and saw no reason why Imbolc the Peace-Weaver might not visit them once in a while.

Imbolc, who sat nearest Stort as if she knew him best of all, said, 'It is time now, Jack and Katherine, time to cross the water together and find my sister the Shield Maiden. Despite that general belief that you're the Shield Maiden, I am no longer quite sure.'

Jack looked surprised but Katherine just shrugged. She'd never understood why the hydden had connected her with some legend of theirs anyway. Jack was another matter – with his hydden/human heritage, she just knew he was destined for great things.

Imbolc smiled gently at them: 'I still think you have your part to play, Katherine and I'm sure it's you who will find my sister, but I think you know where she is better than I do myself! Which is as it should be. Take Bedwyn Stort with you, for when the time comes for you to return to the human world he will show you what to do. Until then you shall be his teachers for the one thing no book, even in the great library of Brum, nor any teacher, be he as great as your Master Brief, can reveal, which is the nature of love. He needs to learn that, if he is to help see through the great task that lies ahead of him, as we all do if we are to play our part. So . . . ready yourselves and let the ferryman see us safely to the other side!'

Strangely, out of earshot of Imbolc, Stort tried to protest.

But Jack shook his head.

'You're coming too,' he said, 'and not just to help us get home but because we want you with us along the way.'

'Me especially?' said Stort, delighted.

'Yes, you,' said Jack.

They didn't linger long because the ferryman was tired and he wanted to get home. They said their farewells quietly to old friends and new, but if they hoped to slip away unnoticed they were mistaken.

This was Wardine, not Brum.

By the time they were ready dawn was near and the bank was lined with villagers.

The bonfire was poked to set sparks flying, and folk said goodbye the proper way, with blessing and tears, hopes and a sense of loss, and with sombre excitement for what the coming months and the New Year would bring.

'It'll bring us the Shield Maiden,' said Katherine, who was beginning to think she knew exactly where that young lady was to be found, even if no one including Jack had got the point, excepting maybe Brief, who was wise in many things.

While for once that inquirer after knowledge, that creator of theories and that most practical and daring of scientists, that linguist and bibliophile, Bedwyn Stort, could not work it out at all.

'My dear friend,' observed the Master Scrivener to Stort as he said a private farewell to his assistant, 'it happens in the Spring, or so I have been told.'

Which left Stort none the wiser for the moment, but with something to think about in the months ahead.

Meanwhile with the festival of Lammas over, the biggest festival of all was on the way: Samhain, or Winter.

A time of old tales and shadows, of fires and dark decay, of transformation and rebirth; and the deep, deep music of great change.

Time to journey.

Time for Jack and Katherine, their last moments come, their portersacs ready and their farewells done, to board the ferry and cross the river to the further shore, and finally to leave Wardine, in the company of their good and much loved friend Bedwyn Stort.

Time for others to watch them go with hopeful heart and wave goodbye as the fire burned and sparks sped into the dawning sky.

Time for a new beginning to things.

Time for the ferryman to turn against the river's current and reach for the mooring and help his mortal cargo on to a land that was old but to them seemed new.

Which done, they turned and looked back a final time and waved. Then they were gone, just like that.

Not that folk could hope to see much against the glorious dazzle of the rising sun – and anyway, Wardiners had their own business to attend to and their own journeys to make.

VII

SHIELD MAIDEN

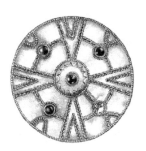

86

RETURN

Nine months later, as the last days of April approached and Spring began to turn to Summer, Jack and Katherine neared Woolstone once more. They had thought that Stort would travel with them all the way, but he decided to stop short at the lake on the far side of which were the Devil's Quoits. He had no wish to cross those waters again.

Of the time since Wardine, when they all journeyed together across Englalond, seeing many wonders, sleeping under the stars, discovering the nature of love, passion and friendship . . . of that time more may be guessed than is actually known. None of those concerned ever spoke much of it to others.

But let this be said now.

It was several months into their journey before it dawned on Jack, and on Stort more slowly still, who the Shield Maiden might be and from where she might come. Katherine knew the truth long before either of them did, her days growing slower as they went, her loving passion for Jack deepening with each day, as did her friendship for Stort. Oh yes, Katherine knew, but she kept her knowledge as a silent smile, and perhaps as licence to feel sick and be irritable for a few weeks.

Until one day along the way Jack and Stort got it.

'Er . . . um!' said Jack rather desperately.

'Aah!' declared Stort in a strangled kind of way.

Then, as if seeing the blinding light of the rising for the first time ever, they understood that Katherine was with child.

They wanted to fuss her after that but she soon reacted to what she felt were their unnecessary attentions.

'I'm not ill Jack, just . . . just . . .'

She wanted to return to the human world and get back home before their child was born.

She wanted that more than anything.

'So what do we do to get back?' asked Jack, gazing across the lake towards the Devil's Quoits.

Stort scratched his head and hummed a bit.

Then he said, 'The key thing is to well . . . sort of . . . I mean, when you reach the henge . . . which you won't be able to see easily – the first bit is submerged . . . to . . . well you kind of . . . um . . . dance in the water . . . but avoid turning sinister, that's certainly important.'

'Thanks,' said Jack ironically, 'that's as clear as mud. I don't think Katherine's in any condition to swim across a gravel pit.'

'We'll construct a raft then,' said Stort enthusiastically, 'and hope it doesn't sink too soon.'

'I don't want it to sink at all,' Jack said. 'She's pregnant!'

'Yes, well, sinking is problematic but possibly not in the way you think,' replied Stort. He was already eyeing the water and sizing up the flotsam and jetsam along the shore for items that might make a raft.

'Leave it to me, Jack! I see a way.'

'We could walk around the lake,' said Jack, not sure he liked the sound of Stort's 'way'.

'Not the same,' said Stort. 'If you want to change back to human size you'll have to go via the lost entrance to the henge and even then . . . well now . . . let's see . . .'

He set to and built a raft out of the materials along the shore which included some polystyrene that had a familiar look about it and bubble wrap, worn by time and weather. But finally, when Stort was finished, Jack eyed the ramshackle craft he had made with alarm.

Not so Katherine.

Her time was near.

'Let's go!' she said.

'If we sink . . .' muttered Jack.

'You won't,' said Stort.

They had a final night, a final fire, reminiscing about all that had happened, glad at what they had heard about Brum and their friends from folk along the way.

Lord Festoon was back and reinstated, Brunte now an uneasy ally; the Fyrd were biding their time and letting Brum and Englalond be, as if the Sinistral knew there was something there of which to be afraid.

'There is,' said Jack, hand on Katherine's stomach. 'Or there soon will be. The Shield Maiden!'

'Will you go back to Brum now?' asked Jack of Stort.

He nodded vaguely.

'I'll certainly be thereabout by the time you get to Woolstone,' he said. 'There's the lost gem still to find and I have an idea about that . . .'

But, for the time being, Jack and Katherine weren't interested in lost gems and new ideas. They had more immediate concerns and only half-listened to his talk.

The gem of Spring was Stort's concern now.

'Imbolc's got a last journey to make and the pendant to give up and then . . . she'll be free at last to go to Beornamund. That's the thing, that's how it will be. But I need to get back before the last day of Spring to lend her a hand . . .'

The night was over, their journey almost so, and they all wanted to get home.

Katherine heaved herself onto the cumbersome raft with Jack's help. He and Stort pushed it out into the water with a following wind and then Jack climbed aboard.

'Don't linger and watch us, Stort,' he called back, 'because if we fall in I don't want you coming to save us. It'll confuse the issue.'

Stort did something else, and something surprising.

He waded after them until he was alongside, a tender, diffident look on his face.

'I . . . I wanted . . .'

Katherine understood.

She took his hand and held it to her belly.

'Wait,' she said softly.

Stort did not have to wait long. He felt the baby's movement as if it was a call of love from across the far distance of time and space. As the craft sailed on he was left standing with a look of wonder on his face.

Then they turned from him towards the far side of the lake and their future, Jack at the helm of the strange craft, with a freshening wind filling its bubble-wrap sail and speeding them towards the far shore.

As they neared it the wind grew stronger still and wild and fickle, turning them about and then about again.

'Jack!'

'Katherine!'

And so it was that yards from the shore and somewhere over the submerged entrance to the henge they capsized and fell together into the water, shocked by the cold but laughing at their predicament. By then they were near enough to the Devil's Quoits to swim and paddle and finally wade ashore, having somehow turned and twisted the dance to which Stort had referred until they were human again, their clothes in tatters, their lives and laughter intact.

They waited till dark, made themselves decent as best they could from material they found along the shore, and tramped the last miles by hydden ways they had learnt to find.

They had a final night under the stars, keeping each other warm, thinking of Stort, sharing their memories, feeling the Shield Maiden moving: a hand, a foot, the slow turning bulge of a head across Katherine's belly.

'Jack?'

'Mmm?'

'I think . . . Jack . . . *Jack!*'

He sat up quickly.

'I think it's almost time.'

'Then I'd better get you home.'

It was the last day of April – and so the last day of Spring – when they arrived under cover of darkness of Woolstone. They came up to the garden across the fields and into the henge on the same side as when Jack had left it so long before in pursuit of Katherine. Hydden then, they were human now, Katherine needing to be supported the last few yards in among the trees.

But they couldn't see much beyond them . . .

Someone had built a new bonfire by the two conifers, to celebrate the coming of Beltane or Summer, on the morrow. It was so large that it obscured all view of the house.

'I think Arthur's come home before us,' said Jack softly. 'Now, can you make it up to the house?'

Katherine shook her head and sat on the grass by one of the trees. She could not go further and did not want to.

'Here,' she whispered between the pains, 'here is where she must be born, betwixt and between our two worlds, yours and mine. Here in the protective circle of the henge.'

87

DISCOVERY

That same night, Bedwyn Stort stood in the driving rain in the dark of night on Waseley Hill. He was on the very threshold of Brum and looking forward to getting back after his long trek from Wardine in the company of his friends until the past few days when he had been alone.

It was true that matters of the heart were unverifiable, but there were always new theories to put to the test.

His theory now was that if ever there was a night when the Shield Maiden was going to be born it was this night, the last of Spring, when one season becomes another.

Which being so, if ever there was a moment to bear out the truth of Beornamund's prophecy that the lost gem of Spring would show itself at the right time, it was this; as for the place, it had surely to be where that fragment of the mythic Sphere was originally lost, which was there on the hill where the CraftLord's workshop had once been.

So Stort stood alone in the dark, waiting and rather afraid. For the rain had been heavier than heavy and the little River Rea, which flowed out on the slopes above him, was already a raging torrent at his side, its banks near bursting, its waters seeming to want to reach up and drag him down.

But he was not going to move an inch.

The hydden who had survived the monsters of the deep of the lake by the Devil's Quoits and the horrors of dangling beneath a hot air balloon was pretty sure he could survive some rain on Waseley Hill in the pursuit of scientific inquiry.

Which might have been true had there not been rain freakish and strange across Brum for weeks past. Rain heavy and rain persistent; rain such as fell nowhere else in Englalond through that time.

So that as Stort stood by the torrent of the river which should have been no more than a safe and easy stream, it was backing up behind him all unknown. Backing in a way that was far beyond any Bilgesnipe's control.

Stort could not hope to see the great wave of water that was racing *up* the hill through the dark, roiling and boiling so powerfully that it ripped away the very surface of the night-bound earth before it. But he heard it as a dull and dangerous roar, and it put into him a fear like no other he had ever felt, born of the certainty of his own imminent destruction.

'But I am not going to move and Master Brief would most certainly chide me if I did. Let this roaring thing come, whatever it may be. Though it may take me into its maw and chew me up, yet if I have the satisfaction of finding the truth of the lost gem it will be enough and I shall die happy – or at least happy-ish!'

So there he stood, the rain teeming down, the river rushing in a torrent past his feet and the roar of its vast return ever louder. Until there came a moment as terrible as it was fearful.

The rain suddenly stopped, as if driven off the hill by the force of water rushing up it. The river ceased to flow, made still and impotent by its own return. Everything was silent and most dangerous.

'Now is the hour and the moment!' Stort whispered to himself. 'Now must the Shield Maiden surely be born. Now we shall see what we shall see!'

It was then that Imbolc came out of the still darkness that had descended, on the last moments of her journey down the years. She assumed no guise, for she had no more strength to do so.

She was a woman so old she seemed part of the Earth and the Universe as well.

'Come and stand by me,' she told Stort, 'and you'll be safe and see what you must.'

Stort did so.

'Hold my hand,' she said, which he did fearfully, for Stort was afraid of her touch. He had nearly died when she touched him on Waseley Hill years before.

She smiled and said, 'Never fear, Bedwyn Stort, you survived once and have proved yourself most worthy since. No harm shall ever come to you from a touch such as mine, only love.'

So he held her hand and took strange comfort from it.

'Now listen carefully,' Imbolc continued. 'My sister is born this night and that means my time is run. Yet I have strength left for one last thing but I need your help to do it!'

Her voice was drowned by the roaring that mounted up behind them as the water tore into them, ripped the earth from beneath their feet and raged on up the hill, sucking the river bed dry. Yet it did not move them from where they stood.

Then for a moment all was still again but for the muted clamour of the water now above, turning, falling, boiling at the source before beginning its descent.

But Stort had stopped attending to that, for he had seen something in the mud of the river bed, sucked dry of its flow for a few moments. It glowed dully, the muted gleam of a light nearly obscured.

He went to the river bed, Imbolc with him.

'It's a great rock,' he said, 'and there's something beneath it.'

'It is not a rock but Beornamund's old forge, dislodged by the water which now returns and will carry it to oblivion,' explained Imbolc. 'You have no time to search out what's there.'

But Stort ignored her and let go her hand.

He went on his knees in the mud and reached under the fallen forge which had been exposed by the wave of water. He pushed his hand through mud and gravel, he sought the source of the light, he touched it with the tips of his fingers but could not quite grasp it.

'It's the gem,' he cried out desperately, 'but I cannot quite grasp it, it's too far under, it slips from my fingers . . .'

The earth beneath him trembled as the wave of water began rushing back down the hill again, gathering strength as it went.

'Come back,' Imbolc called, 'I cannot protect you, Bedwyn Stort, not if you stay there. Come back!'

But Stort did not.

Again and again he thrust his hand and arm under the stone, sure that if only he could reach far enough and grasp tight enough the gem of Spring would be found at last.

The earth shook more, Stort reached too far, and the forge, great and heavy, shaken by the power of the approaching water, slipped a mite and then a mite more and pinned Stort where he lay, even as his hand found the gem and held it fast.

'I touch it, I feel its beauty, but can I say I have found what I cannot see?' cried Stort. 'I cannot! Nor can I move. Imbolc wish me well, for I fear that like you I am about to lose this mortal life!'

Brave words of a brave hydden, but not the truth.

For above him the sky cracked open, and in that great crack he saw the fires of heaven as once he had before.

From them came light, and then a shadow that fell across all the Earth and Stort's face and formed the silhouette of a mortal as great as the sky above.

A great hand reached out of the sky and, grasping the forge, heaved it off Stort's arm and chest.

Stort looked up in surprise and relief and found himself staring at great Beornamund himself.

The wave hit them then, but Beornamund stood guardian of them both, the water flying safely over their heads, blocked by his giant hand.

Until all was still again and the crisis over.

Stort, sitting in mud, his clothes half torn from his back, opened his fist and saw therein, nestling in his palm, the lost gem of Spring in whose deep depths shone the light of bright new life.

'Give it me,' commanded Beornamund.

Which Stort willingly did, for such a thing should not be directly held for long by mortal hand.

Then Beornamund turned to Imbolc, who seemed now to tower above Stort as well, her head among the stars, and he put the gem into its proper place, which was in the old pendant that hung around her neck.

Suddenly the glow of the heavens reflected from the gem lit her face and all her youth and beauty returned. She gazed at Beornamund lovingly and she knew what to do.

She took the pendant from her neck and knelt down to Stort.

'You have earned the right to be its bearer until the Shield Maiden is ready for it. Keep it secret and safe. Tell no one. Bear the burden as only you can, bear it for her with the same love you have for Mother Earth and all things in her and on her. Will you do this for my sister and for me?'

'I will,' said Bedwyn Stort, his eyes closing with fatigue. 'That I will . . .' And before his eyes closed finally into dreamless sleep he saw Beornamund take Imbolc in his arms. The heavens closed about them and they were gone.

Stort was woken not long after, not by the sun, nor the singing of birds, nor the fresh gold breeze. He was woken by the cool run of the water of the tiny stream in which he lay, which was the source of all things – of legends and of cities, of myths and great doings, and of a solitary hydden who was wet and cold and muddy but had in his hand a pendant from which a gem shone forth.

A pendant that was too great a burden for any mortal to carry, even for a Shield Maiden, unless he did so with love and kept his gaze on the stars.

Bedwyn Stort stood up in the dawn, stowed the pendant in the deepest pocket in his suit of Harris tweed, and set off downslope towards Brum through the dawn, to find his friends and to tell them of his adventures and discoveries, with the exception of just one of them, the most important, which if the Mirror gave him strength he would keep to himself until the day came when the Shield Maiden was old enough to wear the pendant around her neck.

88

THE SEASON TURNS

It was as dawn lightened the curtains of the Foales' bedroom overlooking the garden that Margaret imagined she heard a baby's cries.

She had had such dreams before, throughout her adult life, expressing her longing to bear the children she never could.

So she woke that dawn into the familiar waking dream and turned thankfully to Arthur beside her, one arm going over his back, the other to the comfort of his stomach.

Never a dawn went by that she did not wake into the joy that he had come home. Nor did she let slip a moment of gratitude that he filled the house again with his life and energy.

Of his adventures in the Hyddenworld and Brum, of the hydden he knew there and of Katherine and Jack, he spoke frequently, but never enough for Margaret not to long to know more.

But of how he had learnt to pass through the henge from one world to another, and back again, a discovery like many such in the history of the world, made simultaneously by others, he said little. He had followed that path in pursuit of a gem that he had never found, and to find a way, if one existed, to save Katherine and Jack from the dangers that threatened them.

In each of those endeavours, as it seemed, he had failed, and badly. That Katherine and Jack might one day find their way home he naturally hoped, but he tried not to think about it and to accept that their wyrd might have already taken them on different paths – paths over which he had no control.

So Arthur was back and he was not going to return to the Hyddenworld again.

He had found a way to win Marshal Brunte round, or maybe Brunte had won him round, you could never be sure with him. Either way, Brunte and Festoon were reconciled in their joint wish to destroy the Sinistral and all their Fyrd armies. That achieved, he had made his way back to Woolstone. He came back as he had hoped he might on February 1st, the first day of Spring, so he and Margaret could share the passage of the new season and renew their love, which they had duly done.

'Never again,' she said.

'Never!' he declared. 'I'll not even go back into the henge, but I'll let the grass grow and leave it to the creatures of the night and those of other worlds including that of the hydden.'

So the weeks of Spring had passed, the weather grown warm and Summer beckoned.

'We'll make a fire to welcome Beltane in,' Margaret had said a few days before, using the pagan name for Summer, the start of whose season is celebrated on May 1st.

So together they built a bonfire, as Jack and Katherine had once done, to celebrate a life lived, to welcome new life in. And with each thing they put on it, each thing to burn, each thing to say goodbye to, she had seemed to hear a baby's cries.

She said nothing, for their childlessness grieved Arthur too. Not of the cries she heard by day or the troubling dreams she had by night. Nothing. He was tired from his long journey and wished for nothing but rest, sleep, good food, hearty conversation, and days with the woman he loved.

'Leave it until Summer,' he would say of things that needed discussion. 'Leave it until then.'

So when she woke that dawn Margaret had every reason to believe that what she heard was her own longing and imagining and that the last thing she should do was wake Arthur.

She snuggled into his back, she turned onto her own, she heard the cries again.

'I'm imagining it,' she told herself, turning on her side and covering her ears with her hands.

Silence for a time and a sense of relief.

But sorrow too, for she missed Katherine and Jack and wished for their return as she had so long wished for Arthur's.

'I came back and so will they,' he told her again and again.

But there is nothing so insistent as a baby's cry. It cannot be ignored.

She heard it again and then again, carried on the dawn breeze through the open window.

She sat up in bed and listened.

It was real all right, if faint and only occasional. Real as Arthur. Real as herself.

'Arthur!?'

The baby cried out again.

Margaret got up at once, went to the window, opened the curtain and the window too, as wide as it would go.

'*Arthur!*'

He did not stir and Margaret was not going to hesitate any more. She pulled on her dressing gown and slippers, hurried downstairs into the conservatory, opened its doors and went outside onto the broken patio.

The baby's cries were angry now.

'Arthur!' Margaret called louder still up towards their window.

He might have been dead to the world so far as a baby was concerned, but when Margaret put that tone in her voice he was awake and up and over to the window in no time.

He peered out and saw her on the lawn, her hair as wild and dishevelled as his own.

'What is it, for goodness sake?'

'Listen!'

He listened and heard. The cries of a baby so clear now and so demanding it might have been the tolling of a cathedral bell summoning a congregation.

'It's coming from the henge,' she said.

All she saw then was Arthur disappear from view and all she could guess was that he was coming down to join her.

But that was not soon enough.

The baby's cries grew louder still and so, despite her fear of the henge itself, she ran down the garden towards it thinking of nothing, expecting nothing, fearful of everything.

Round the bonfire, through the trees and then into the cool depth of the henge, where she stopped and looked but heard no more.

Until gradually there came to her that quietest and most beautiful of sounds – the first contented suckling of a newborn child.

Margaret saw them first, Arthur moments later, a stick in his hand as if he expected attack. He dropped it at once.

'Katherine?' whispered Margaret, going towards them rather doubtfully, for she looked quite different than before.

'Jack?' queried Arthur a shade nervously, for Jack's hair was longer now, his frame bigger.

Together, with their baby, they looked like creatures of the wild but Margaret embraced them all.

'Welcome home my dears,' she said, with tears in her eyes. 'Welcome home.'

They helped Katherine up to the house, the baby in Jack's arms. He and Arthur quickly moved Clare's old bed into the conservatory because that's where Katherine wanted to be. Same bed, same place, same view, but now new life and a different season.

They washed her, and the baby, and Jack had a bath and they fed and talked and looked at each other and the baby in disbelief.

The day advanced.

The chimes sounded protectively as they always had.

Arthur checked the bonfire with Jack's help. Margaret hovered, as happy as she had ever been.

'I'll sit with Katherine and the baby when you light the fire,' she said.

Which Jack did at dusk, Arthur preferring to oversee things from a distance and then when the fire was well set to retreat back to the conservatory and watch it grow.

Jack stayed down there awhile, his silhouette large and strong by the fire, while he thought of many things and stared past it and its smoke and sparks into the henge, towards the Hyddenworld. He felt a longing to go back one day.

'Not yet,' he whispered to himself, 'not yet. So many things to do.'

Then he retreated back up the garden as Arthur had done, to join his family and watch the bonfire from the safe distance of the house, its light bright in the eyes of their daughter, the Shield Maiden.

Spring was over now and Summer just begun.

We very much hope you enjoyed *Hyddenworld: Spring*. If you have a comment or query about the book or the series write to the author directly at william@williamhorwood.co.uk. Readers can join his emailing list for news of future events and titles on his website: www.williamhorwood.co.uk

www.panmacmillan.com